JUN   2008

ESSEX COUNTY VOL.2:

GHOST STORIES

BY JEFF LEMIRE

Top Shelf Productions
Atlanta / Portland

ISBN 978-1-891830-94-5
1. Farm Life
2. Hockey
3. Graphic Novels

Essex County Volume 2: Ghost Stories © 2007 Jeff Lemire.
Edited by Brett Warnock and Chris Staros. Published by
Top Shelf Productions, PO Box 1282, Marietta, GA 30061-
1282, USA. Publishers: Brett Warnock and Chris Staros. Top
Shelf Productions® and the Top Shelf logo are registered
trademarks of Top Shelf Productions, Inc. All Rights Reserved.
No part of this publication may be reproduced without
permission, except for small excerpts for purposes of review.
Visit our online catalog at www.topshelfcomix.com.

Visit Jeff Lemire at www.jefflemire.com/.

First Printing, September 2007. Printed in Canada.

 Canada Council   **Conseil des Arts**
for the Arts   **du Canada**

We acknowledge the support of the Canada Council for the Arts
which last year invested $20.1 million in writing and publishing throughout
Canada.

Nous remercions de son soutien le Conseil des Arts du Canada,
qui a investi 20,1 millions de dollars l'an dernier dans les lettres et l'édition à
travers le Canada.

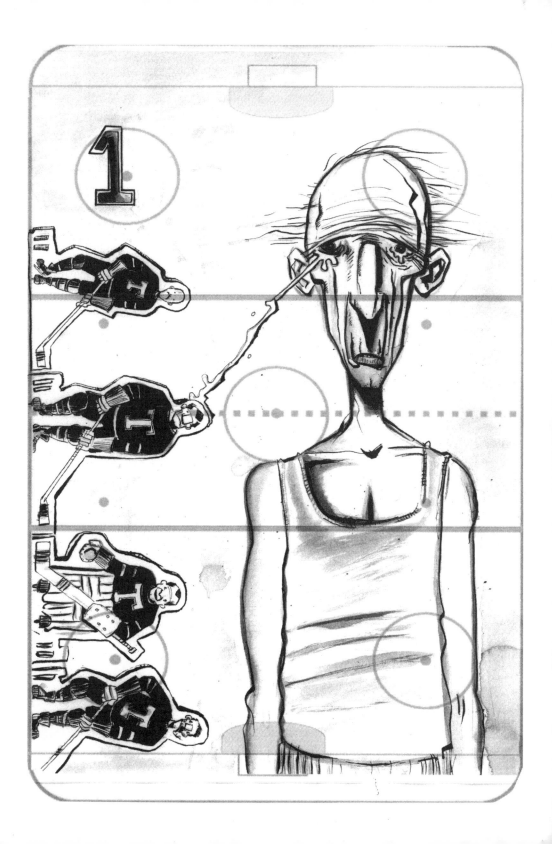

"Hockey captures the essence
of Canadian experience in the New World.
In a land so inescapably and inhospitably cold,
hockey is the chance of life, and
an affirmation that despite the deathly
chill of winter we are alive."
-Stephen Leacock

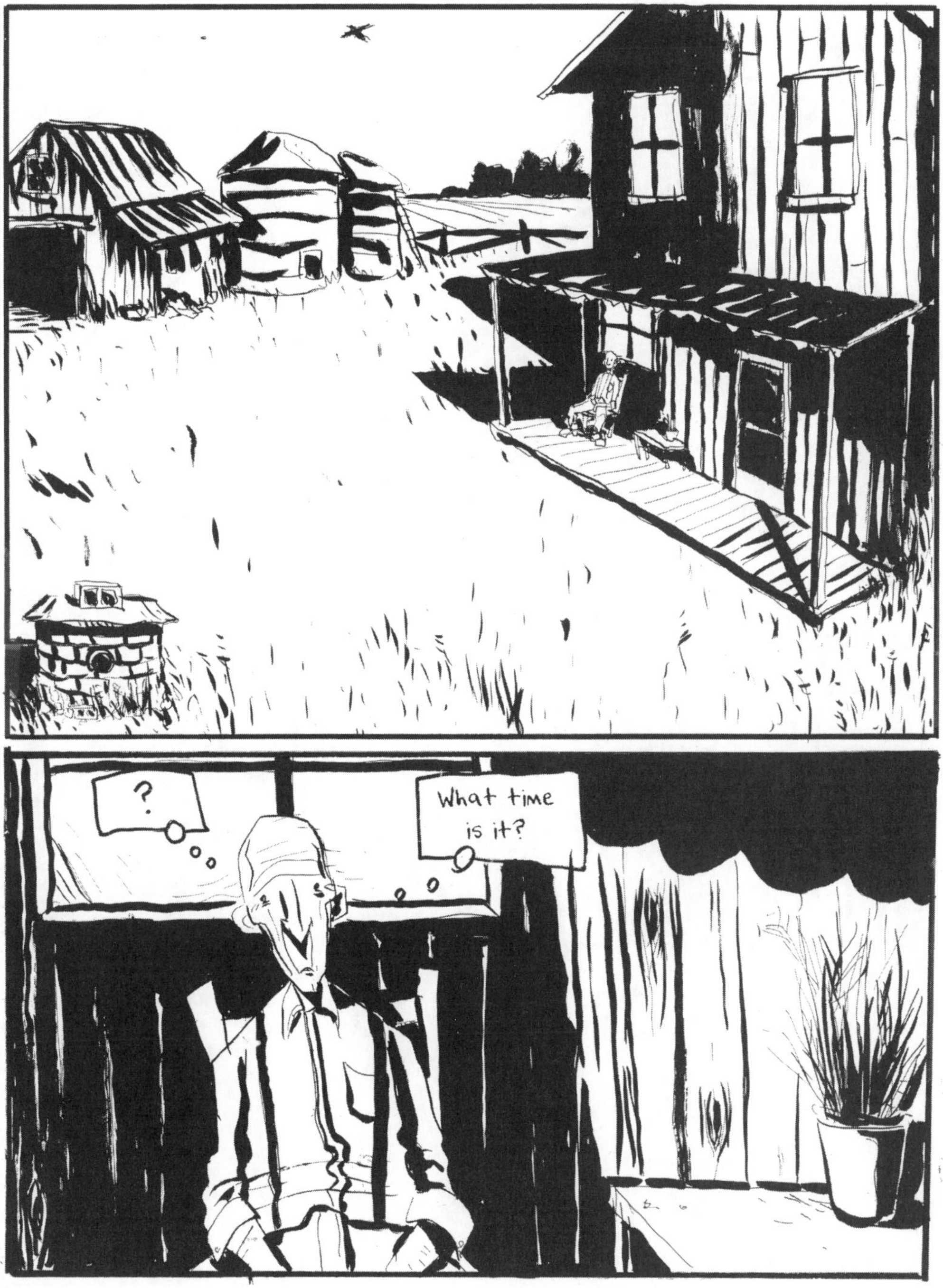
?
What time is it?

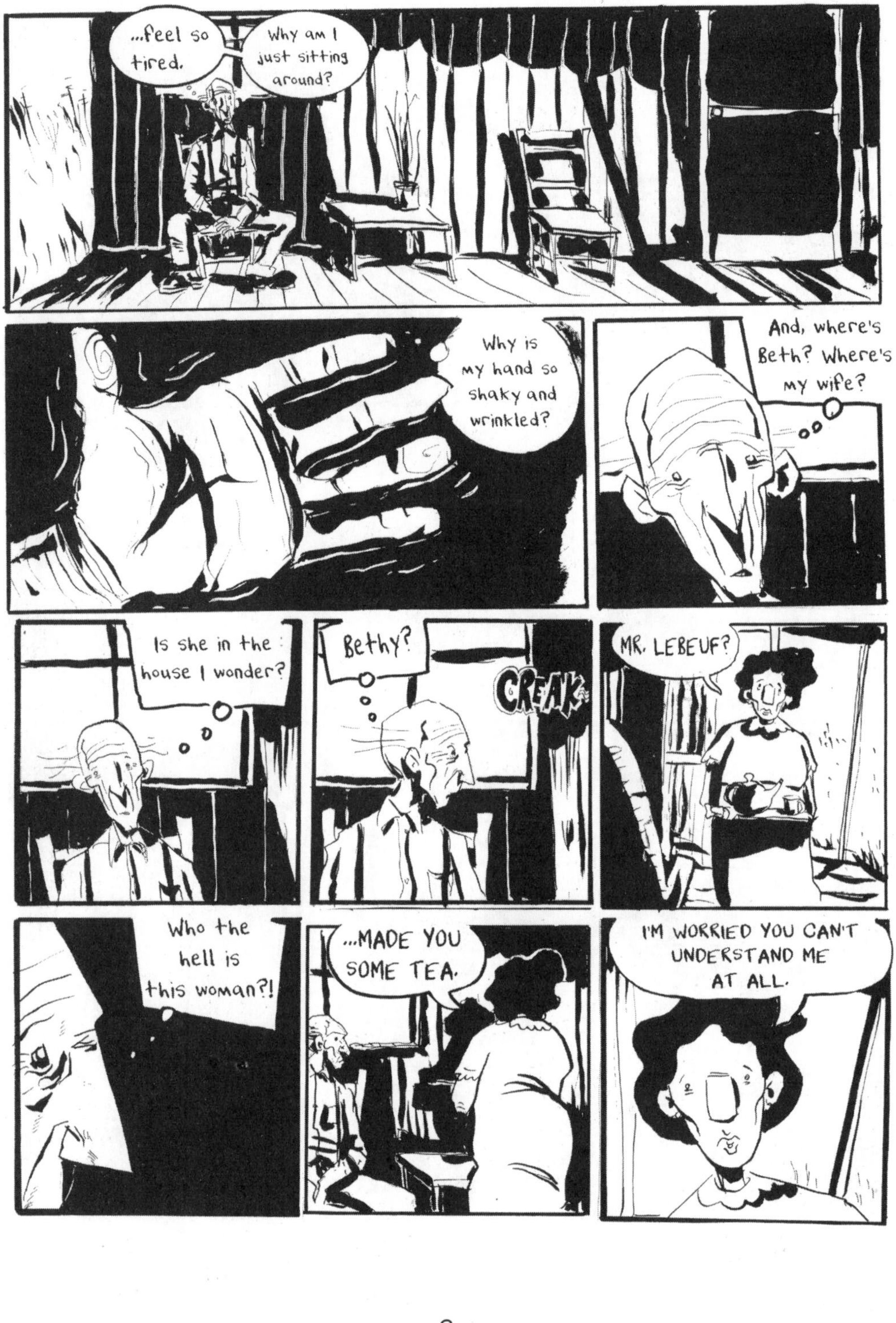
...feel so tired.
Why am I just sitting around?
Why is my hand so shaky and wrinkled?
And, where's Beth? Where's my wife?
Is she in the house I wonder?
Bethy?
CREAK
MR. LEBEUF?
Who the hell is this woman?!
...MADE YOU SOME TEA.
I'M WORRIED YOU CAN'T UNDERSTAND ME AT ALL.

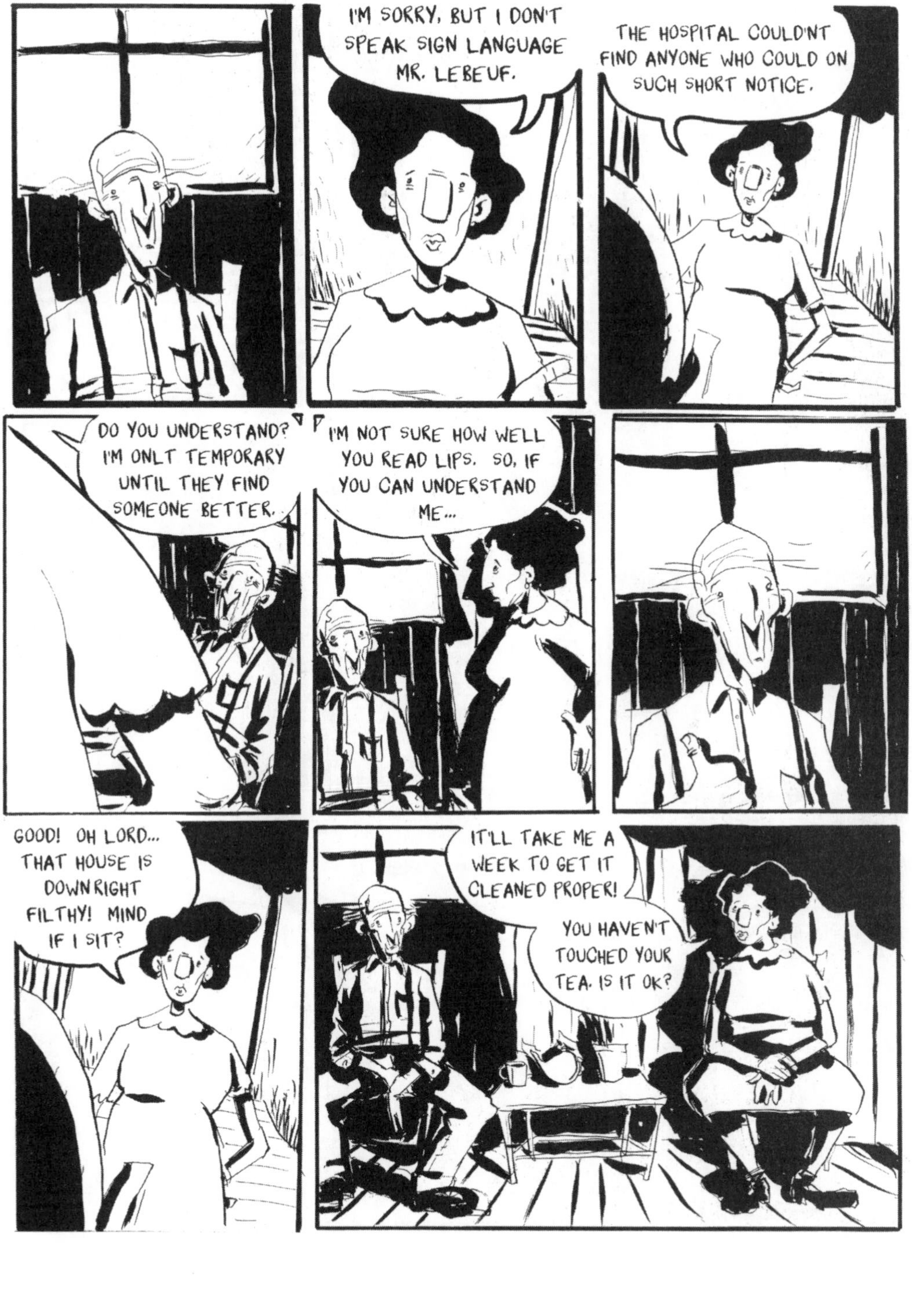
I'M SORRY, BUT I DON'T SPEAK SIGN LANGUAGE MR. LEBEUF.
THE HOSPITAL COULDN'T FIND ANYONE WHO COULD ON SUCH SHORT NOTICE.
DO YOU UNDERSTAND? I'M ONLT TEMPORARY UNTIL THEY FIND SOMEONE BETTER.
I'M NOT SURE HOW WELL YOU READ LIPS. SO, IF YOU CAN UNDERSTAND ME...
GOOD! OH LORD... THAT HOUSE IS DOWNRIGHT FILTHY! MIND IF I SIT?
IT'LL TAKE ME A WEEK TO GET IT CLEANED PROPER!
YOU HAVEN'T TOUCHED YOUR TEA. IS IT OK?

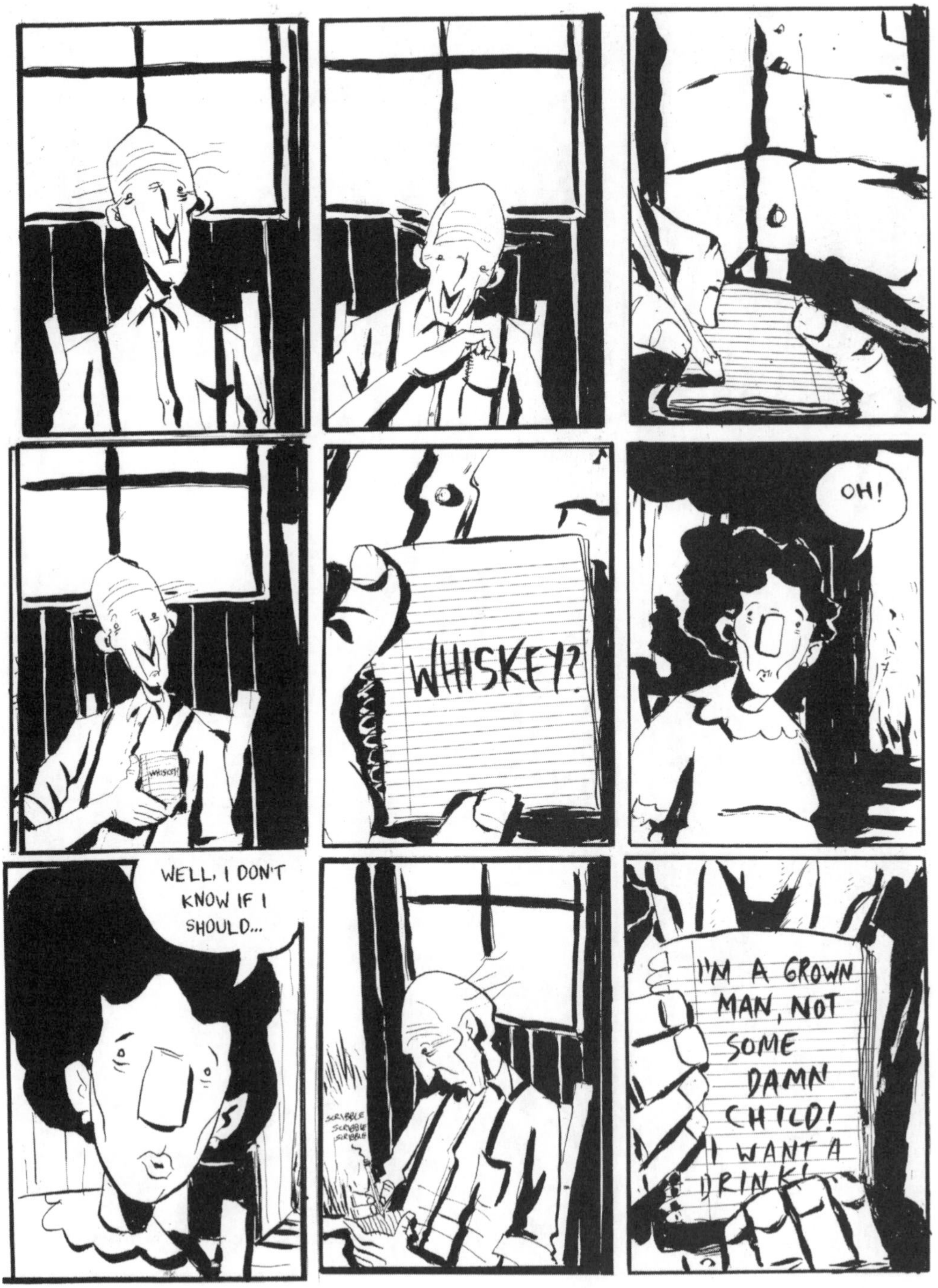
WHISKEY?
OH!
WELL, I DON'T KNOW IF I SHOULD...
SCRIBBLE SCRIBBLE SCRIBBLE
I'M A GROWN MAN, NOT SOME DAMN CHILD! I WANT A DRINK!

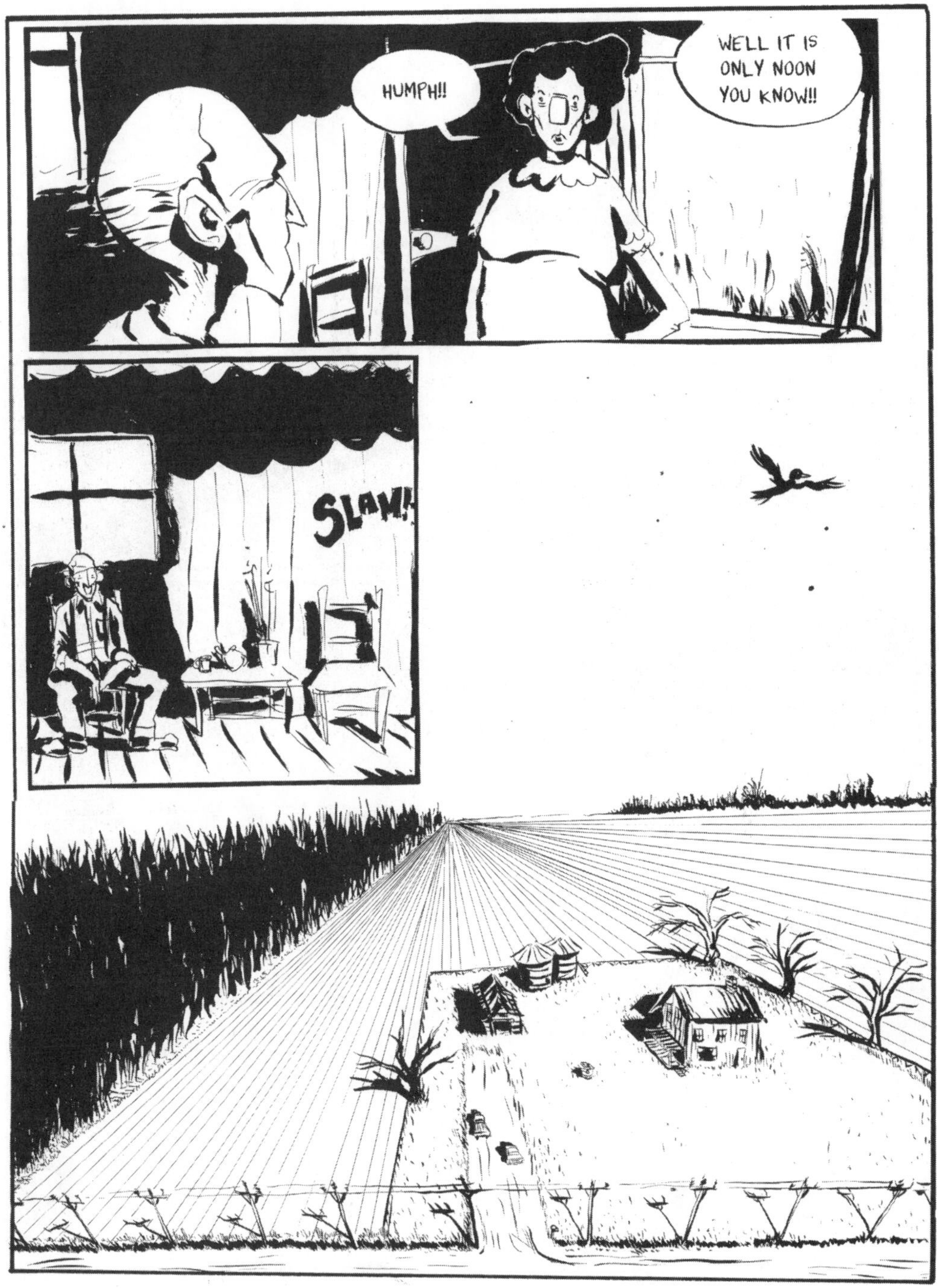
HUMPH!!
WELL IT IS ONLY NOON YOU KNOW!!
SLAM!!

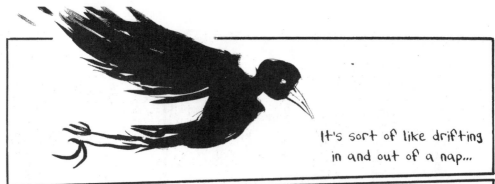

It's sort of like drifting in and out of a nap...

...Moments of clarity still come...

My mind will snap to attention and I'll know who I am, and where I am, just as clear as I ever did.

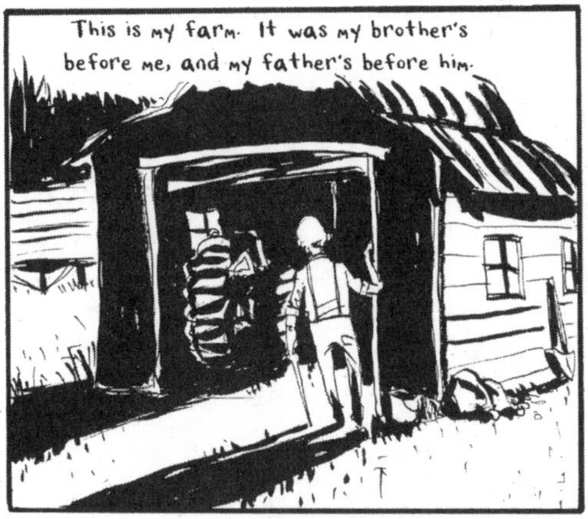
This is my farm. It was my brother's before me, and my father's before him.

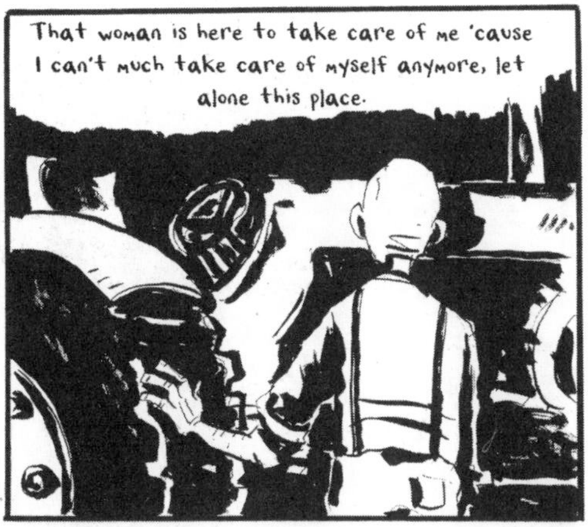
That woman is here to take care of me 'cause I can't much take care of myself anymore, let alone this place.

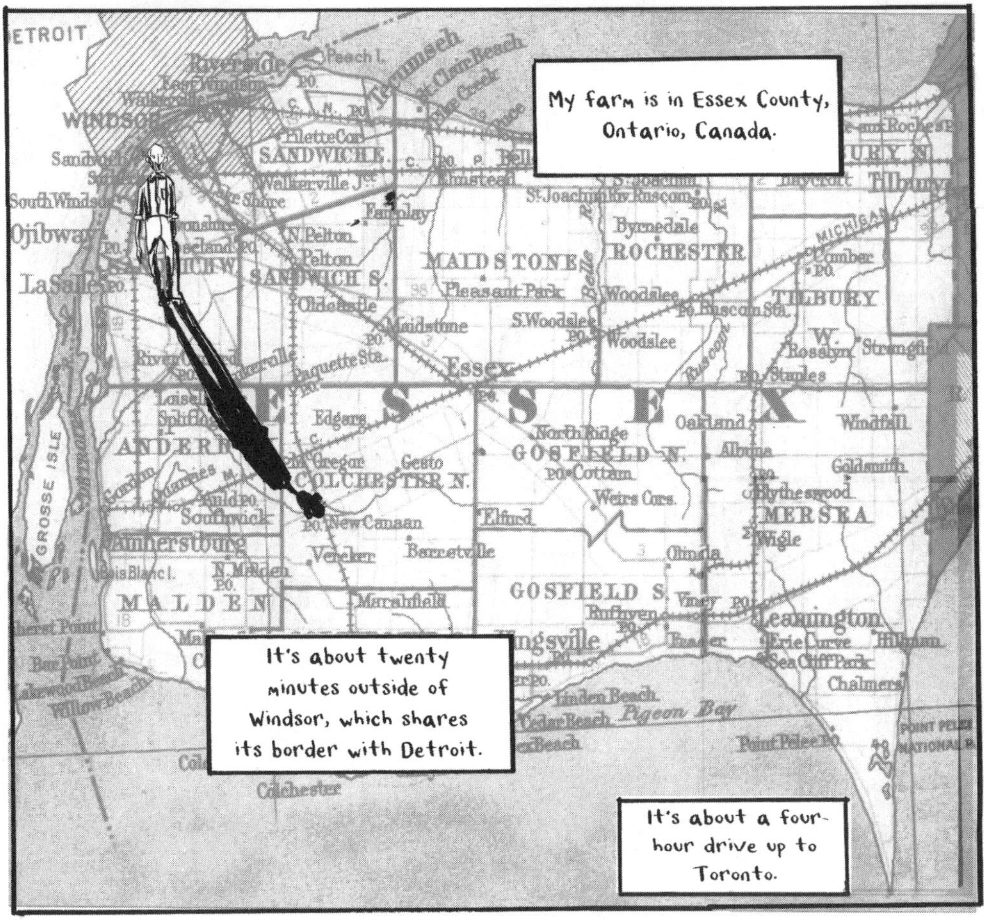
My farm is in Essex County, Ontario, Canada.
It's about twenty minutes outside of Windsor, which shares its border with Detroit.
It's about a four-hour drive up to Toronto.
DETROIT
MAIDSTONE
ROCHESTER
TILBURY
ESSEX
GOSFIELD S.
MERSEA
Leamington
Pigeon Bay
GROSSE ISLE

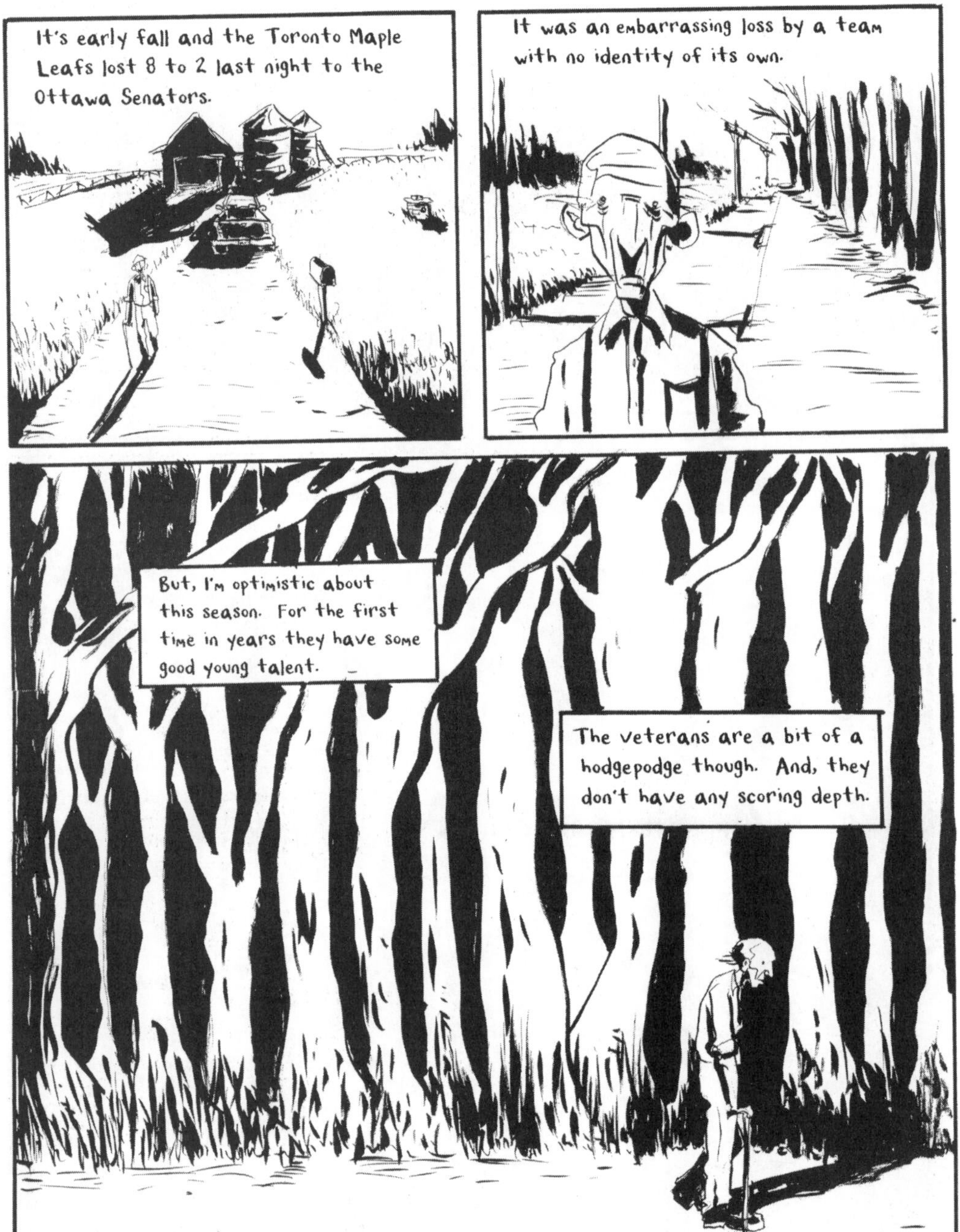
It's early fall and the Toronto Maple Leafs lost 8 to 2 last night to the Ottawa Senators.
It was an embarrassing loss by a team with no identity of its own.
But, I'm optimistic about this season. For the first time in years they have some good young talent.
The veterans are a bit of a hodgepodge though. And, they don't have any scoring depth.

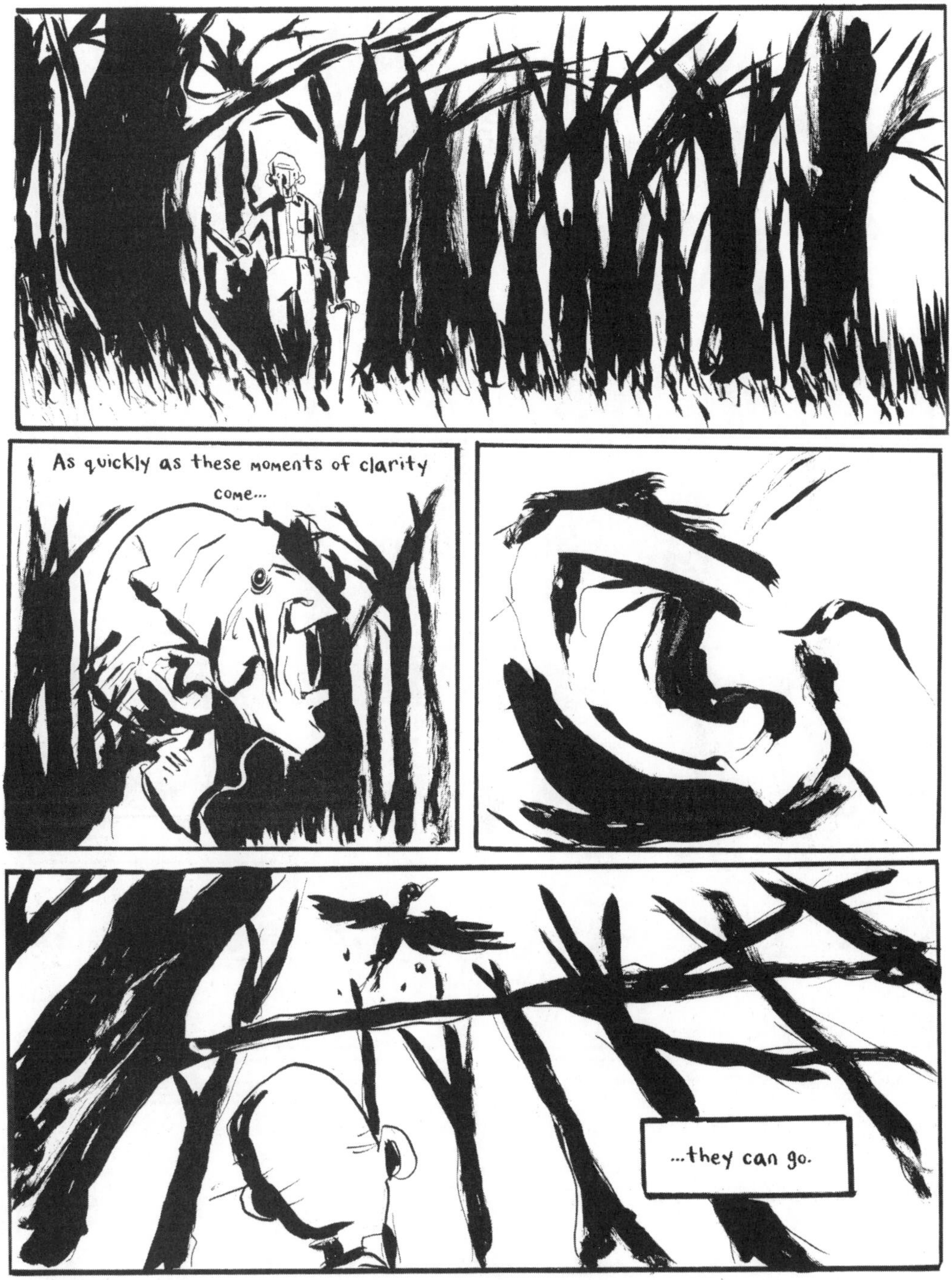
As quickly as these moments of clarity come...
...they can go.

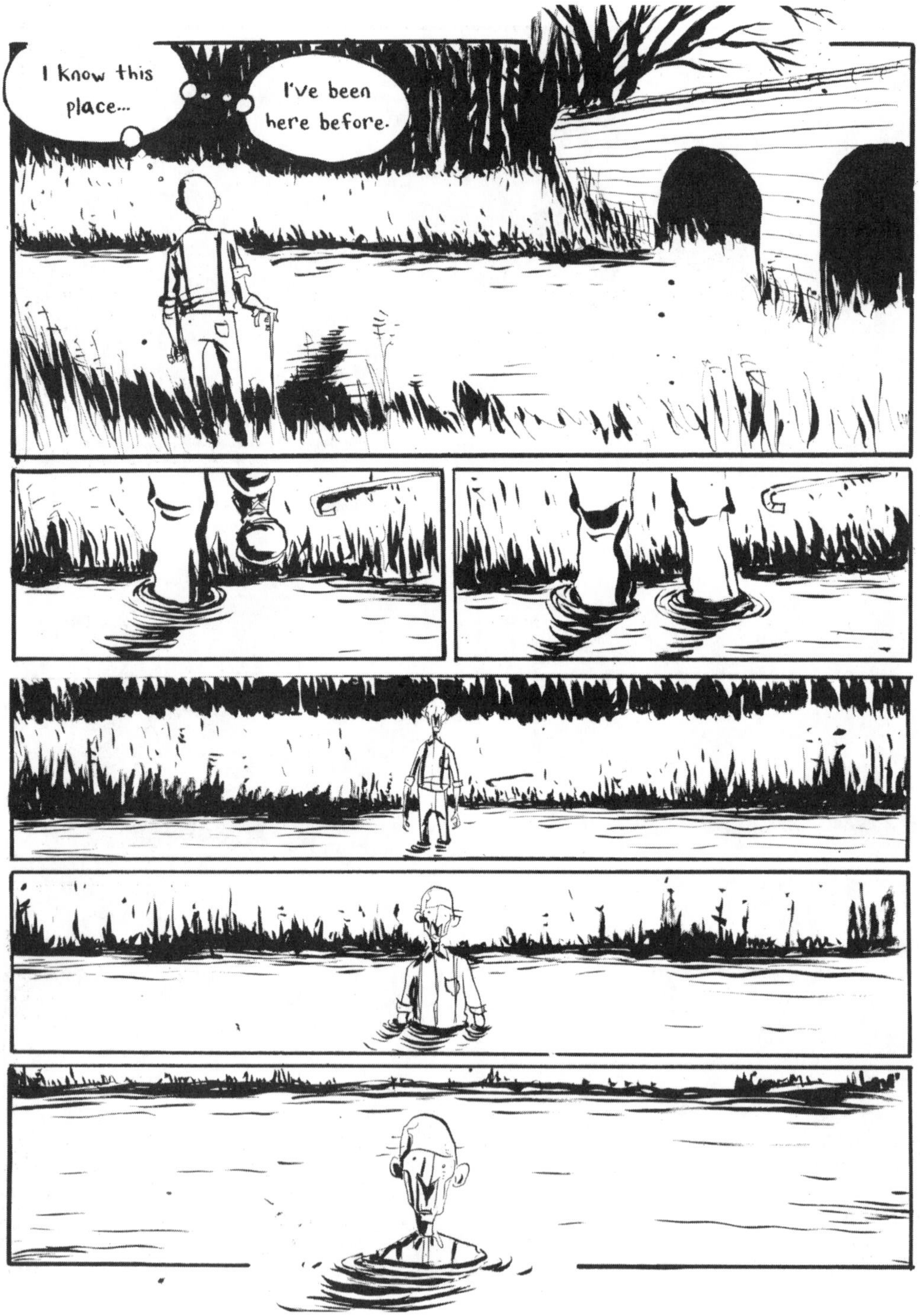
I know this place...
I've been here before.

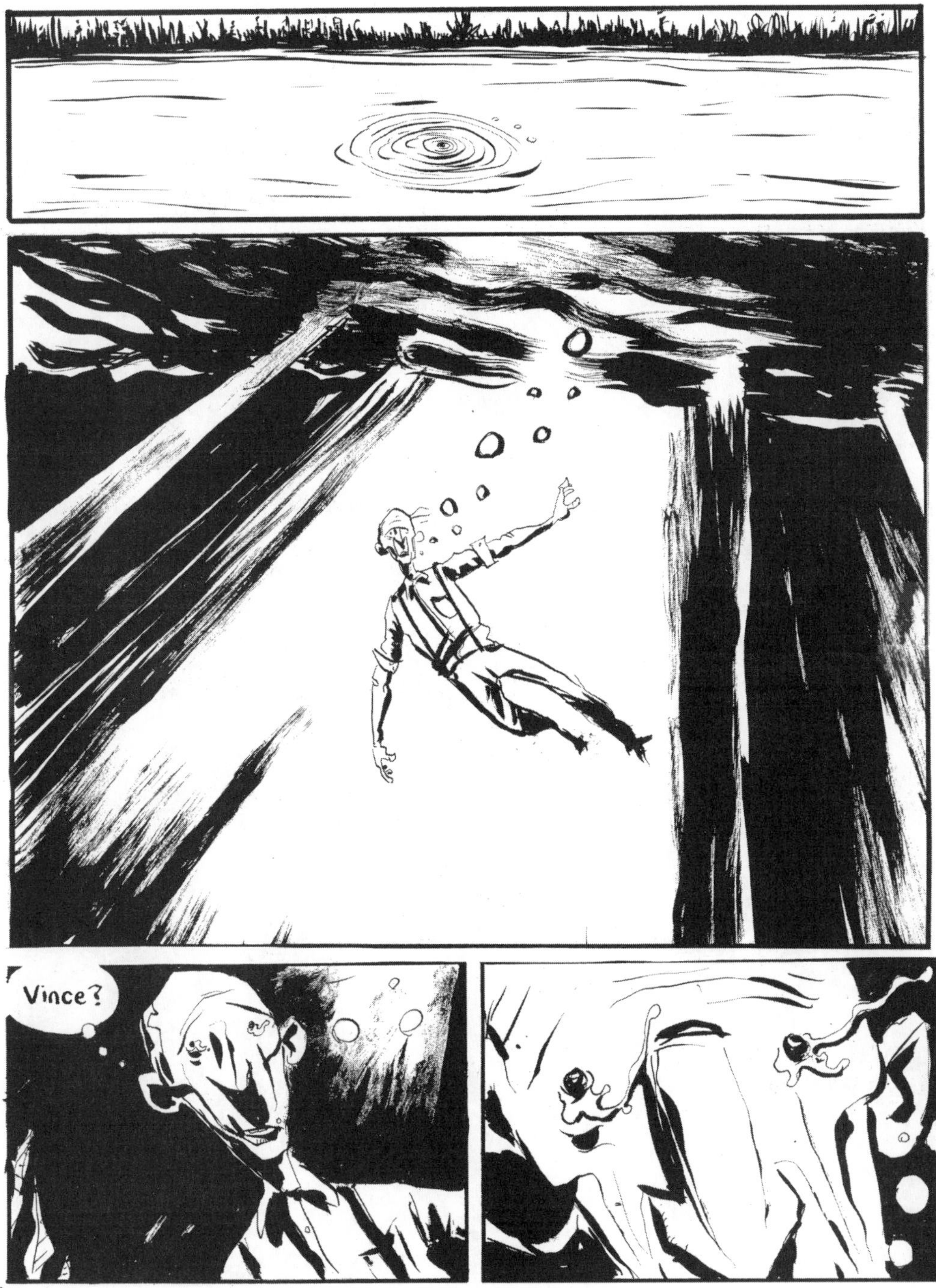
Vince?

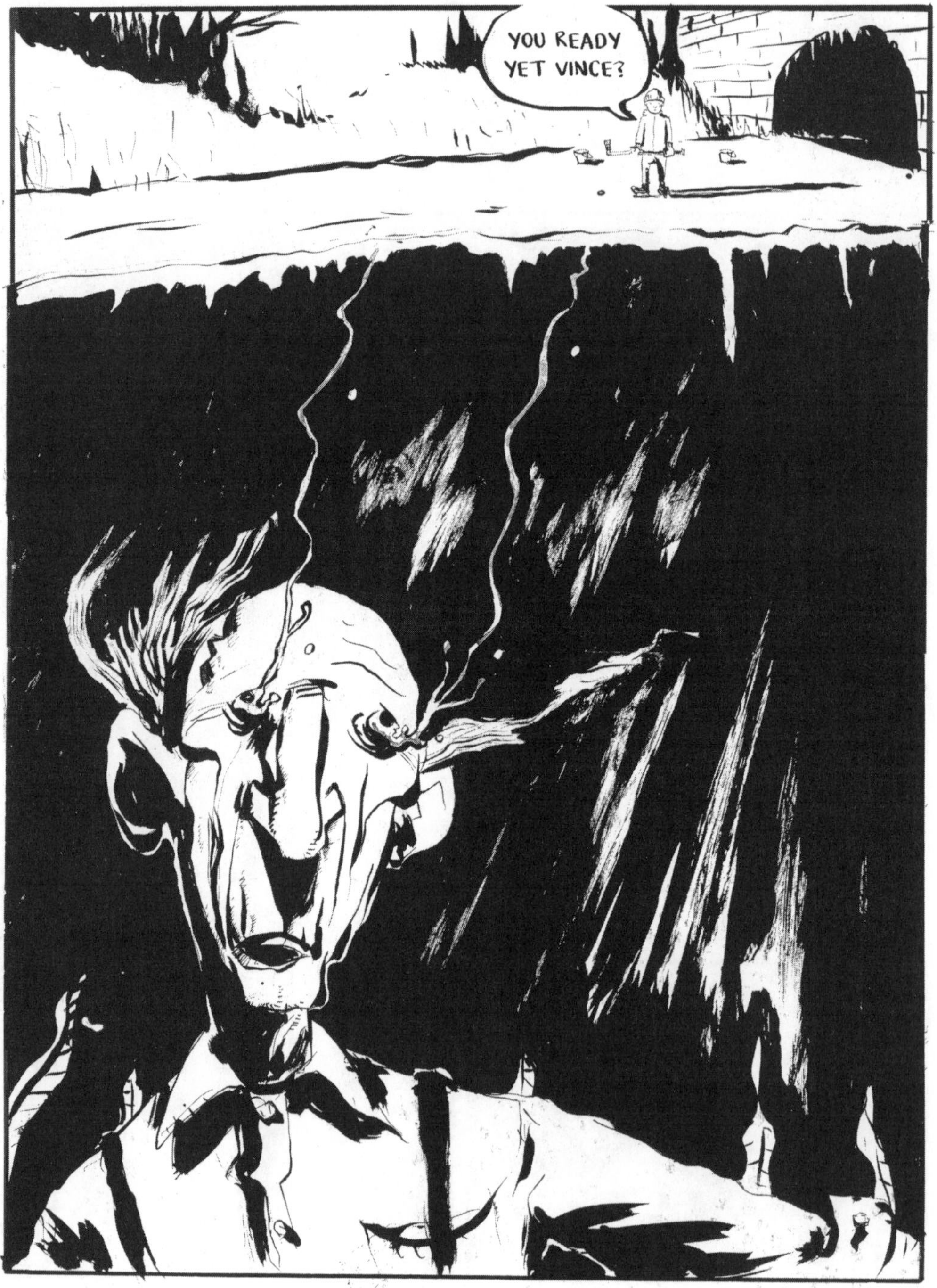
YOU READY YET VINCE?

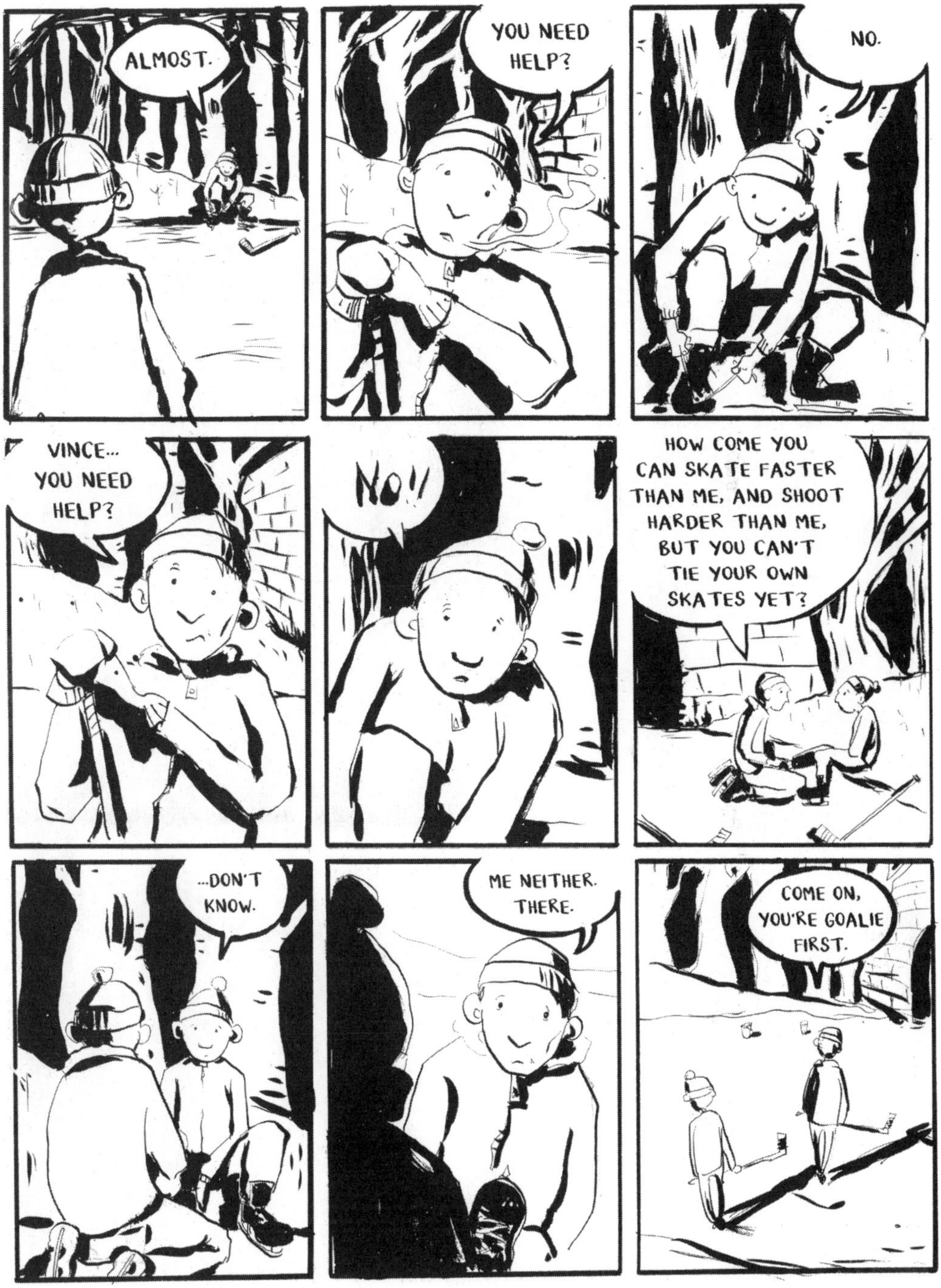
ALMOST.
YOU NEED HELP?
NO.
VINCE... YOU NEED HELP?
NO!!
HOW COME YOU CAN SKATE FASTER THAN ME, AND SHOOT HARDER THAN ME, BUT YOU CAN'T TIE YOUR OWN SKATES YET?
...DON'T KNOW.
ME NEITHER. THERE.
COME ON, YOU'RE GOALIE FIRST.

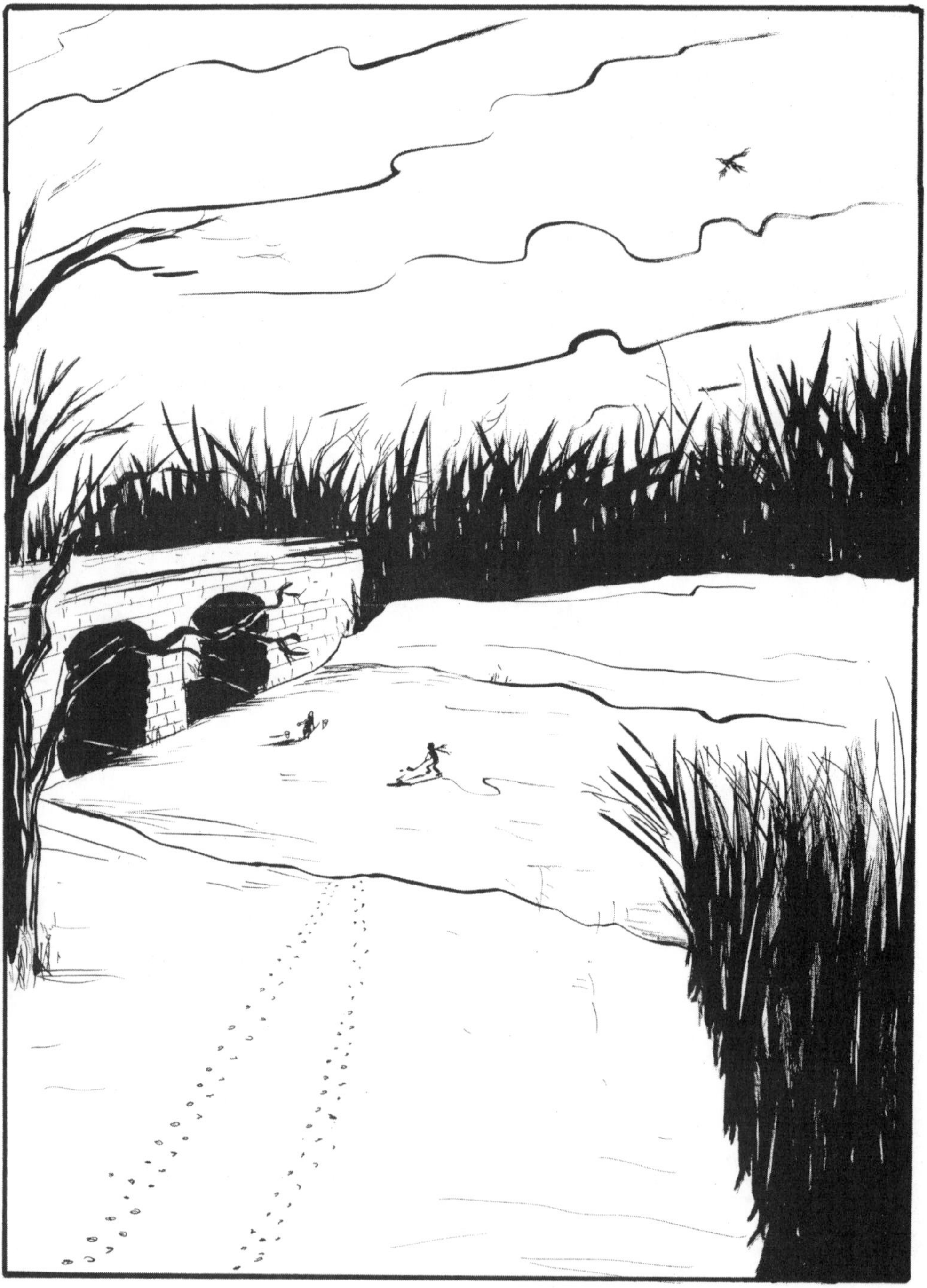

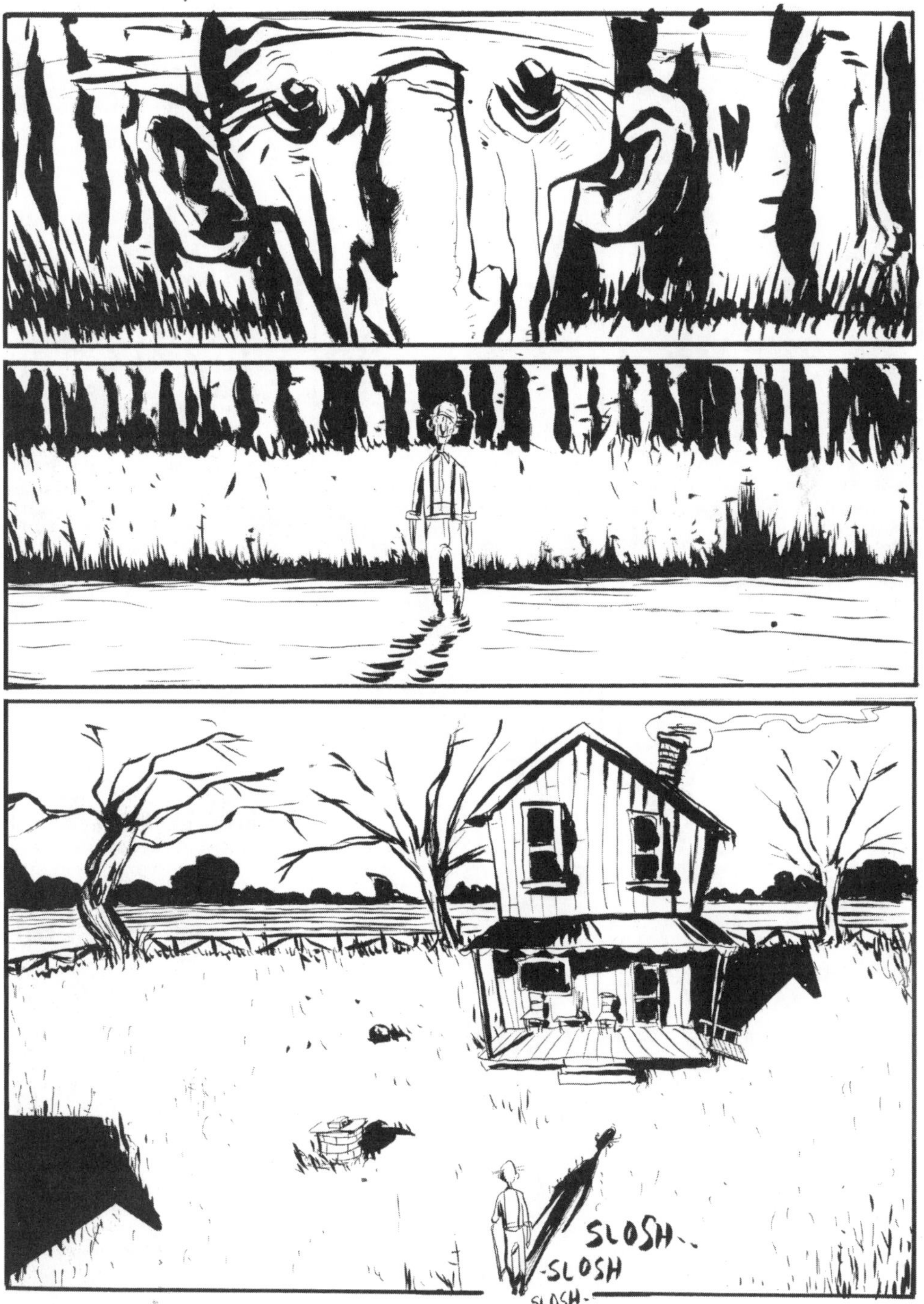
SLOSH..
-SLOSH
SLOSH-

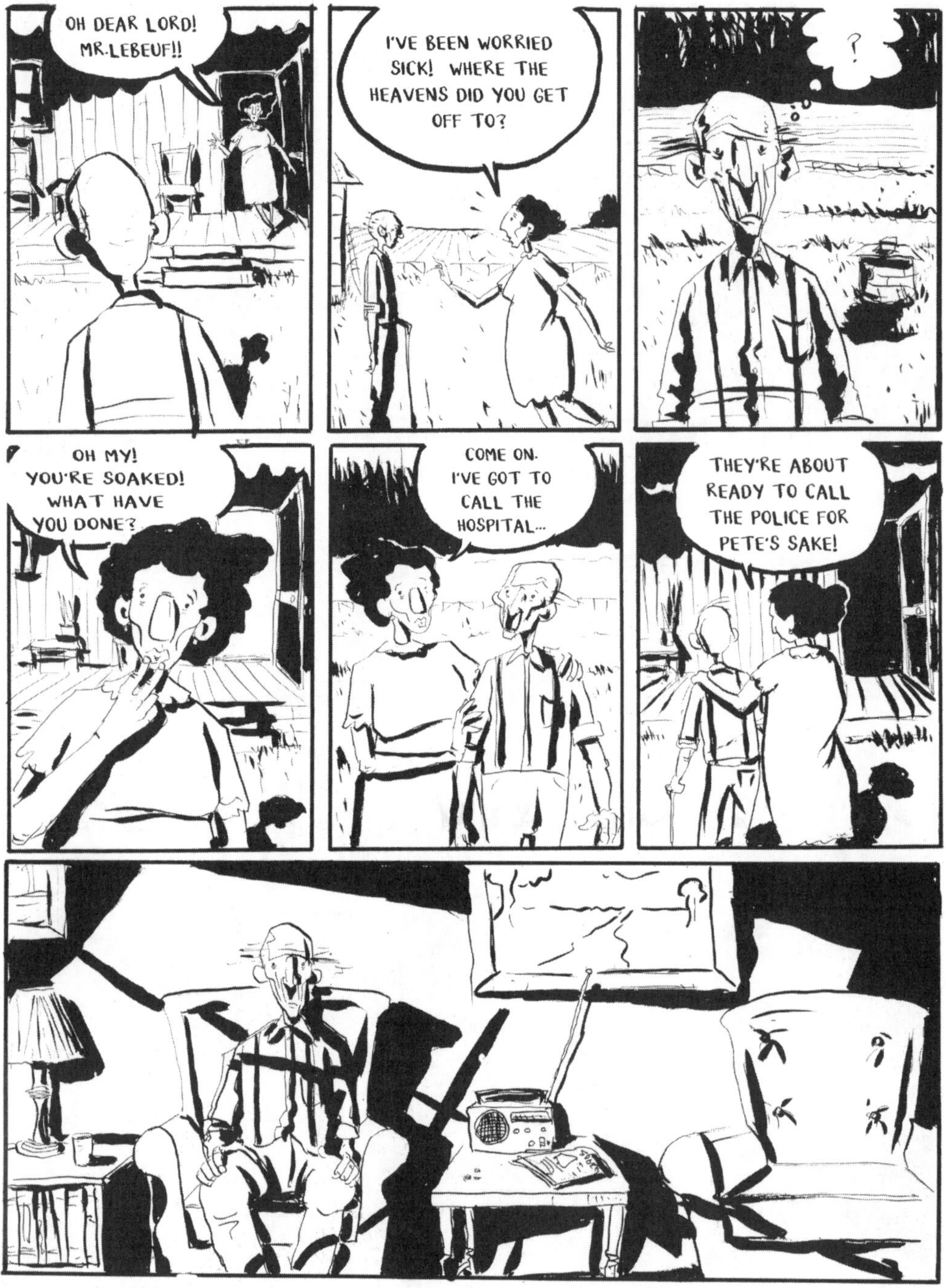
OH DEAR LORD! MR.LEBEUF!!
I'VE BEEN WORRIED SICK! WHERE THE HEAVENS DID YOU GET OFF TO?
?
OH MY! YOU'RE SOAKED! WHAT HAVE YOU DONE?
COME ON. I'VE GOT TO CALL THE HOSPITAL...
THEY'RE ABOUT READY TO CALL THE POLICE FOR PETE'S SAKE!

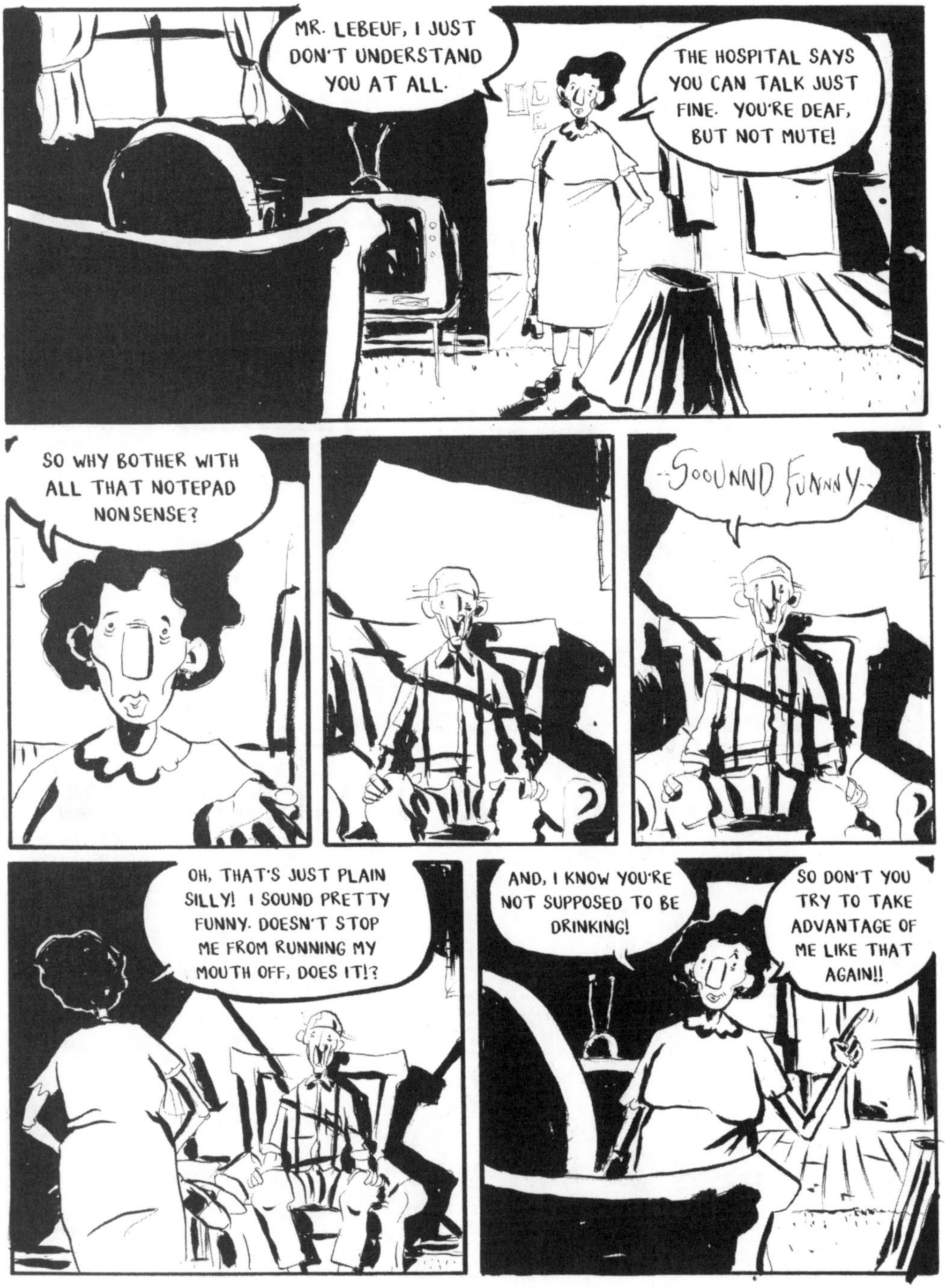
MR. LEBEUF, I JUST DON'T UNDERSTAND YOU AT ALL.
THE HOSPITAL SAYS YOU CAN TALK JUST FINE. YOU'RE DEAF, BUT NOT MUTE!
SO WHY BOTHER WITH ALL THAT NOTEPAD NONSENSE?
SOOUNND FUNNNY
OH, THAT'S JUST PLAIN SILLY! I SOUND PRETTY FUNNY. DOESN'T STOP ME FROM RUNNING MY MOUTH OFF, DOES IT!?
AND, I KNOW YOU'RE NOT SUPPOSED TO BE DRINKING!
SO DON'T YOU TRY TO TAKE ADVANTAGE OF ME LIKE THAT AGAIN!!

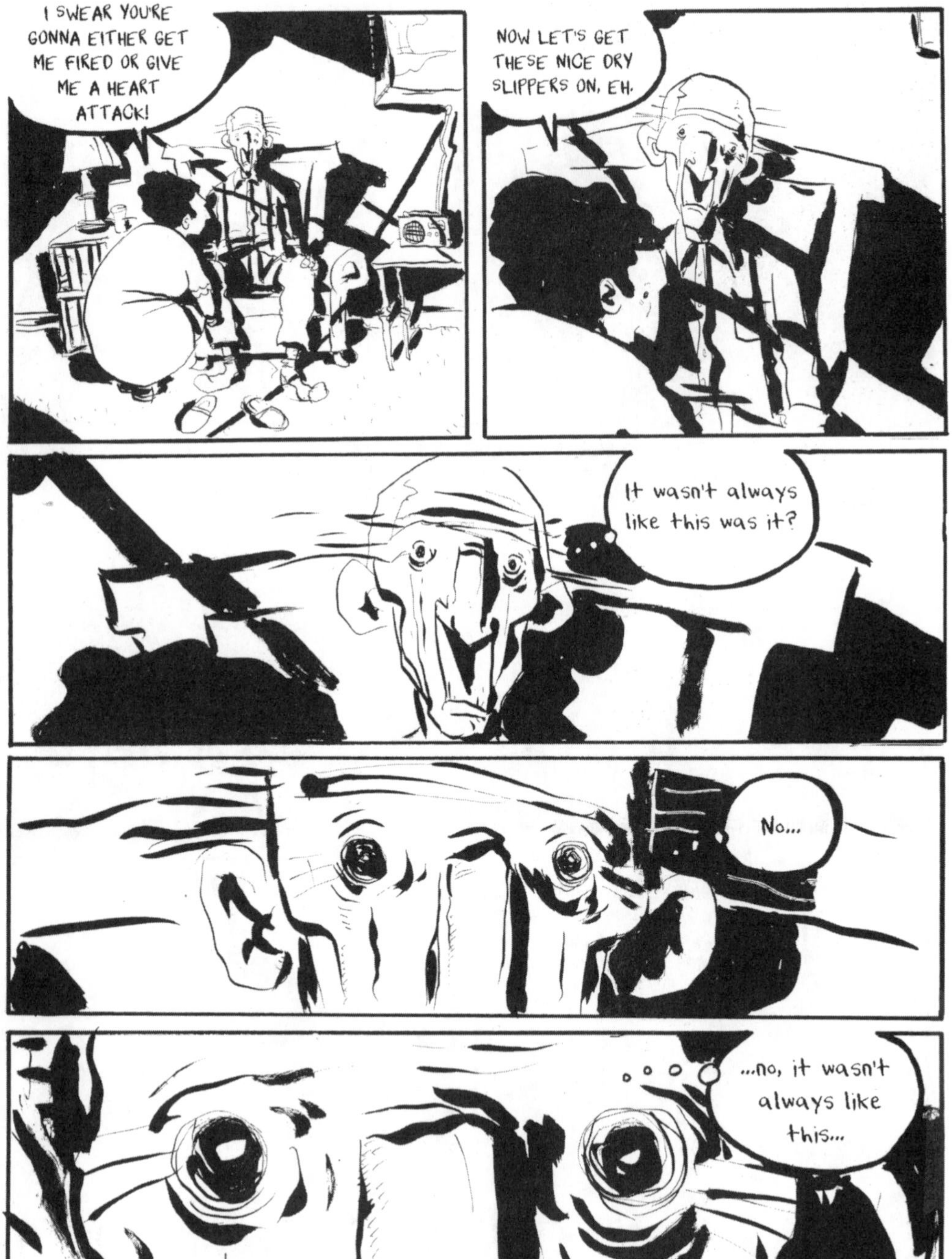
I SWEAR YOU'RE GONNA EITHER GET ME FIRED OR GIVE ME A HEART ATTACK!
NOW LET'S GET THESE NICE DRY SLIPPERS ON, EH.
It wasn't always like this was it?
No...
...no, it wasn't always like this...

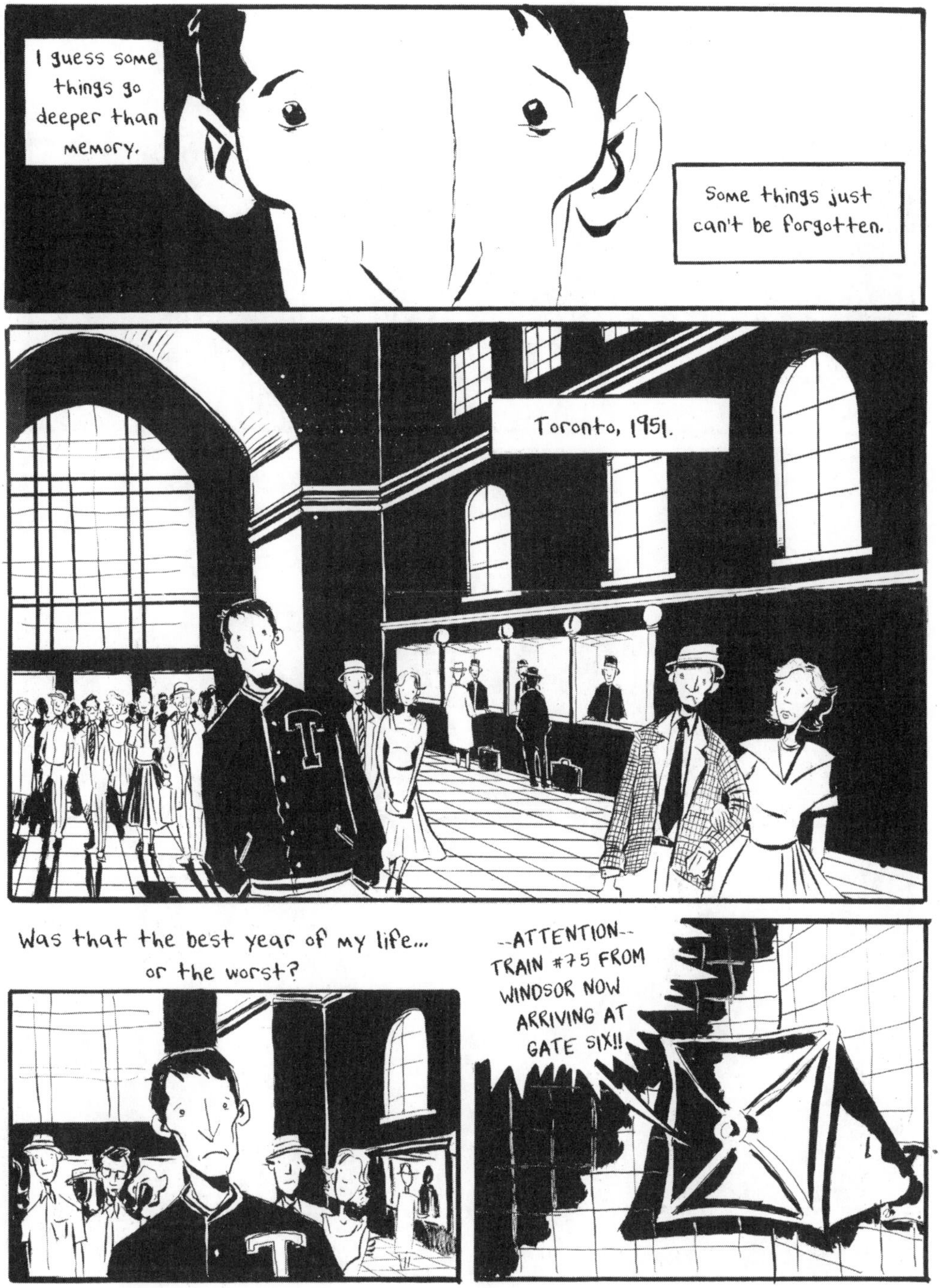
I guess some things go deeper than memory.
Some things just can't be forgotten.
Toronto, 1951.
Was that the best year of my life... or the worst?
--ATTENTION-- TRAIN #75 FROM WINDSOR NOW ARRIVING AT GATE SIX!!

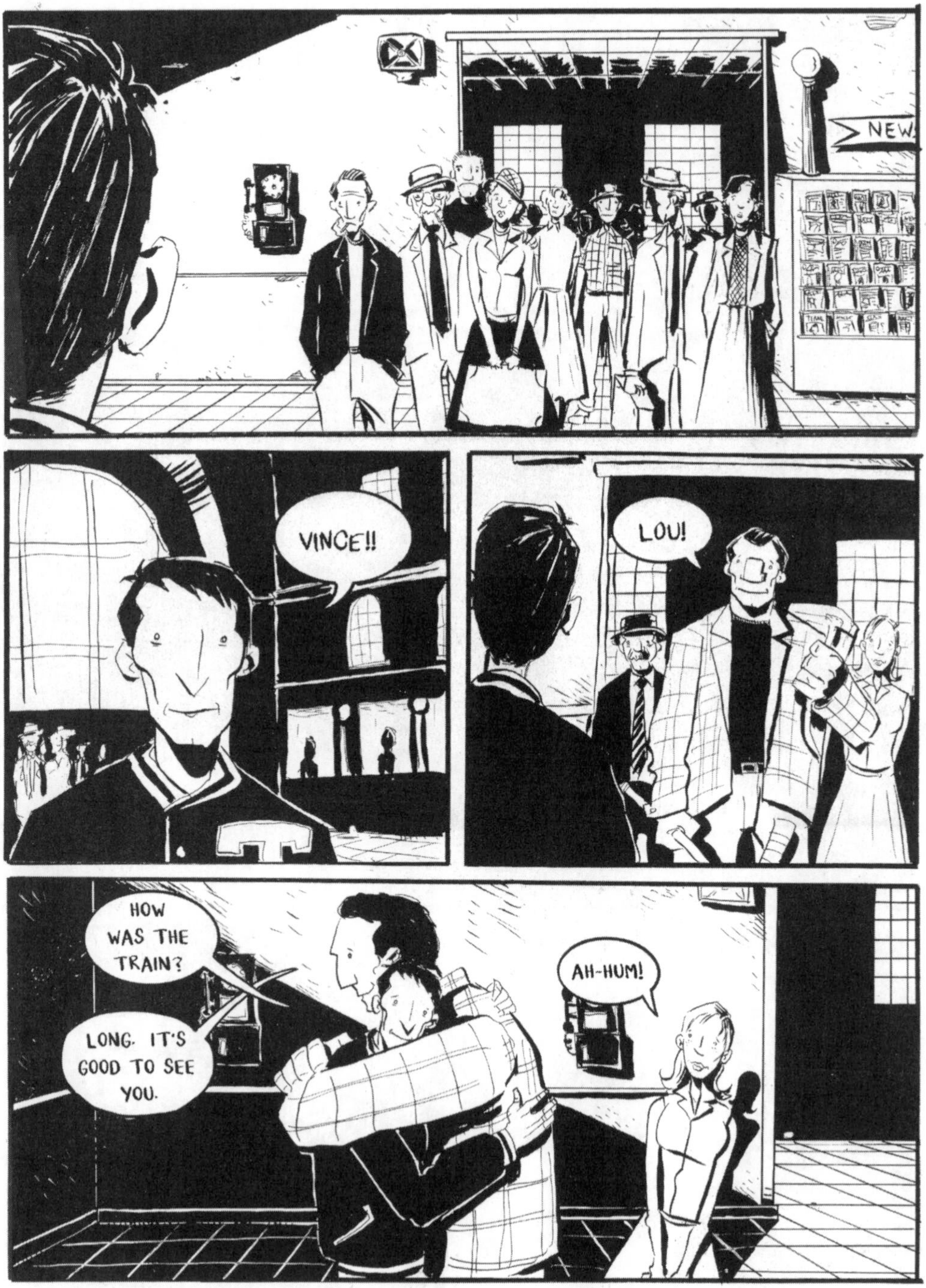
NEWS
VINCE!!
LOU!
HOW WAS THE TRAIN?
LONG. IT'S GOOD TO SEE YOU.
AH-HUM!

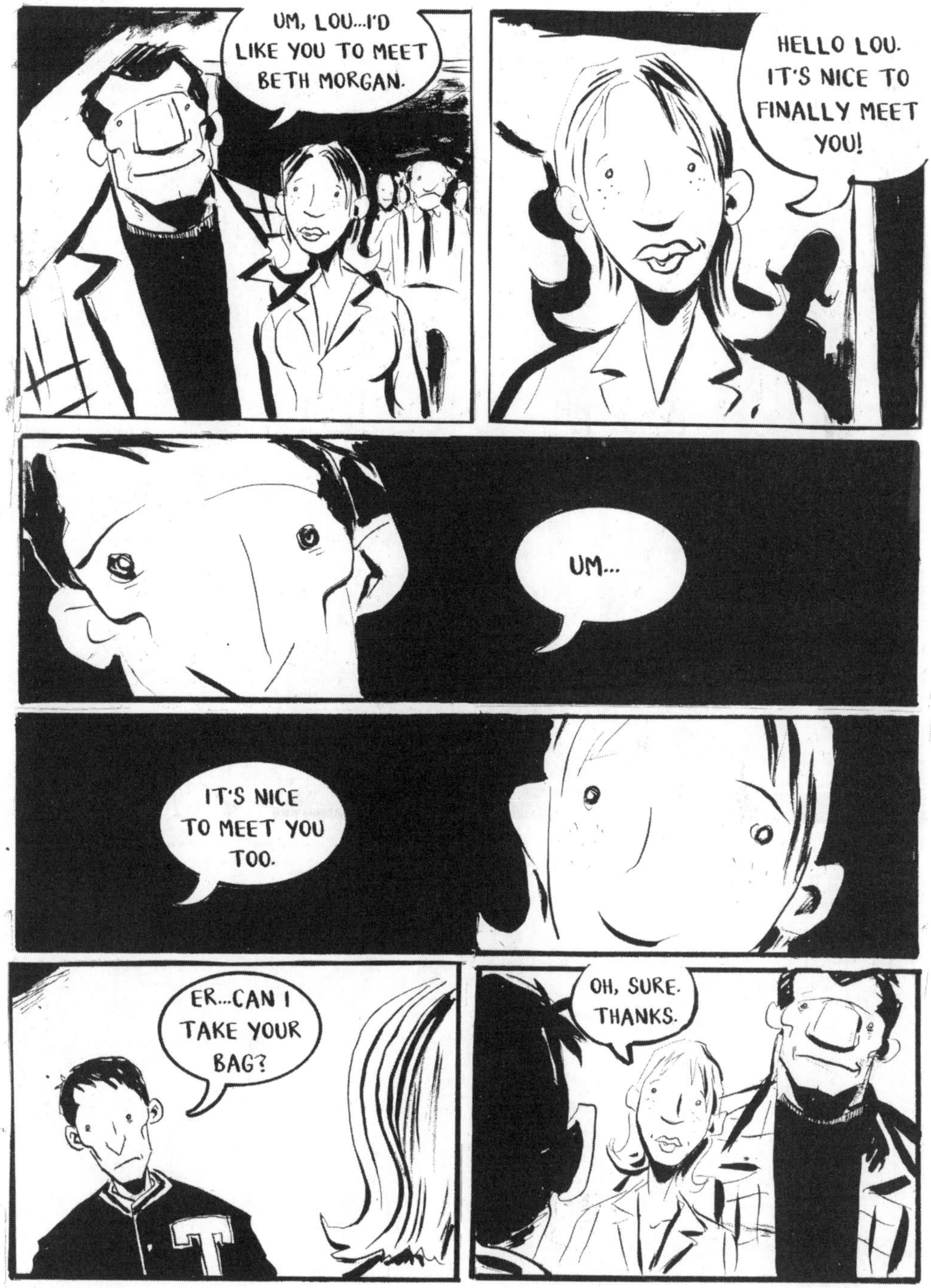
UM, LOU...I'D LIKE YOU TO MEET BETH MORGAN.
HELLO LOU. IT'S NICE TO FINALLY MEET YOU!
UM...
IT'S NICE TO MEET YOU TOO.
ER...CAN I TAKE YOUR BAG?
OH, SURE. THANKS.

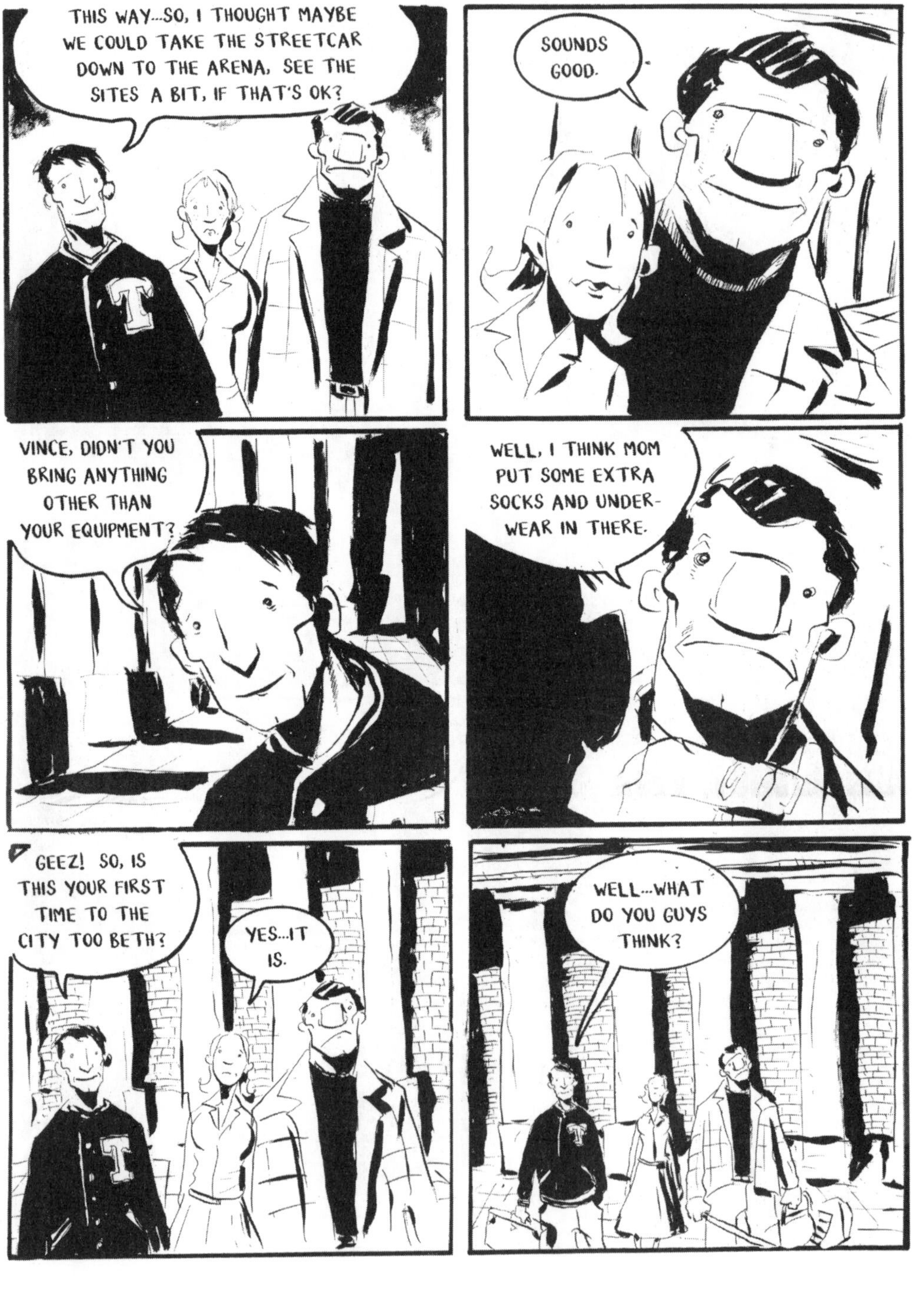
THIS WAY...SO, I THOUGHT MAYBE WE COULD TAKE THE STREETCAR DOWN TO THE ARENA, SEE THE SITES A BIT, IF THAT'S OK?
SOUNDS GOOD.
VINCE, DIDN'T YOU BRING ANYTHING OTHER THAN YOUR EQUIPMENT?
WELL, I THINK MOM PUT SOME EXTRA SOCKS AND UNDER-WEAR IN THERE.
GEEZ! SO, IS THIS YOUR FIRST TIME TO THE CITY TOO BETH?
YES...IT IS.
WELL...WHAT DO YOU GUYS THINK?

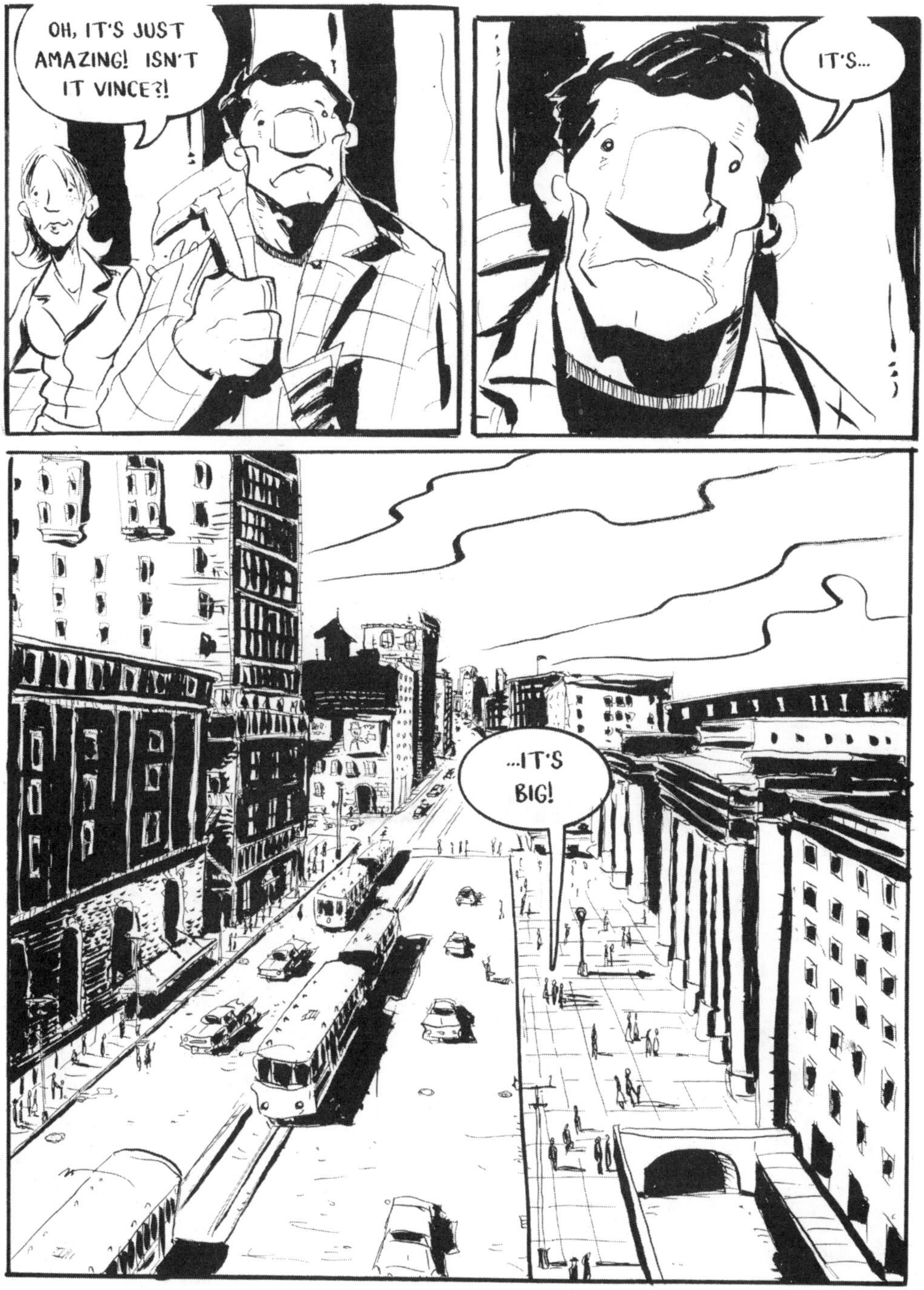
OH, IT'S JUST AMAZING! ISN'T IT VINCE?!
IT'S...
...IT'S BIG!

1951. The year my "little" brother followed me to Toronto to play hockey for a now defunct semiprofessional hockey club called THE GRIZZLIES. We played out of the old Ricoh Coliseum downtown. I was in my third year with the team, and I'd established myself as a reliable third line centerman.

The Grizzlies were struggling to hold on to a playoff spot when the scouts got wind of a young winger from Essex County who had scored thirty goals in his last junior season. The fact that he also happened to be my younger brother only sweetened the deal for them. A day after his 18th birthday they had him on a train to the city...

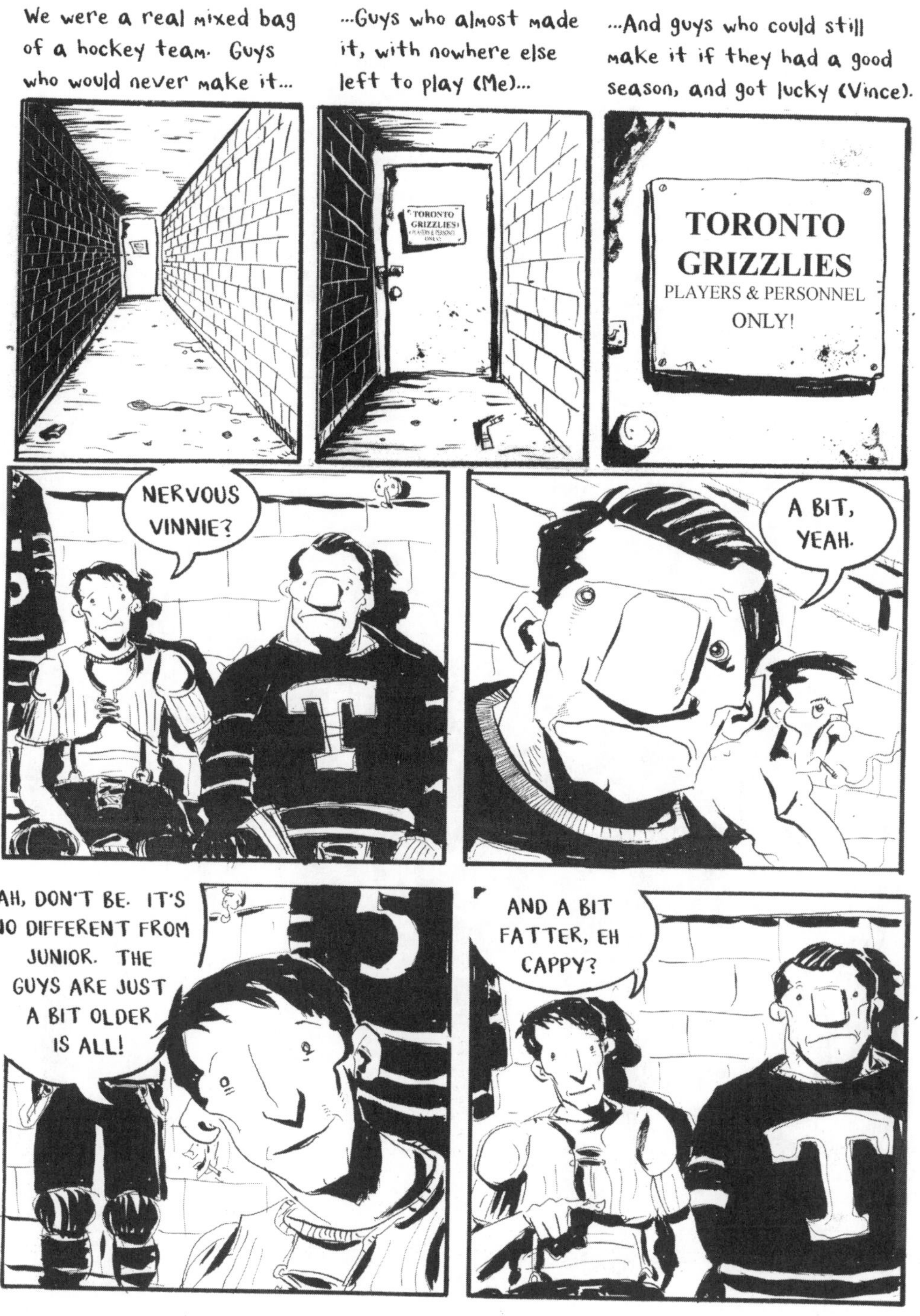
We were a real mixed bag of a hockey team. Guys who would never make it...
...Guys who almost made it, with nowhere else left to play (Me)...
...And guys who could still make it if they had a good season, and got lucky (Vince).
TORONTO GRIZZLIES PLAYERS & PERSONNEL ONLY!
NERVOUS VINNIE?
A BIT, YEAH.
AH, DON'T BE. IT'S NO DIFFERENT FROM JUNIOR. THE GUYS ARE JUST A BIT OLDER IS ALL!
AND A BIT FATTER, EH CAPPY?

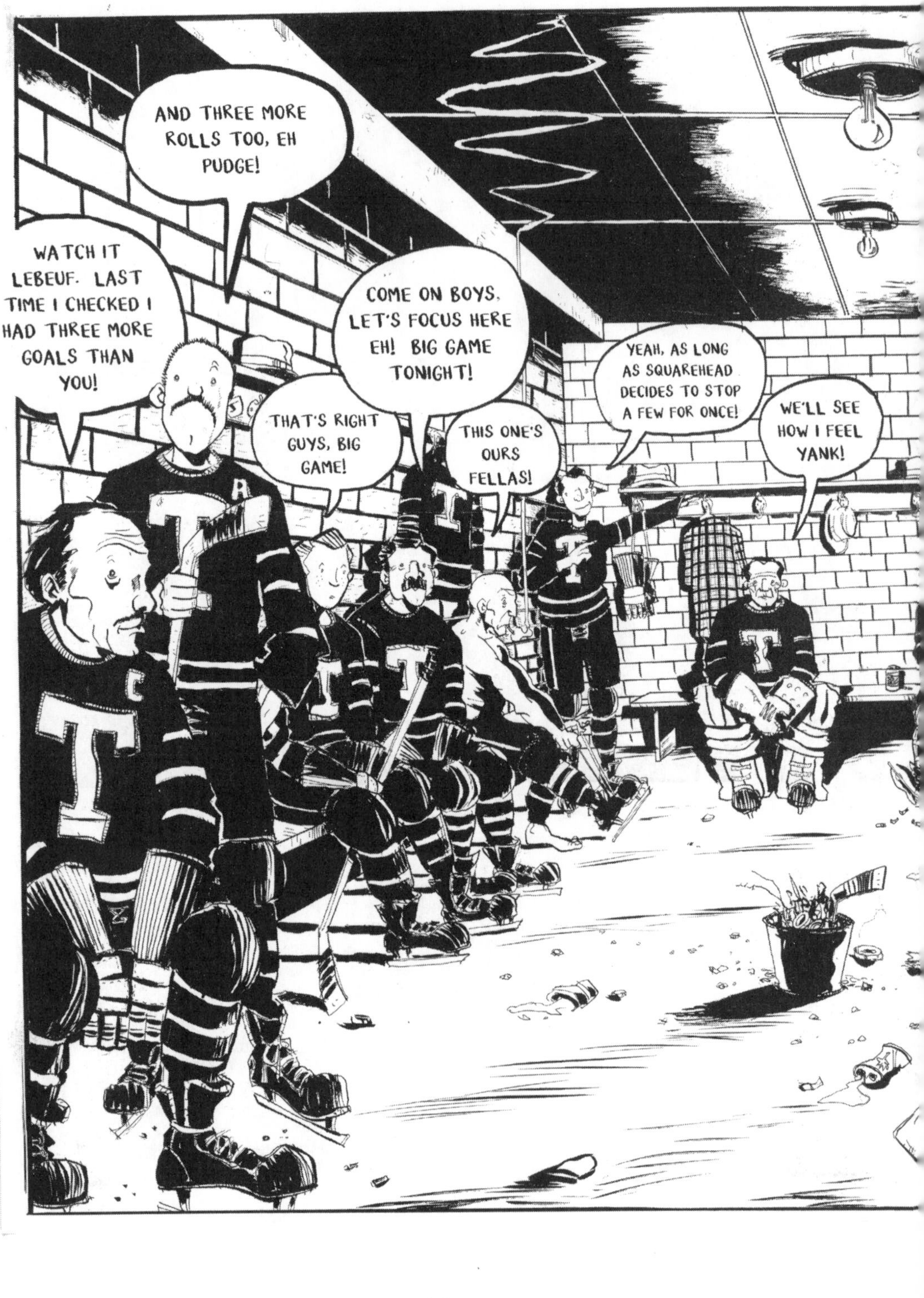
WATCH IT LEBEUF. LAST TIME I CHECKED I HAD THREE MORE GOALS THAN YOU!
AND THREE MORE ROLLS TOO, EH PUDGE!
COME ON BOYS, LET'S FOCUS HERE EH! BIG GAME TONIGHT!
THAT'S RIGHT GUYS, BIG GAME!
THIS ONE'S OURS FELLAS!
YEAH, AS LONG AS SQUAREHEAD DECIDES TO STOP A FEW FOR ONCE!
WE'LL SEE HOW I FEEL YANK!

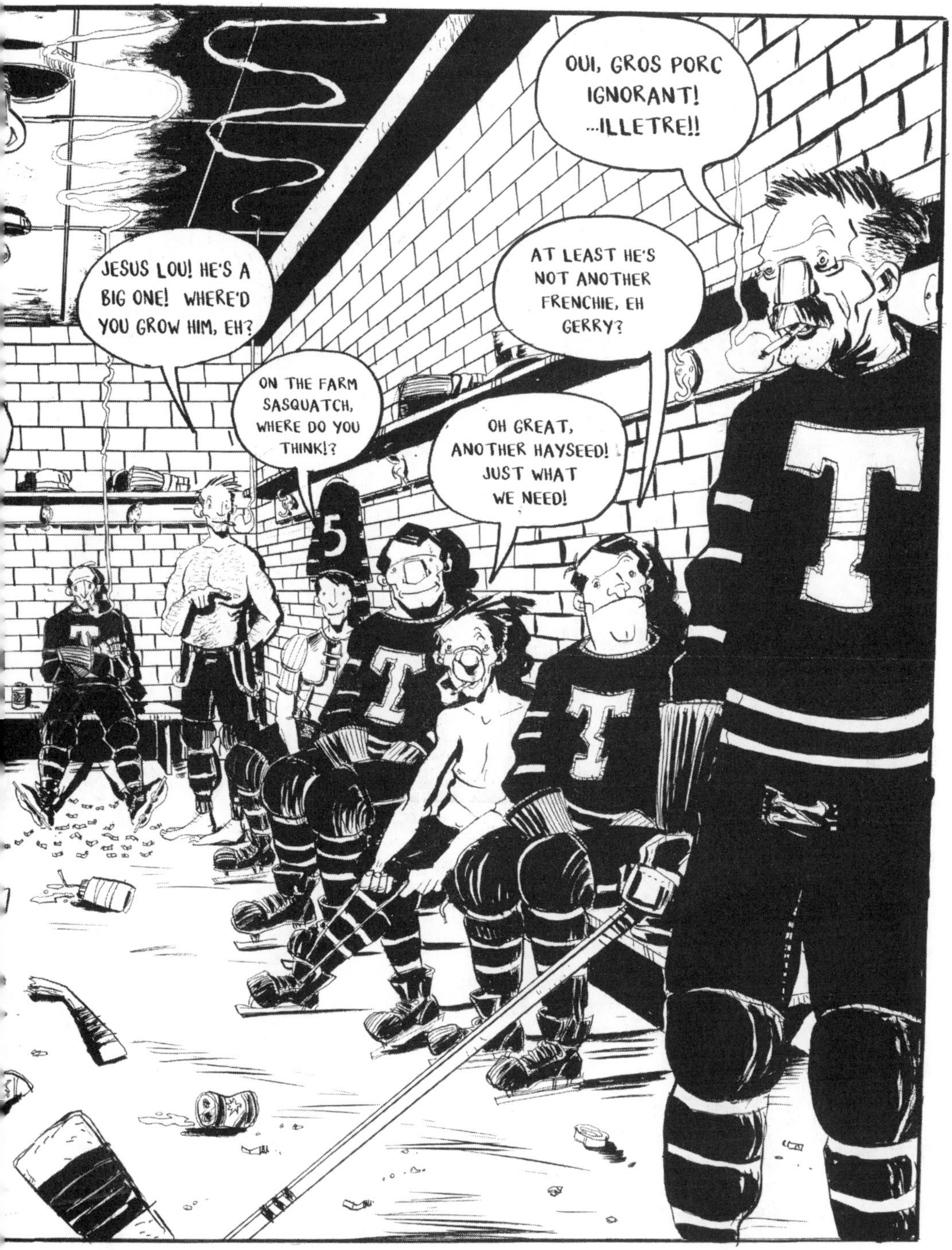
JESUS LOU! HE'S A BIG ONE! WHERE'D YOU GROW HIM, EH?
ON THE FARM SASQUATCH, WHERE DO YOU THINK!?
OH GREAT, ANOTHER HAYSEED! JUST WHAT WE NEED!
AT LEAST HE'S NOT ANOTHER FRENCHIE, EH GERRY?
OUI, GROS PORC IGNORANT! ...ILLETRE!!

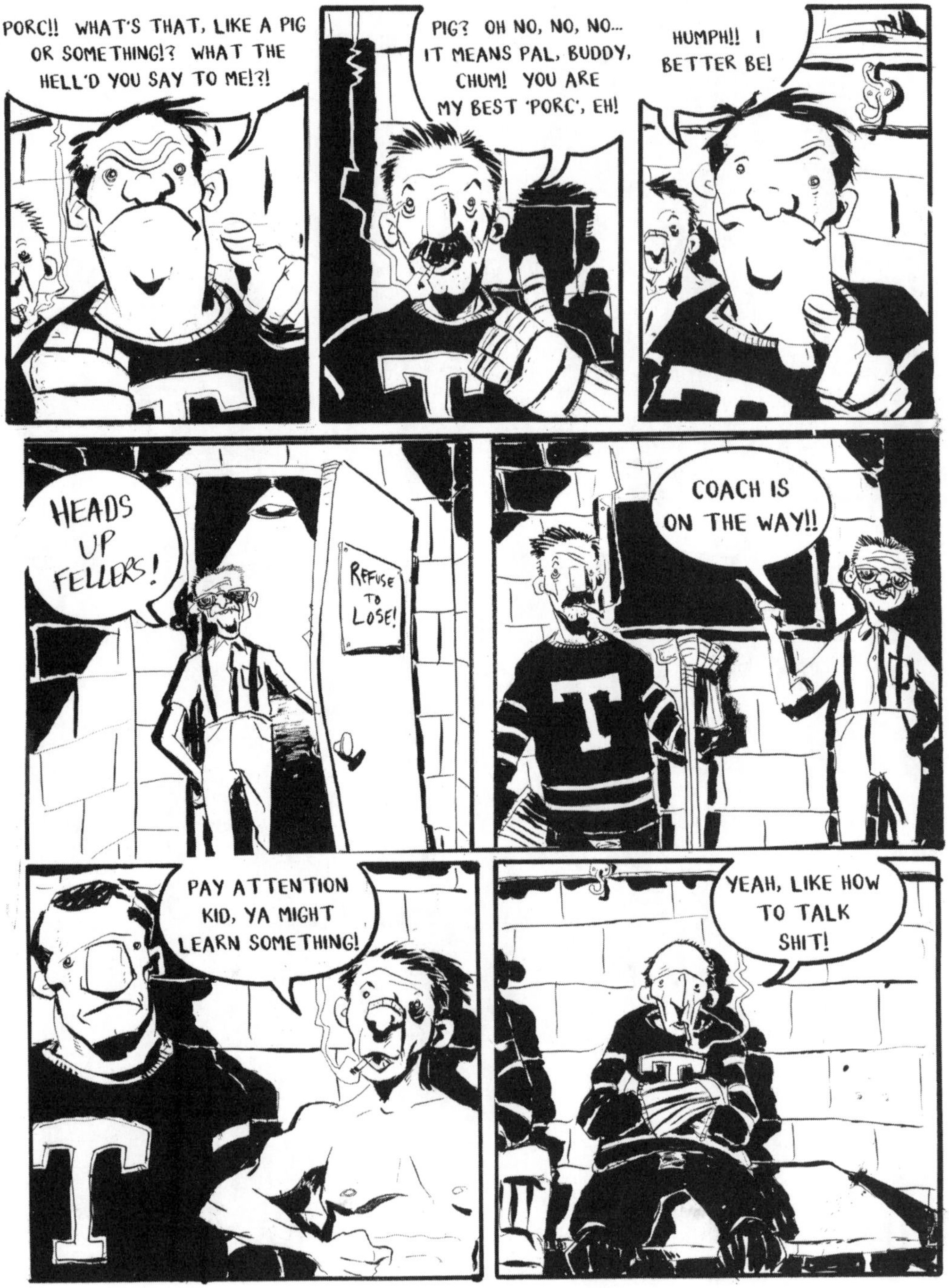
PORC!! WHAT'S THAT, LIKE A PIG OR SOMETHING!? WHAT THE HELL'D YOU SAY TO ME!?!
PIG? OH NO, NO, NO... IT MEANS PAL, BUDDY, CHUM! YOU ARE MY BEST 'PORC', EH!
HUMPH!! I BETTER BE!
HEADS UP FELLERS!
REFUSE TO LOSE!
COACH IS ON THE WAY!!
PAY ATTENTION KID, YA MIGHT LEARN SOMETHING!
YEAH, LIKE HOW TO TALK SHIT!

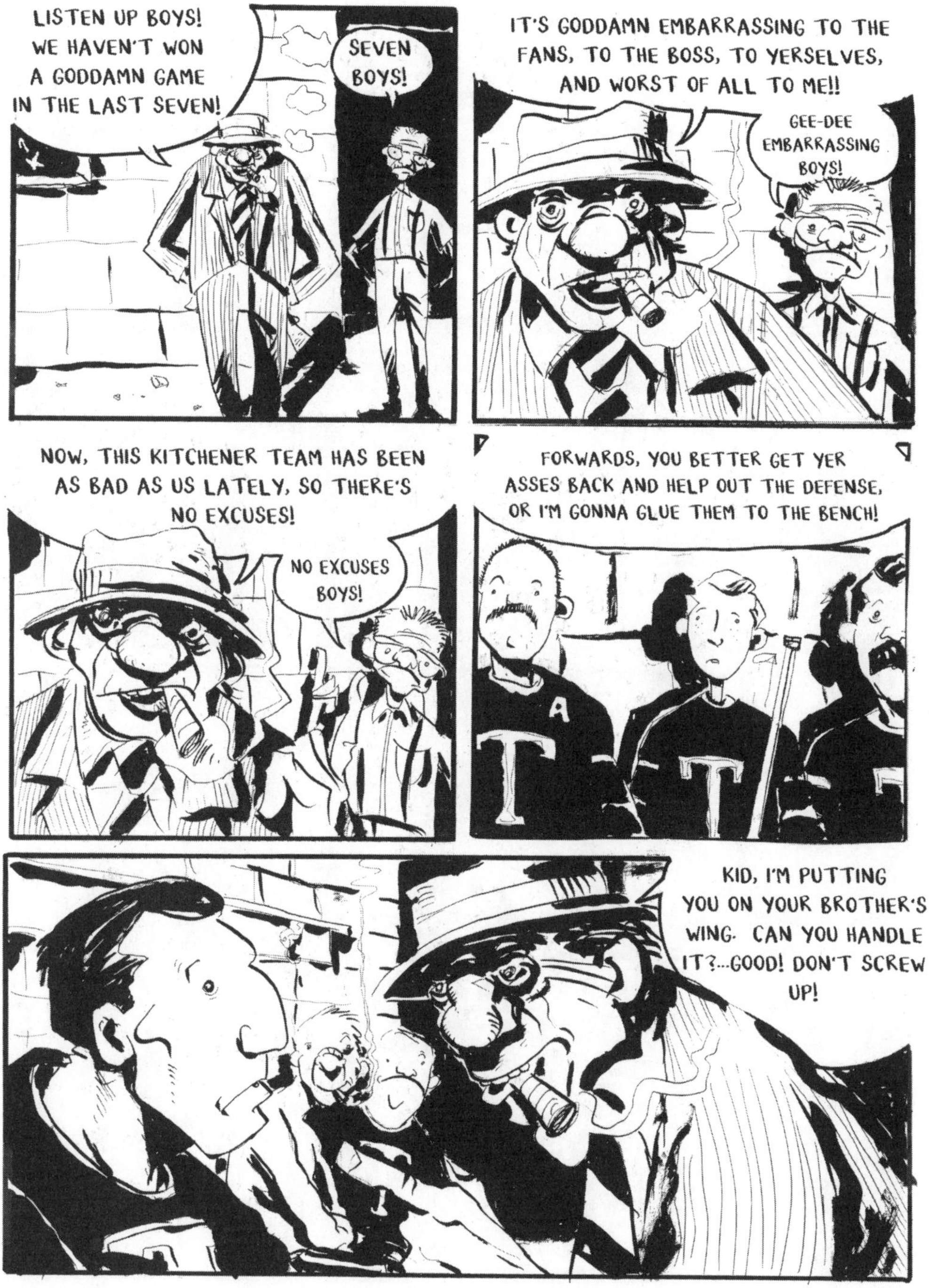
LISTEN UP BOYS! WE HAVEN'T WON A GODDAMN GAME IN THE LAST SEVEN!
SEVEN BOYS!
IT'S GODDAMN EMBARRASSING TO THE FANS, TO THE BOSS, TO YERSELVES, AND WORST OF ALL TO ME!!
GEE-DEE EMBARRASSING BOYS!
NOW, THIS KITCHENER TEAM HAS BEEN AS BAD AS US LATELY, SO THERE'S NO EXCUSES!
NO EXCUSES BOYS!
FORWARDS, YOU BETTER GET YER ASSES BACK AND HELP OUT THE DEFENSE, OR I'M GONNA GLUE THEM TO THE BENCH!
KID, I'M PUTTING YOU ON YOUR BROTHER'S WING. CAN YOU HANDLE IT?...GOOD! DON'T SCREW UP!

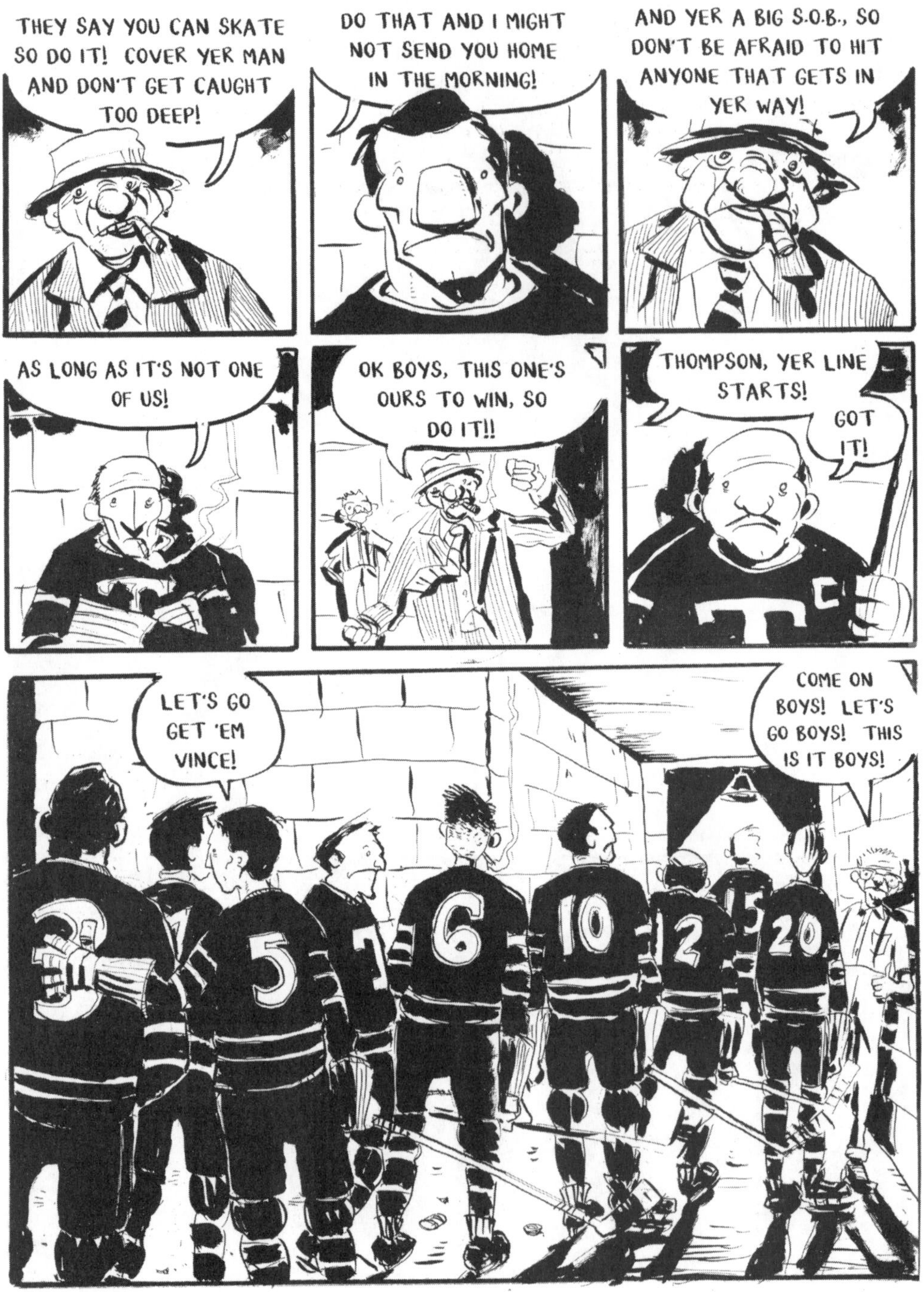
THEY SAY YOU CAN SKATE SO DO IT! COVER YER MAN AND DON'T GET CAUGHT TOO DEEP!
DO THAT AND I MIGHT NOT SEND YOU HOME IN THE MORNING!
AND YER A BIG S.O.B., SO DON'T BE AFRAID TO HIT ANYONE THAT GETS IN YER WAY!
AS LONG AS IT'S NOT ONE OF US!
OK BOYS, THIS ONE'S OURS TO WIN, SO DO IT!!
THOMPSON, YER LINE STARTS!
GOT IT!
LET'S GO GET 'EM VINCE!
COME ON BOYS! LET'S GO BOYS! THIS IS IT BOYS!

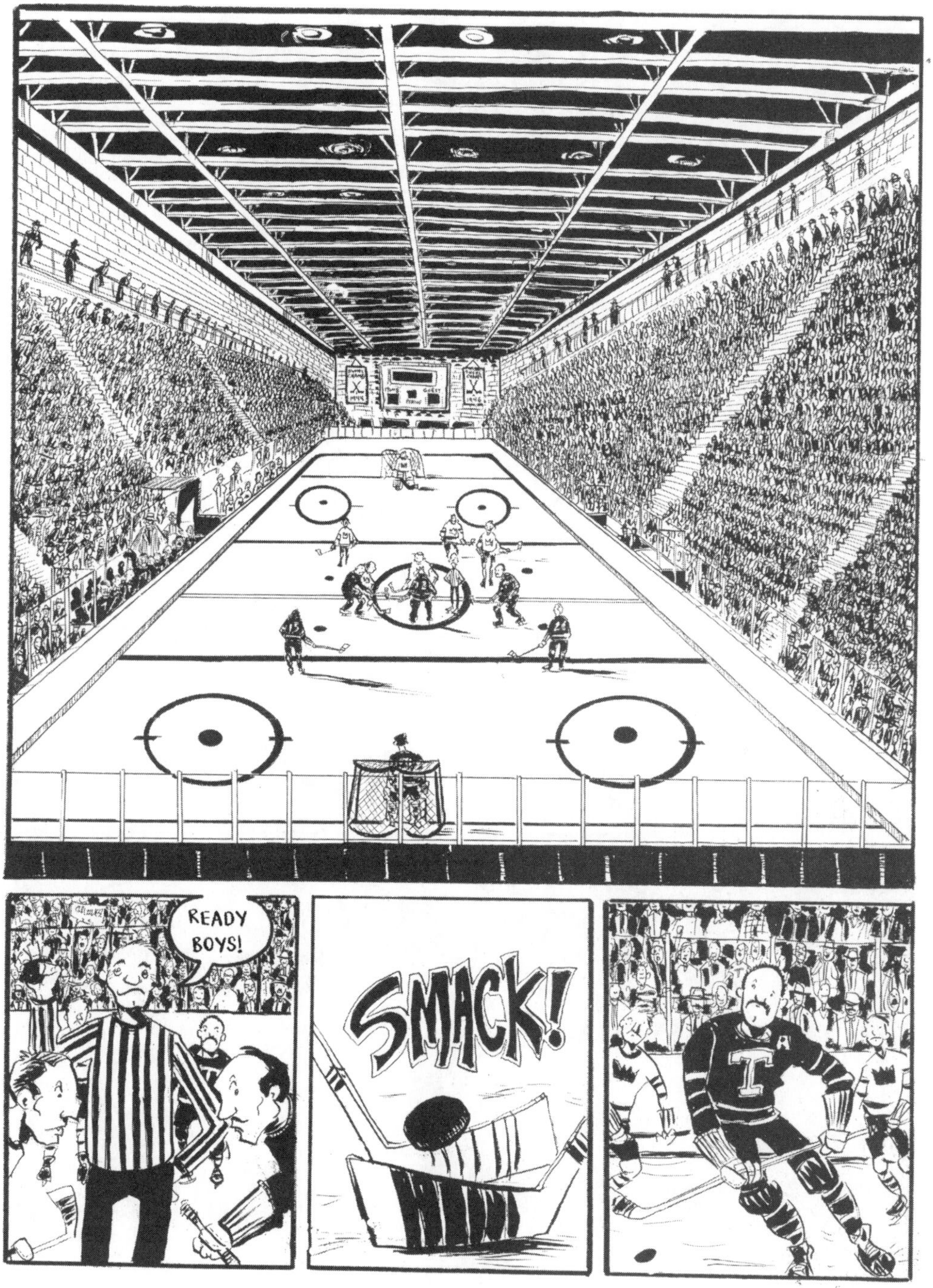
READY BOYS!
SMACK!

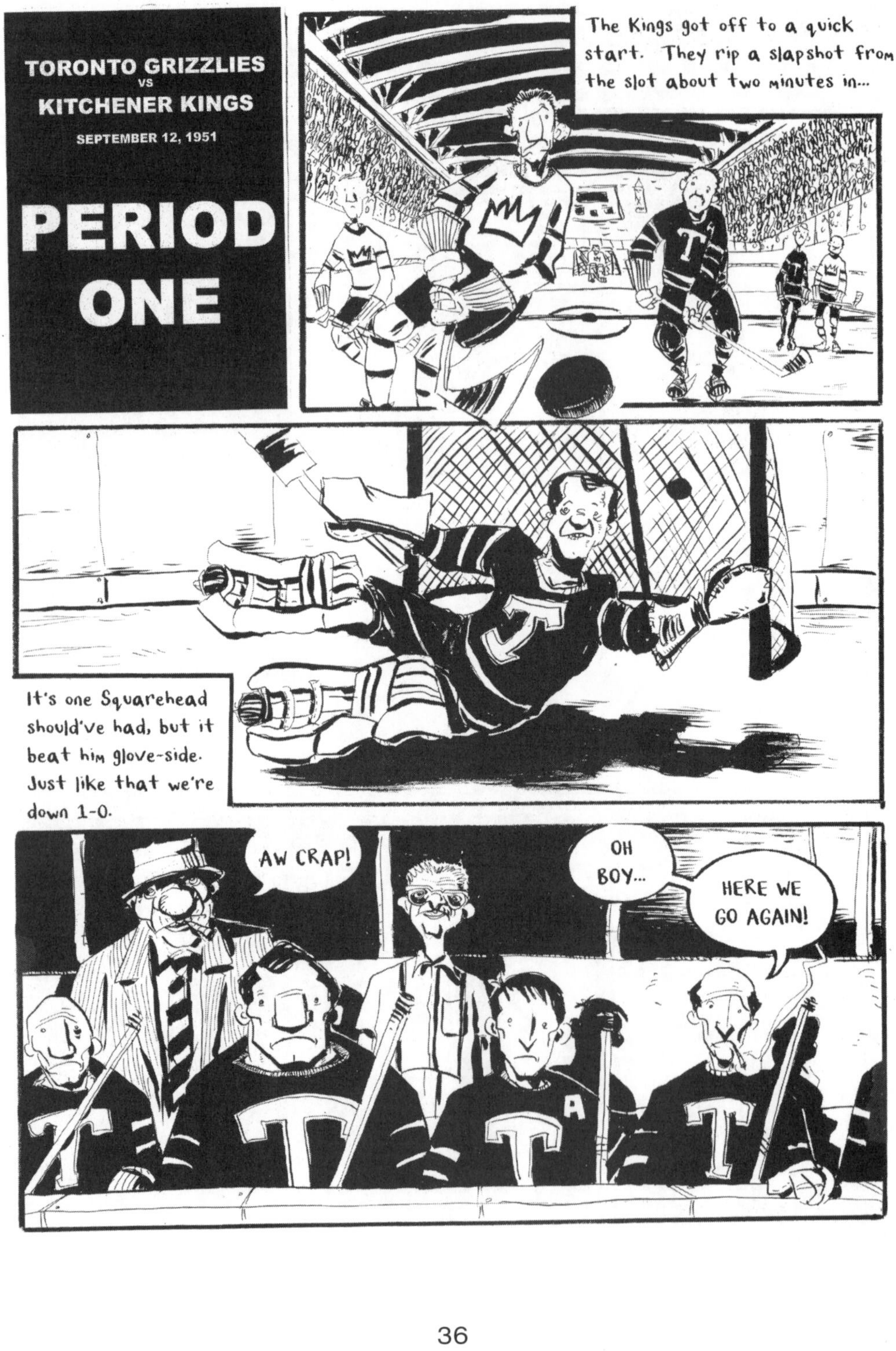

TORONTO GRIZZLIES
VS
KITCHENER KINGS
SEPTEMBER 12, 1951
PERIOD ONE
The Kings got off to a quick start. They rip a slapshot from the slot about two minutes in...
It's one Squarehead should've had, but it beat him glove-side. Just like that we're down 1-0.
AW CRAP!
OH BOY...
HERE WE GO AGAIN!

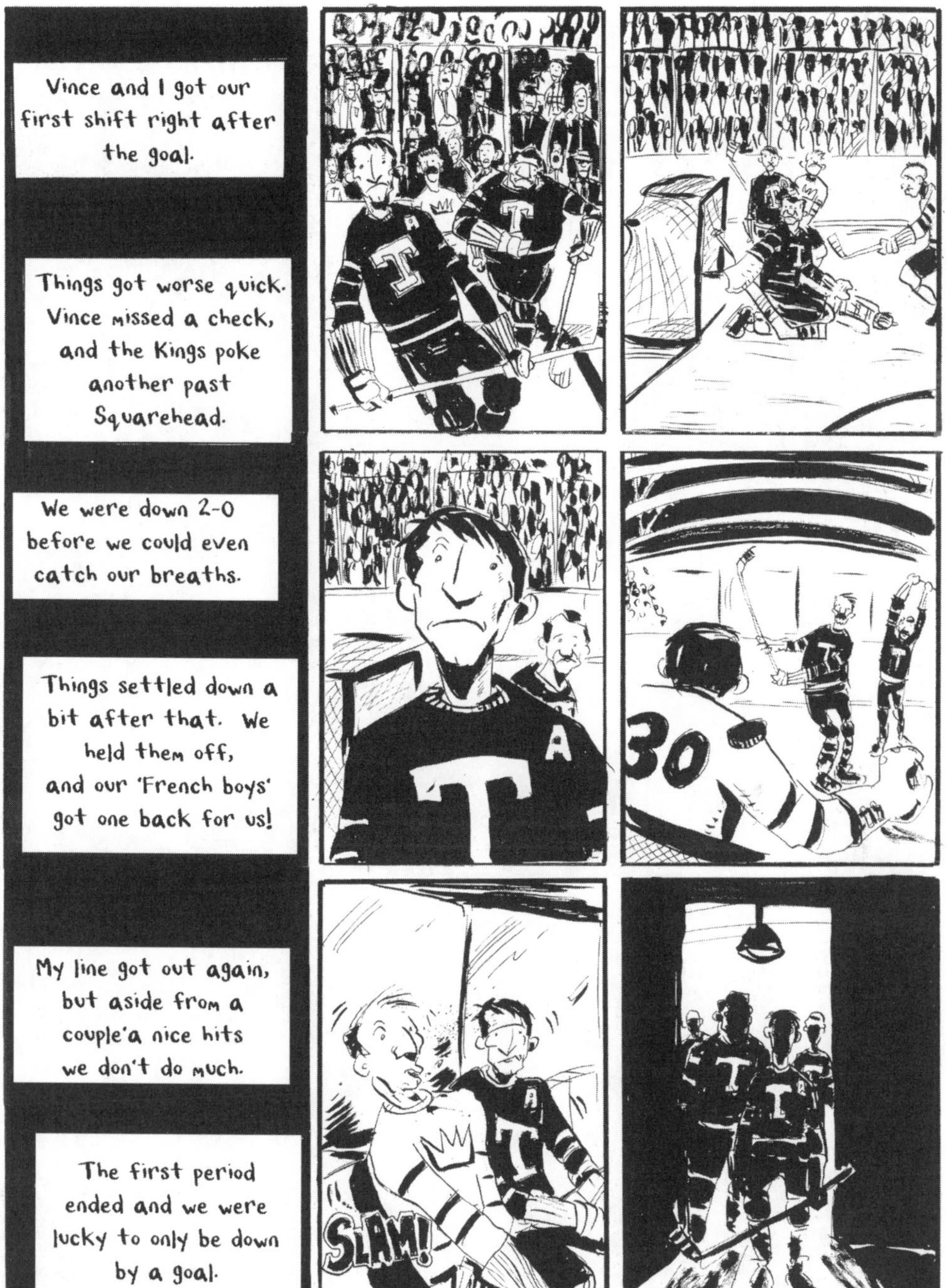
Vince and I got our first shift right after the goal.
Things got worse quick. Vince missed a check, and the Kings poke another past Squarehead.
We were down 2-0 before we could even catch our breaths.
Things settled down a bit after that. We held them off, and our 'French boys' got one back for us!
My line got out again, but aside from a couple'a nice hits we don't do much.
SLAM!
The first period ended and we were lucky to only be down by a goal.

PERIOD TWO

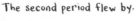
The second period flew by.

No goals half way through, but things started to get chippy.

Vince was still playing quiet...almost timid.

His head hadn't caught up with everything yet.

I knew he could take this game and win it by himself if he wanted to.

I just needed to get him going!

So, with about six minutes left in the period I picked a fight...

...and I made sure I lost.

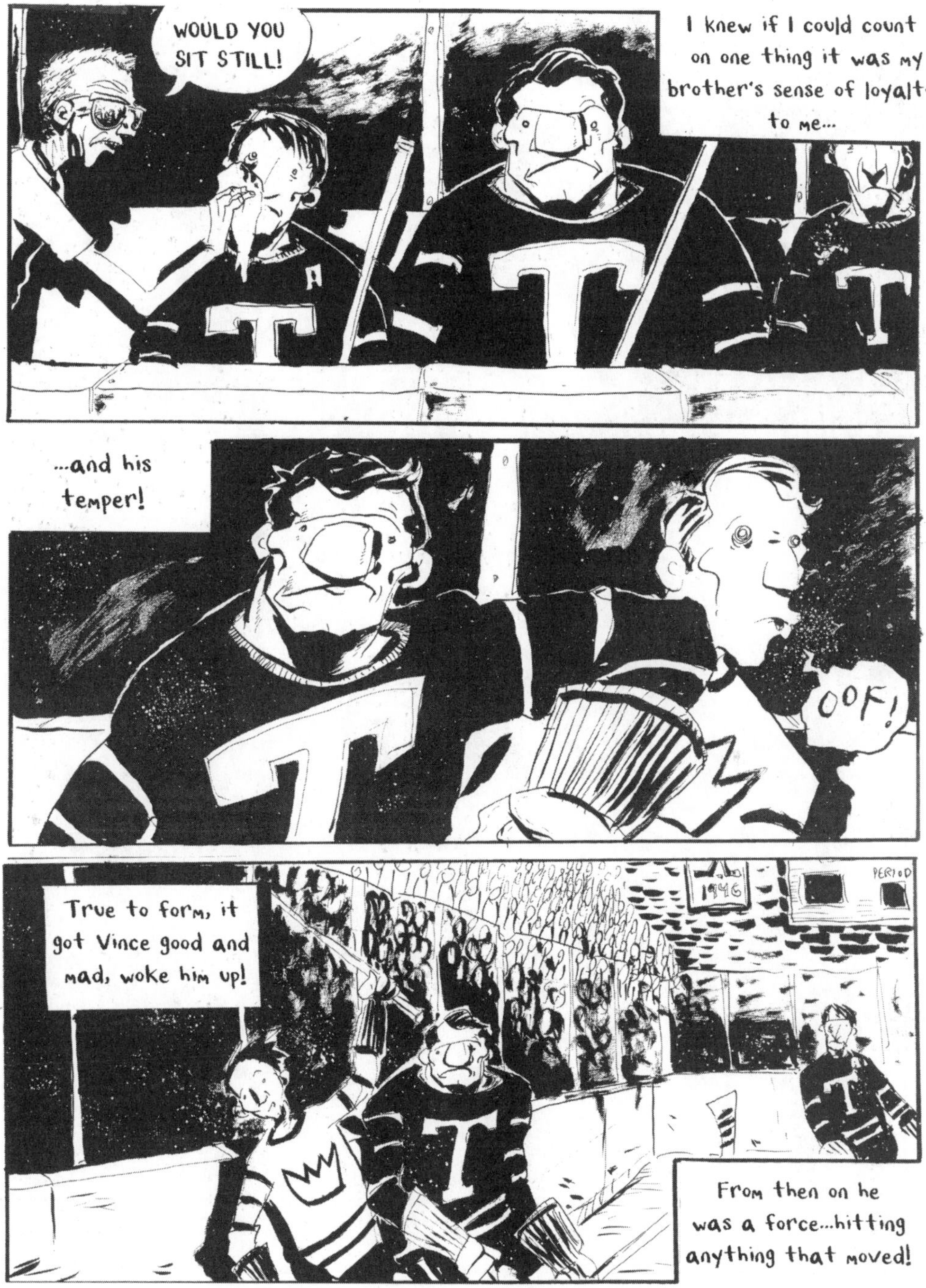
WOULD YOU SIT STILL!
I knew if I could count on one thing it was my brother's sense of loyalty to me...
...and his temper!
OOF!
True to form, it got Vince good and mad, woke him up!
1946
PERIOD
From then on he was a force...hitting anything that moved!

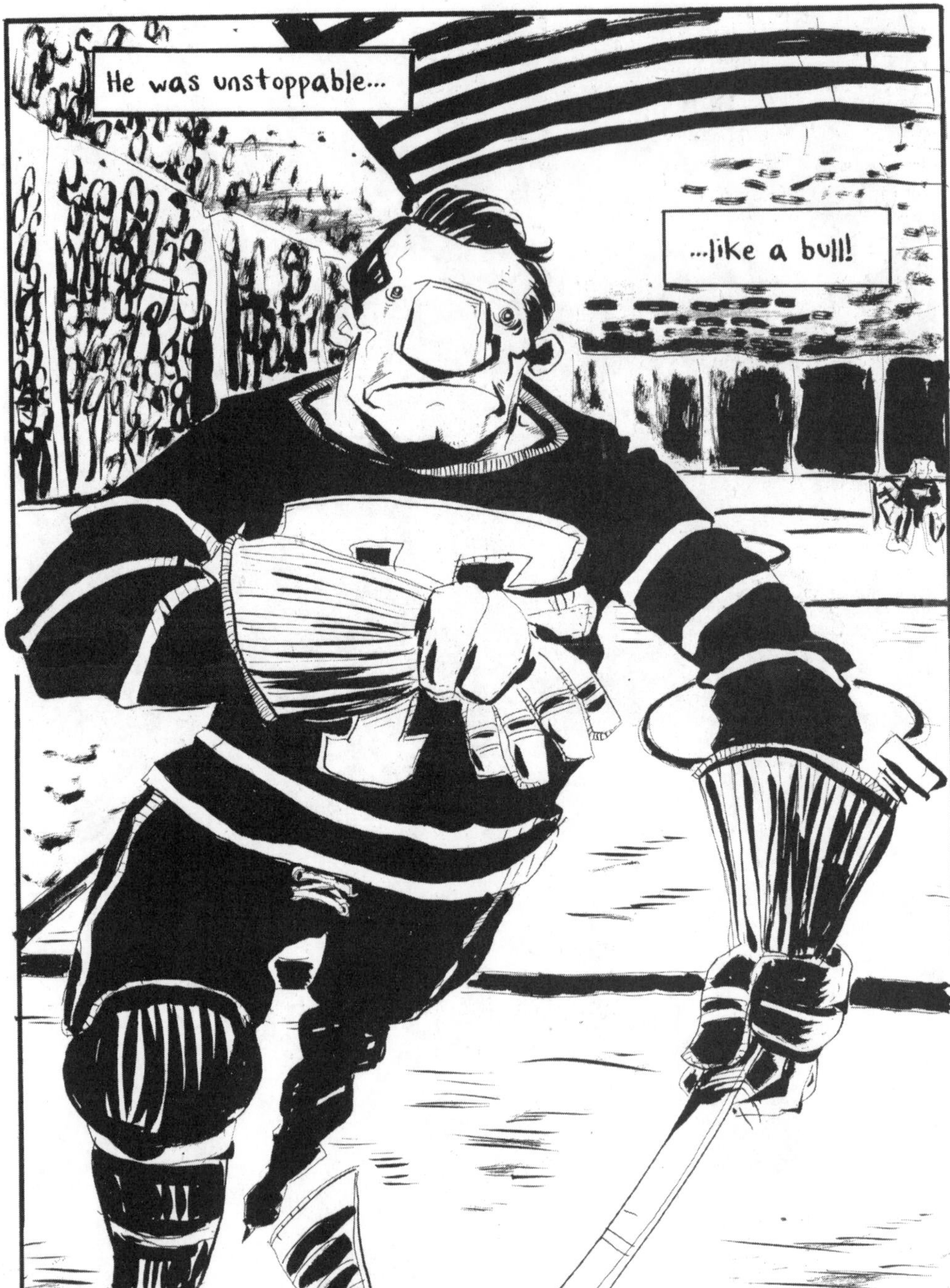
He was unstoppable...
...like a bull!

PERIOD THREE

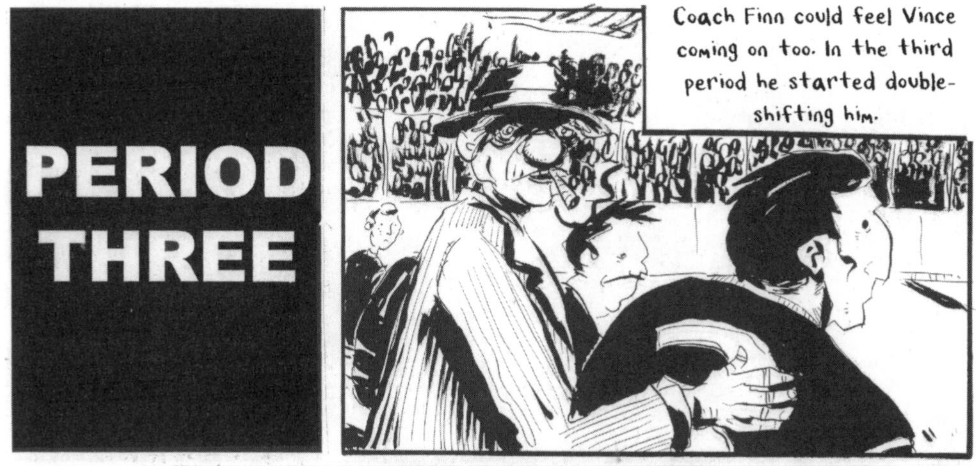
Coach Finn could feel Vince coming on too. In the third period he started double-shifting him.

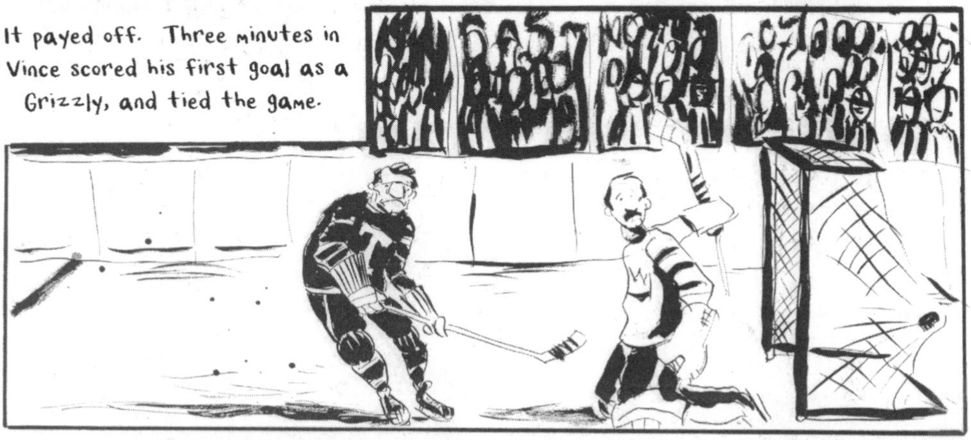
It payed off. Three minutes in Vince scored his first goal as a Grizzly, and tied the game.

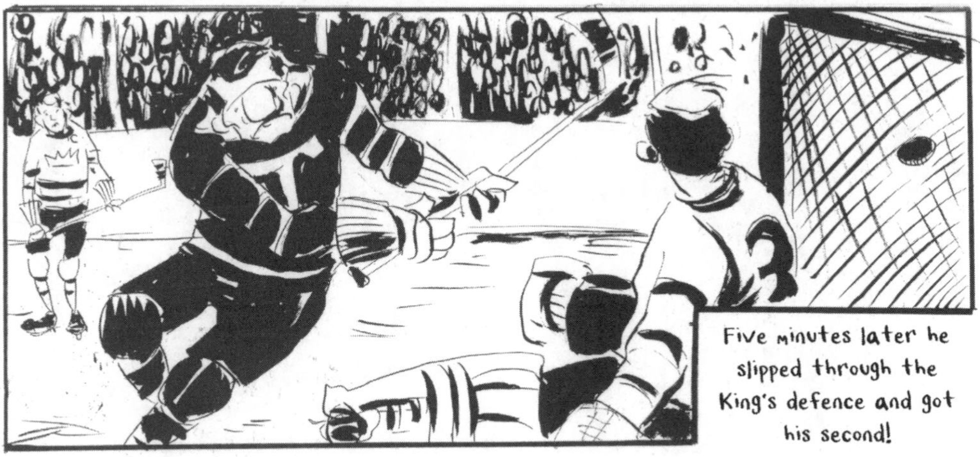
Five minutes later he slipped through the King's defence and got his second!

THAT'S IT BOYS!

The Kings didn't know what hit 'em, and we weren't about to let our feet offa their throats!

With four minutes left Vince set me up for the insurance goal!

When the final whistle blew, we'd won.

WELL, I'll BE DAMNED!

The fans had a new hero.

And The Grizzlies had a new star!

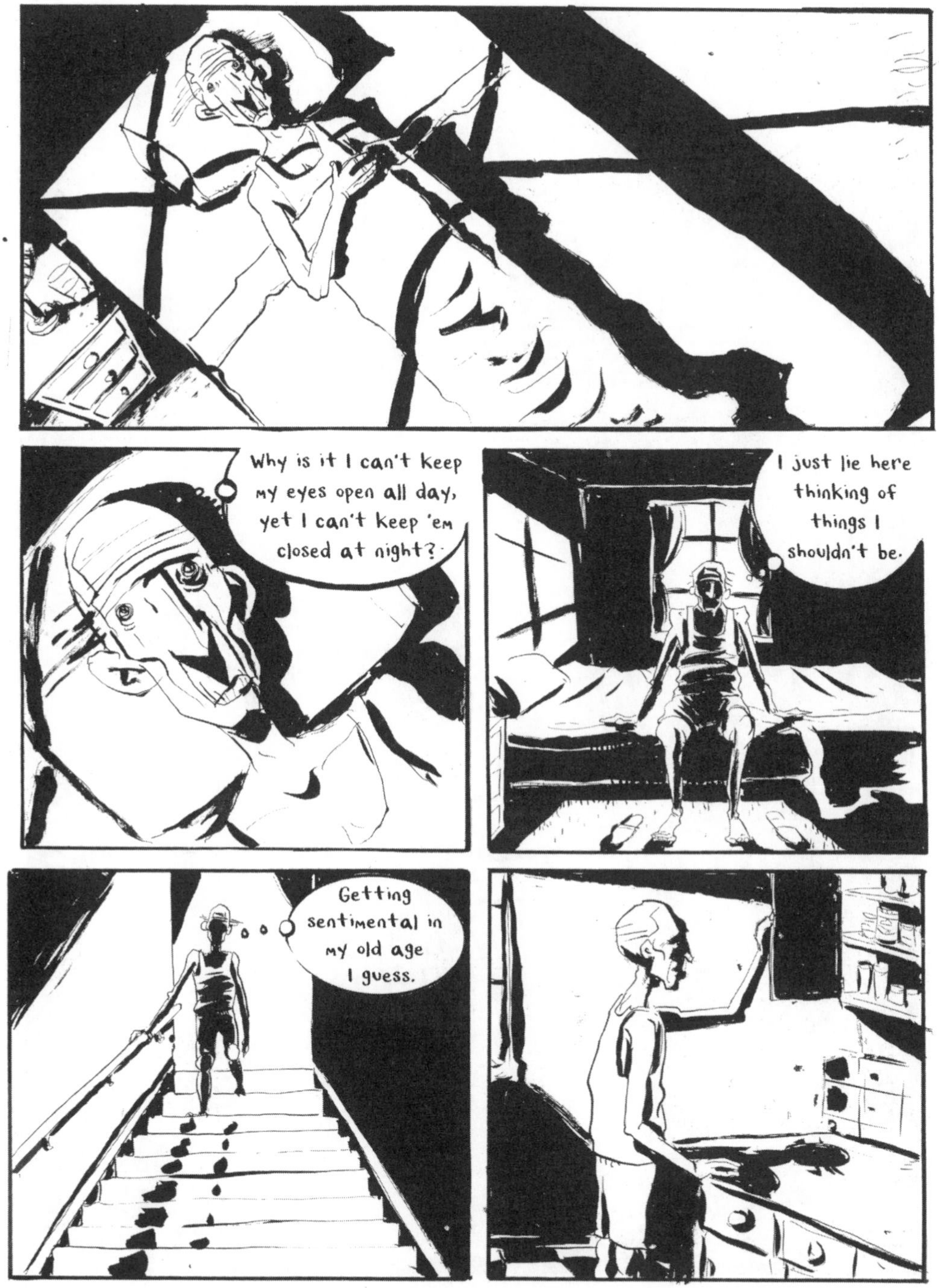
Why is it I can't keep my eyes open all day, yet I can't keep 'em closed at night?
I just lie here thinking of things I shouldn't be.
Getting sentimental in my old age I guess.

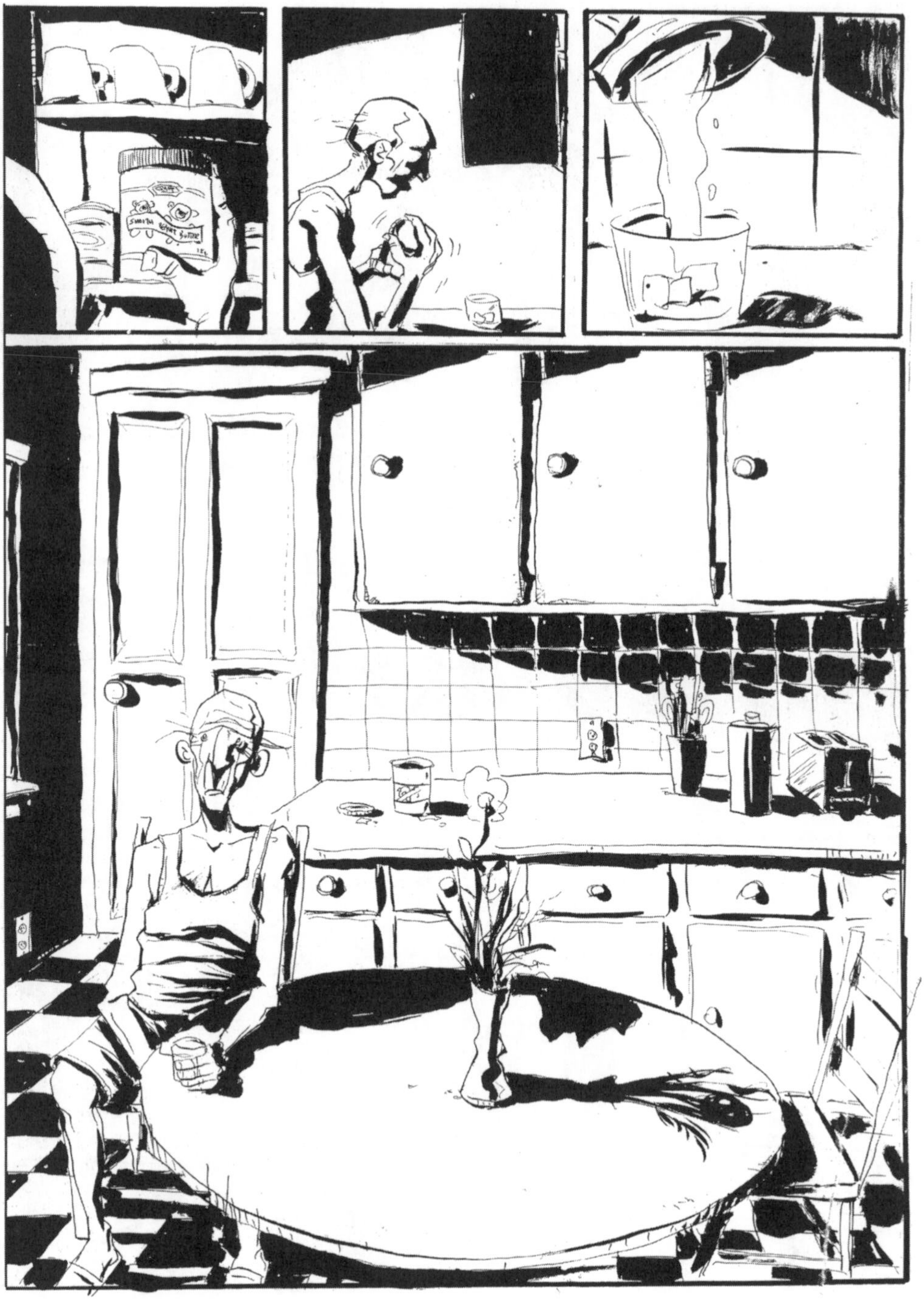

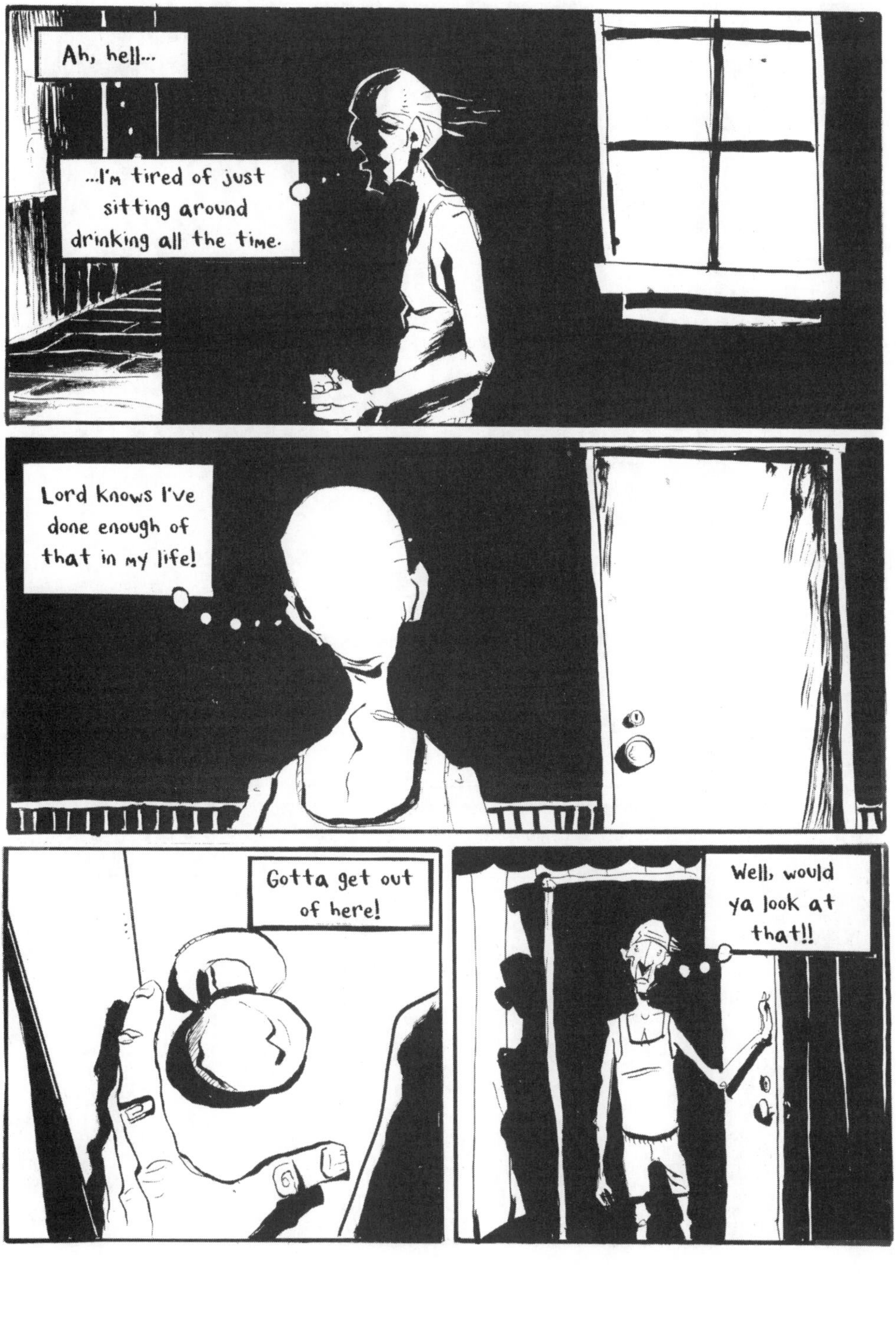
Ah, hell...
...I'm tired of just sitting around drinking all the time.
Lord knows I've done enough of that in my life!
Gotta get out of here!
Well, would ya look at that!!

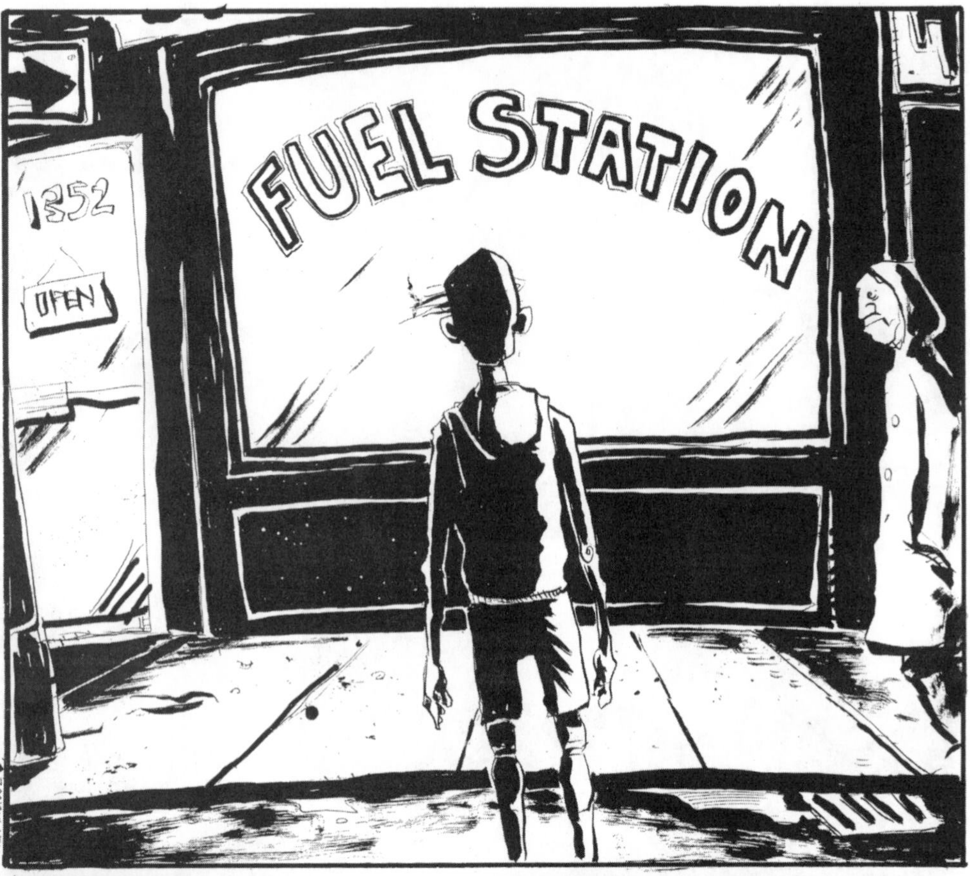
FUEL STATION
1352
OPEN

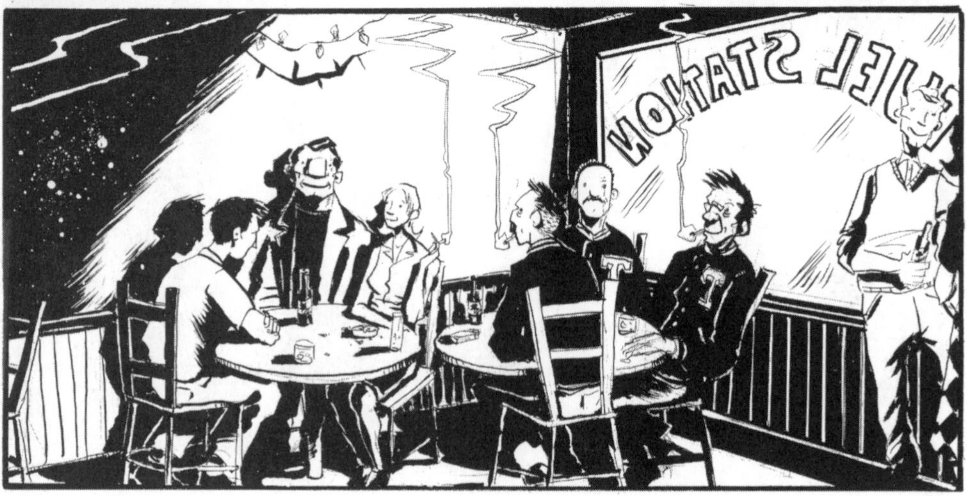

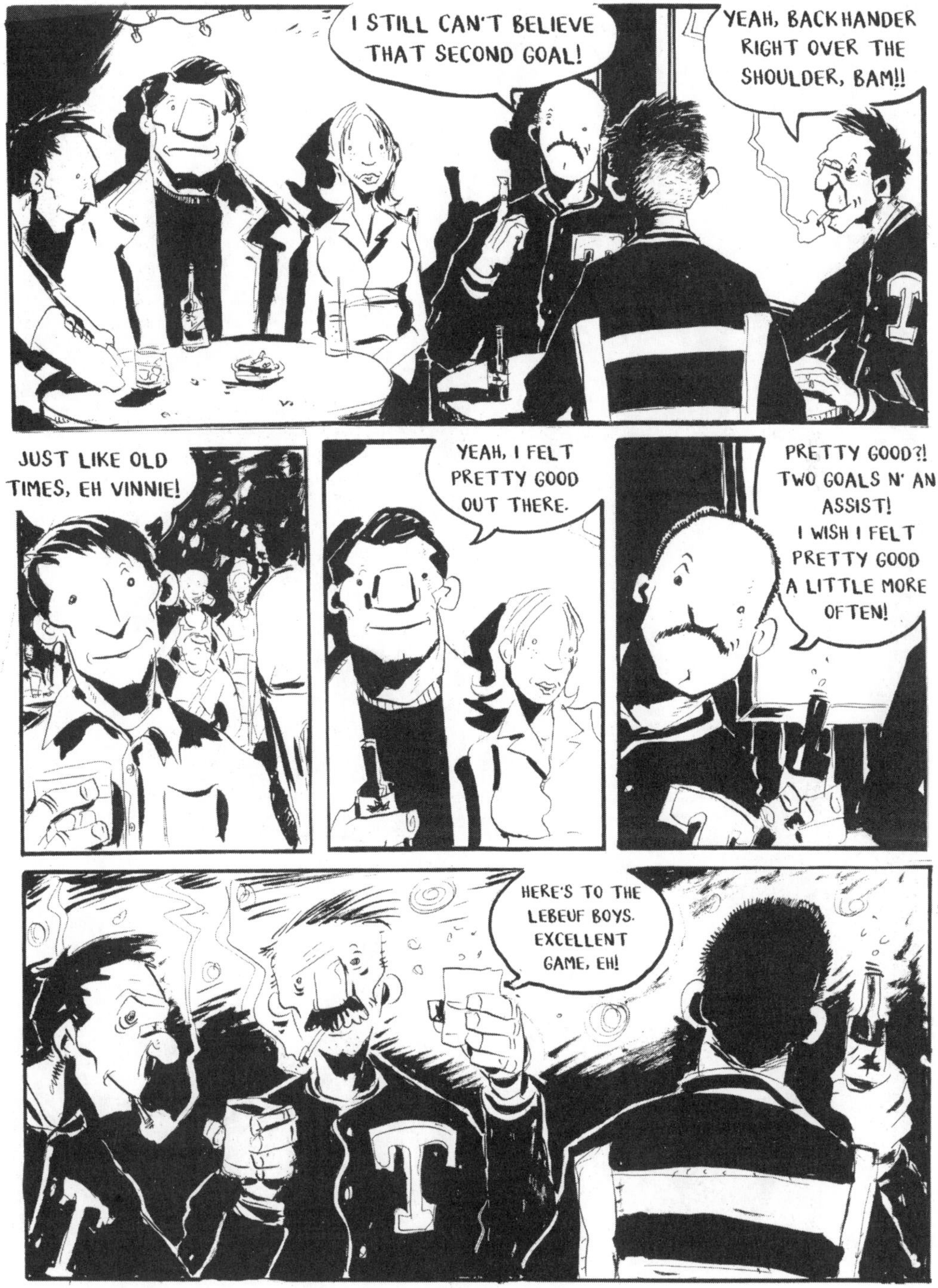
I STILL CAN'T BELIEVE THAT SECOND GOAL!
YEAH, BACKHANDER RIGHT OVER THE SHOULDER, BAM!!
JUST LIKE OLD TIMES, EH VINNIE!
YEAH, I FELT PRETTY GOOD OUT THERE.
PRETTY GOOD?! TWO GOALS N' AN ASSIST! I WISH I FELT PRETTY GOOD A LITTLE MORE OFTEN!
HERE'S TO THE LEBEUF BOYS. EXCELLENT GAME, EH!

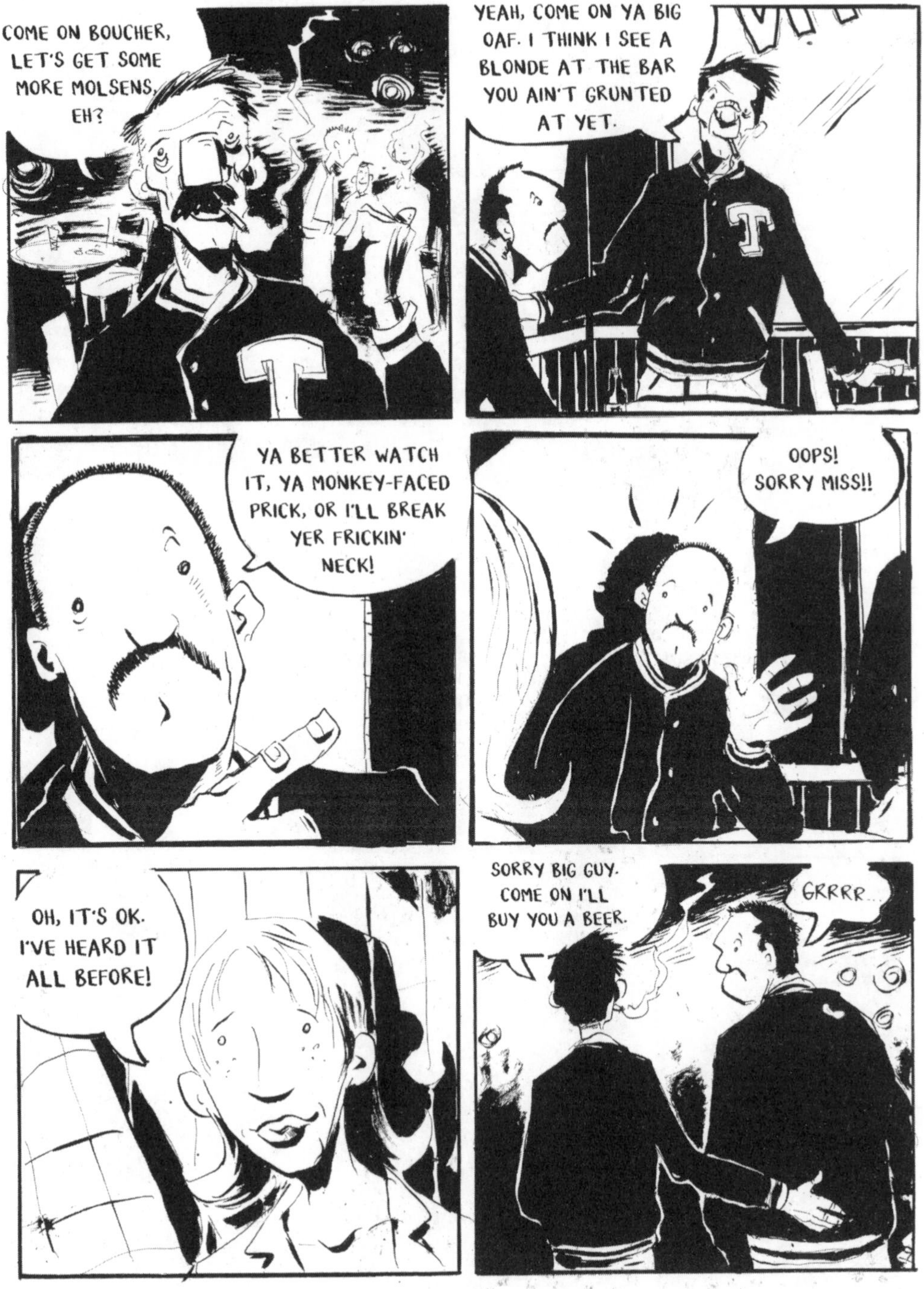
COME ON BOUCHER, LET'S GET SOME MORE MOLSENS, EH?
YEAH, COME ON YA BIG OAF. I THINK I SEE A BLONDE AT THE BAR YOU AIN'T GRUNTED AT YET.
YA BETTER WATCH IT, YA MONKEY-FACED PRICK, OR I'LL BREAK YER FRICKIN' NECK!
OOPS! SORRY MISS!!
OH, IT'S OK. I'VE HEARD IT ALL BEFORE!
SORRY BIG GUY. COME ON I'LL BUY YOU A BEER.
GRRRR...

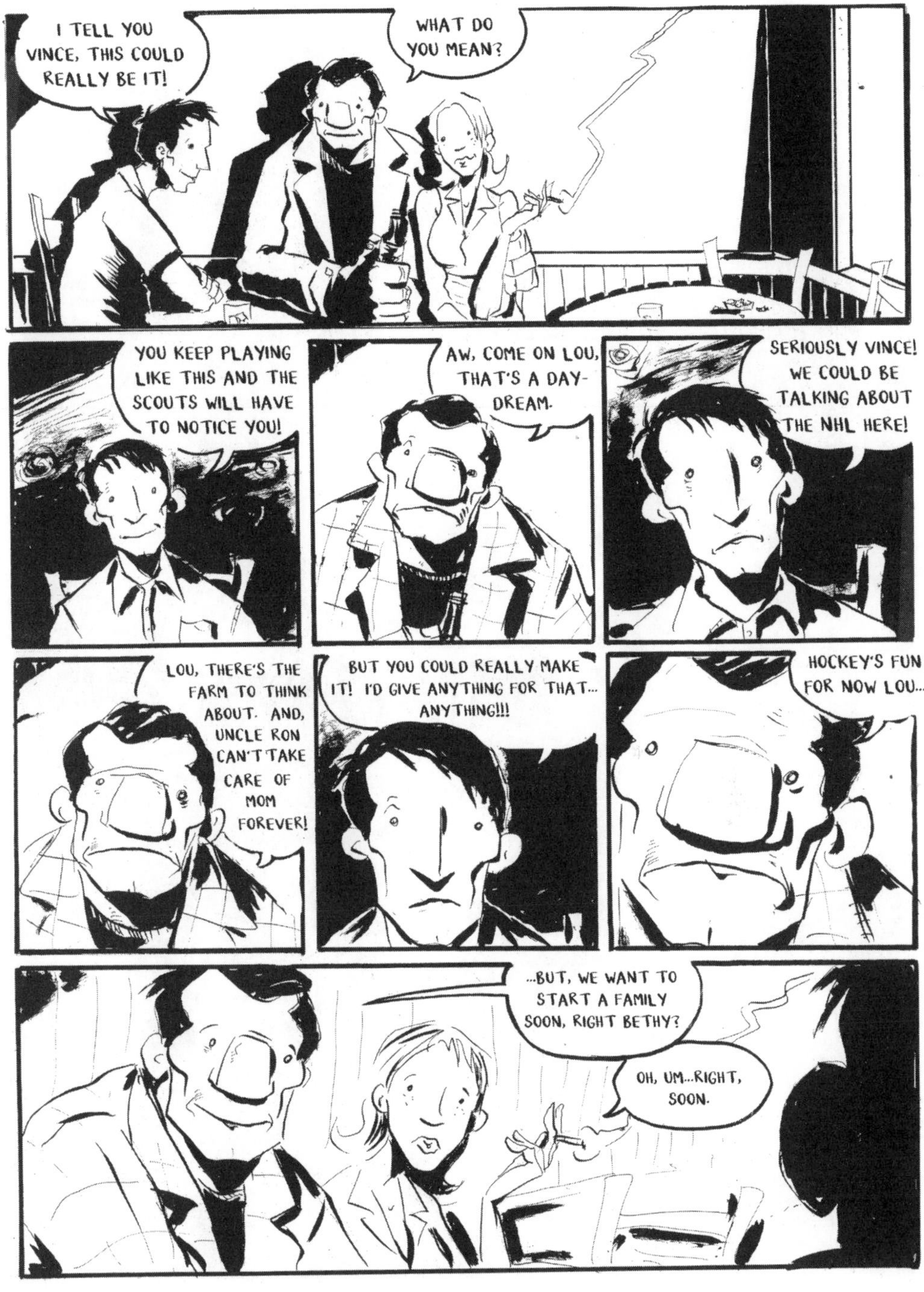
I TELL YOU VINCE, THIS COULD REALLY BE IT!
WHAT DO YOU MEAN?
YOU KEEP PLAYING LIKE THIS AND THE SCOUTS WILL HAVE TO NOTICE YOU!
AW, COME ON LOU, THAT'S A DAY-DREAM.
SERIOUSLY VINCE! WE COULD BE TALKING ABOUT THE NHL HERE!
LOU, THERE'S THE FARM TO THINK ABOUT. AND, UNCLE RON CAN'T TAKE CARE OF MOM FOREVER!
BUT YOU COULD REALLY MAKE IT! I'D GIVE ANYTHING FOR THAT... ANYTHING!!!
HOCKEY'S FUN FOR NOW LOU...
...BUT, WE WANT TO START A FAMILY SOON, RIGHT BETHY?
OH, UM...RIGHT, SOON.

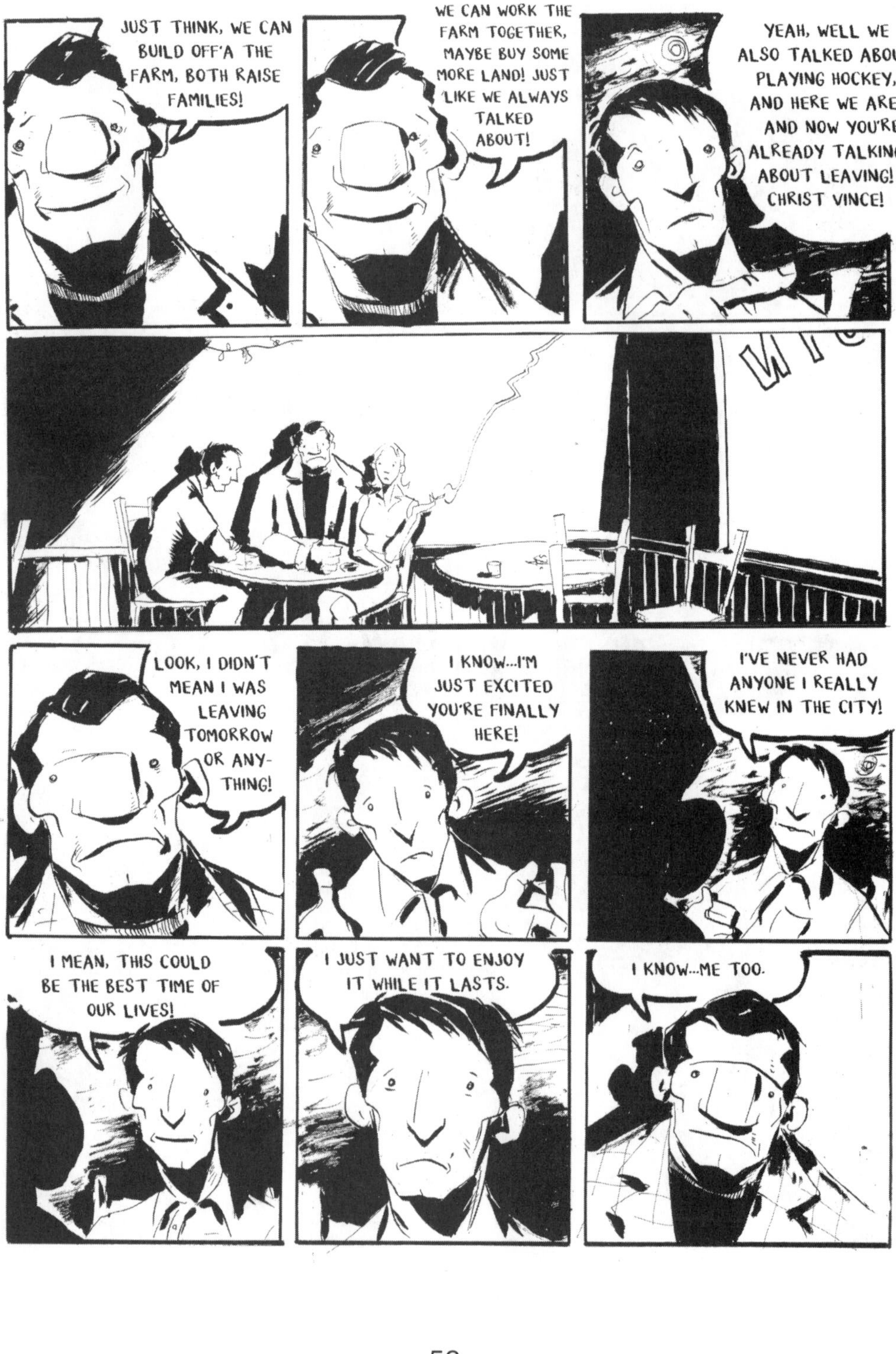
JUST THINK, WE CAN BUILD OFF'A THE FARM, BOTH RAISE FAMILIES!
WE CAN WORK THE FARM TOGETHER, MAYBE BUY SOME MORE LAND! JUST LIKE WE ALWAYS TALKED ABOUT!
YEAH, WELL WE ALSO TALKED ABOUT PLAYING HOCKEY, AND HERE WE ARE! AND NOW YOU'RE ALREADY TALKING ABOUT LEAVING! CHRIST VINCE!
LOOK, I DIDN'T MEAN I WAS LEAVING TOMORROW OR ANY-THING!
I KNOW...I'M JUST EXCITED YOU'RE FINALLY HERE!
I'VE NEVER HAD ANYONE I REALLY KNEW IN THE CITY!
I MEAN, THIS COULD BE THE BEST TIME OF OUR LIVES!
I JUST WANT TO ENJOY IT WHILE IT LASTS.
I KNOW...ME TOO.

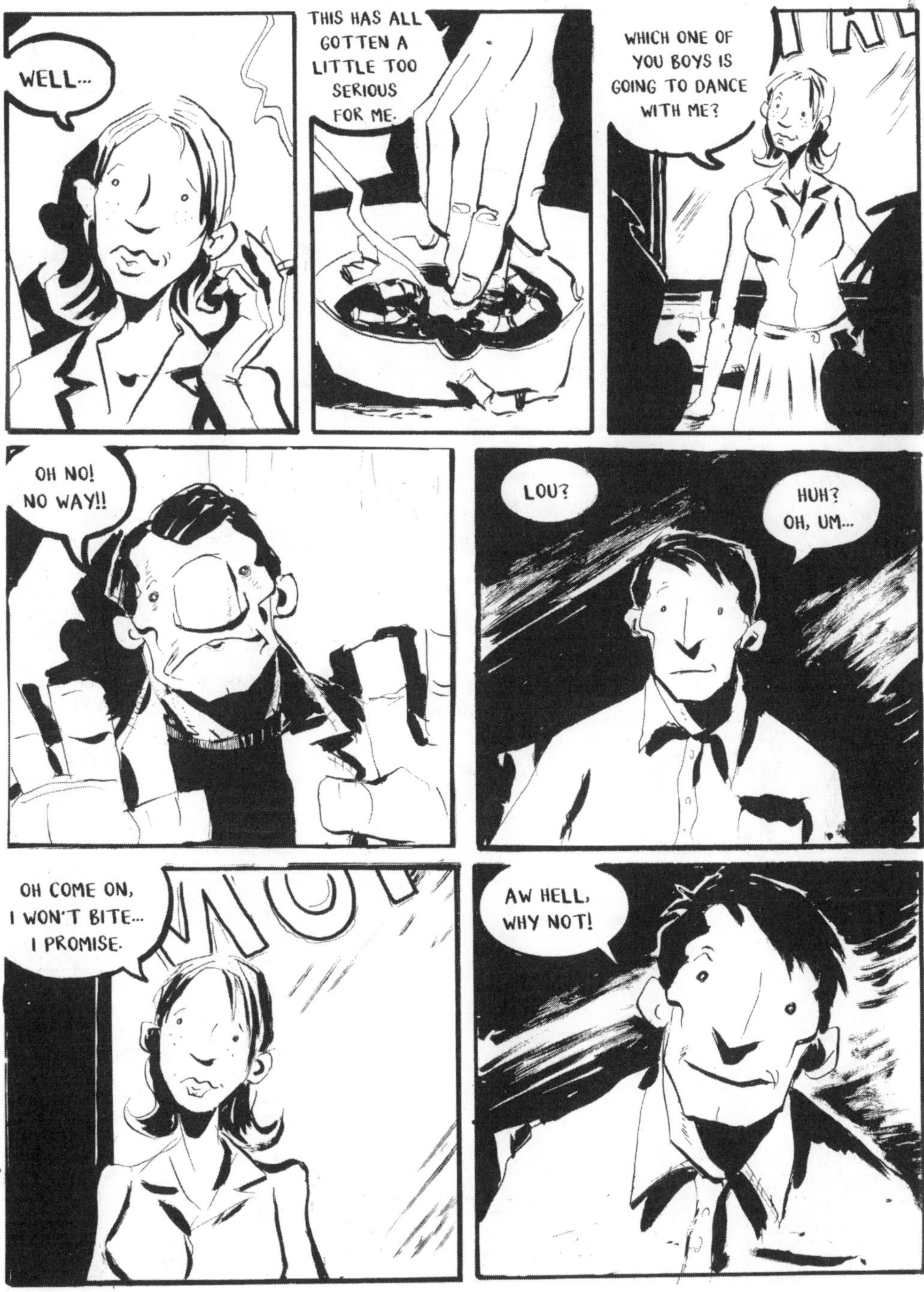
WELL...
THIS HAS ALL GOTTEN A LITTLE TOO SERIOUS FOR ME.
WHICH ONE OF YOU BOYS IS GOING TO DANCE WITH ME?
OH NO! NO WAY!!
LOU?
HUH? OH, UM...
OH COME ON, I WON'T BITE... I PROMISE.
AW HELL, WHY NOT!

OPEN

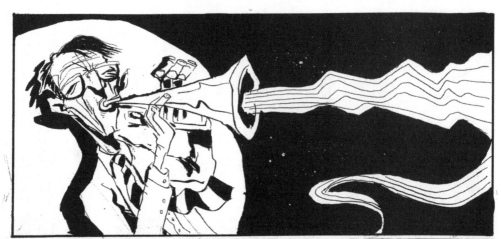

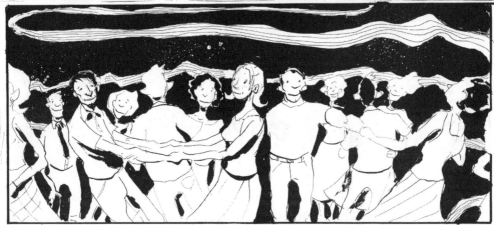

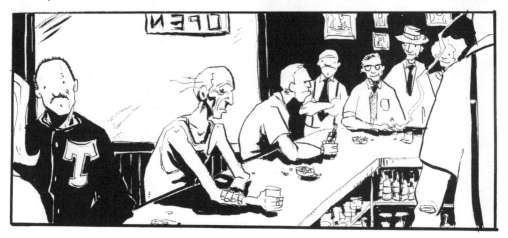

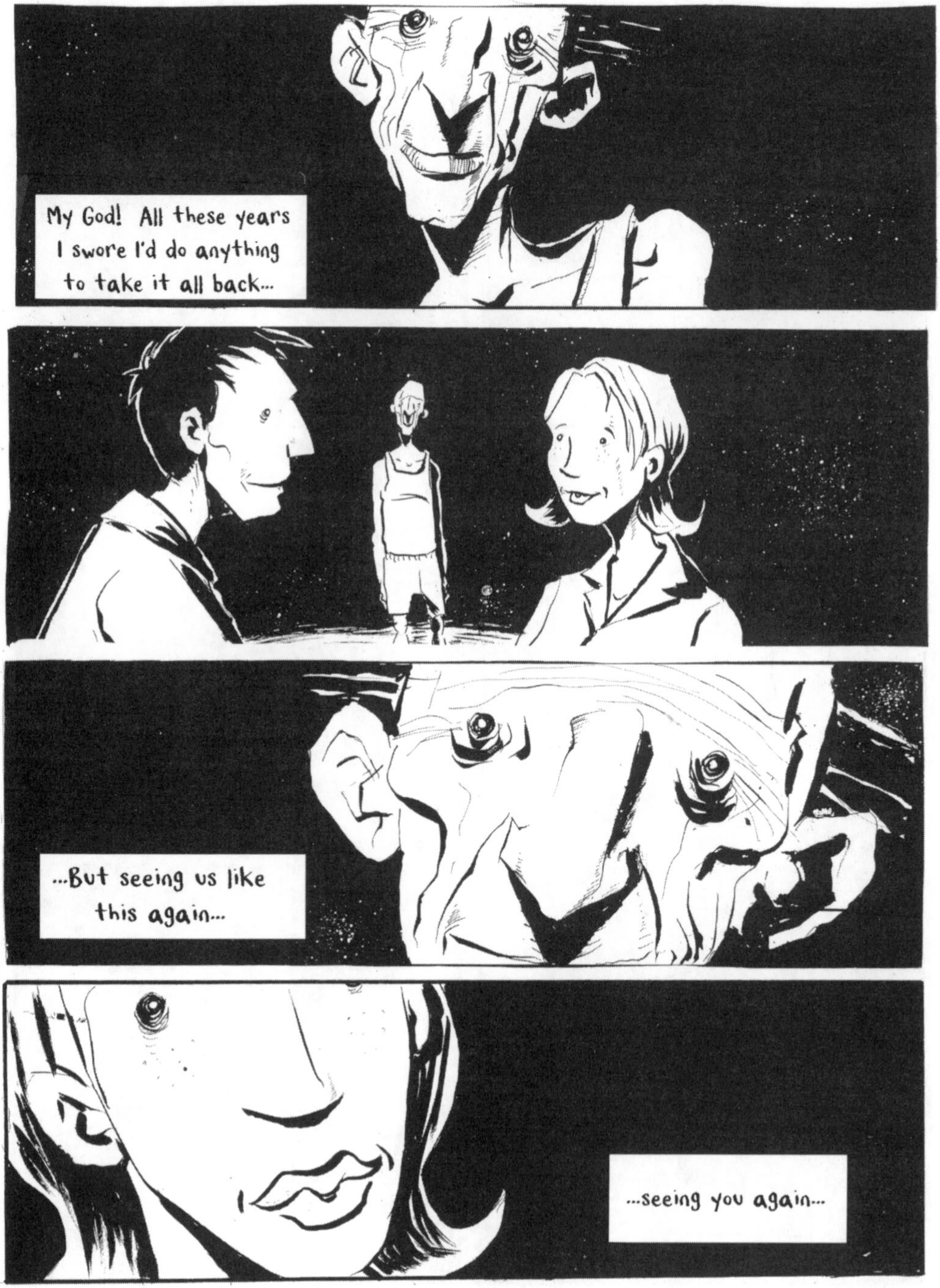
My God! All these years I swore I'd do anything to take it all back...
...But seeing us like this again...
...seeing you again...

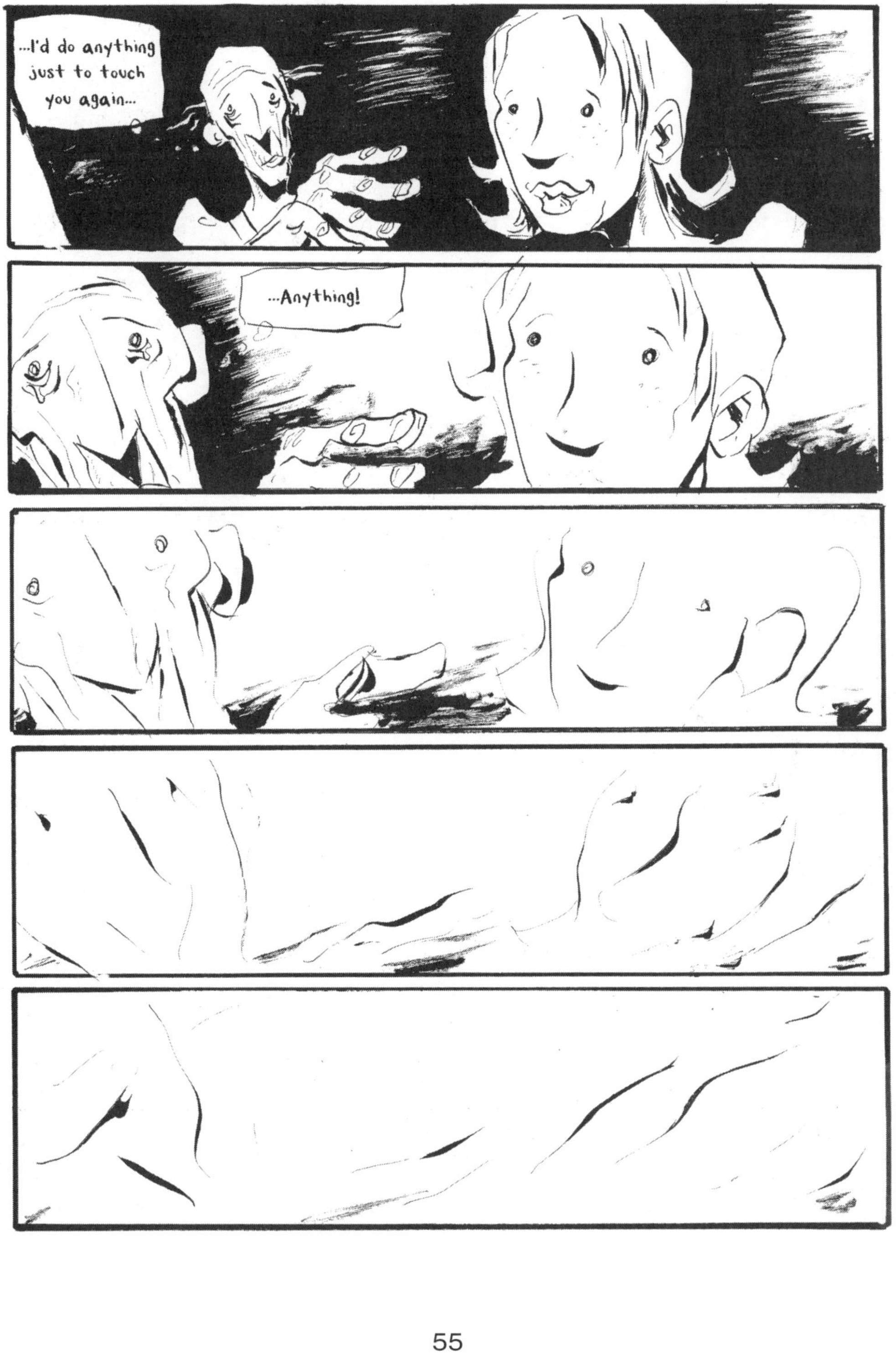
...I'd do anything just to touch you again...
...Anything!

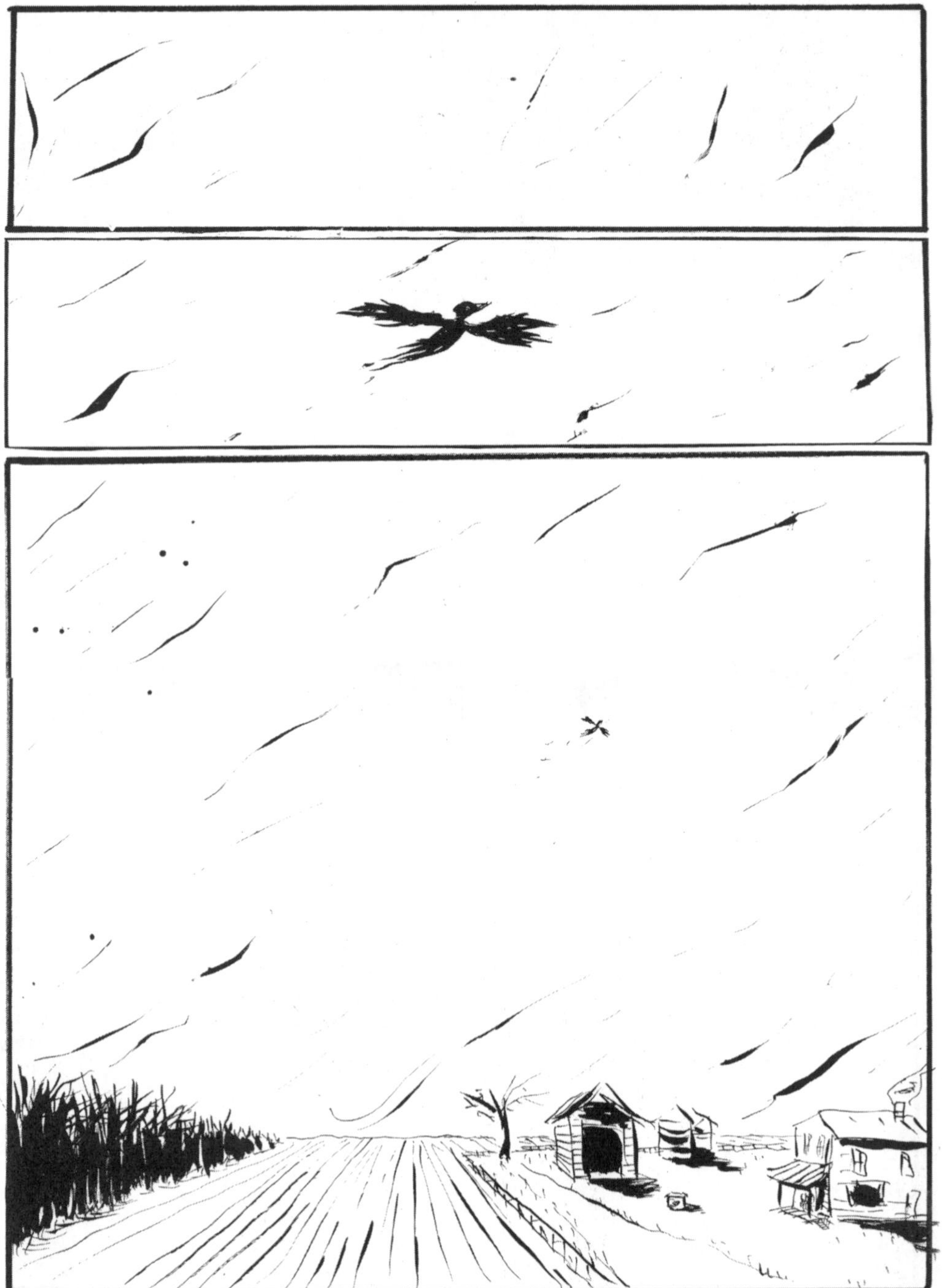

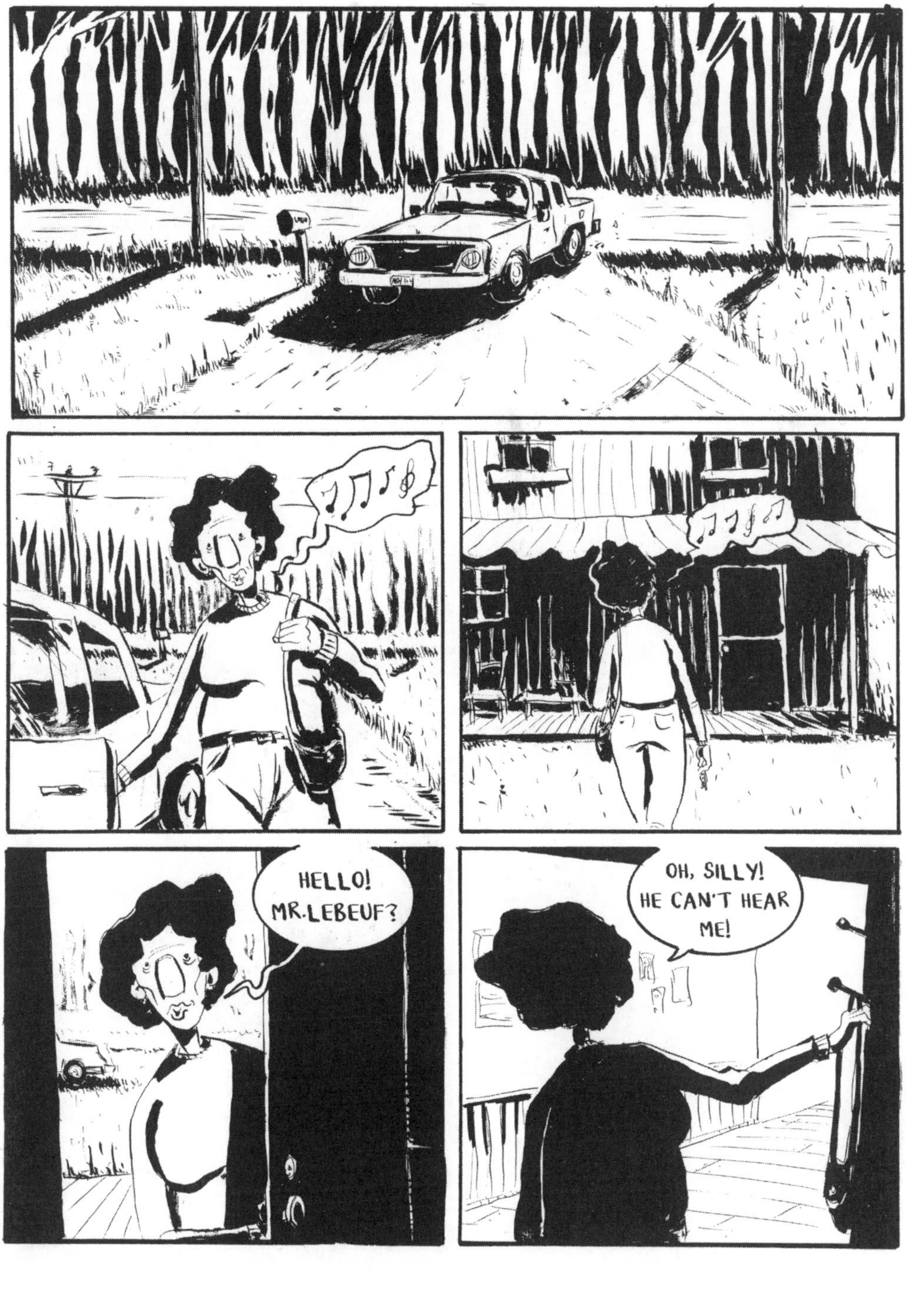
HELLO! MR.LEBEUF?
OH, SILLY! HE CAN'T HEAR ME!

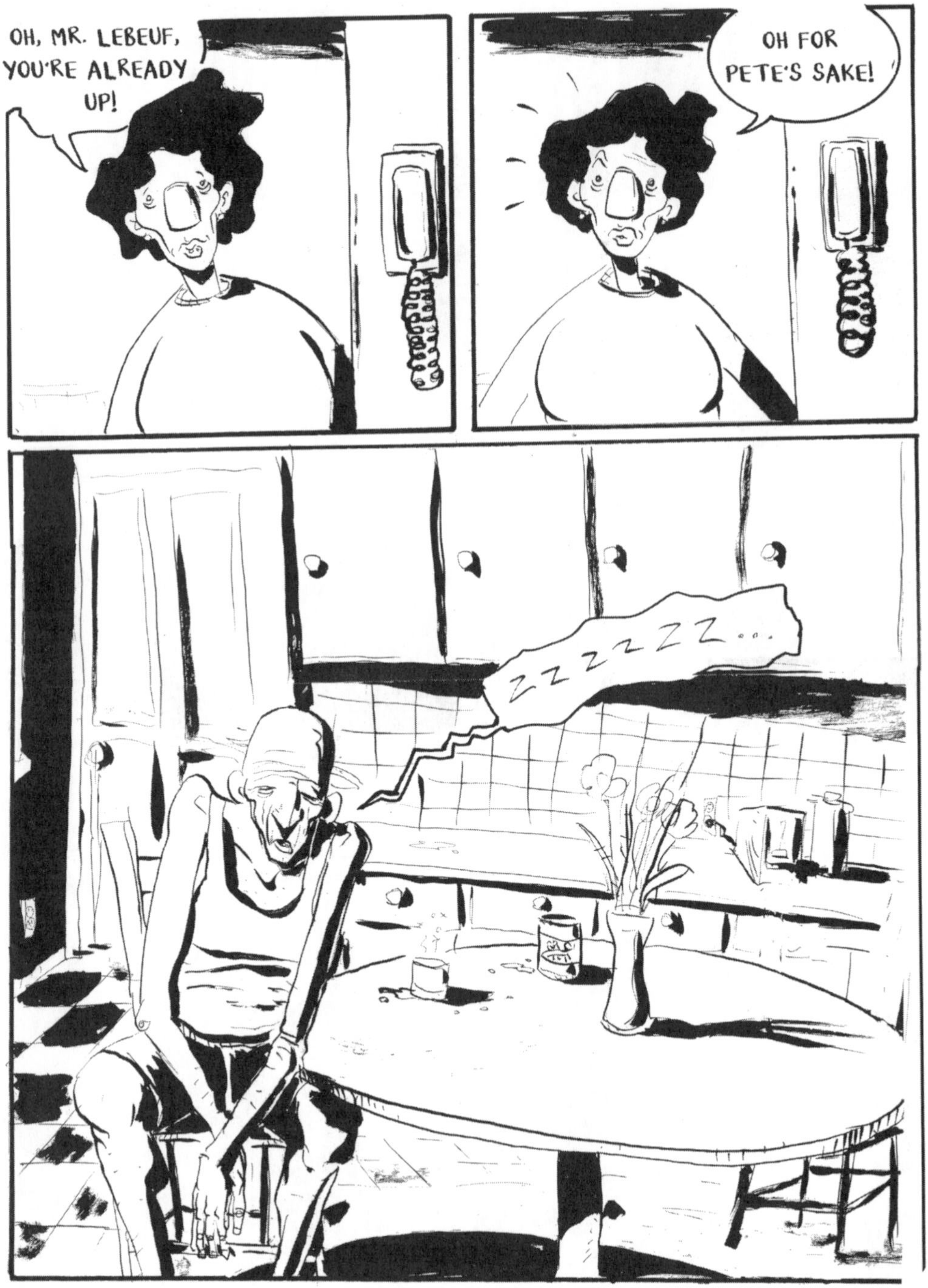
OH, MR. LEBEUF, YOU'RE ALREADY UP!
OH FOR PETE'S SAKE!
ZZZZZZZ...

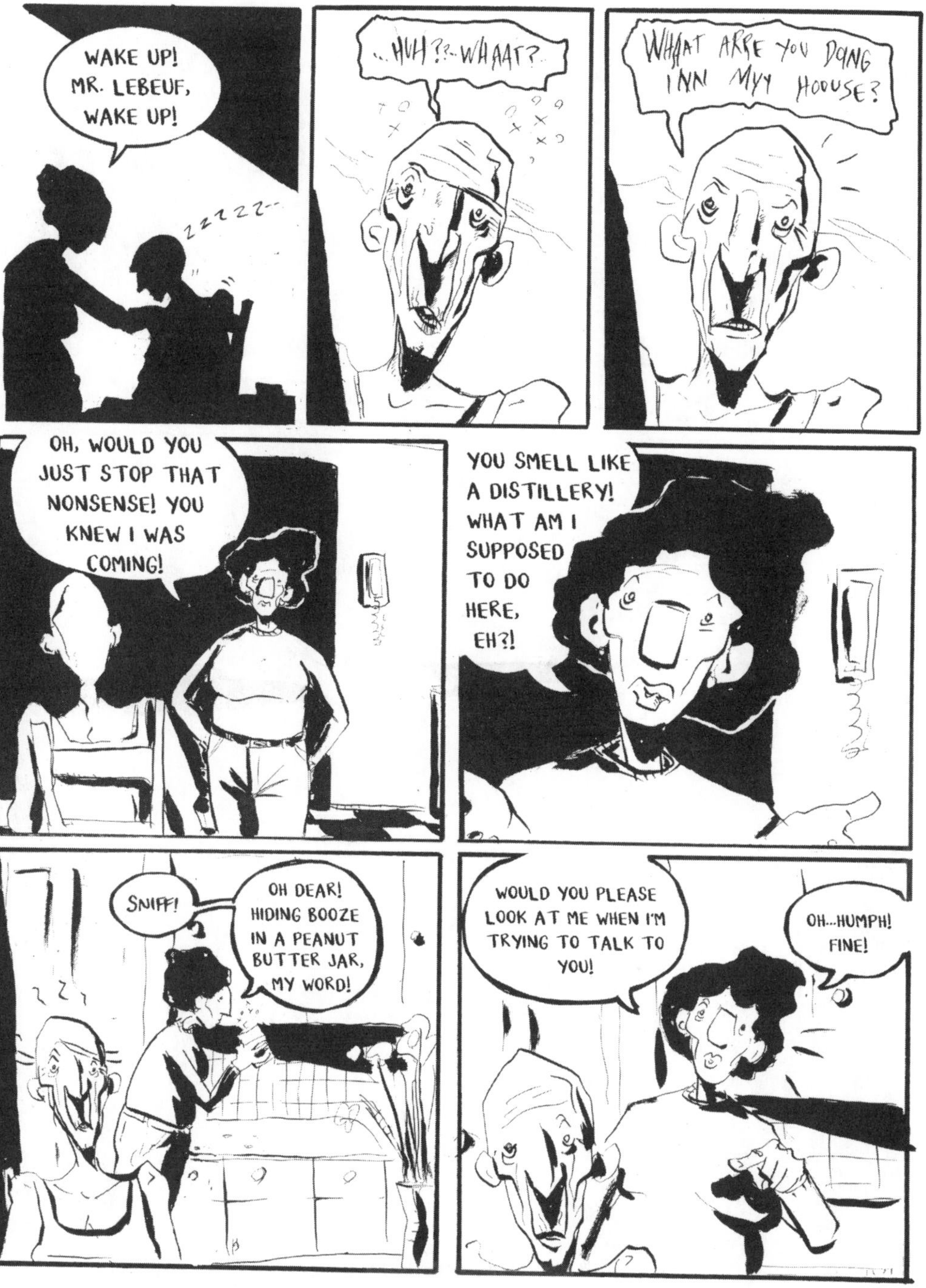
WAKE UP! MR. LEBEUF, WAKE UP!
ZZZZZ
...HUH?!?...WHAAT?
WHAAT ARRE YOU DOING INN MYY HOOUSE?
OH, WOULD YOU JUST STOP THAT NONSENSE! YOU KNEW I WAS COMING!
YOU SMELL LIKE A DISTILLERY! WHAT AM I SUPPOSED TO DO HERE, EH?!
SNIFF!
OH DEAR! HIDING BOOZE IN A PEANUT BUTTER JAR, MY WORD!
WOULD YOU PLEASE LOOK AT ME WHEN I'M TRYING TO TALK TO YOU!
OH...HUMPH! FINE!

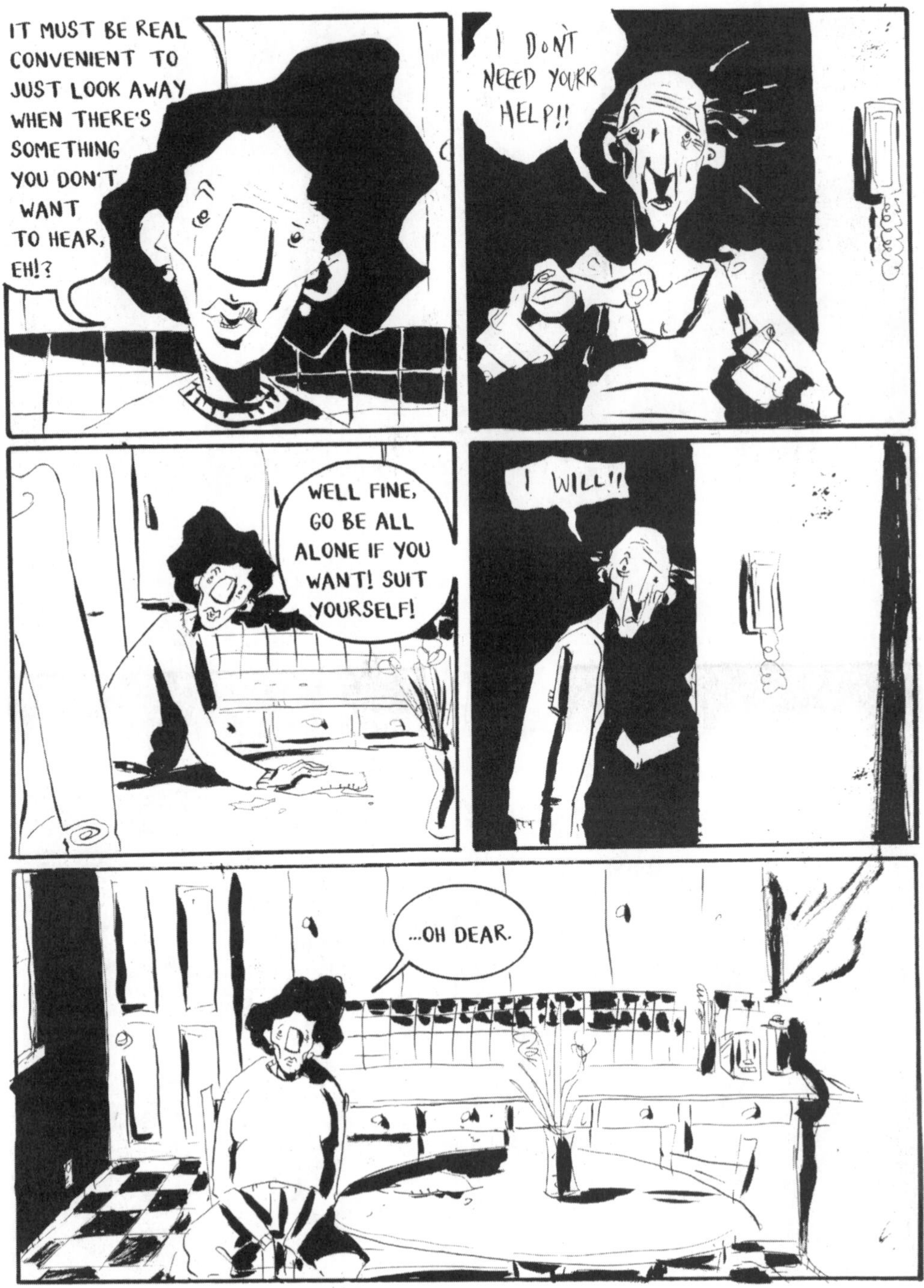
IT MUST BE REAL CONVENIENT TO JUST LOOK AWAY WHEN THERE'S SOMETHING YOU DON'T WANT TO HEAR, EH!?
I DON'T NEEED YOURR HELP!!
WELL FINE, GO BE ALL ALONE IF YOU WANT! SUIT YOURSELF!
I WILL!!
...OH DEAR.

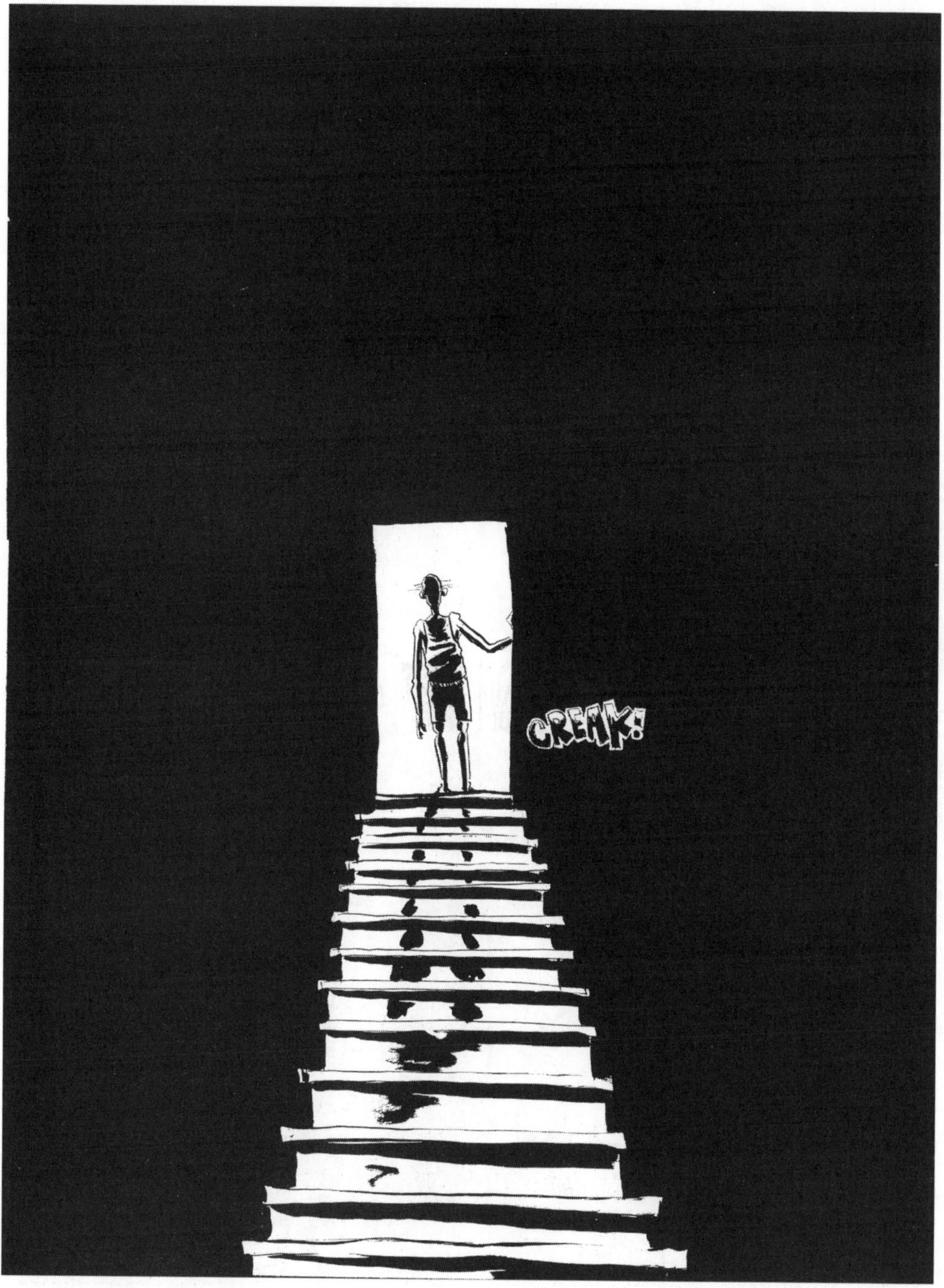
CREAK!

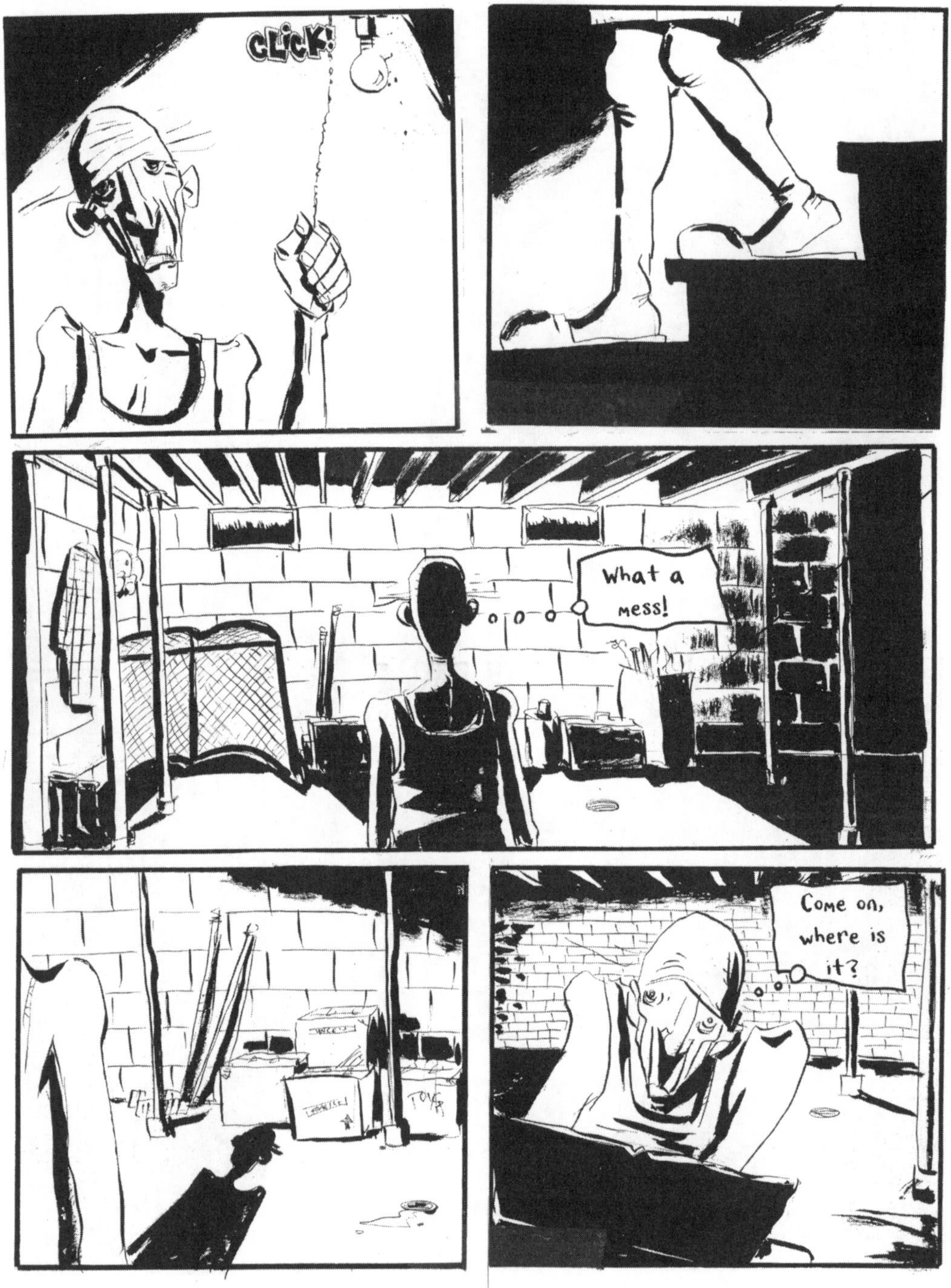
CLICK!
What a mess!
Come on, where is it?

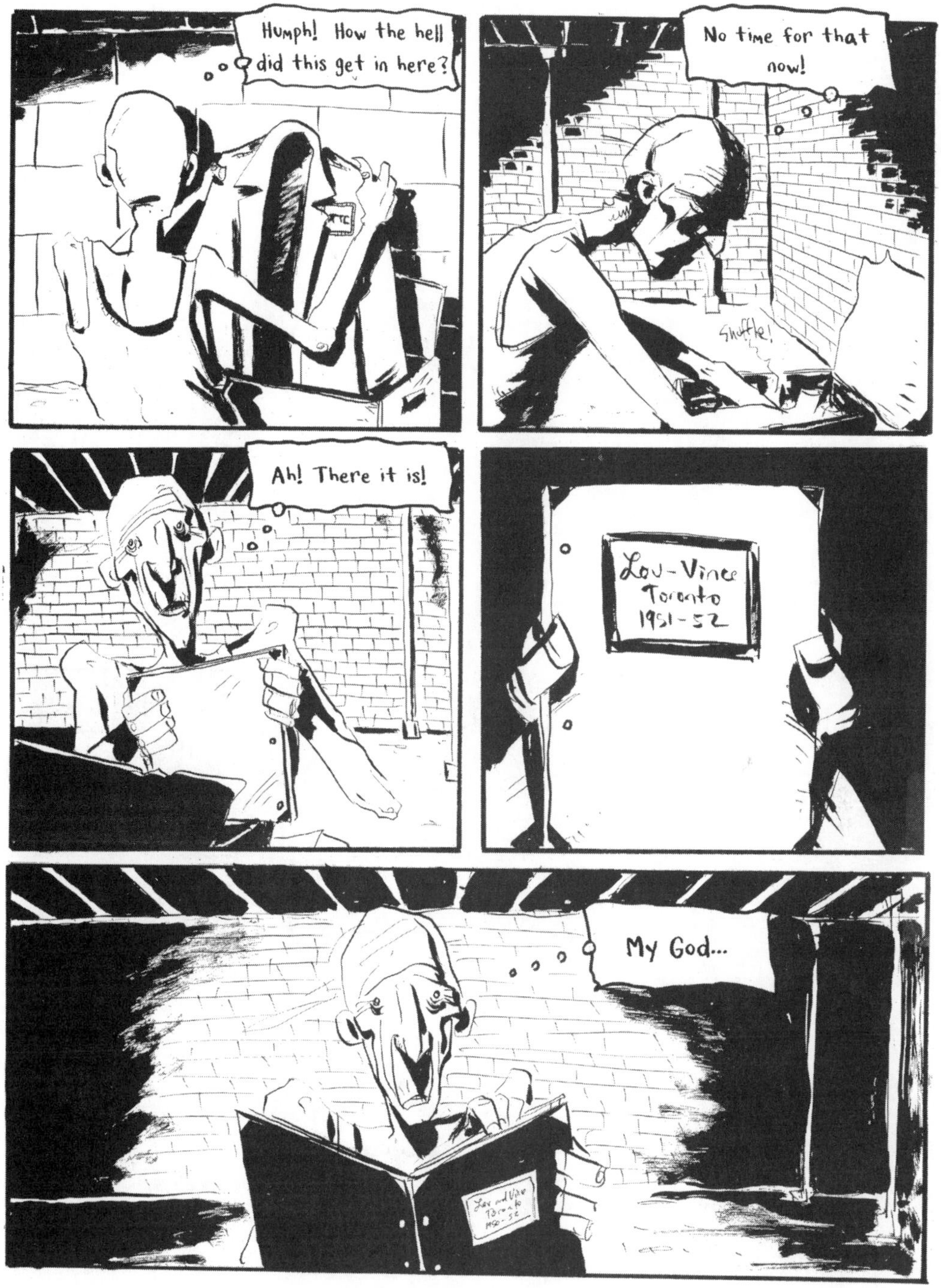
Humph! How the hell did this get in here?
No time for that now!
Shuffle!
Ah! There it is!
Lou-Vince
Toronto
1951-52
My God...

Vince and the Team bus   '51

GRIZZLIE BROS. DRAW NEW FANS

By NEIL MacCARL

The smashing success of the two Oshawa Curling club in carrying off the two blue-ribbon awards in double rink competition, the Ontario Tankard and the Governor-General's Trophy, should not come as a surprise to the close followers of the curling game.

There have been plenty of tipoffs in the past five years that the Oshawa club was producing some excellent young curlers as shown by their victories in the Ontario Junior Tankard for three successive years, 1947, 1948 and 1949. And all Oshawa victory in the Governor-General's play in 1948 added further to their prestige, although the club had never managed to score in a major event such as the Tankard.

An All-Oshawa Show

But it was an all-Oshawa show yesterday as A. J. Parkhill and Dr. J. Brock scored in the Tankard final at Toronto Curling club while William Minnett and Rev. J. Pereyma were winning the Governor-General's final at Granite club.

It took a strong finish, particularly by Dr. Brock, to give Oshawa its first Tankard victory. After eight ends of play, Dr. Brock was trailing J. C. W. Leeds of Kingston 13-3, while Parkhill of Oshawa had a four-shot lead over H. M. Reid of Kingston, which gave the Kingston entry a combined lead of six shots.

Dr. Brock was down 10-4 after 11 ends, but Kingston failed to score in the remainder of the game, while Oshawa counted 11 shots in finish one shot behind.

Youngsters Shine

The Oshawa victory in the Tankard adds weight to the theory that curling isn't an old man's game. Bud Moore, who played lead for A. J. Parkhill, is only 19, and probably one of the youngest members ever to play on a Tankard winner. And Allan Morrison, second shot, is only two years older.

Despite their comparative youth, these two lads have been playing for six years, and even played on three junior Tankard winners. Morrison also played on a Governor-General's trophy winner in 1948.

It is the same story with regard

to the Governor-General's winners, W. Minnett and Rev. Pereyma, the winning Skips, both played on the Oshawa trophy winner in 1948.

Minnett defeated C. Renwick of Wingham 19-11 for an eight-shot margin which compensated for Rev. Pereyma's 17-11 defeat by J. R. Roe in the final round.

In the consolation play, H. Foryshe and Percy Slatch of Lindsay took the Burden trophy, defeating Kitchener 28-23. Forsythe lost 13-10 to Carl Asmussen, and his 1950 Brier rink from Kitchener, but Slatch trounced J. Locke 18-6.

Kitchener didn't miss out altogether on the silverware as W. A. Clarke and Allan Slark took the Globe and Mail trophy by defeating Brockville 42-25. Slark defeated G. Bigford 17-6 and Clarke beat T. G. Goodison 25-11.

STORY REVERSED THIS TIME BLUES WIN IN FINAL MINUTE

Queen's University provided a smaller-than-usual Hart House Athletic Night crowd with plenty of thrills before they went down to a heart-breaking 35-34 defeat at the hands of the University of Toronto Blues last night.

A foul shot of

LETHBRIDGE LEAFS BEAT AMBRI-PROTTI

Ambri, Italy, Feb. 9—(CP)—Lethbridge Maple Leafs last night walloped the Ambri-Protti hockey team 22-1.

BAGNATO BUSY GETTING BOUTS FOR NEWSBOYS

Hardly had the welts and bruises subsided on the frames and features of last year's contestants when another Newsboys' boxing show comes along. This latest edition of a program that was instituted about a quarter of a century ago, is scheduled for a week Monday night (Feb. 19) at the Gardens. All proceeds go to the Toronto Newsboys' Welfare fund, and this boxing show is the fund's only source of revenue.

Vic Bagnato is again matchmaking the Newsboys' program, and announces that as he lined up a top team of Montreal scrappers to take on the best from this province in the feature matches.

Star of the Montreal squad is the Quebec bantam champion, Frankie Fitzgerald, who made such a smash hit on last year's show, in besting Oakwood's fiery Maurice Mousseau. Bagnato hasn't yet decided who should represent Ontario against the capable Mousseau.

LEBEUF BOYS DOMINATE

San Franci Rodovich, fo Southern Cal... hhe with a pre in his $100,000 the old Natio Federal Ju man yesterd...

B G

MA

Mar Mar

Oct. 3, 1951

Dear Mom,

Sorry I haven't written in a while.
Things have been real busy here. Lou is
fine, and says "Hi!" The team is
a real good bunch of guys, and
we've been playing a lot better lately.

We leave for a road trip up North
to Parry Sound on Saturday. Should
be nice this time of year.

The city sure is busy. So many people,
always going. Lou really likes it.
I guess it's ok for some people,
but it's not for me. I can't
wait to come back home this
summer. Hope Uncle Ken got
the winter wheat off in time.

I'll write soon. Beth is coming up
again after we get back. Looking
forward to that! Bye Mom.

xoxo Vince

Me, Vince and the Boys Nov '51

TORONTO DAILY STAR: Fri. March 16, 1951

Speaking on Sport
By MILT DUNNELL — Sports Editor

Grizzlies Win
Fourth In A Row

They set the playoff dates, as you've been told. And they discussed the 70-game schedule without getting past centre ice. But the feature event of the program wasn't even mentioned in the routine handouts, if you can believe these insiders and those routines. The way we got it, the Leafs' Conn Smythe was practically on trial for his life. Some of those interviews which Smythe gave were his return from Florida got him indicted by his fellow-barons of the ice industry. They made good many at the time, but some of the sentences hurt they will when used as evidence by owners who had been wronged by Smythe's barbs...

Vincent Lebeuf
Junior City Fight Entries Close April 16

Wave Goodbye to th

By RED BURNETT
Star Staff Correspondent

Chicago, March 16—Jack Stewart, winner of the fifth goal that sent Harry Lumley last night...

HABITANTS HOP TO THIRD SPOT
HOWE NEAR MARK

Montreal, March 16 — (CP) — Montreal's one-and-seventy Canadiens are back in third place in the National Hockey League standings today, thanks to rookie Bernie (Boom Boom) Geoffrion...

N.H.L. S

Lev on fam bus Oct 51

TORONTO DAILY STAR: Mon. Nov. 7, 1955

Speaking on Sport

Phil Might Even Pay For The Privilege

TORONTO'S MINOR LEAGUE GRIZZLIES ON A ROLL

STEWART TRIES TIPTOE BUT LEAFS STILL DON'T BEAT GUMP

One Day, Clancy Dreams of 1st Place
The Next, He's Fearful of Cellar

By RED BURNETT
Star Staff Correspondent

Detroit, Nov. 7—Exemplifying the leading Canadiens, the current NHL race is a promoter's dream and a coach's nightmare...

BELIVEAU 1-MAN GANG
AS CANADIENS BEAT, TIE
BOSTON OVER WEEK-END

By the Canadian Press

Varsity Injuries Take Much of the Joy
Out of Romp Over Western Mustangs

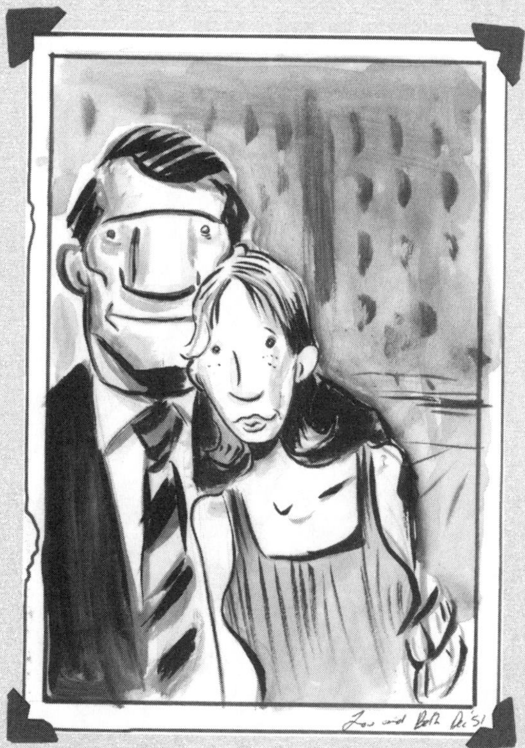
Lou and Beth Dec '51

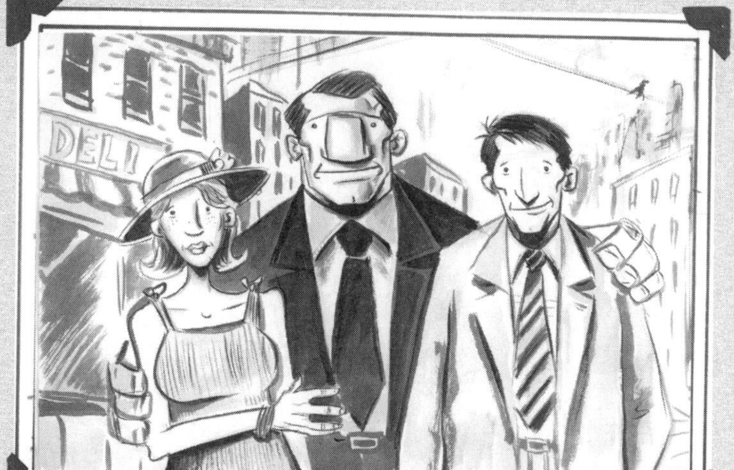
DELI
Vince on the Team Bus '51

GRIZZLIES AND KNIGHTS BRAWL, TIE.

By MILT DUNNELL
Star Staff Correspondent

New York, Dec. 31 — This is supposed to be one of big league hockey's rough spots—one of the U.S. cities in which sales resistance has developed at an alarming rate. And maybe it is. But you couldn't prove it at Madison Square Garden last night, where slightly more than 13,000 clients — biggest crowd of the season—squealed as the Rangers came from behind a two-goal deficit to earn a two-all draw with the Leafs.

That's right, the customers actually celebrated the tie. Earlier in the season you were led to believe they'd rather lose than split the points. If that's the case, they used an unique method of showing their disapproval of last night's draw.

By RED BURNETT

Start of Thomson-Kryzanowski Feud

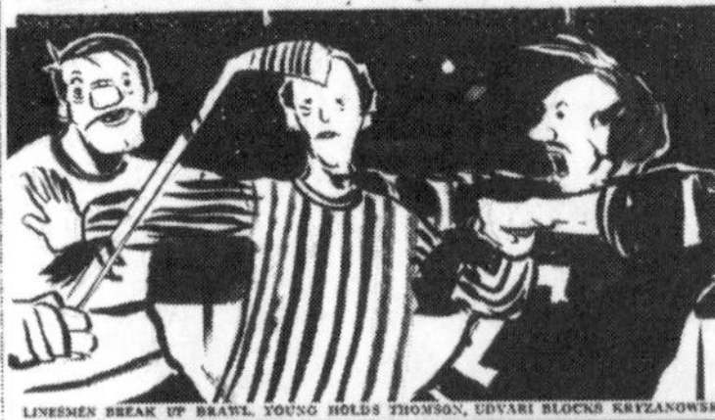

LINESMEN BREAK UP BRAWL, YOUNG HOLDS THOMSON, UDVARI BLOCKS KRYZANOWSKI

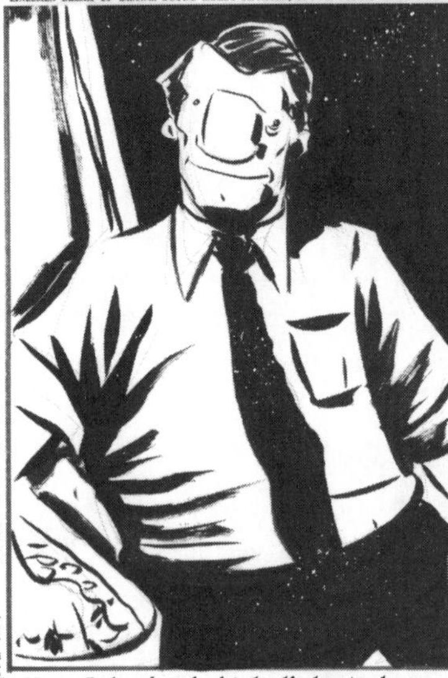

Vince Lebeuf soaks his badly bruised knuckles. "You should see the other guy!"

HAB ROOKIES SET PACE IN WIN OVER RANGERS RED WINGS BOP HAWKS

JUST HAD TO BE 2 REFS TO OGLE TEAM REMATCH

SPEERS' SECOND GOAL GIVES SARACINIS TIE

TRI-BELLS LOSE OUT IN CLOSING MINUTES

NHL Summaries

TWO MORE COLLEGES DESERT COAST GRIDS

BROWN WINS PUCK CROWN

Hit Ref., Jailed!

GRAY BOOSTS LEAD WITH THREE GOALS

AUSSIES BOO TEAM IN 4TH CRICKET TEST

FRANK YOUNG NETS 40 FOR LOOP MARK

PEOPLES IN SLUMP MAHERS PULL AWAY

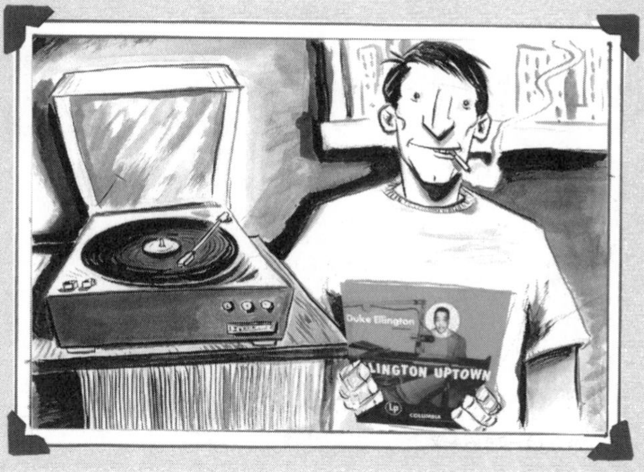
Duke Ellington
LLINGTON UPTOWN
COLUMBIA

Dec 16, 1951.

Dear Mom,

I hope you got that last package of clippings and photographs I sent. Lou bought a new fancy camera and won't stop snapping pictures of us. I guess you'll probably like them though.

We got the care package you sent up with Beth. Thanks. Sorry to hear about Aunt Alma's health. Hopefully she'll pull through.

Only one more week then we'll be off for the holidays! So, we'll be at the train station at 2:30 pm on the 22nd. Don't forget us!

xoxo. Vince

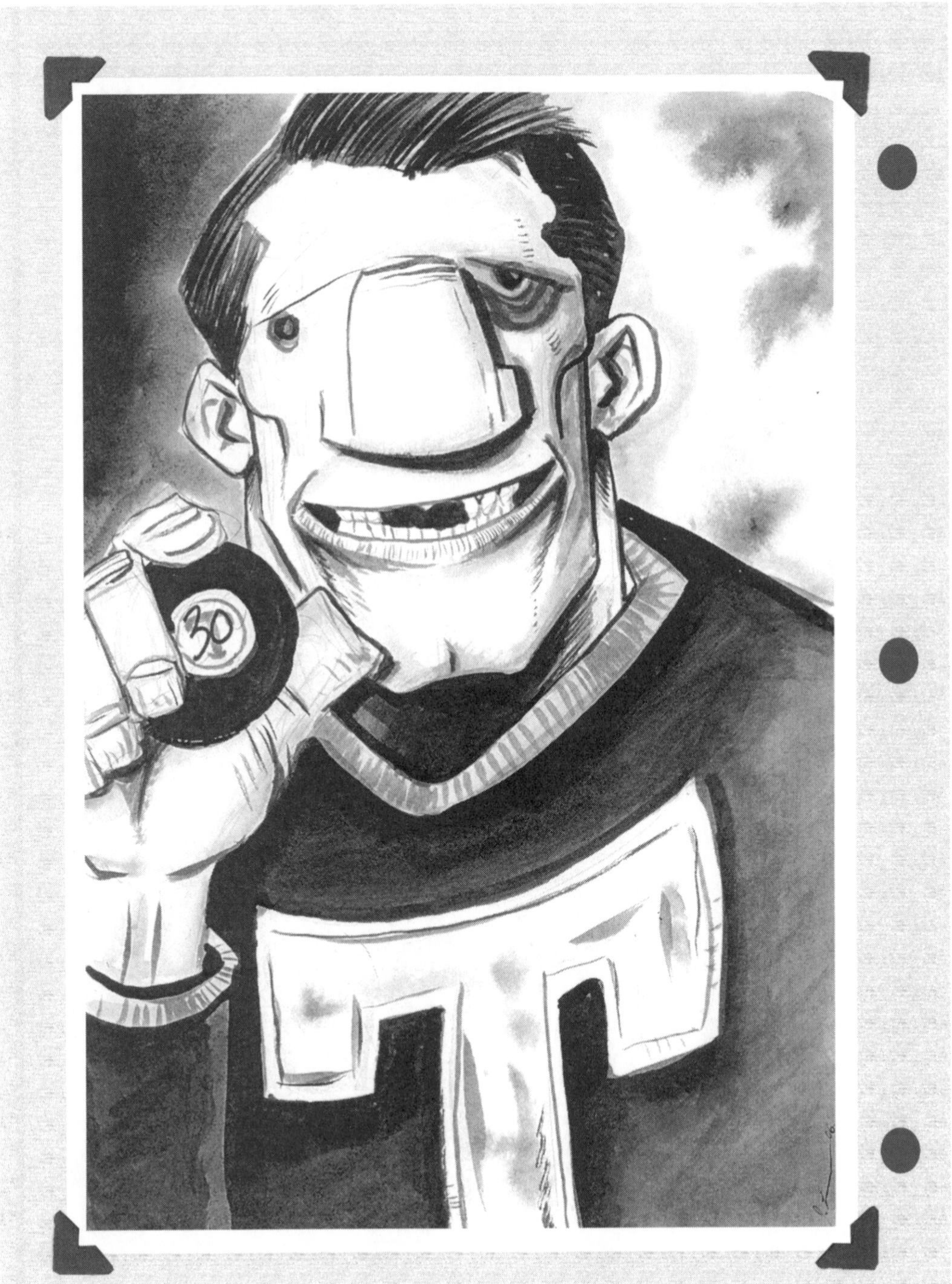
30

Jan 12, 1952.

Dear Mom,

Can you believe it! 30 goals! I asked the newspaper man and he gave me this nice big photograph for you. It's the same one that they ran in the paper on Friday!

We're real close to making the playoffs now. If we do, I won't be home until March at the earliest. So, I hope Uncle Ron can get started on the planting if I don't make it home in time. Have to get going, meeting the boys to celebrate.

xoxo Vince.

LEBEUF GETS 30 AND QUITE A SHINER
DiMaggio Just Can't Get Going
Halifax Team Plays Here
ON ONE UP
HEAD STARS
TING REGENTS
LEBEUF SCORES 30 GOALS!
SPRING Sale AUTO SUPPLIES
BATTERY Sale

GRIZZLIES COACH EARNS PRAISE FOR TURNAROUND

22 TORONTO DAILY STAR: Thurs., Feb. 1, 15-1

Speaking on Sport

By Milt Dunnell—Sports Editor

A Bleat From Miss Duddleydumpple

MISS Daisy Duddleydumpple just called to say she and her gals probably will picket the Gardens. Miss Duddleydumpple, it develops, is chairman of the civil rights committee of the Two's the Quota for a Honeymoon league, which has branches in the U.S., Mexico and some sections of Santa Domingo. The league is anxious to gain a foothold in Canada. Miss Duddleydumpple had heard, we suspected, about the case of Johnny McCormack. Miss Duddleydumpple said she had, and that was the reason for the league's indignation. The league had decided that Connie Smythe should be brought to trial, and that was the reason for the pickets. Miss Duddleydumpple was non-plussed to learn that Smythe is in Florida. How, she wondered, could Smythe, who's nearly two thousand miles away, send one of his slaves to a honeymoon nest of Pittsburgh Hornets.

We asked Miss Duddleydumpple if she knew Smythe. She admitted she didn't. That's just the trouble with a lot of the executives in those high-sounding, well-intentioned international organizations. They're not versed in fundamentals. She wouldn't know, for instance, that Smythe intervened, a year ago, when a beloved Turk Broda, decided to show a waistline bulge, as a badge of the success he'd attained in hockey. Or maybe he might even get around to running for alderman.

By the time Smythe and the physical torture specialists got through, the Turkey could have feathered the end of his belt and let it dangle like a highlander's sporran. And then there was the time the Turk got himself a horse and was looking over the condition books for posh parks like Sunshine, San Mateo and Billings, Montana. Turk tore up his application for membership in the Jockey club a few minutes after Smythe read the announcement in the newspapers. There's no evidence that any pressure was brought to bear. Smythe's an old racing man himself—Shotless Joe, Skating Fool, Blue Ice, remember?—so there's no reason why he should be prejudiced against the turf. You'll find him at Woodbine on King's Plate day—and likely at the daily double cashier's window.

But Miss Duddleydumpple should have some knowledge of things like that before she starts popping off about civil liberties. If they're still in the book, they're in fine type, underneath the clause that says there shall be no assist on a goal for the attacking team when a defending player boots the disc into his own rigging.

Off-Hours Are Their Own — Almost

YOU see, Miss Duddleydumpple, it's like this: playing hockey for a club like the Leafs is partly punching a clock and partly like being a member of a family—a big happy family. You have to be on the job. If the coach says practice at ten, you're ready to go on the ice at ten. The train leaves for New York at 11.30 from Union Station. So you'd better be aboard. If you're not, you'd better bust that rattler to Sunnyside. Otherwise, there's liable to be a chunk of you know what missing from your next pay envelope. That's the

GRIZZLIES CLOSE IN ON PLAYOFFS

Team Trades Captain, Winger To Barrie

WON'T TAKE CUT

HOWL DOWN TENNIS HECKLERS ISN'T CRICKET, AUSSIES TOLD

McCOR
LEA

By RED I

Those checks
Johnny McCormac
for Pittsburgh
next two weeks
very costly to the
demotion of "Lou
when the Maple
Detroit Red Wing
first place in the
blow to the home
There's no dou
too good for the
no doubt that,
ability and perfo
others on the Lea
be spared easier
It could be that
Cormack, the Le
off the nose to
the moment. Co
needs all the b
brains available
place spot. The g
going John had
hearts on the clu
a good hockey br
a hockey stick w
tension. He ha
plays than any o
the N.H.L.
The Leaf front
no rule against
mid-season or at
that McCormack's
Hornets was not a
This could be, b
able to sell that
Order Fr
Hap Day, Leafs
manager and ho
has been watchin
past few games
lost Rudy Migay
an injured ankle.
Smythe in Florid
him they needed
called back today
said McCormack
take Migay's pl
line.
"The Migay-A
Solinger line is t
goals and they ne
take over for Ru
playing very wel
It usually cost
ference between
when he is sent t
a rough jolt to J
days.
Frank Selke
Canadiens will b
McCormack wo
bother them toni
Forum. Selke t
as a second F

TO DAILY STAR: Fri., March 16, 1951

Speaking on Sport

ilt Dunnell—Sports Editor

ers Put Stingeroo On Smythe?

rong about wire-tapping, after all. Our feel-
been that once the coppers get the right to
ephone, you might as well return the gadget
Bell's estate. But we'd have given a hatful
dn't be money—to tune in on the National
s the other day in New York. That wouldn't
it would be close enough to the real thing.
med, via the jungle drums and the hilltop
of the best shows the N.H.L. has put on
owners keep it to themselves. The rich get

ff dates, as you've been told. And they dis-
hedule without getting past centre ice. But
the program wasn't even mentioned in the
u can believe those beacons and those tom-
t it, the Leafs' Conn Smythe was practically
ome of those interviews which Smythe gave
Florida got him indicted by his fellow-barons
ey made good copy at the time, but some of
lilt when used as evidence by owners who
ythe's barbs.
he details, you'd have to guess the complaints
ythe hit Boston on his way north. He told
effect, that the Bruins couldn't sell beans in
re the civic dish. Later, he got into Jim
gesting the Red Wings were the least-penal-
ecause they were past-masters of the beef.
into breaks from
im won-

LEBEUF NAMED CAPTAIN

LOU LEBEUF TAKES ON CAPTAIN'S ROLE FOR ALL-IMPORTANT GAME TOMMOROW NIGHT VS. CHATHAM

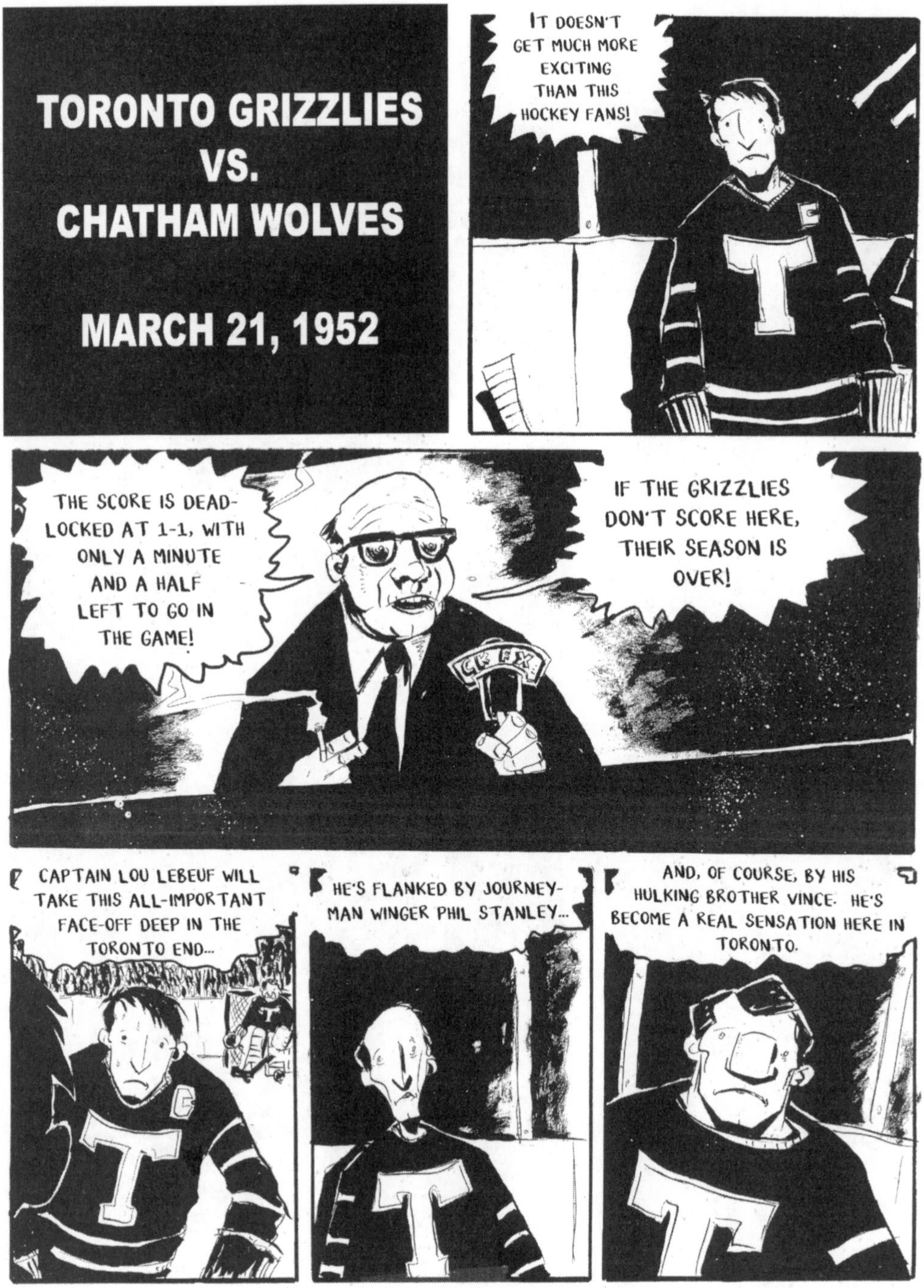
TORONTO GRIZZLIES
VS.
CHATHAM WOLVES
MARCH 21, 1952
IT DOESN'T GET MUCH MORE EXCITING THAN THIS HOCKEY FANS!
THE SCORE IS DEAD-LOCKED AT 1-1, WITH ONLY A MINUTE AND A HALF LEFT TO GO IN THE GAME!
IF THE GRIZZLIES DON'T SCORE HERE, THEIR SEASON IS OVER!
CKFX
CAPTAIN LOU LEBEUF WILL TAKE THIS ALL-IMPORTANT FACE-OFF DEEP IN THE TORONTO END...
HE'S FLANKED BY JOURNEY-MAN WINGER PHIL STANLEY...
AND, OF COURSE, BY HIS HULKING BROTHER VINCE. HE'S BECOME A REAL SENSATION HERE IN TORONTO.

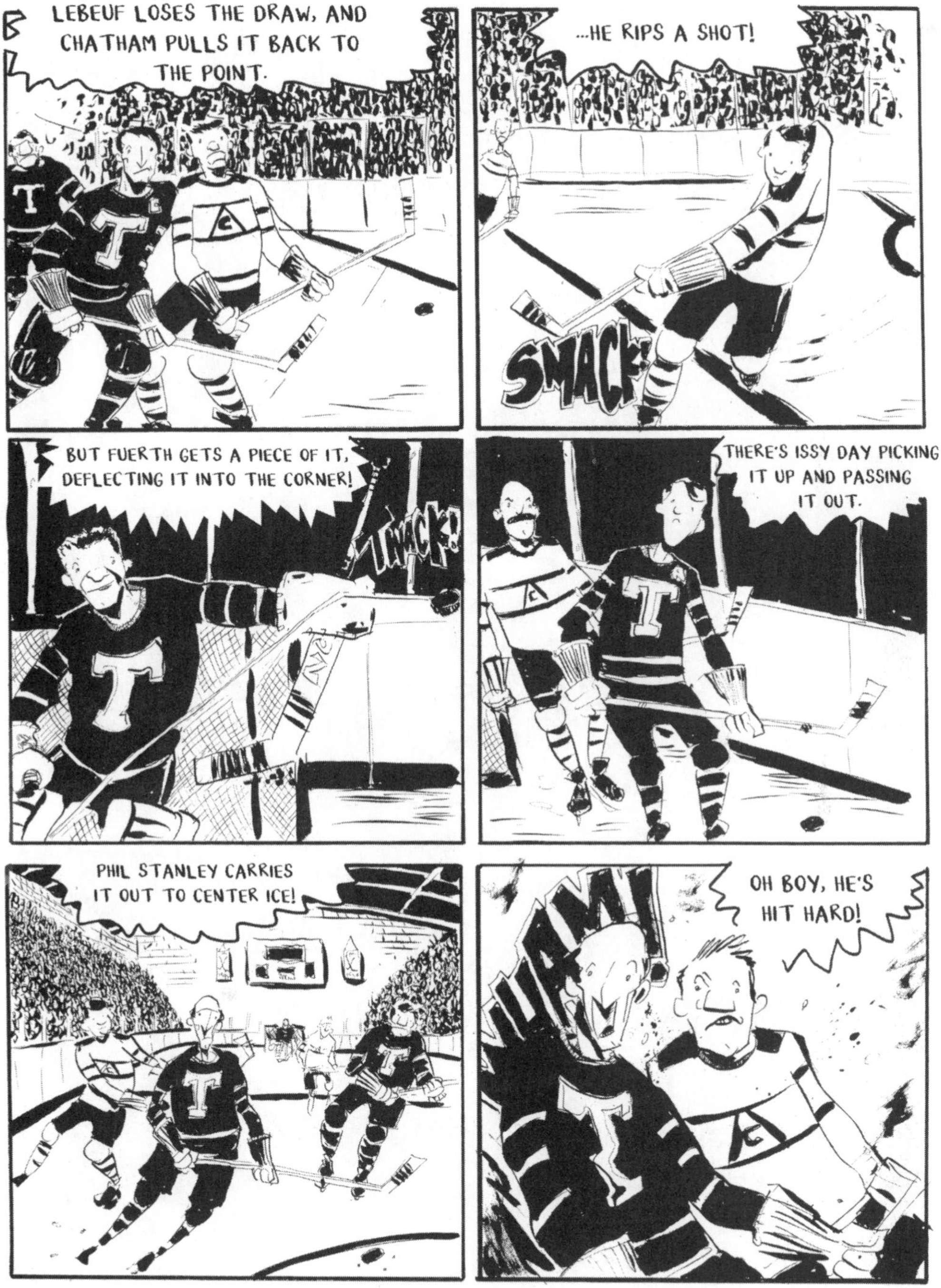
LEBEUF LOSES THE DRAW, AND CHATHAM PULLS IT BACK TO THE POINT.
...HE RIPS A SHOT!
SMACK!
BUT FUERTH GETS A PIECE OF IT, DEFLECTING IT INTO THE CORNER!
THWACK!
THERE'S ISSY DAY PICKING IT UP AND PASSING IT OUT.
PHIL STANLEY CARRIES IT OUT TO CENTER ICE!
WHAM!
OH BOY, HE'S HIT HARD!

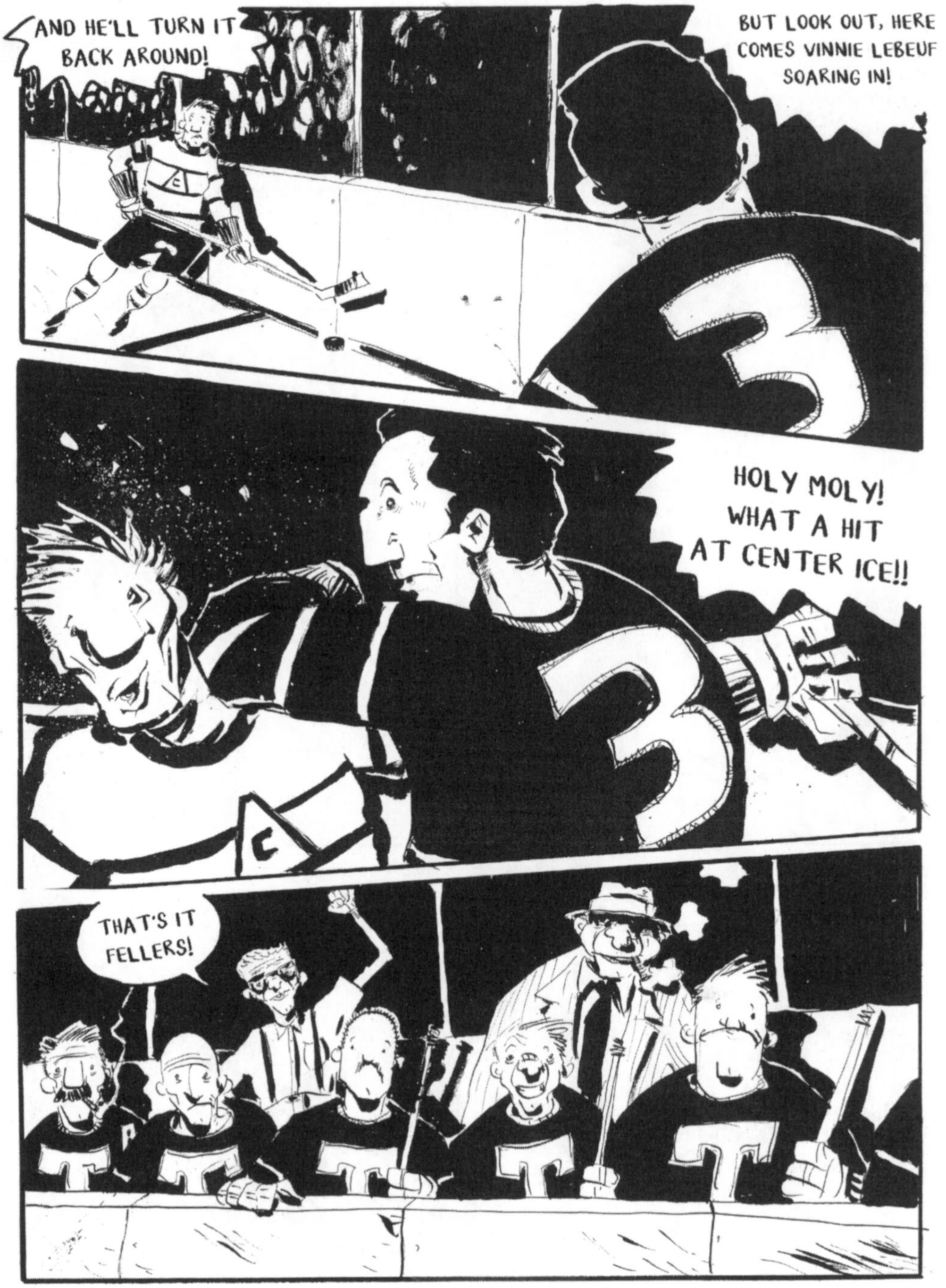
AND HE'LL TURN IT BACK AROUND!
BUT LOOK OUT, HERE COMES VINNIE LEBEUF SOARING IN!
HOLY MOLY! WHAT A HIT AT CENTER ICE!!
THAT'S IT FELLERS!

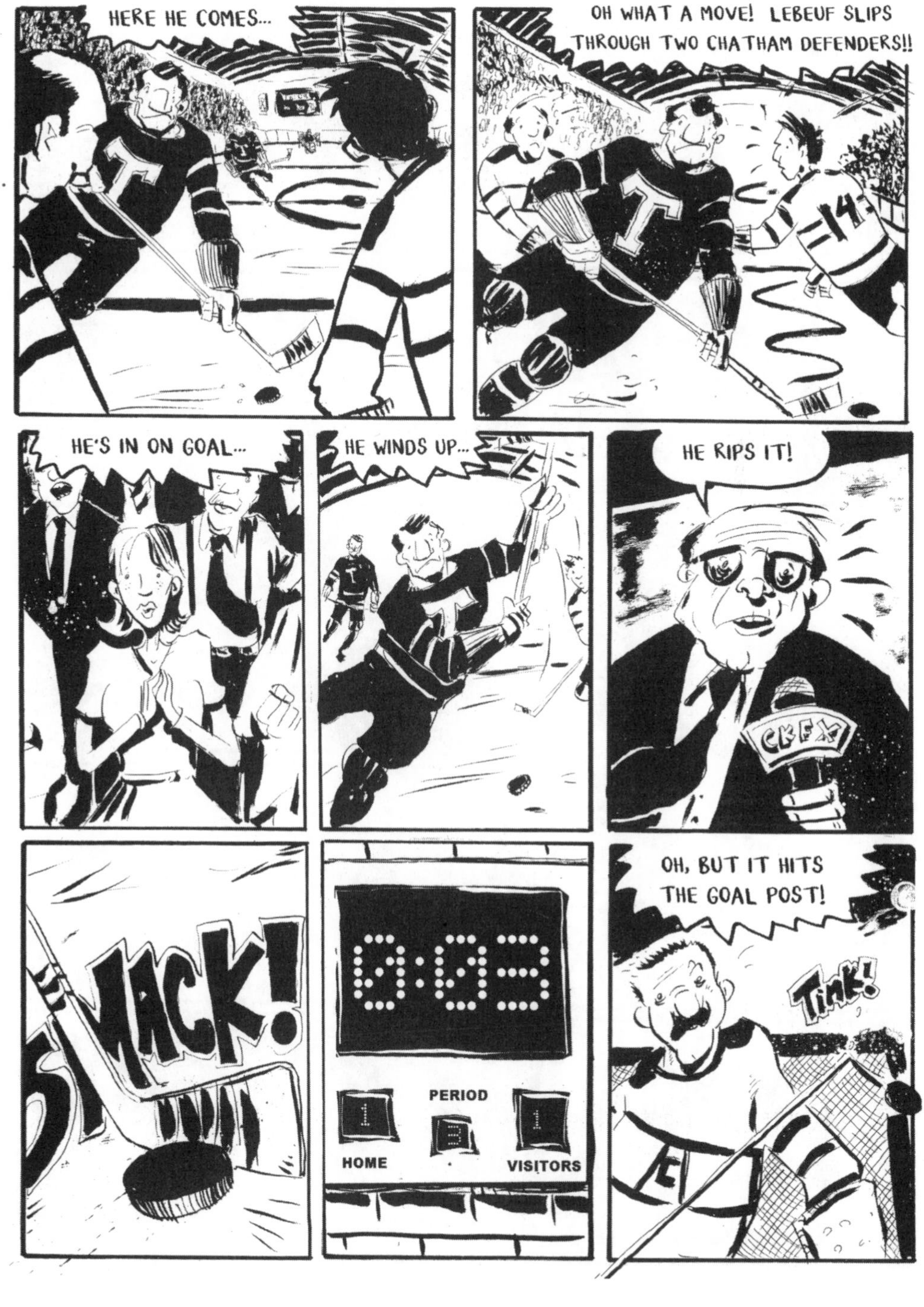
HERE HE COMES...
OH WHAT A MOVE! LEBEUF SLIPS THROUGH TWO CHATHAM DEFENDERS!!
14
HE'S IN ON GOAL...
HE WINDS UP...
HE RIPS IT!
CKFX
SMACK!
0:03
PERIOD
1
3
1
HOME
VISITORS
OH, BUT IT HITS THE GOAL POST!
TINK!

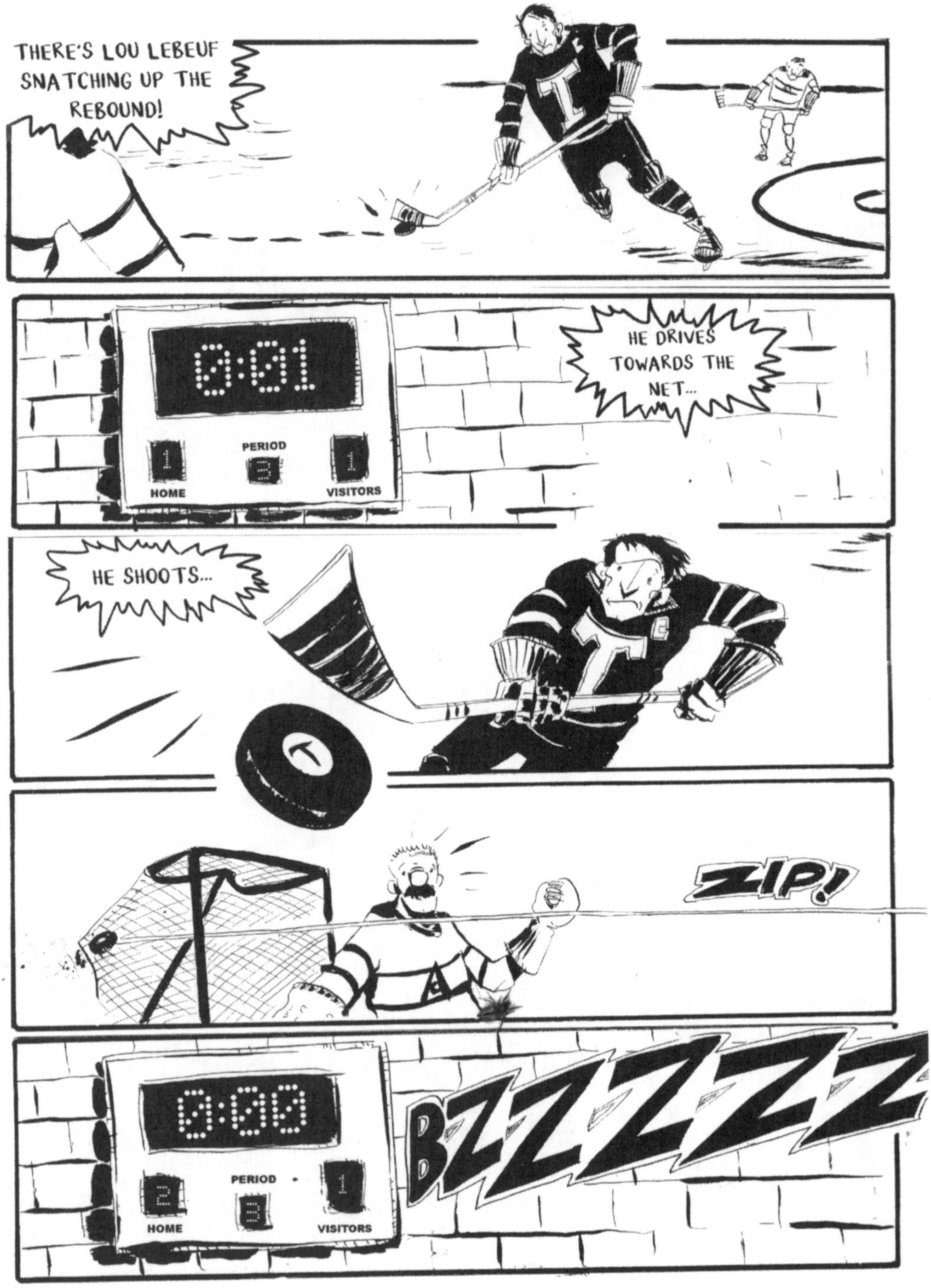

THERE'S LOU LEBEUF SNATCHING UP THE REBOUND!
0:01
PERIOD
HOME
VISITORS
HE DRIVES TOWARDS THE NET...
HE SHOOTS...
ZIP!
0:00
PERIOD
HOME
VISITORS
BZZZZZ

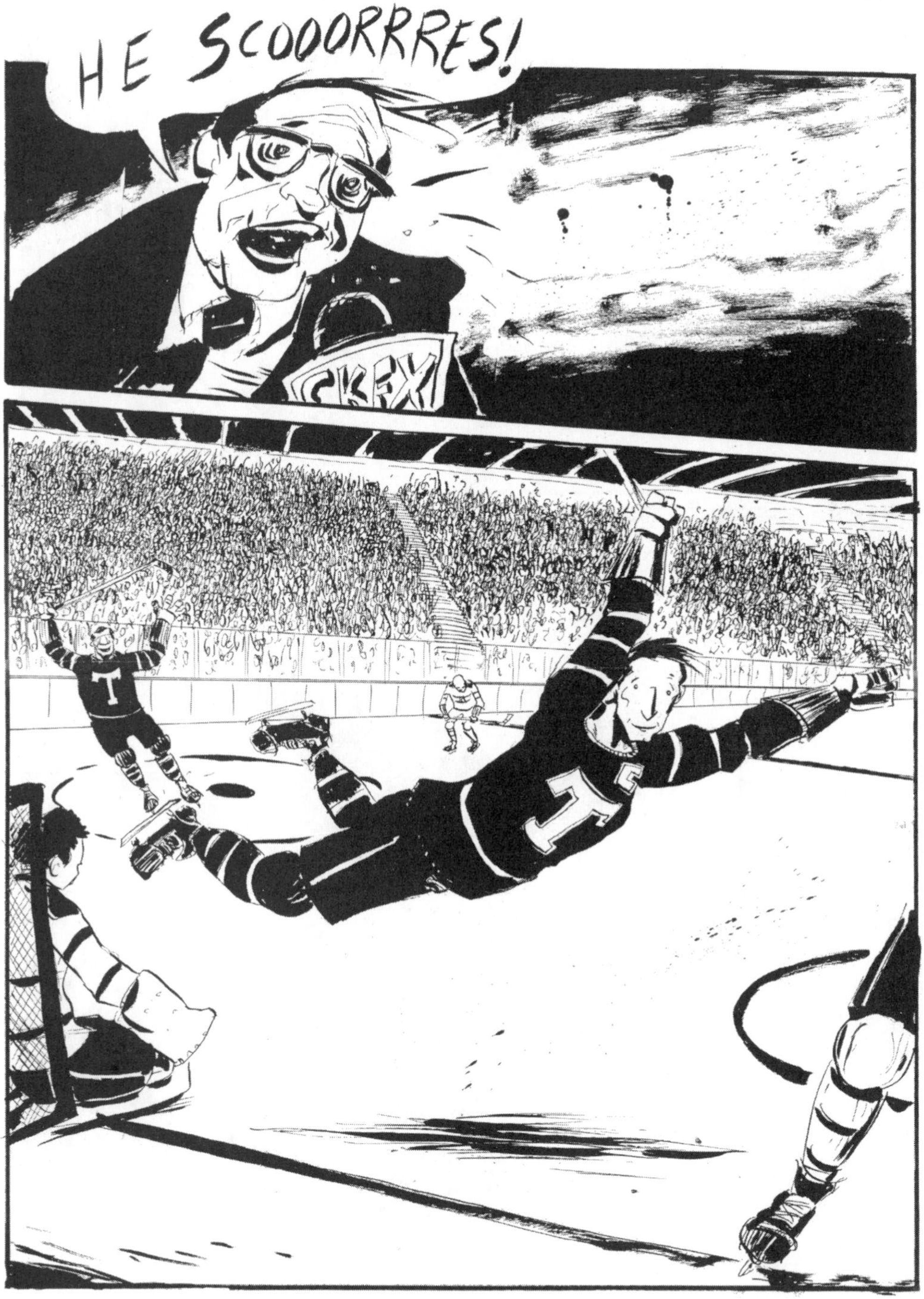
HE SCOOORRRES!
CKFX

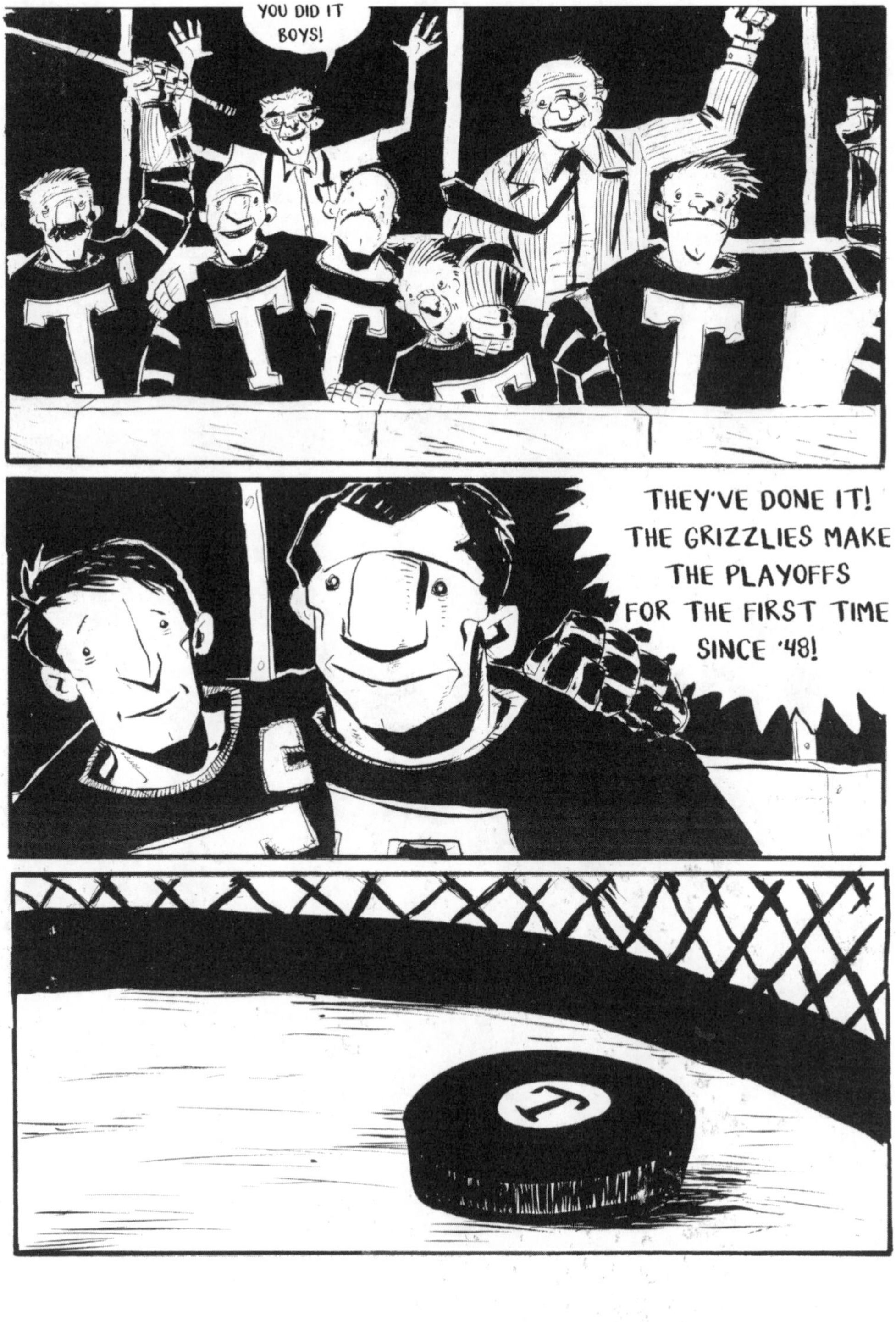
YOU DID IT BOYS!
THEY'VE DONE IT! THE GRIZZLIES MAKE THE PLAYOFFS FOR THE FIRST TIME SINCE '48!

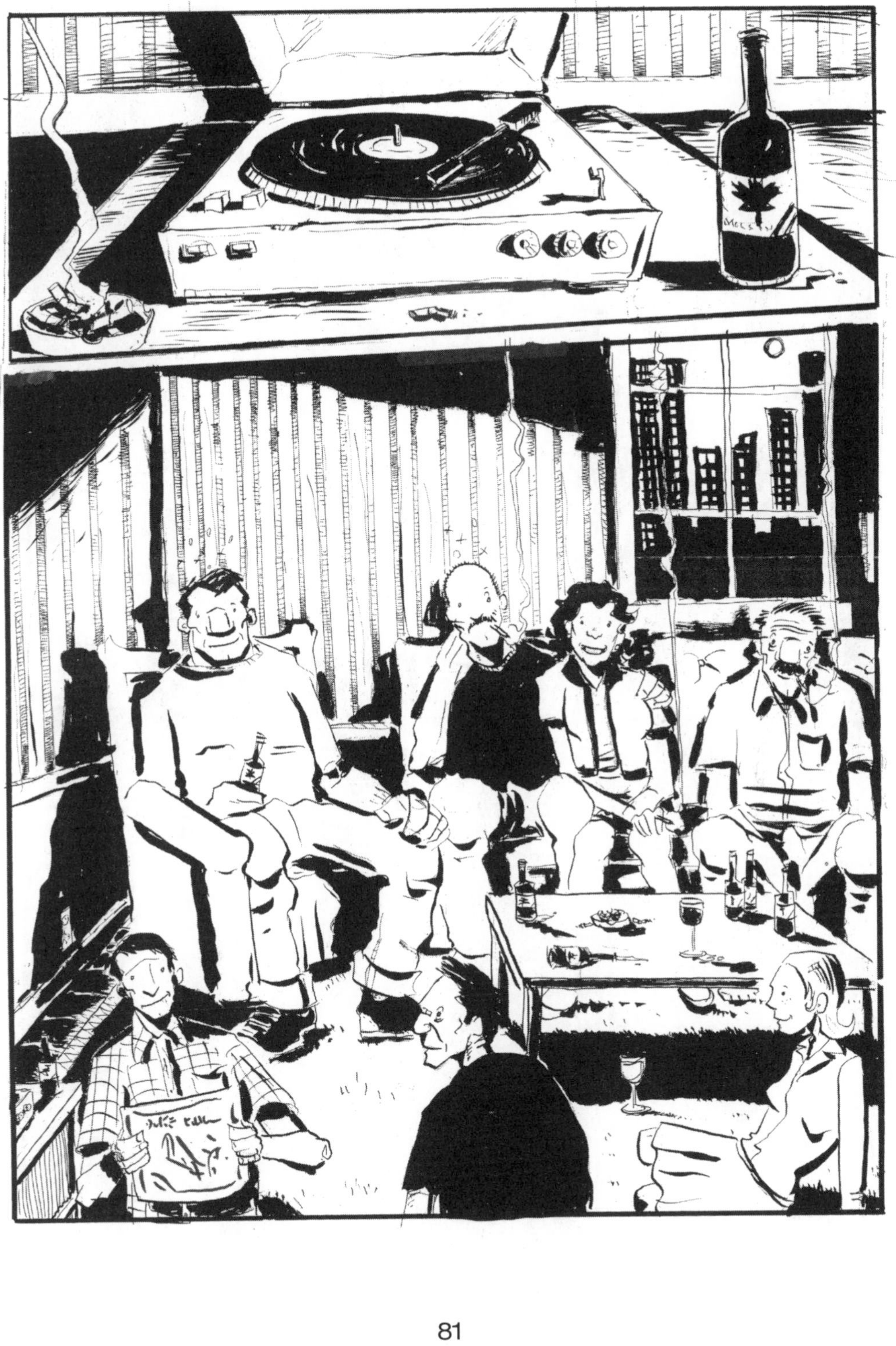

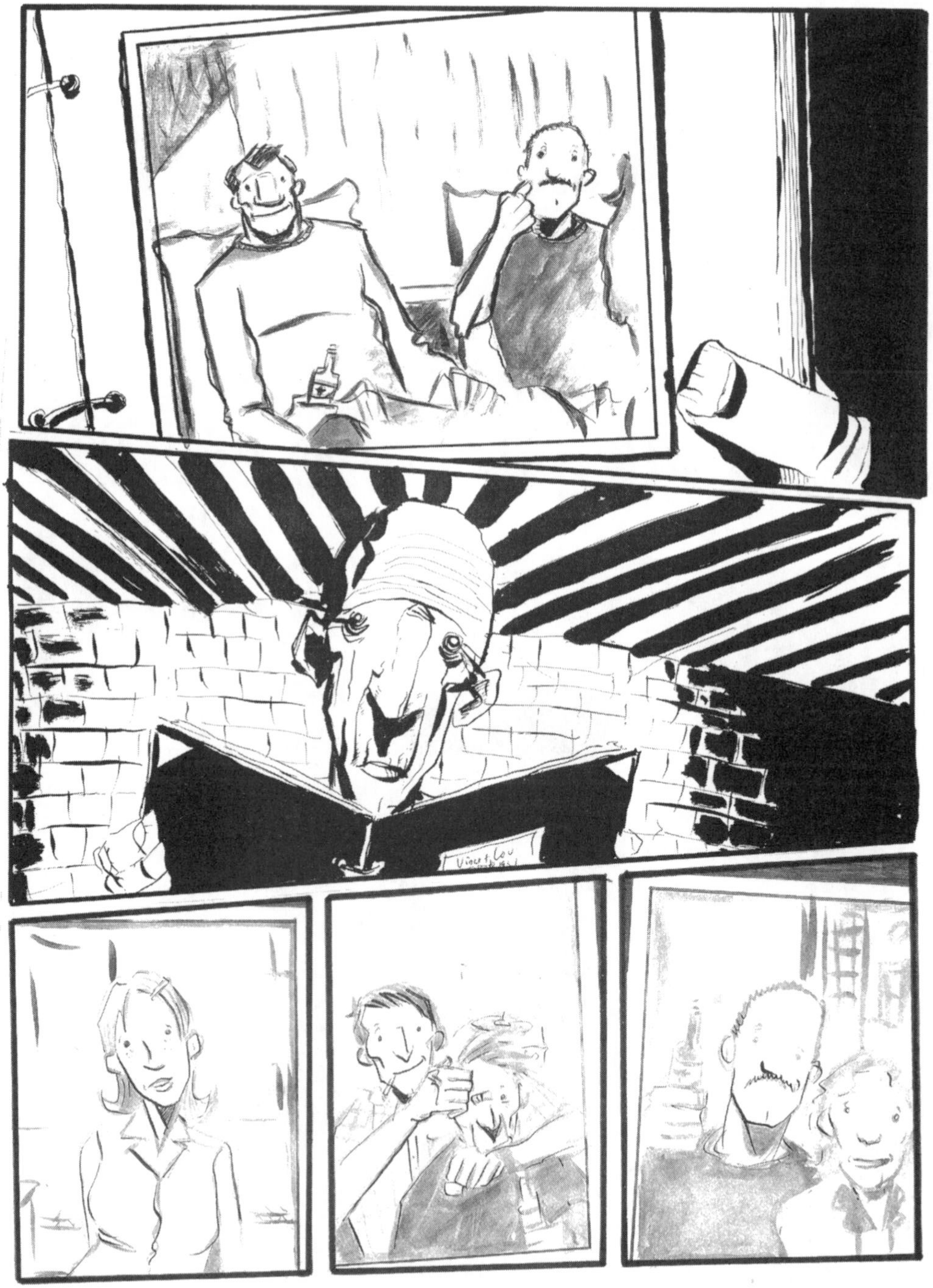
Vince & Lou

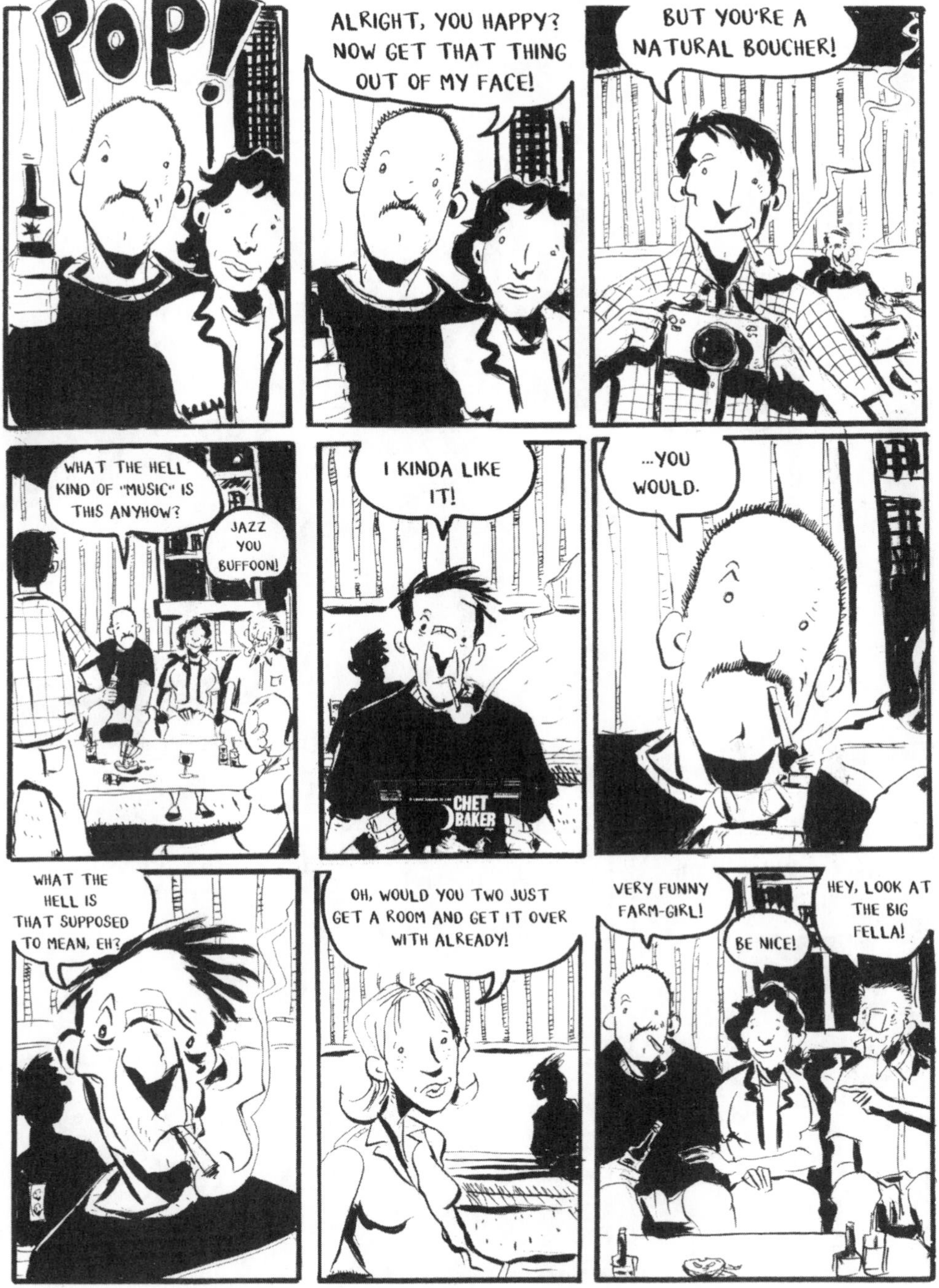
POP!
ALRIGHT, YOU HAPPY? NOW GET THAT THING OUT OF MY FACE!
BUT YOU'RE A NATURAL BOUCHER!
WHAT THE HELL KIND OF "MUSIC" IS THIS ANYHOW?
JAZZ YOU BUFFOON!
I KINDA LIKE IT!
CHET BAKER
...YOU WOULD.
WHAT THE HELL IS THAT SUPPOSED TO MEAN, EH?
OH, WOULD YOU TWO JUST GET A ROOM AND GET IT OVER WITH ALREADY!
VERY FUNNY FARM-GIRL!
BE NICE!
HEY, LOOK AT THE BIG FELLA!

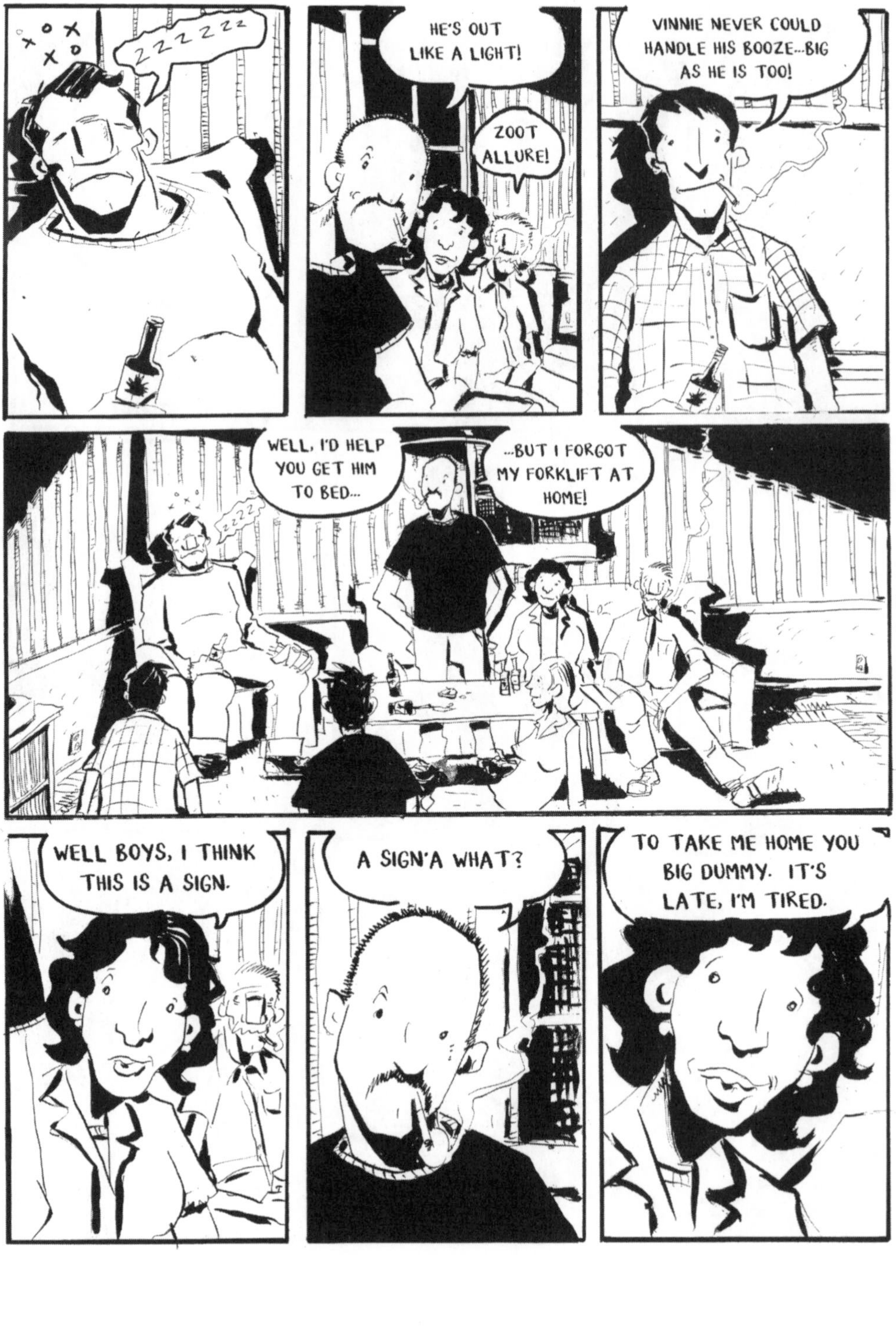
ZZZZZZ
HE'S OUT LIKE A LIGHT!
ZOOT ALLURE!
VINNIE NEVER COULD HANDLE HIS BOOZE...BIG AS HE IS TOO!
WELL, I'D HELP YOU GET HIM TO BED...
...BUT I FORGOT MY FORKLIFT AT HOME!
ZZZZ
WELL BOYS, I THINK THIS IS A SIGN.
A SIGN'A WHAT?
TO TAKE ME HOME YOU BIG DUMMY. IT'S LATE, I'M TIRED.

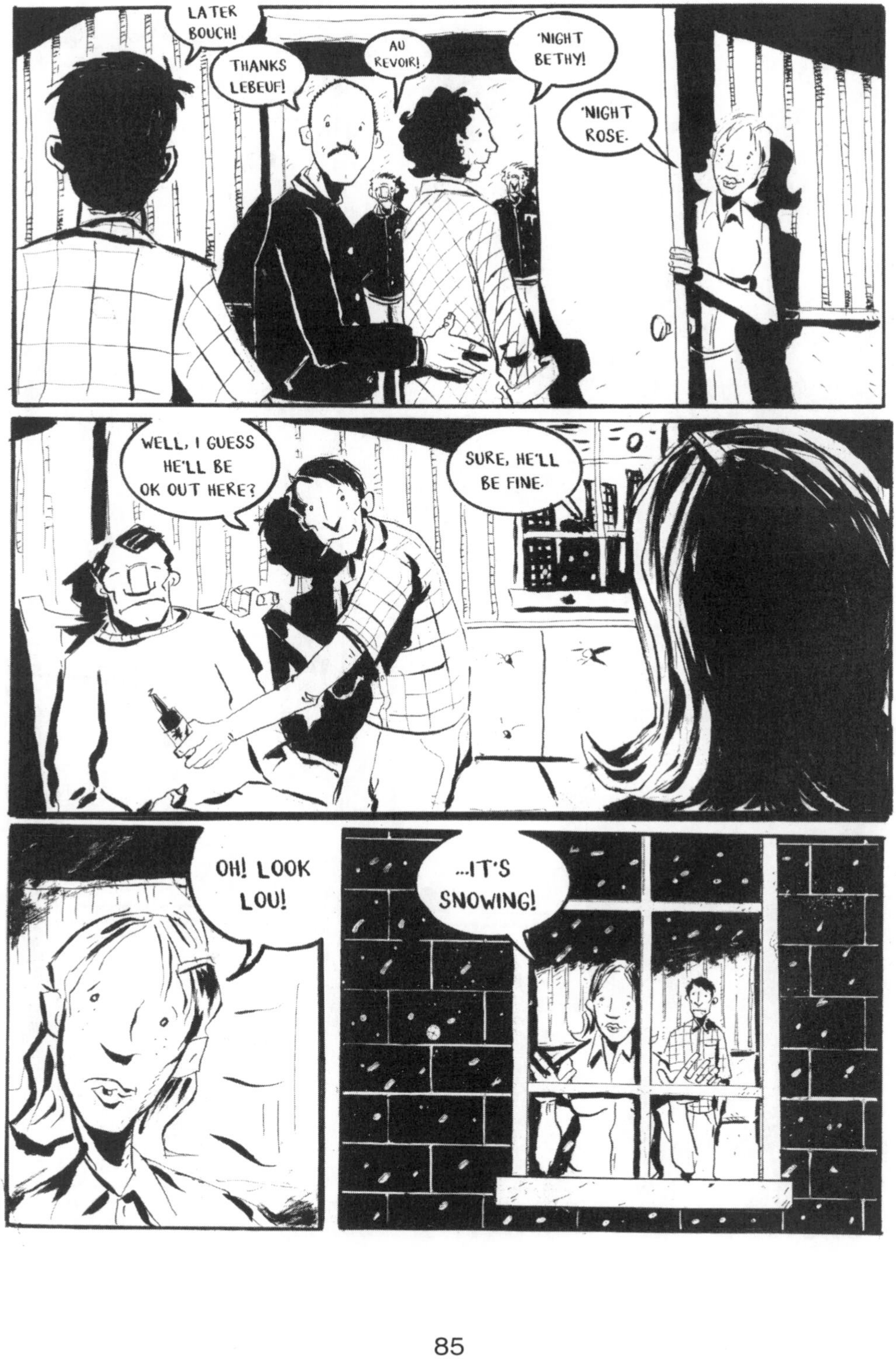
LATER BOUCH!
THANKS LEBEUF!
AU REVOIR!
'NIGHT BETHY!
'NIGHT ROSE.
WELL, I GUESS HE'LL BE OK OUT HERE?
SURE, HE'LL BE FINE.
OH! LOOK LOU!
...IT'S SNOWING!

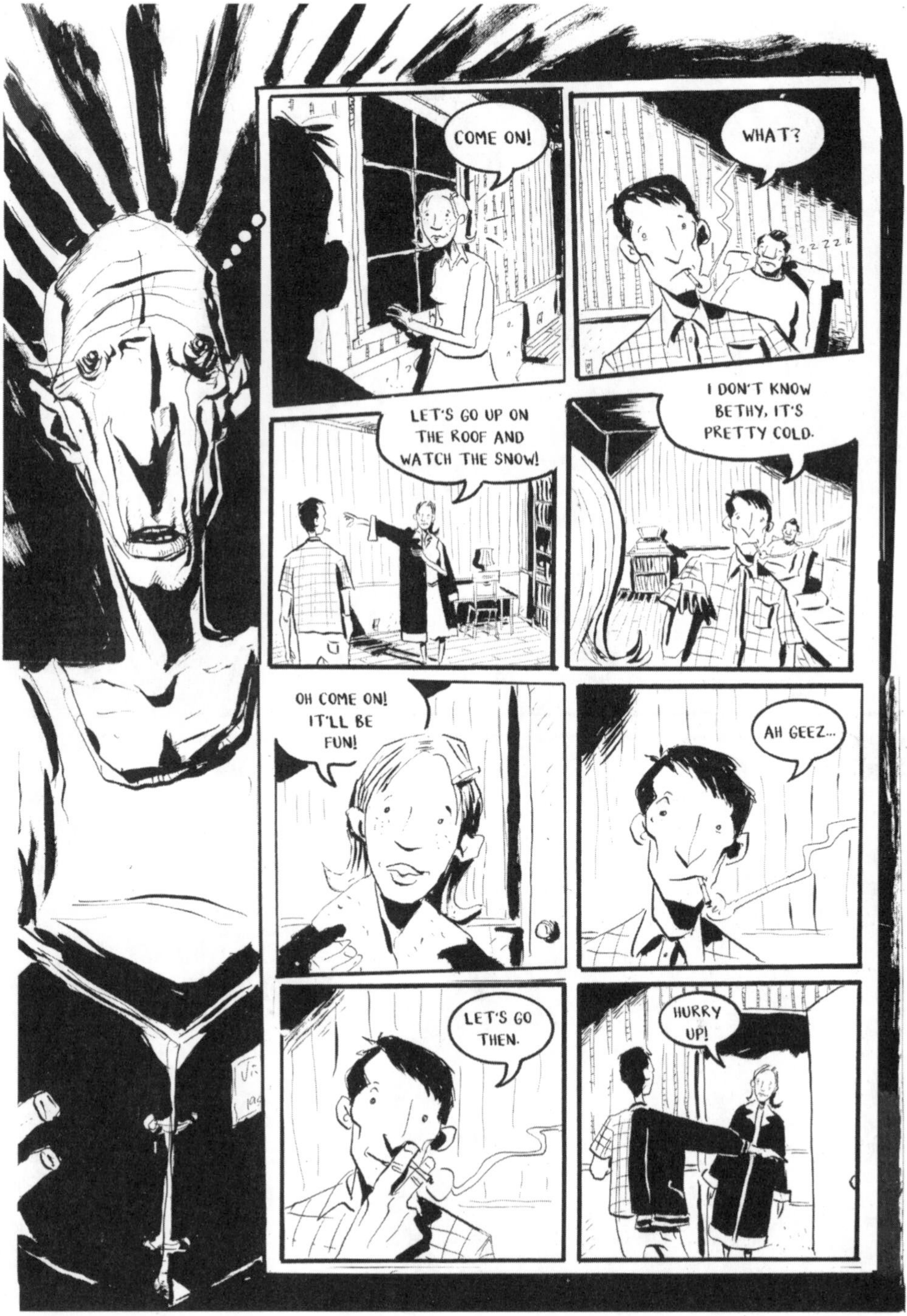
COME ON!
WHAT?
LET'S GO UP ON THE ROOF AND WATCH THE SNOW!
I DON'T KNOW BETHY, IT'S PRETTY COLD.
OH COME ON! IT'LL BE FUN!
AH GEEZ...
LET'S GO THEN.
HURRY UP!

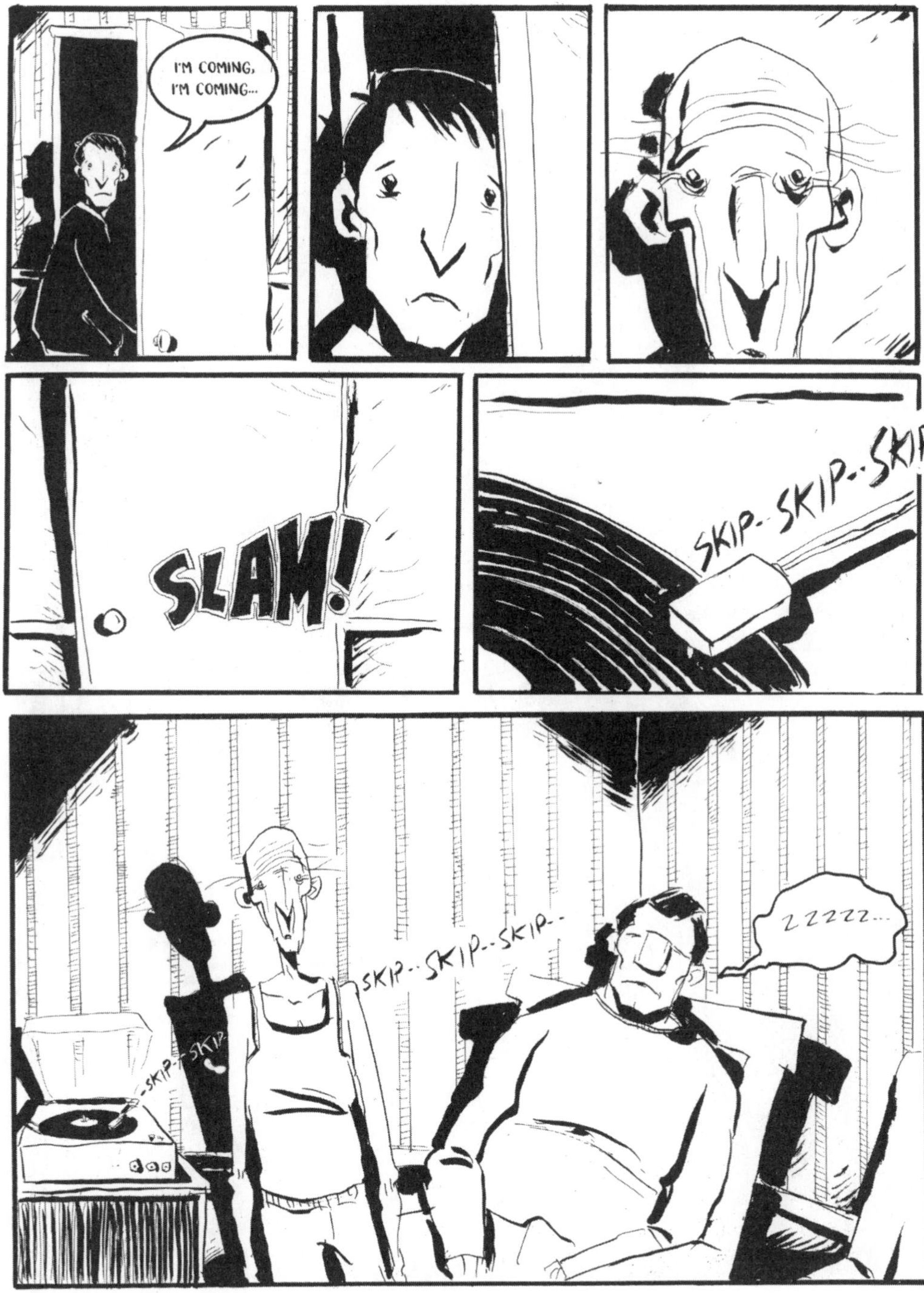
I'M COMING,
I'M COMING...
SLAM!
SKIP..SKIP..SKIP.
SKIP..SKIP..SKIP..
-SKIP-SKIP-
ZZZZZ...

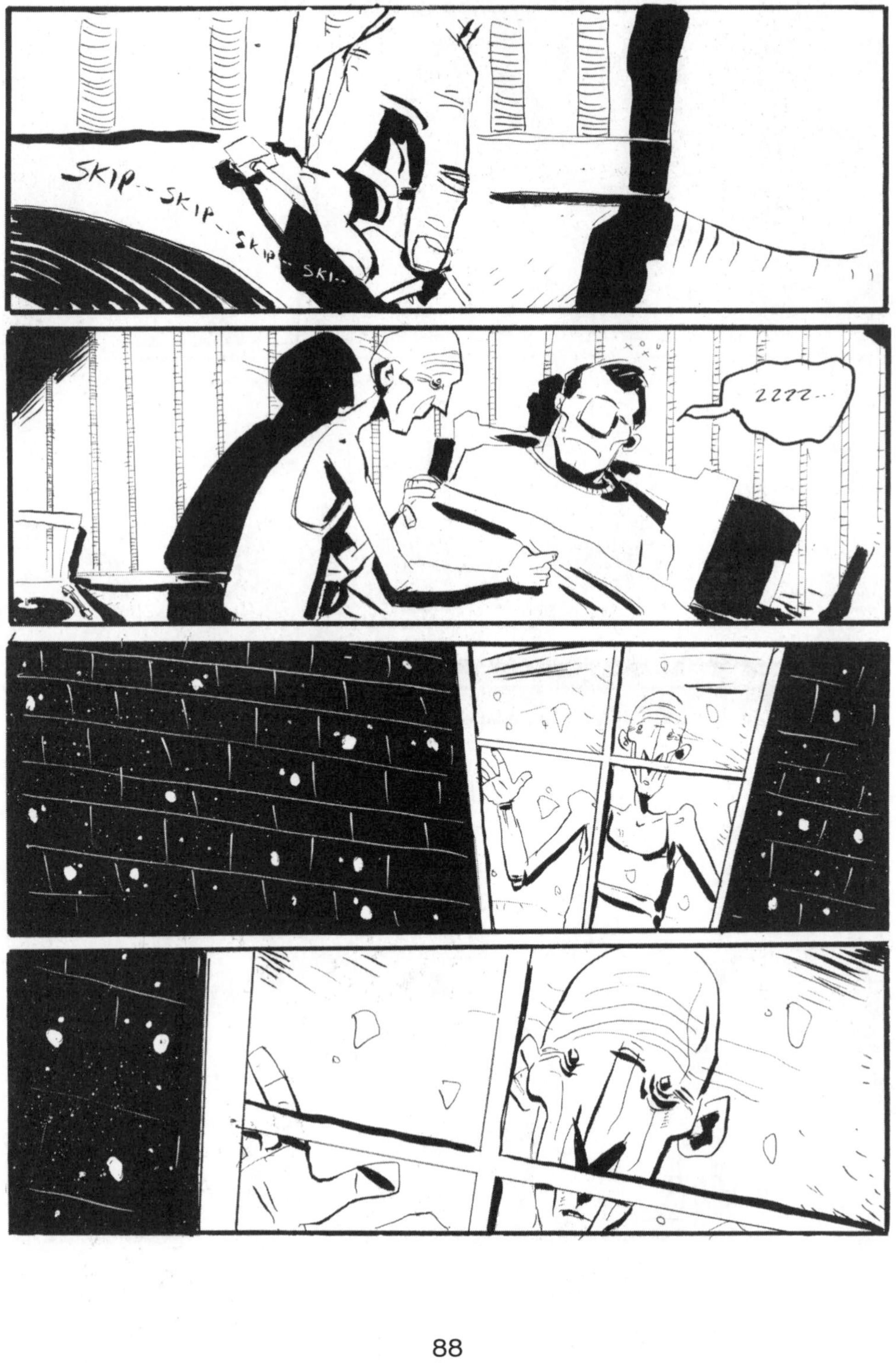
SKIP--SKIP--SKIP--SKI--
ZZZZ...

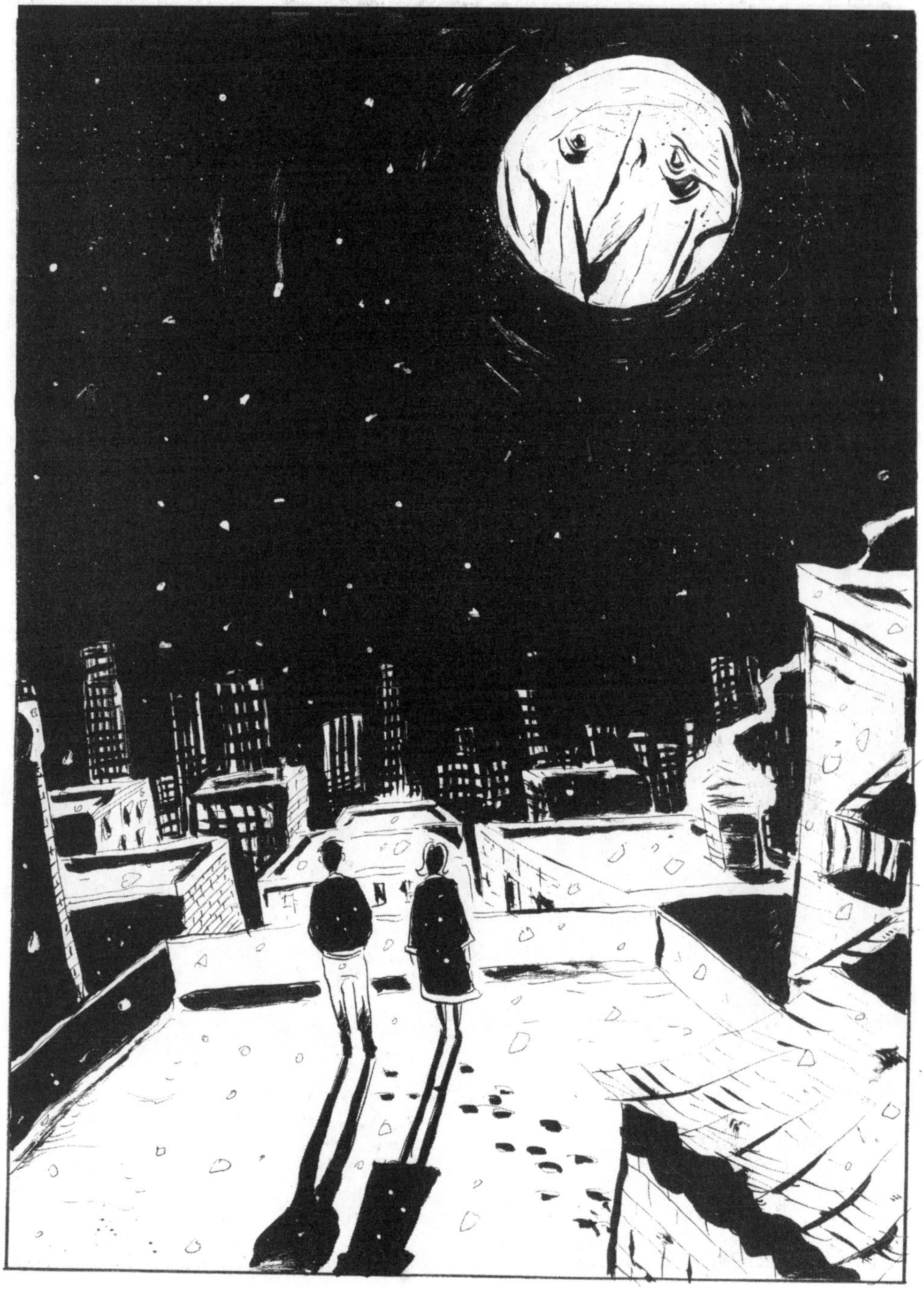

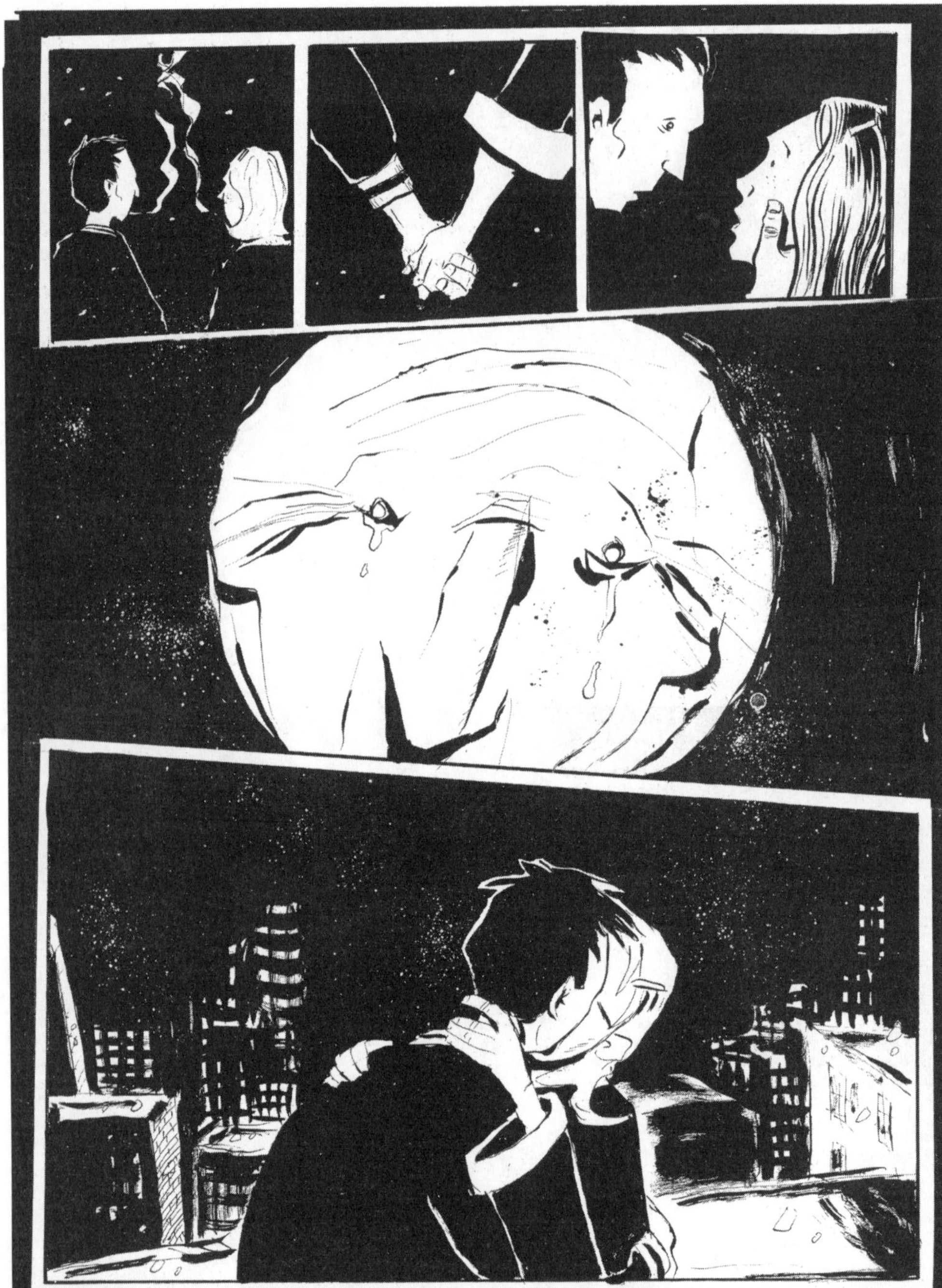

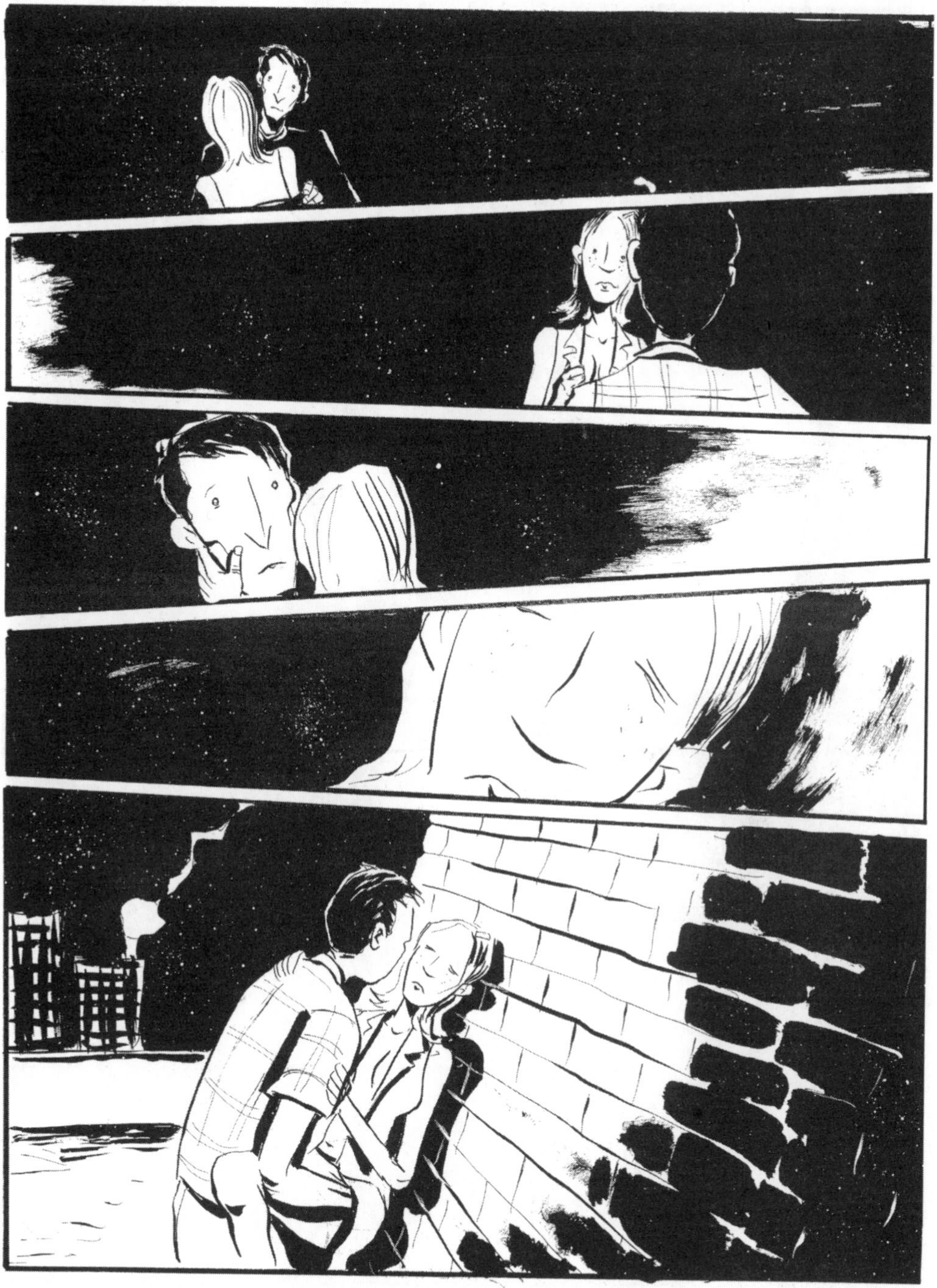

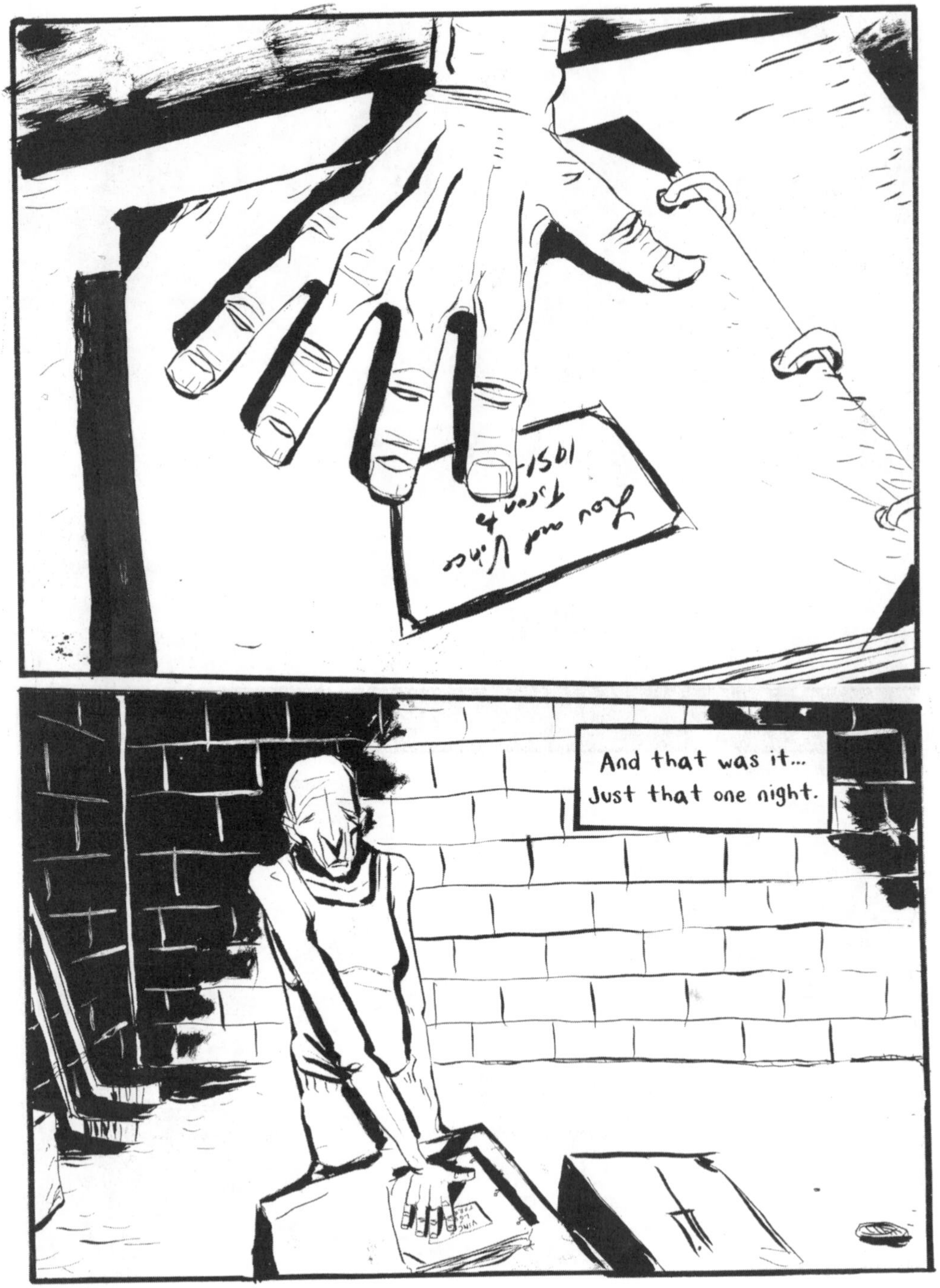
And that was it...
Just that one night.

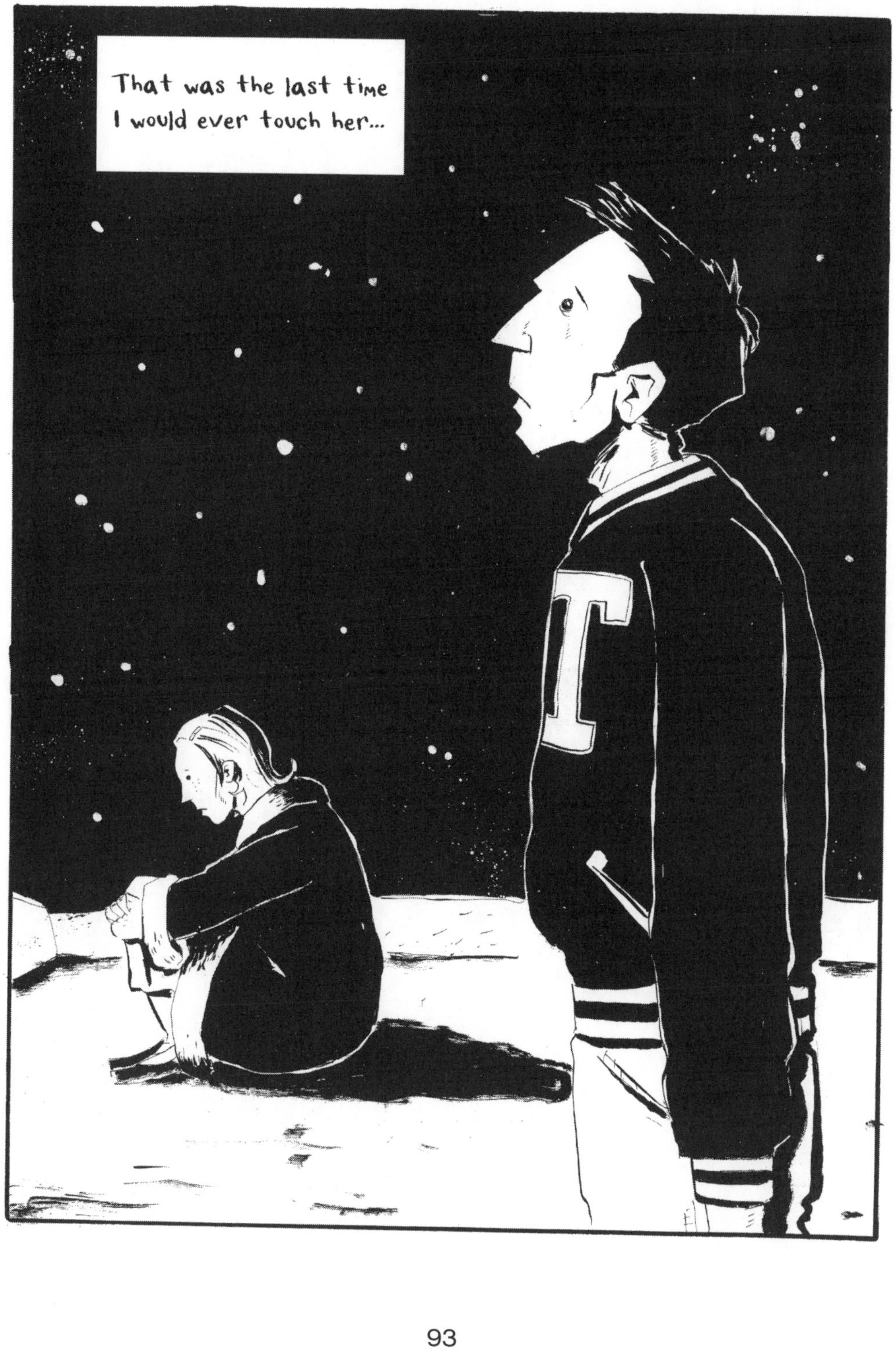
That was the last time
I would ever touch her...

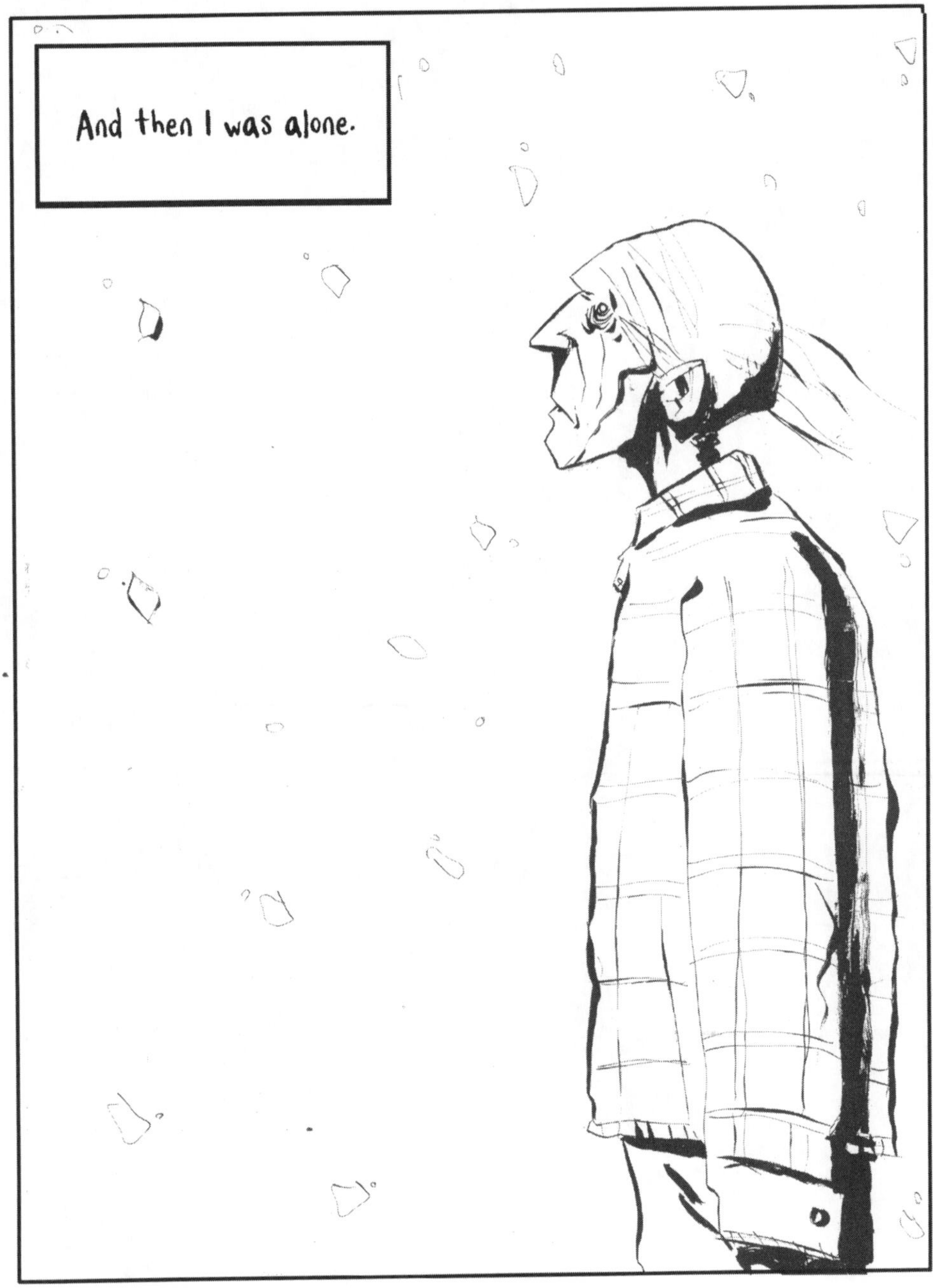
And then I was alone.

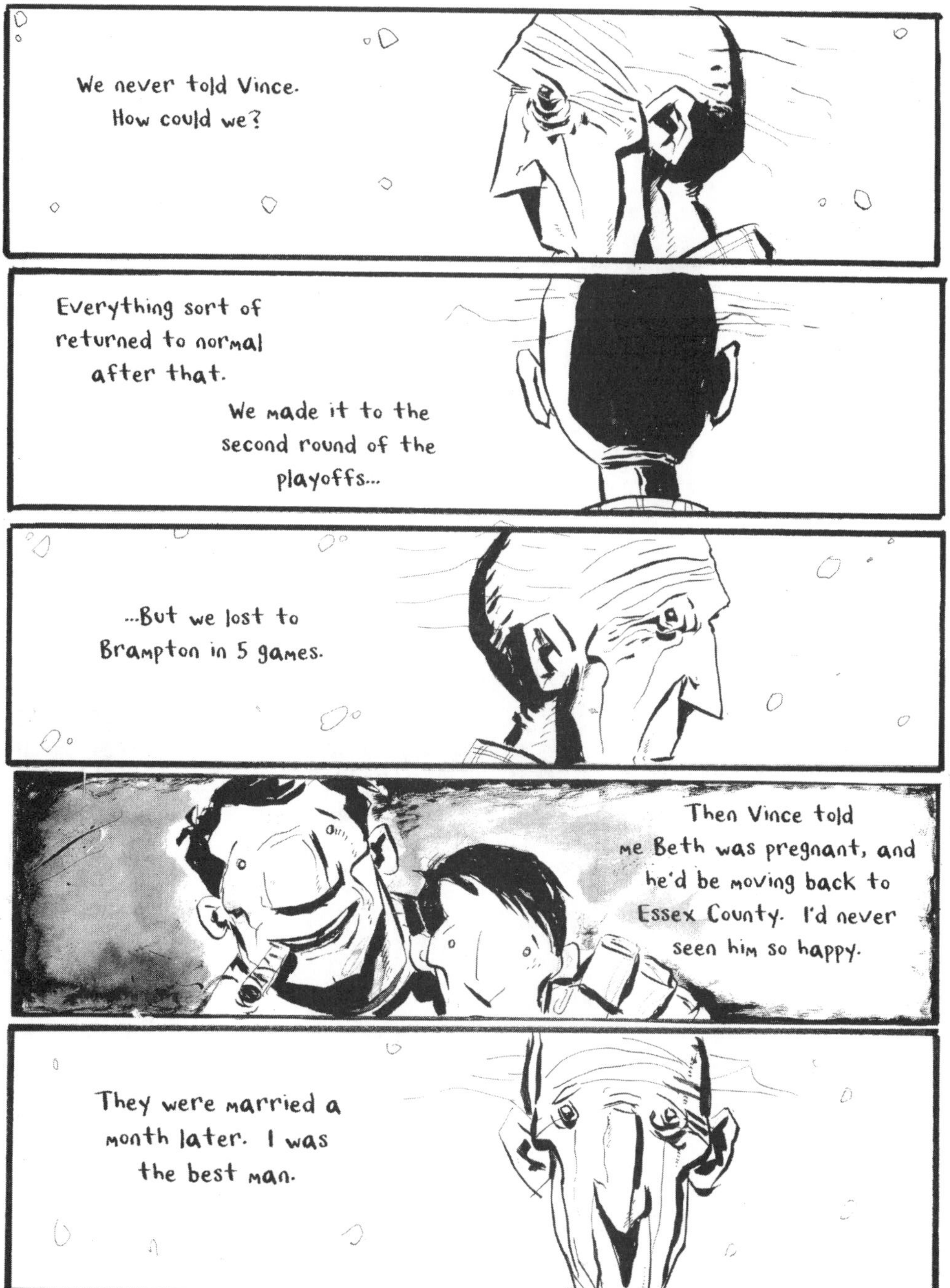
We never told Vince. How could we?
Everything sort of returned to normal after that.
We made it to the second round of the playoffs...
...But we lost to Brampton in 5 games.
Then Vince told me Beth was pregnant, and he'd be moving back to Essex County. I'd never seen him so happy.
They were married a month later. I was the best man.

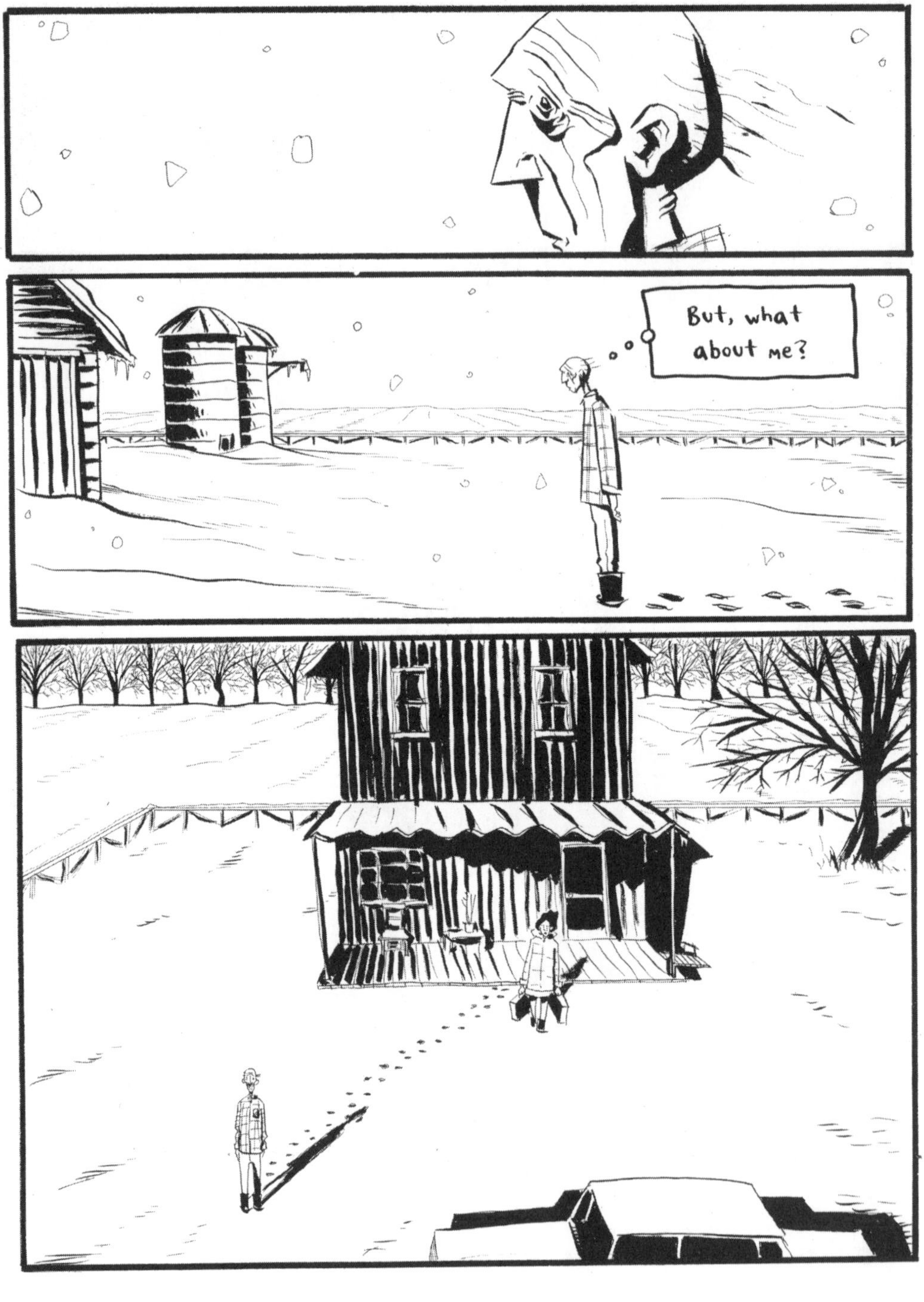
But, what about me?

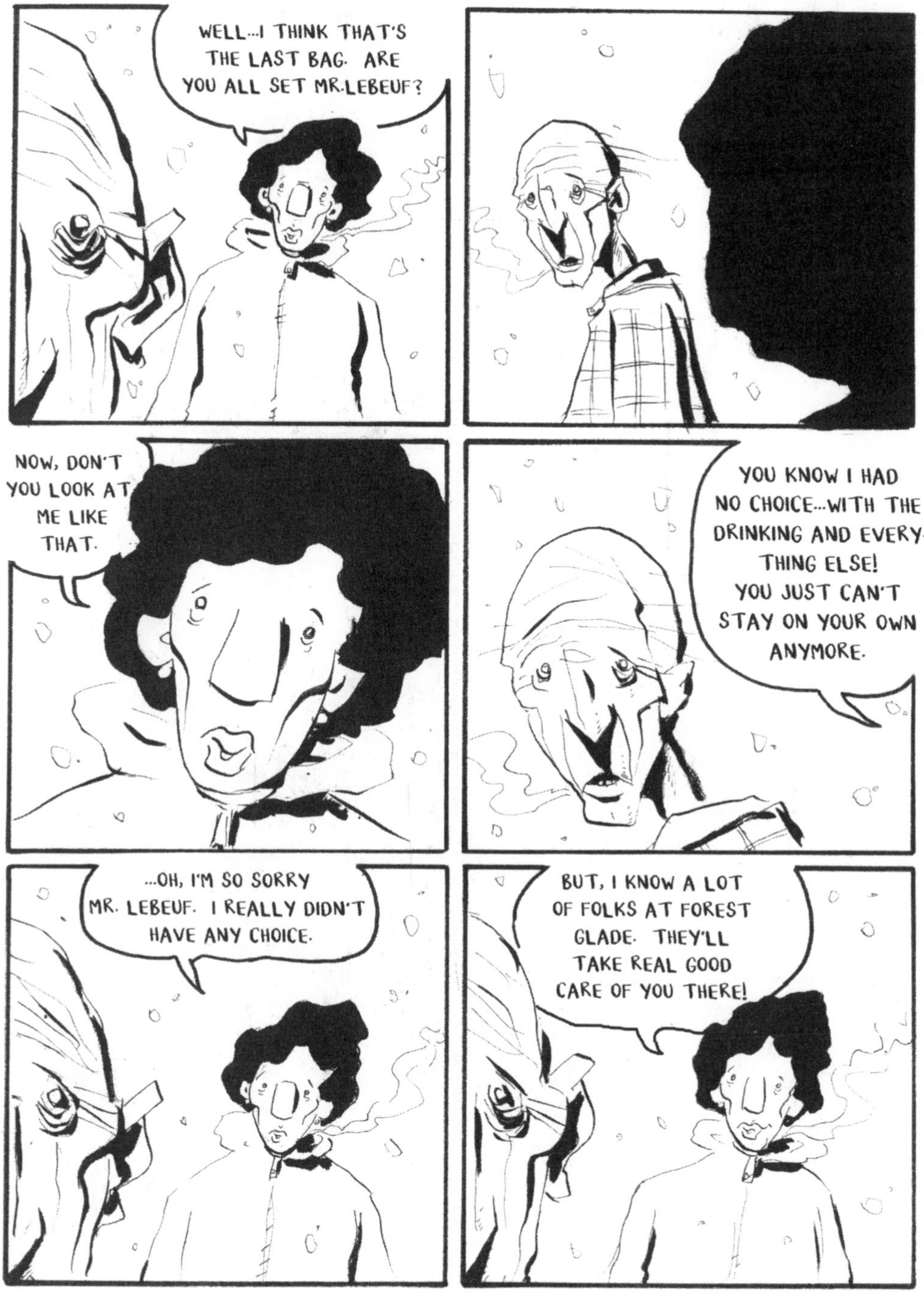
WELL...I THINK THAT'S THE LAST BAG. ARE YOU ALL SET MR. LEBEUF?
NOW, DON'T YOU LOOK AT ME LIKE THAT.
YOU KNOW I HAD NO CHOICE...WITH THE DRINKING AND EVERY-THING ELSE! YOU JUST CAN'T STAY ON YOUR OWN ANYMORE.
...OH, I'M SO SORRY MR. LEBEUF. I REALLY DIDN'T HAVE ANY CHOICE.
BUT, I KNOW A LOT OF FOLKS AT FOREST GLADE. THEY'LL TAKE REAL GOOD CARE OF YOU THERE!

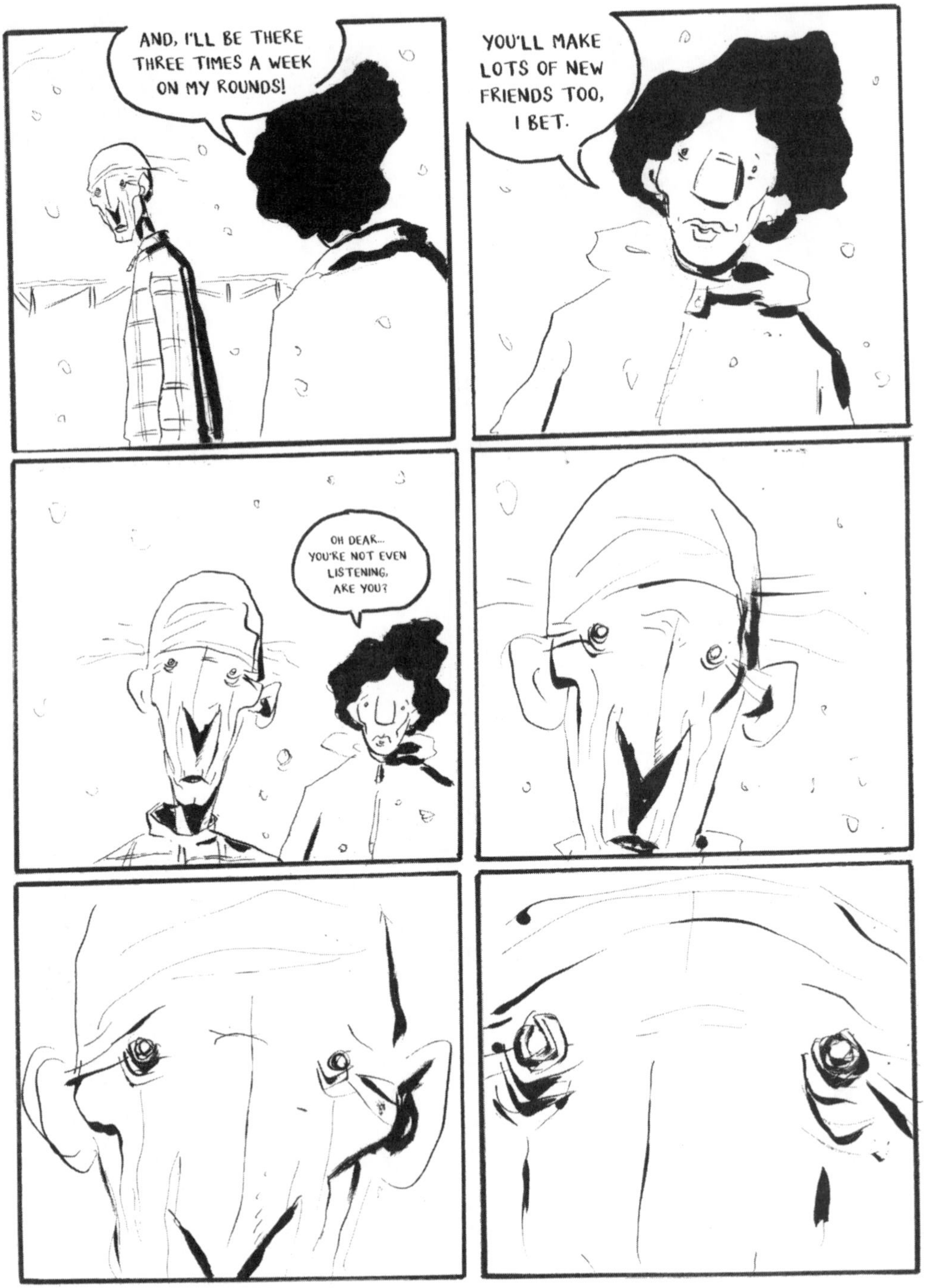
AND, I'LL BE THERE THREE TIMES A WEEK ON MY ROUNDS!
YOU'LL MAKE LOTS OF NEW FRIENDS TOO, I BET.
OH DEAR... YOU'RE NOT EVEN LISTENING, ARE YOU?

I went right back to the
city after the wedding.

I knew I had to stay
away...let them be happy.

I started a new season
with The Grizzlies.

But, it wasn't the same anymore.
My lifelong dream of playing
pro hockey seemed
empty without my brother
beside me.

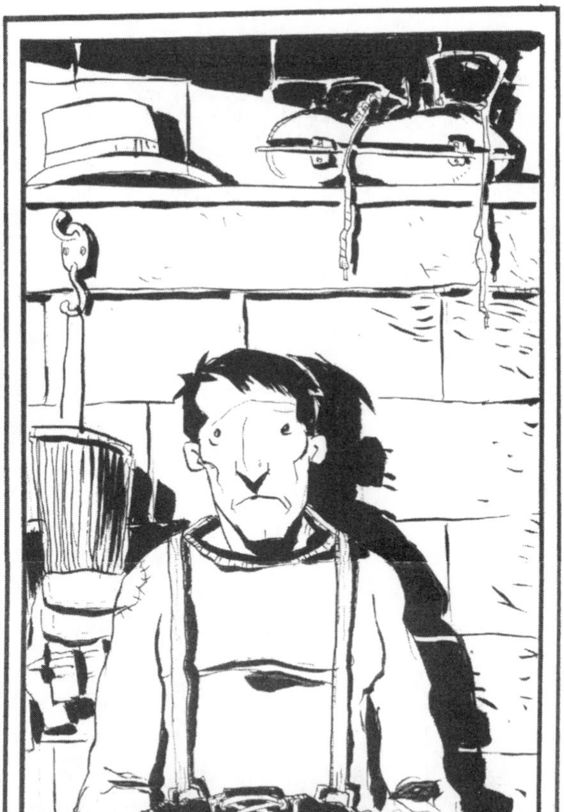

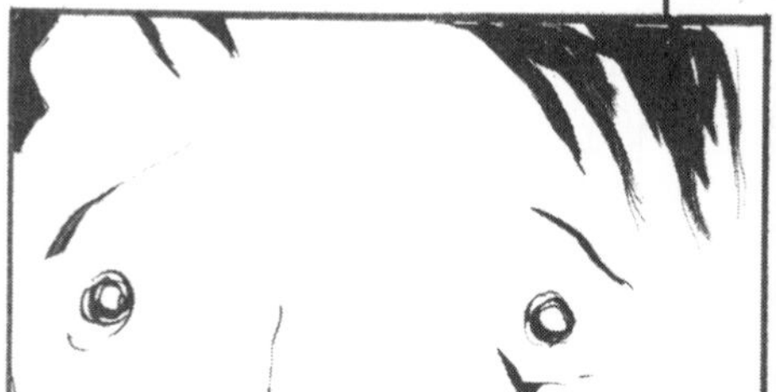

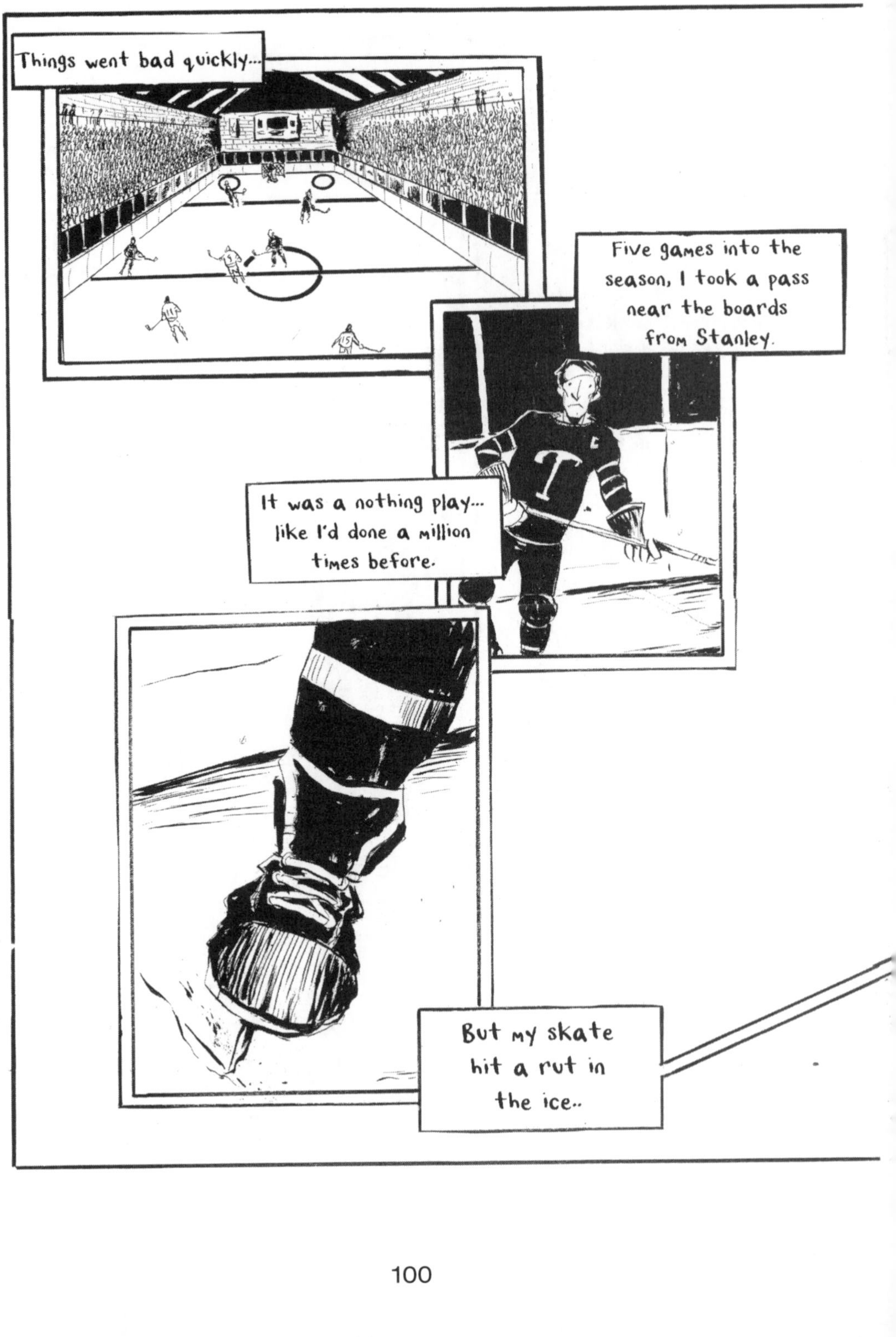
Things went bad quickly...
Five games into the season, I took a pass near the boards from Stanley.
It was a nothing play... like I'd done a million times before.
But my skate hit a rut in the ice..

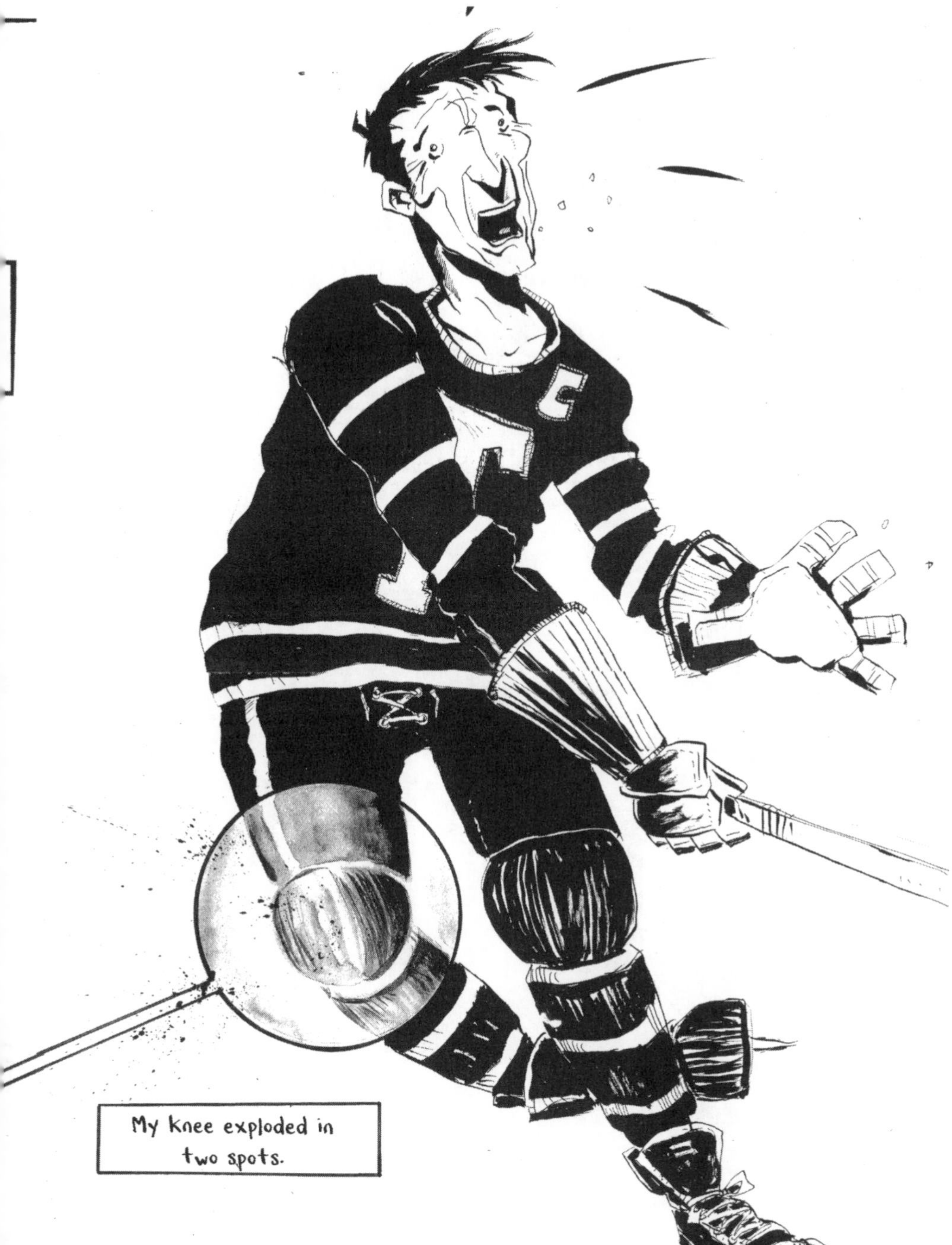
My knee exploded in two spots.

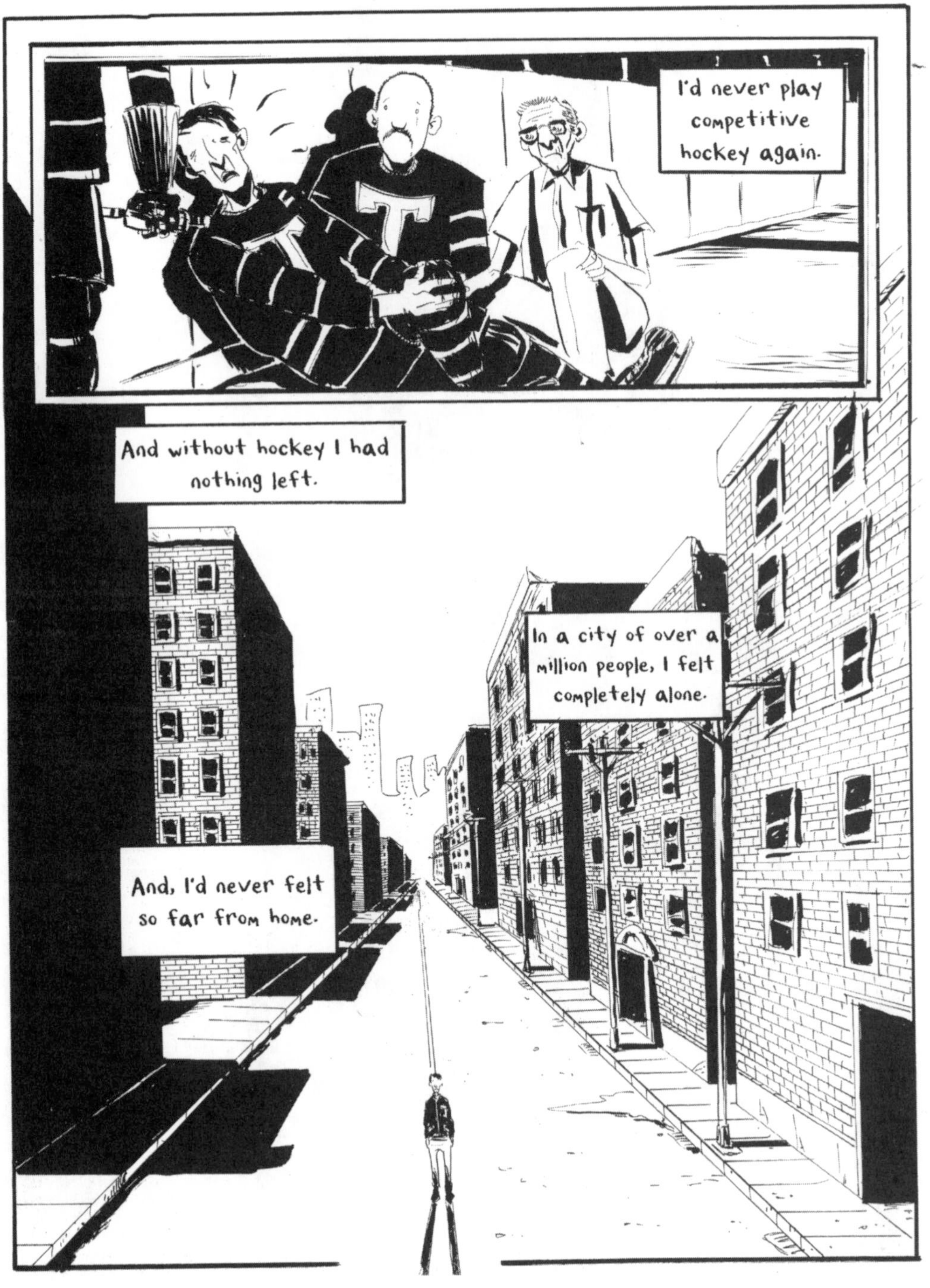
I'd never play competitive hockey again.
And without hockey I had nothing left.
In a city of over a million people, I felt completely alone.
And, I'd never felt so far from home.

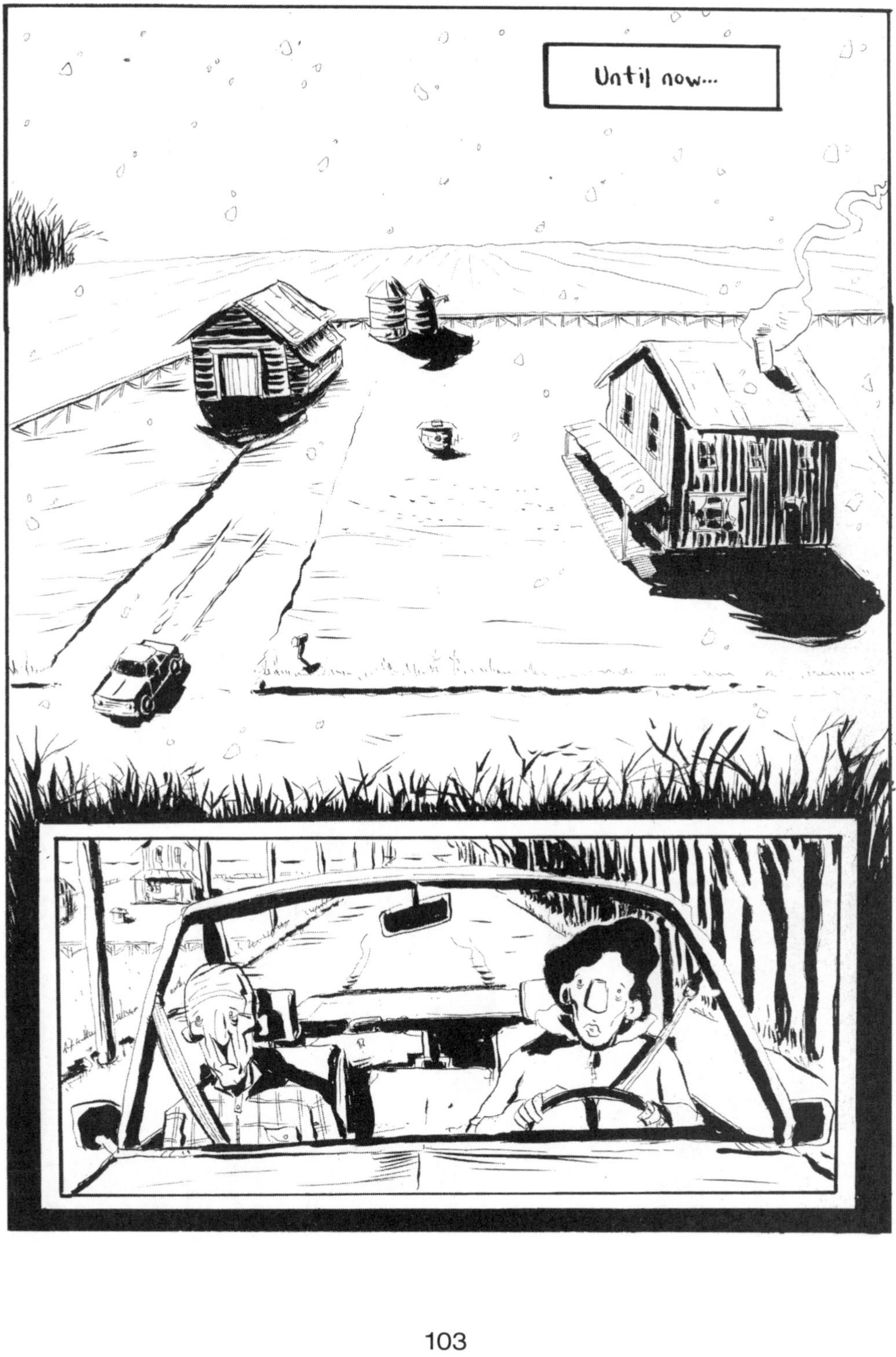
Until now...

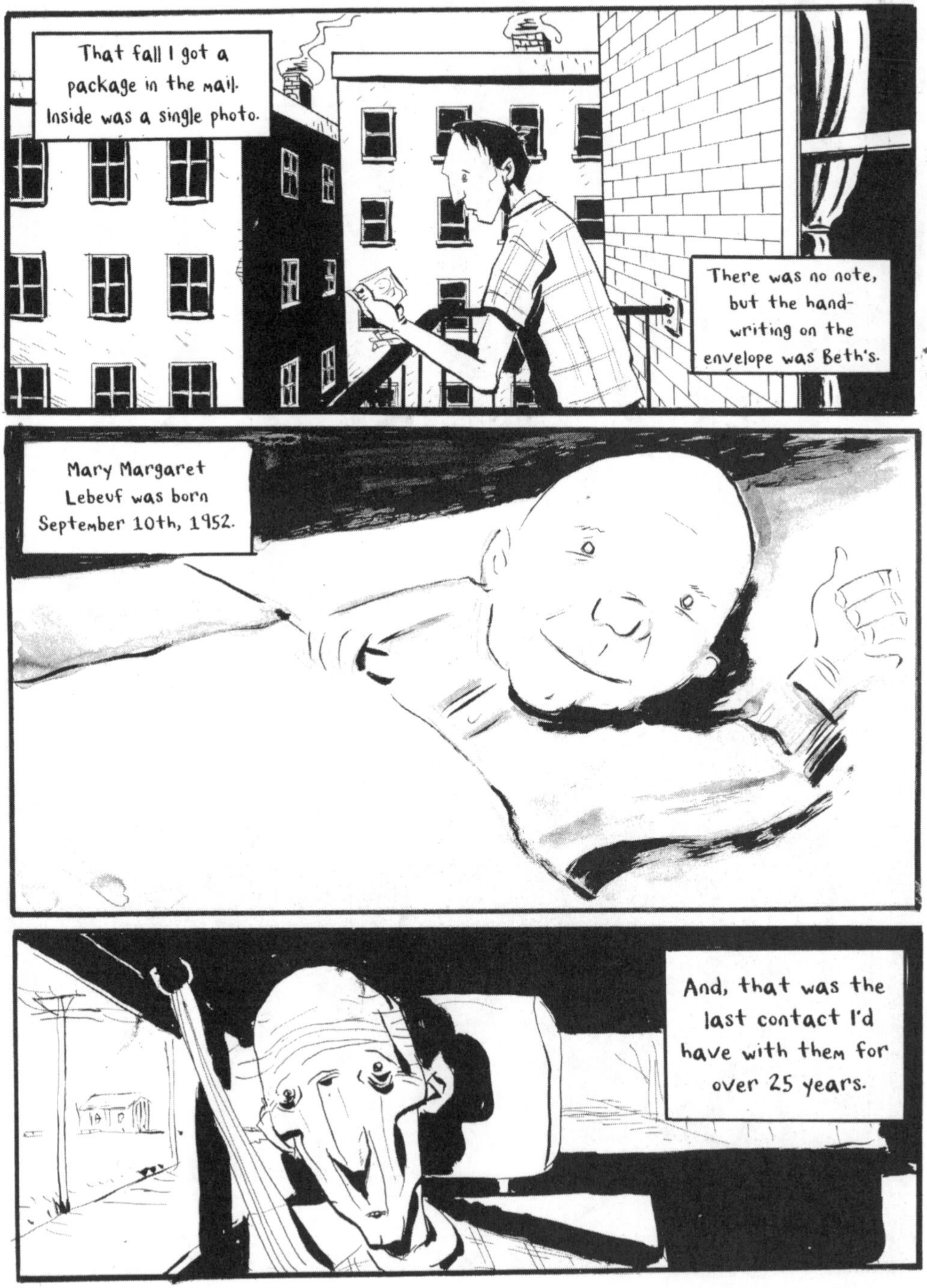
That fall I got a package in the mail. Inside was a single photo.
There was no note, but the hand-writing on the envelope was Beth's.
Mary Margaret Lebeuf was born September 10th, 1952.
And, that was the last contact I'd have with them for over 25 years.

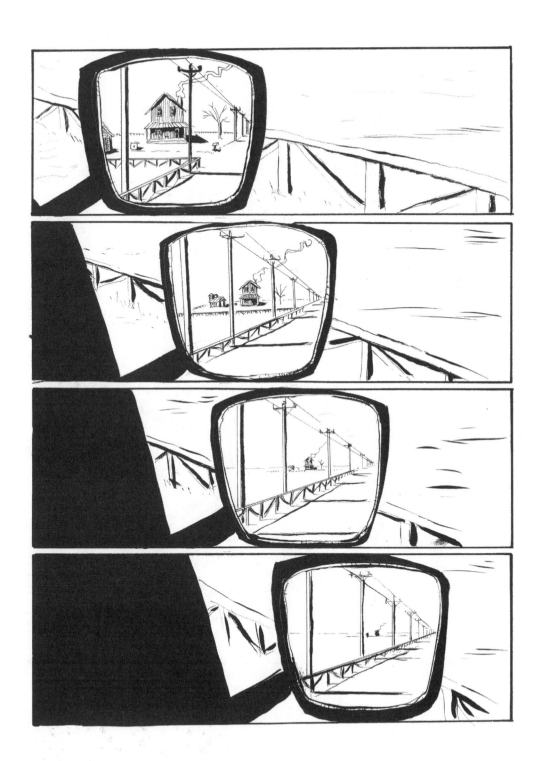

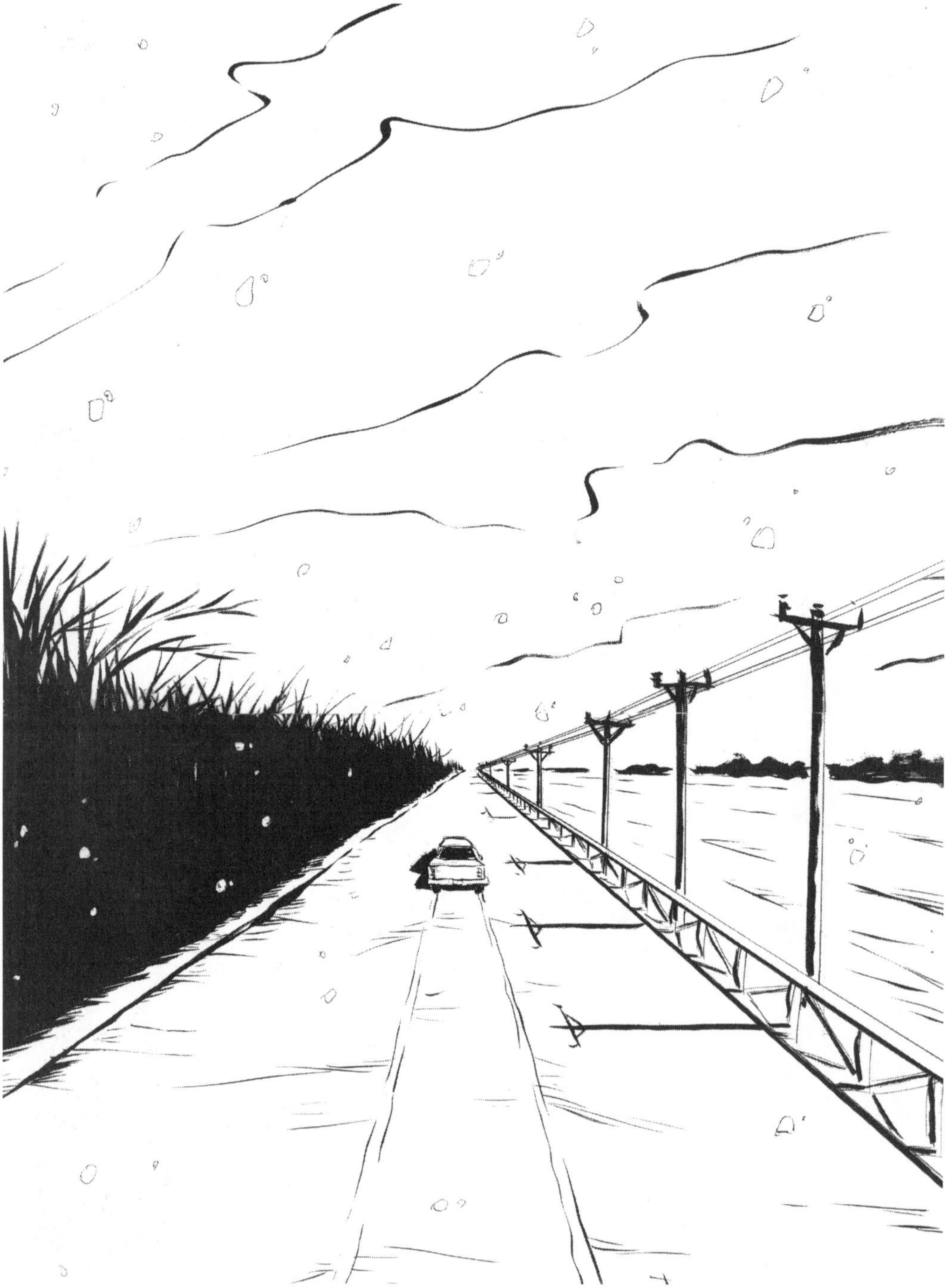

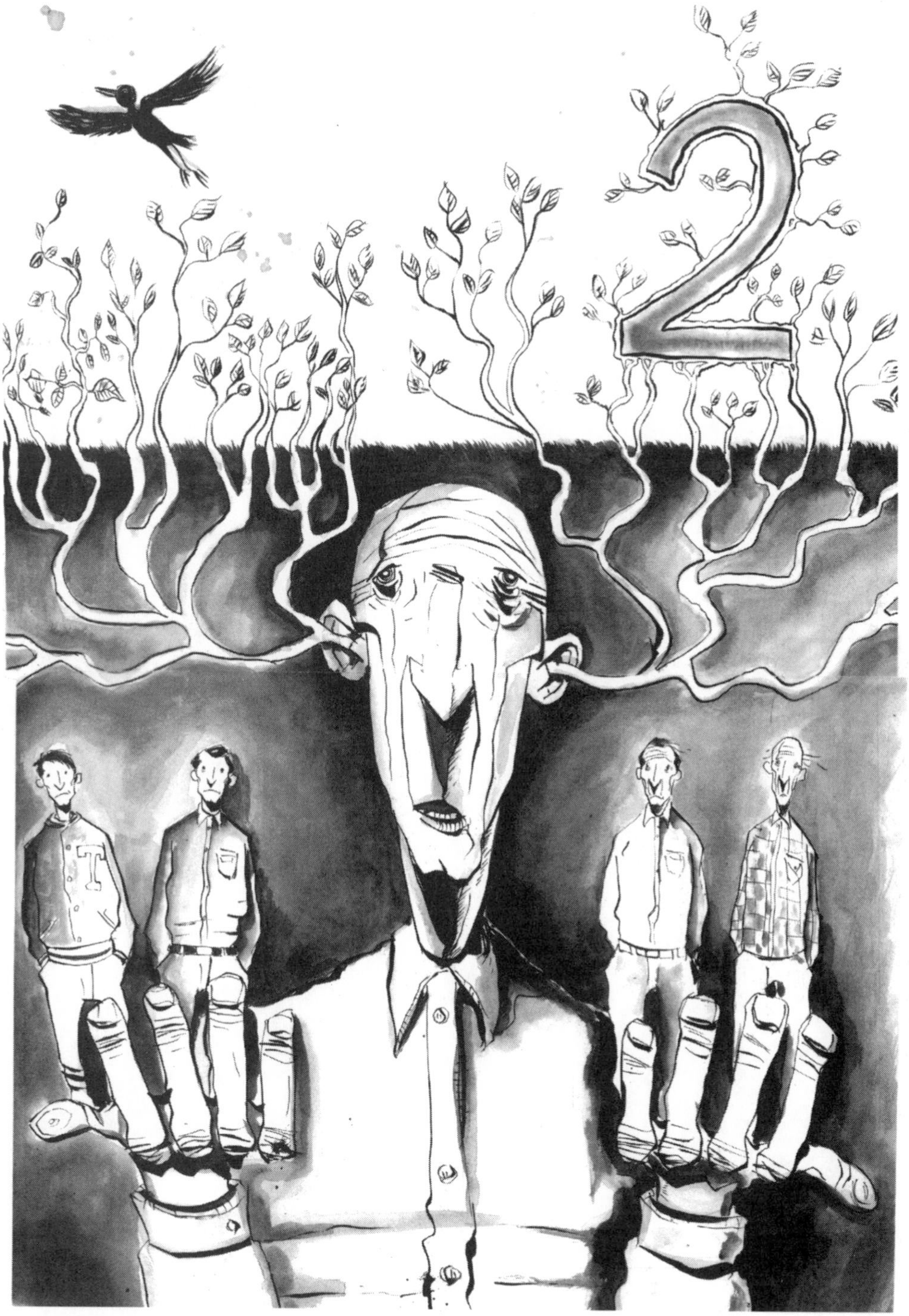
2

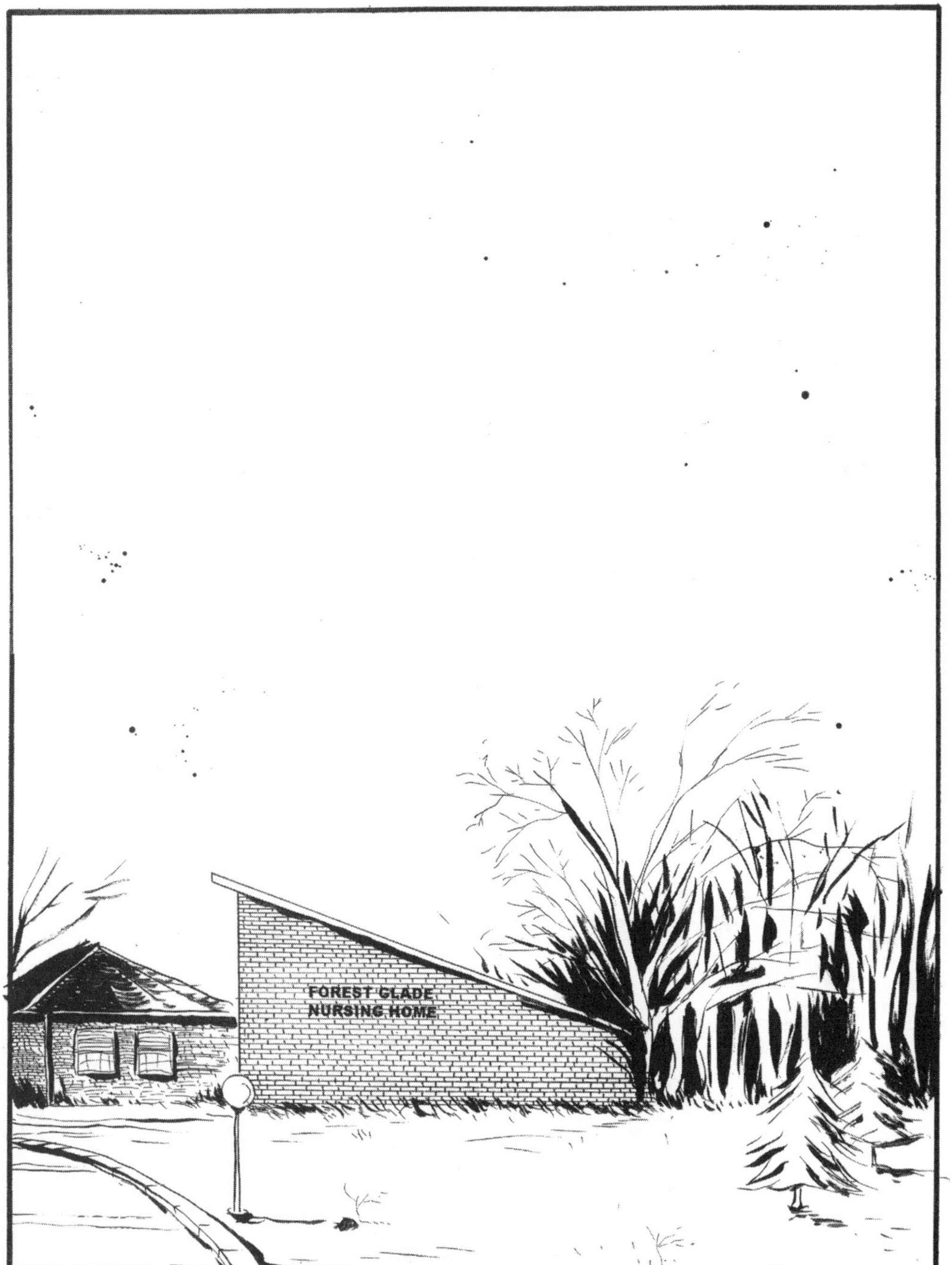
FOREST GLADE
NURSING HOME

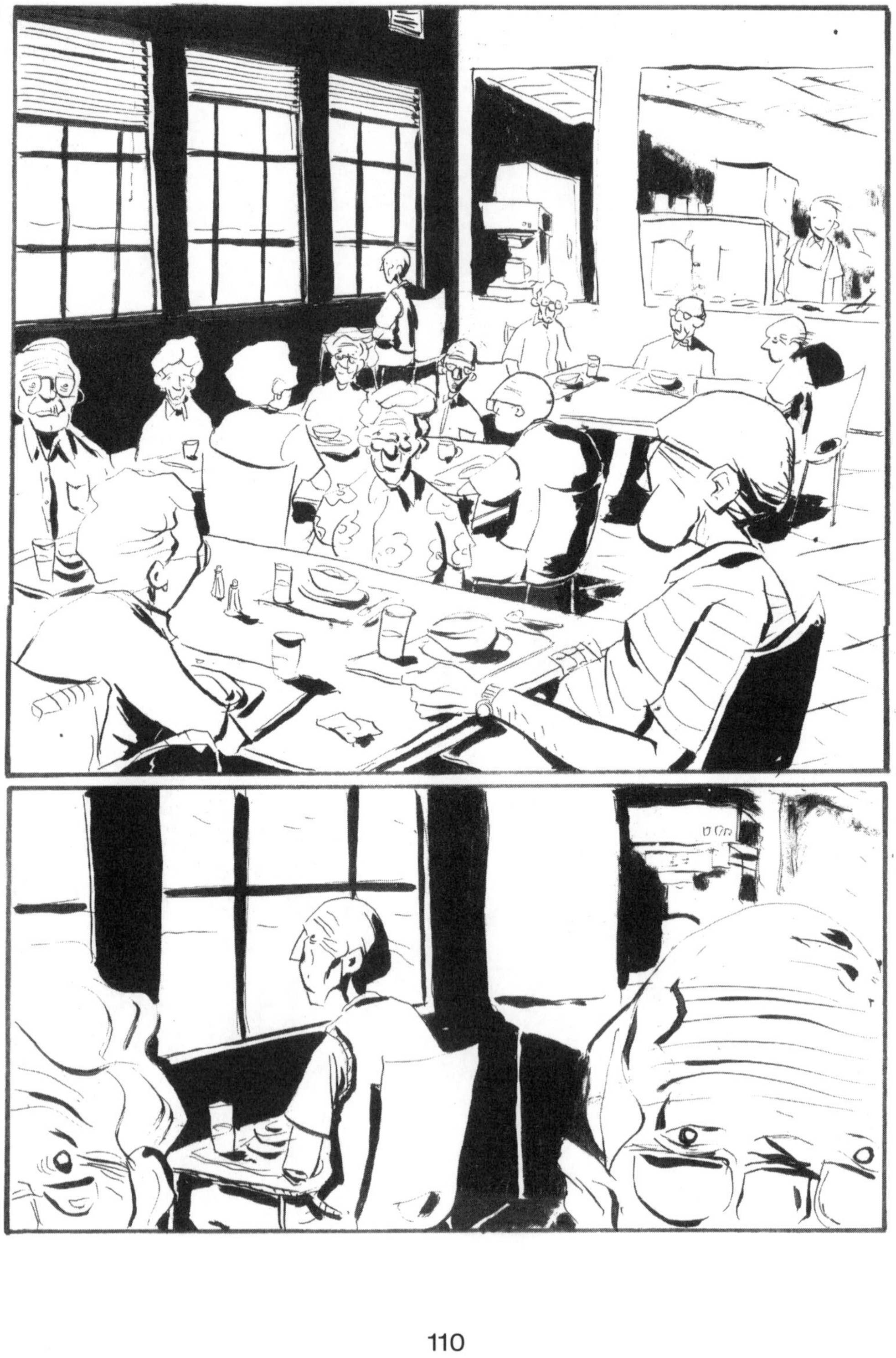

...Wonder how much time I got before work?

SCRATCH SCRATCH...

Ah, plenty of time to finish my breakfast.

Hmm...I always order two eggs, sausage, homefries, and brown toast. What is this crap!?

That's more like it!

DINER

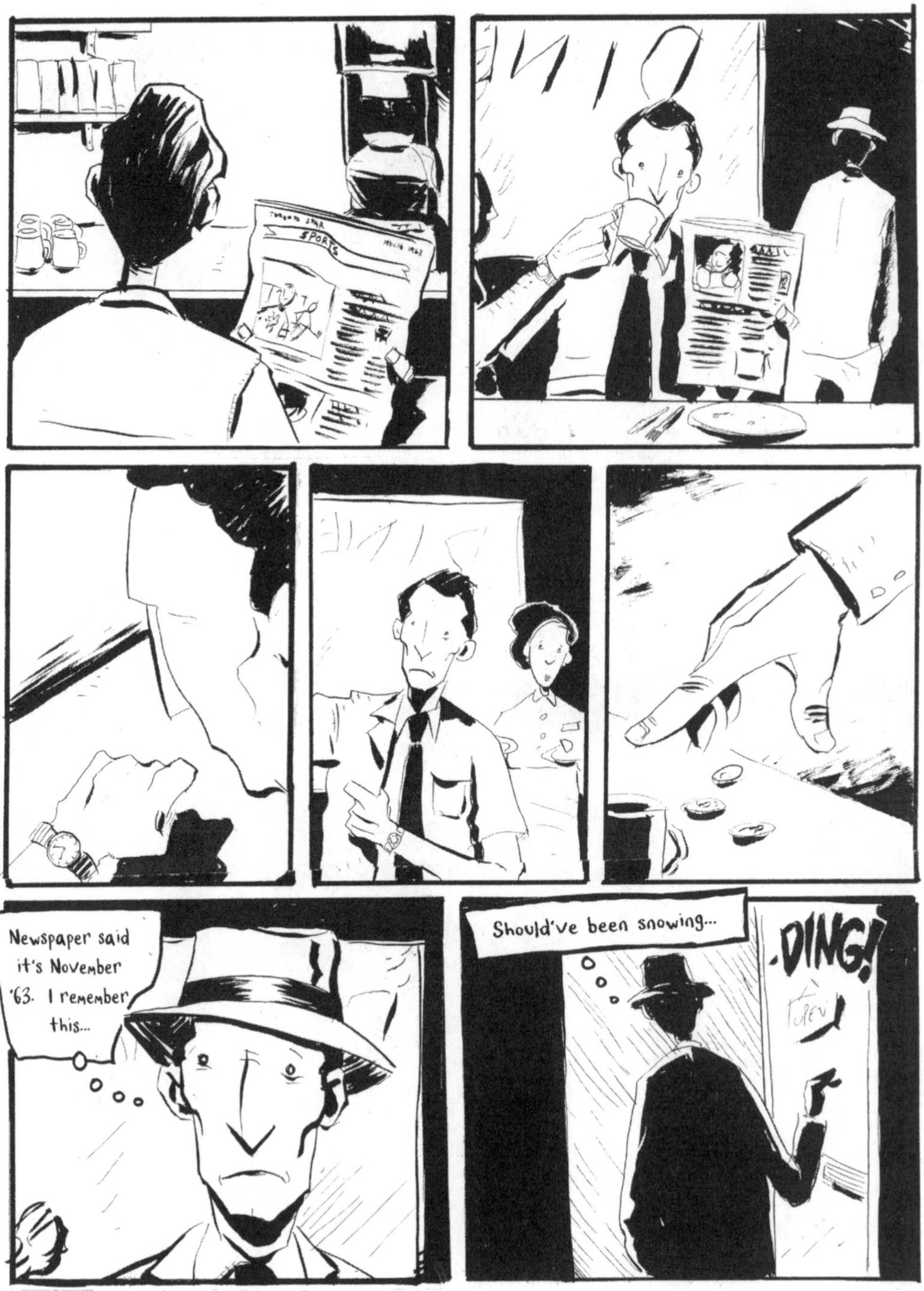

SPORTS
Newspaper said it's November '63. I remember this...
Should've been snowing...
DING!

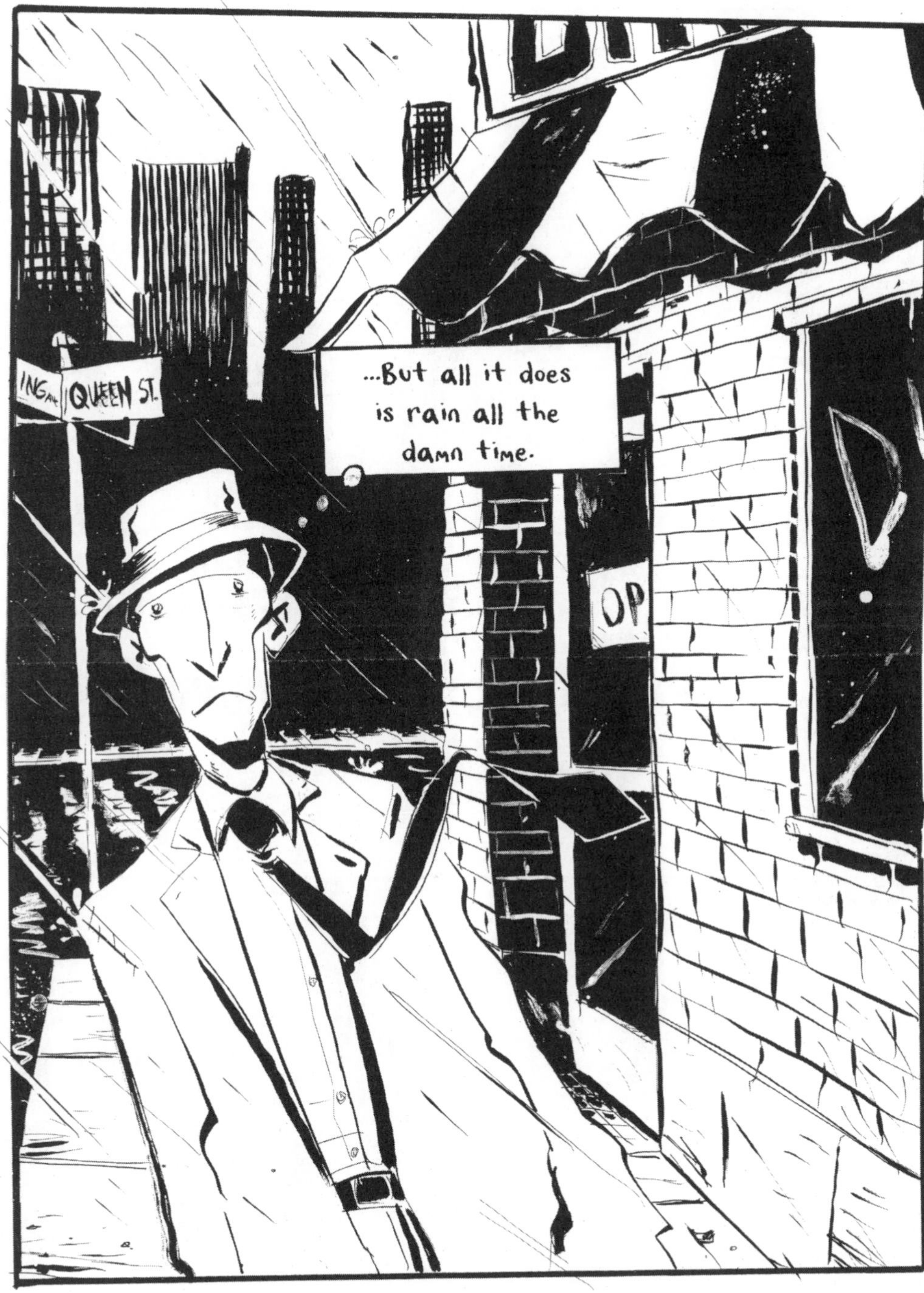
ING
QUEEN ST.
...But all it does is rain all the damn time.
OP

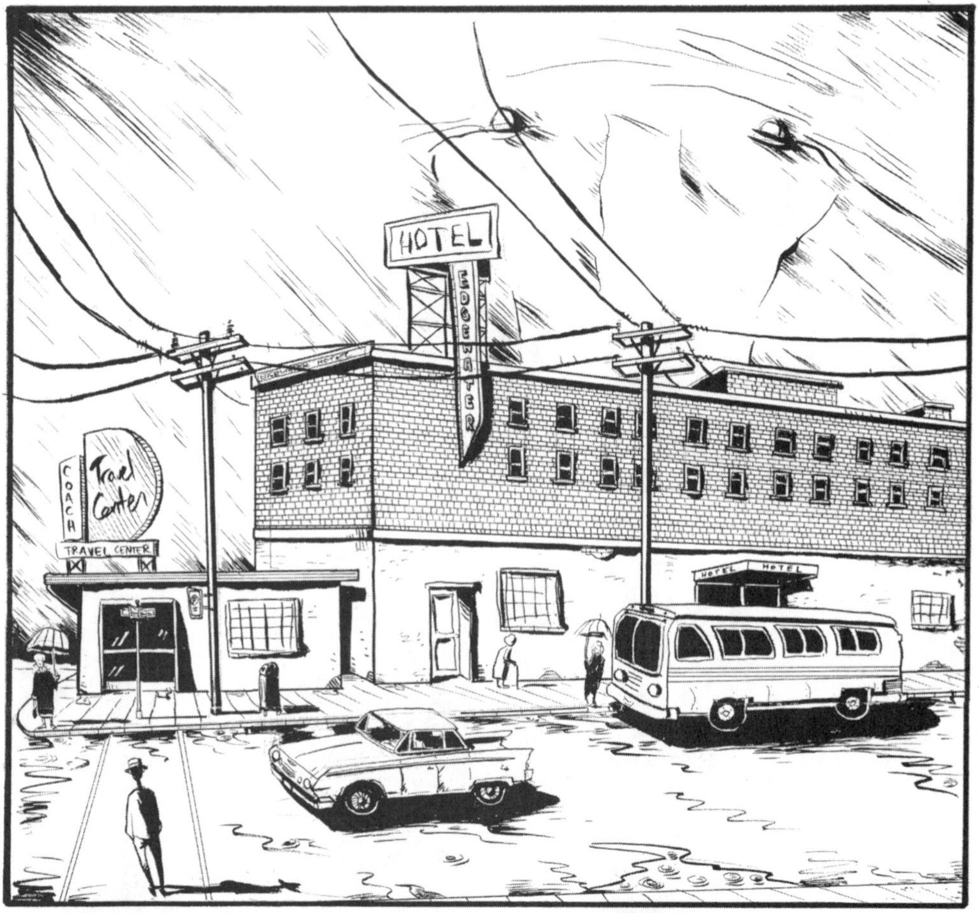
HOTEL
EDGEWATER
COACH
Travel Center
TRAVEL CENTER
HOTEL HOTEL

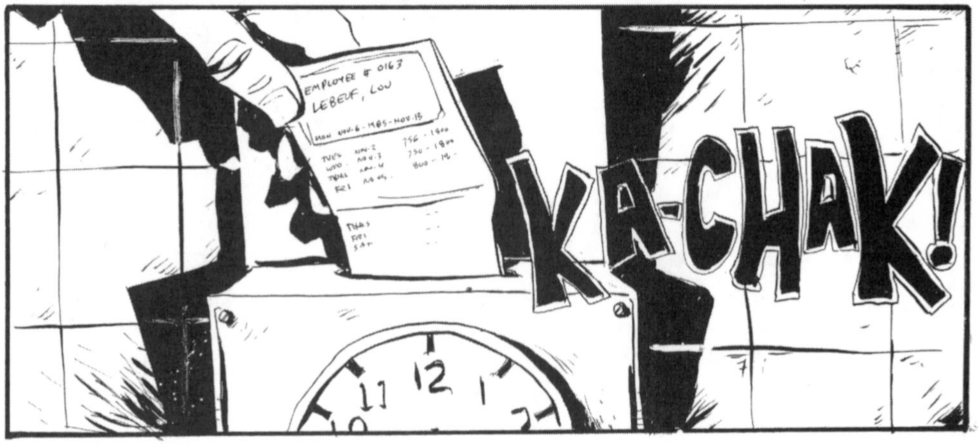
EMPLOYEE # 0163
LEBEUF, LOU
KA-CHAK!

When Vince left, and I got
hurt, I was kind of lost.
I didn't have hockey anymore,
and I needed to find a job fast.

Donnie Gill, one of my old
Grizzly pals, had gotten
a job as a mechanic
for the TTC (Toronto's
Public Transit).

The city was expanding
its transit lines in the
late 50s, so he put in
a word for me, and I applied
to the union.

Before I knew it I was
driving a streetcar full-time.

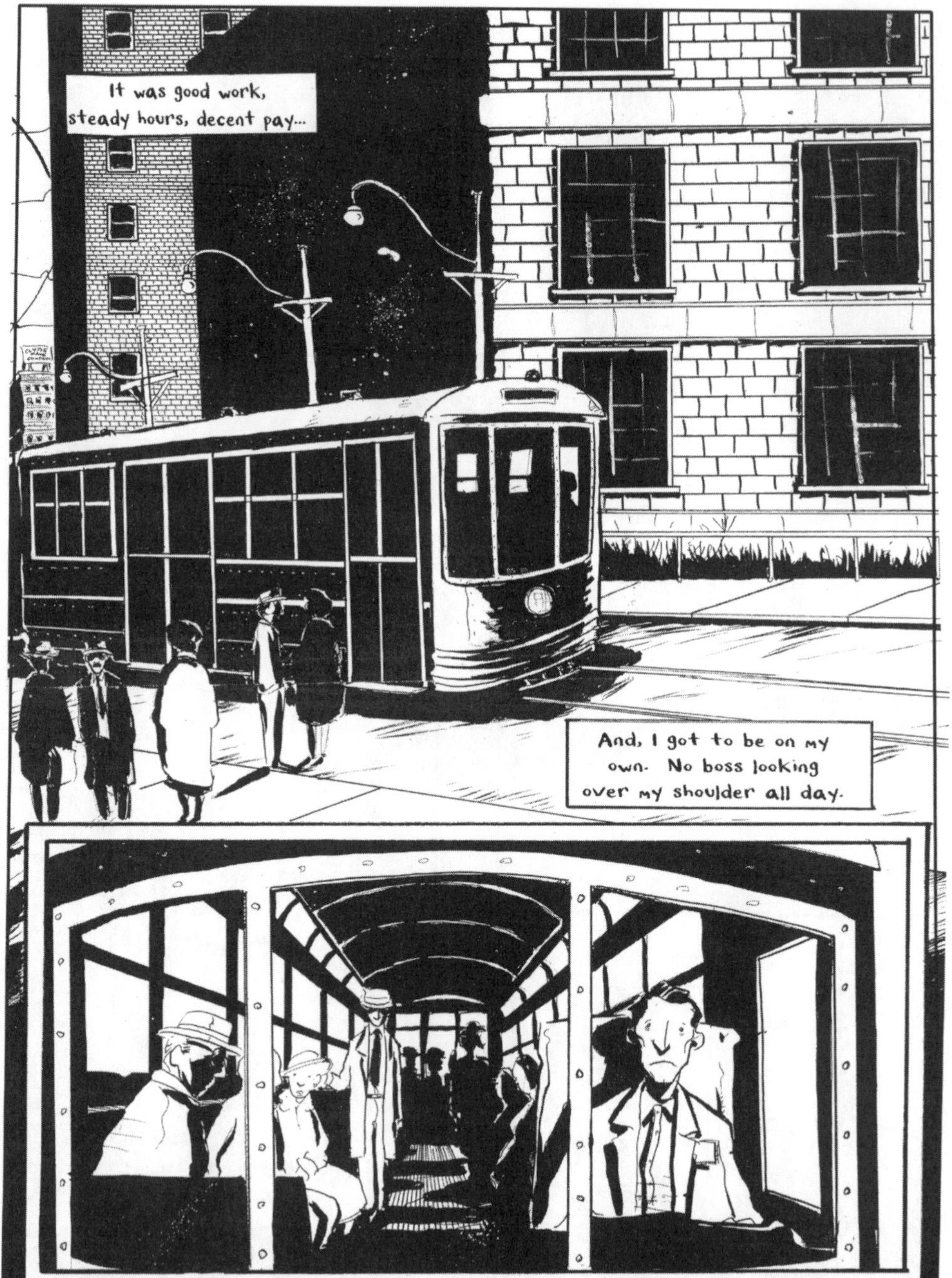
It was good work, steady hours, decent pay...
And, I got to be on my own. No boss looking over my shoulder all day.

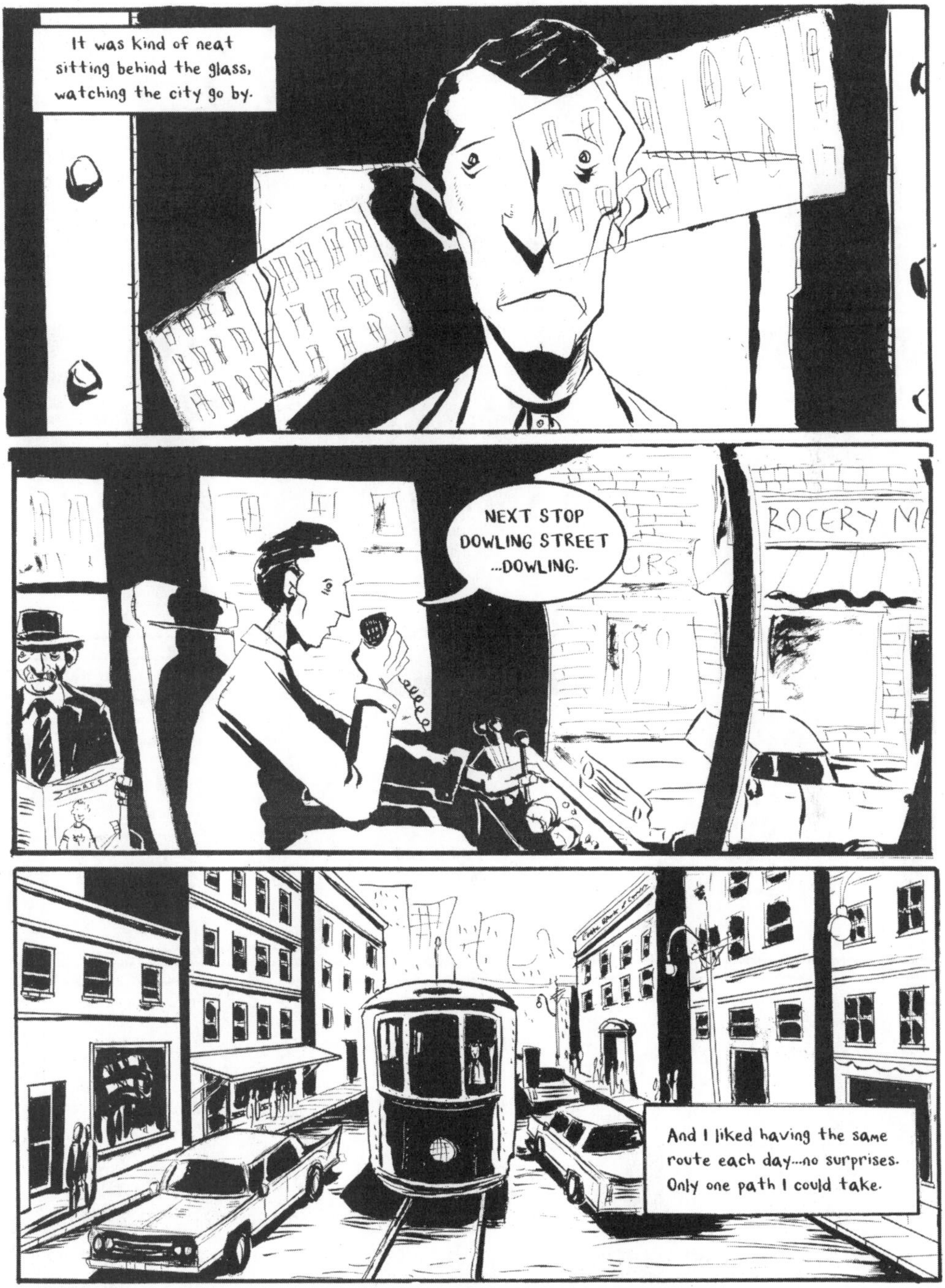
It was kind of neat sitting behind the glass, watching the city go by.
NEXT STOP DOWLING STREET ...DOWLING.
And I liked having the same route each day...no surprises. Only one path I could take.

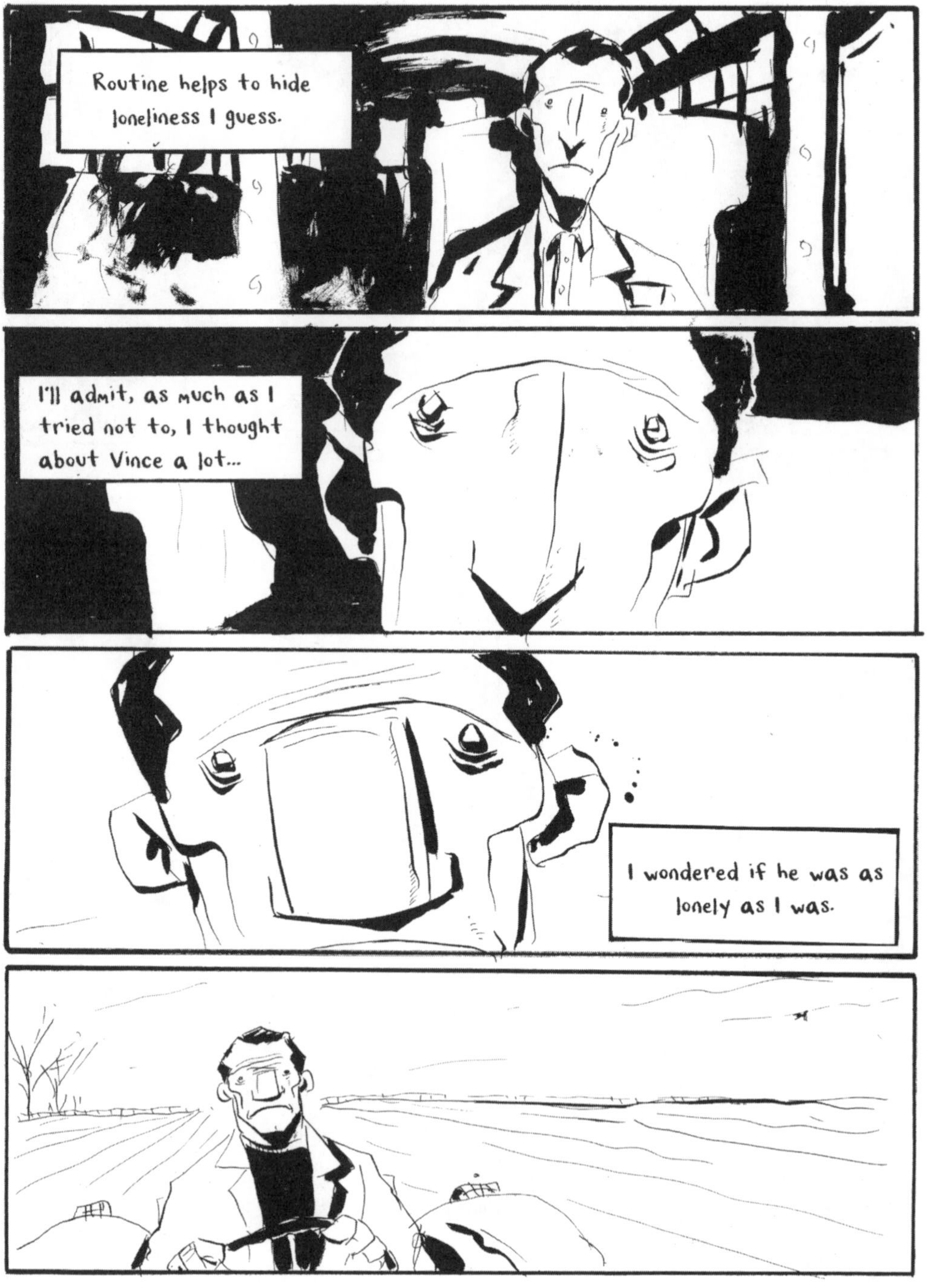
Routine helps to hide loneliness I guess.
I'll admit, as much as I tried not to, I thought about Vince a lot...
I wondered if he was as lonely as I was.

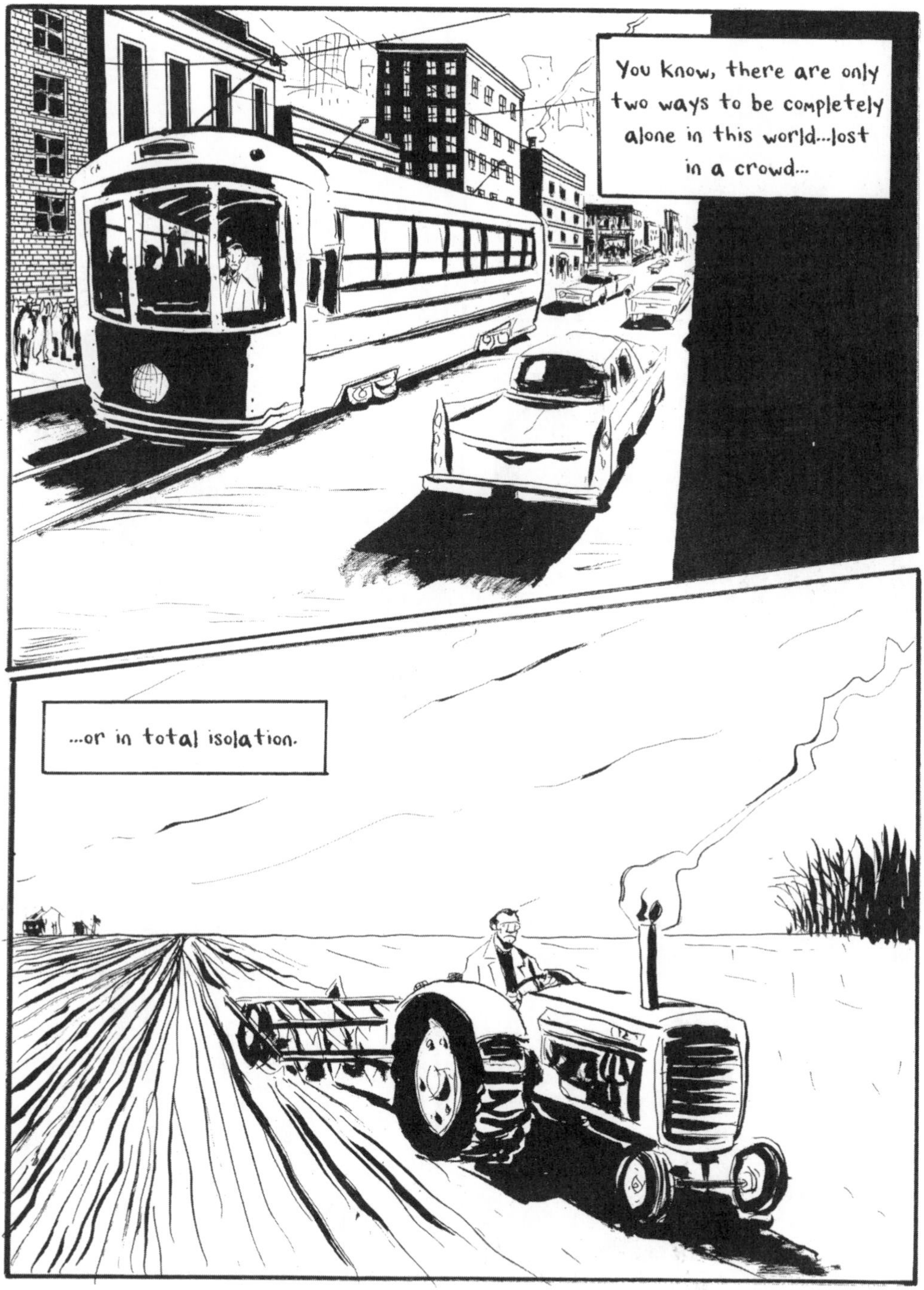
You know, there are only two ways to be completely alone in this world...lost in a crowd...
...or in total isolation.

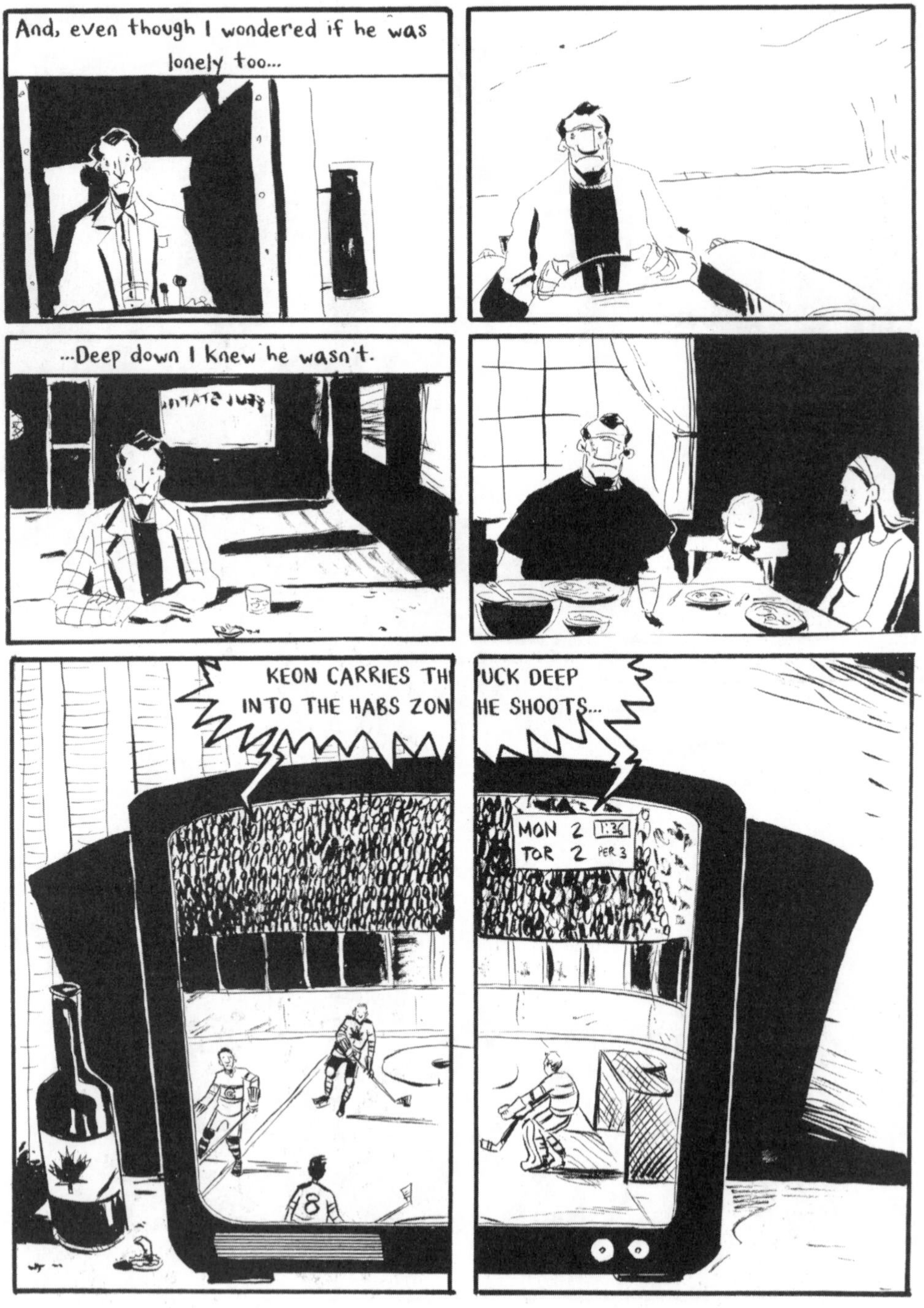
And, even though I wondered if he was lonely too...
...Deep down I knew he wasn't.
KEON CARRIES THE PUCK DEEP INTO THE HABS ZONE HE SHOOTS...
MON 2 1:36
TOR 2 PER 3

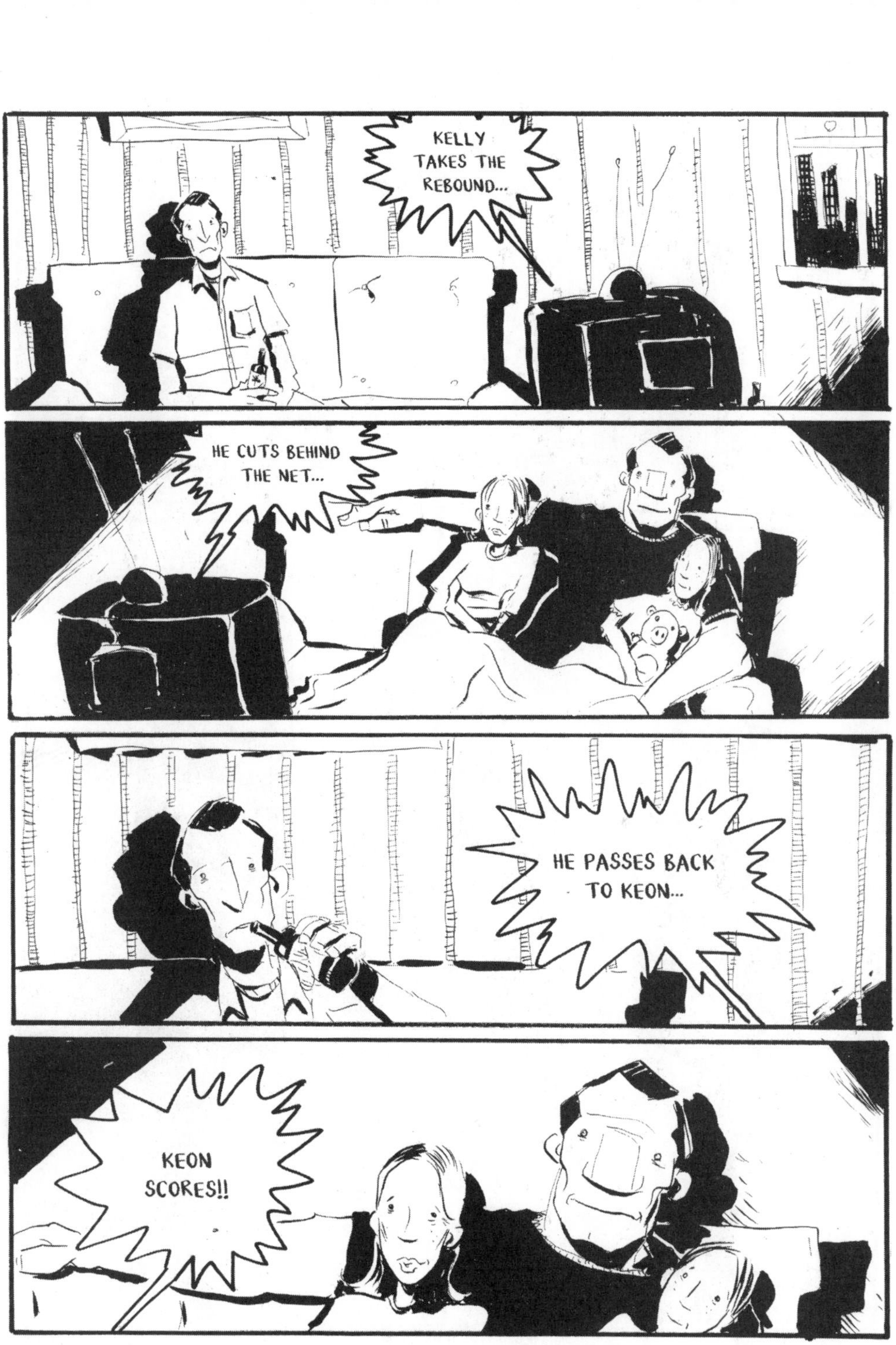
KELLY TAKES THE REBOUND...
HE CUTS BEHIND THE NET...
HE PASSES BACK TO KEON...
KEON SCORES!!

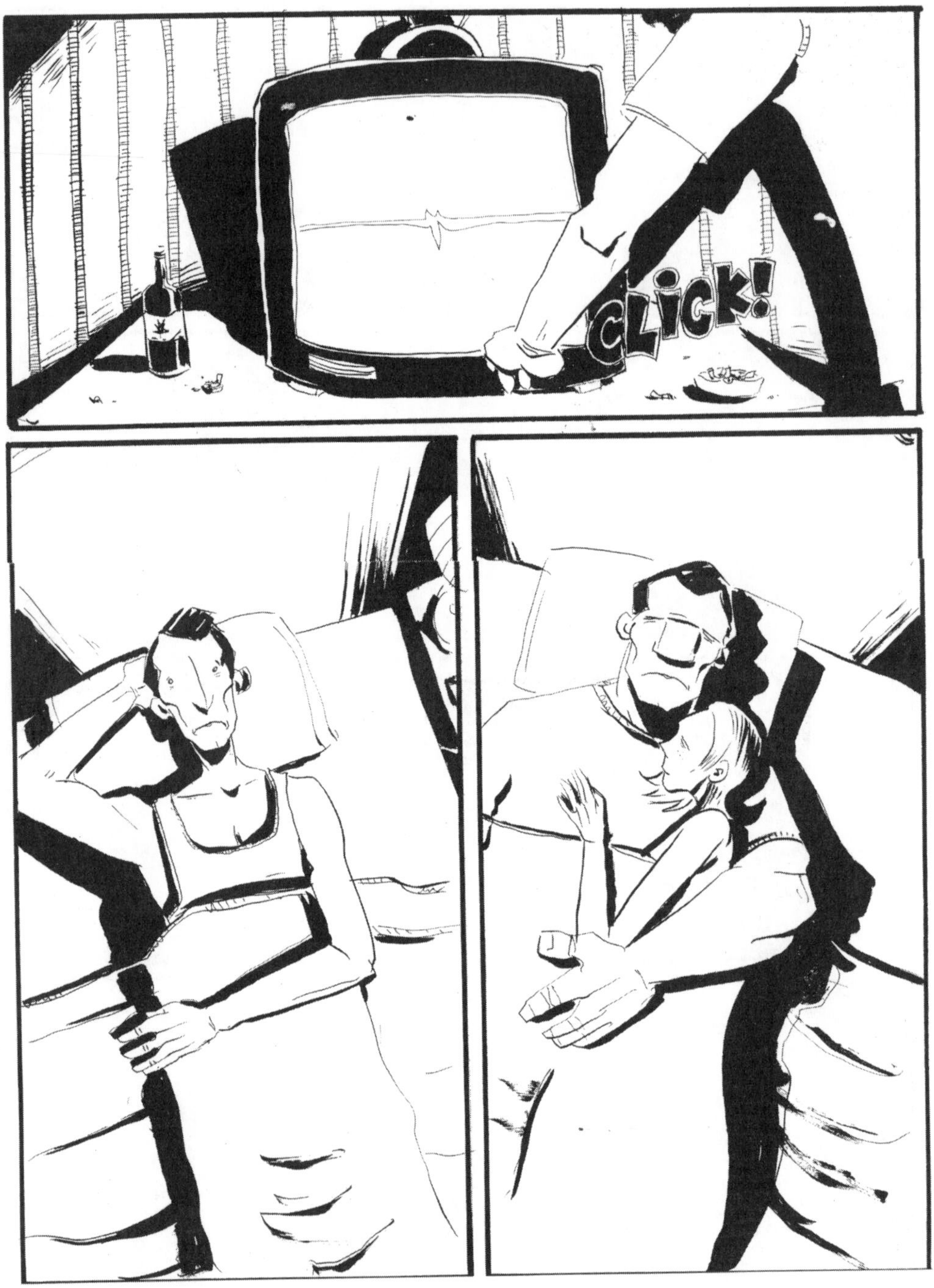
CLICK!

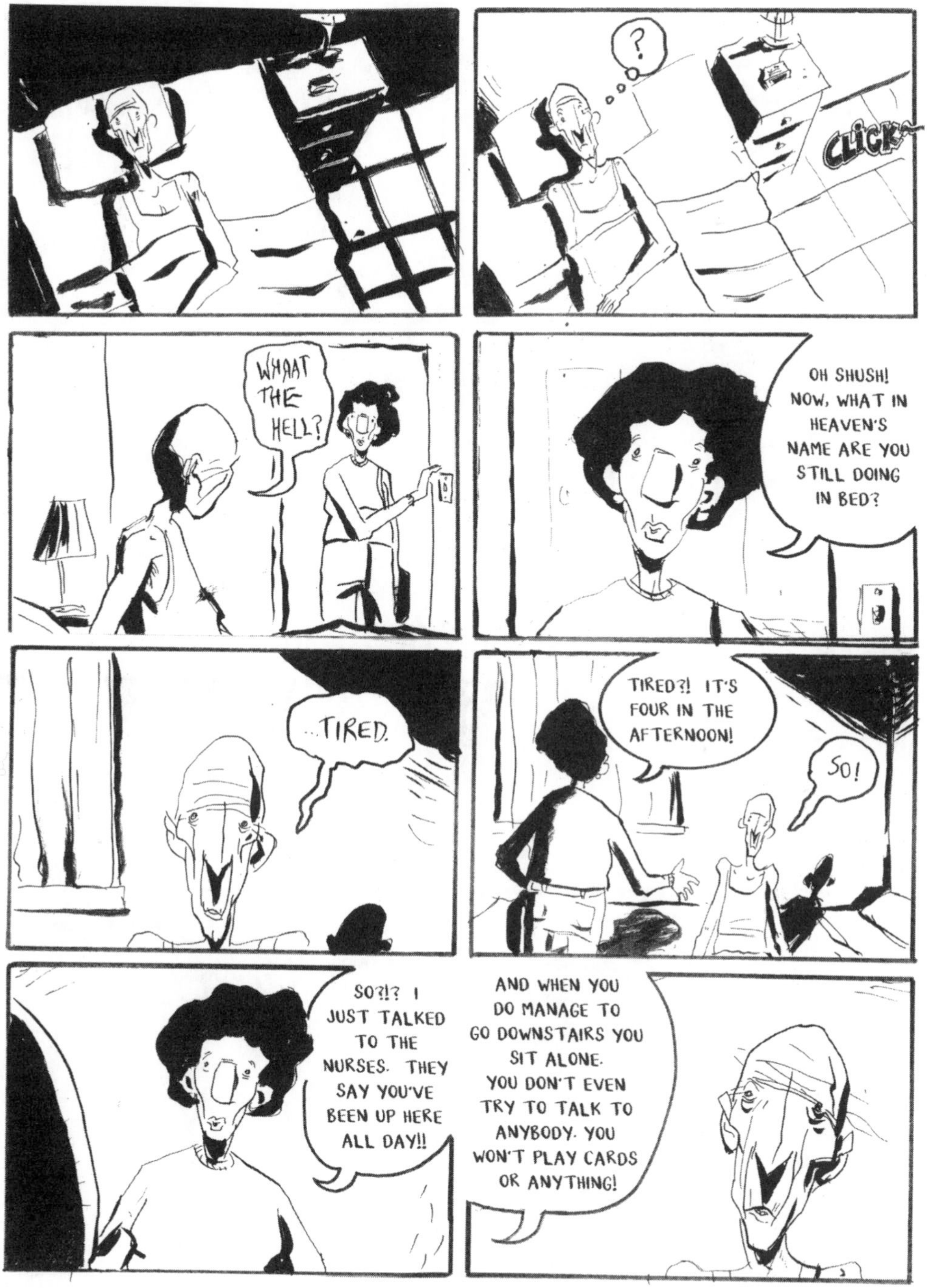
?
CLICK
WHAT THE HELL?
OH SHUSH! NOW, WHAT IN HEAVEN'S NAME ARE YOU STILL DOING IN BED?
...TIRED.
TIRED?! IT'S FOUR IN THE AFTERNOON!
SO!
SO?!? I JUST TALKED TO THE NURSES. THEY SAY YOU'VE BEEN UP HERE ALL DAY!!
AND WHEN YOU DO MANAGE TO GO DOWNSTAIRS YOU SIT ALONE. YOU DON'T EVEN TRY TO TALK TO ANYBODY. YOU WON'T PLAY CARDS OR ANYTHING!

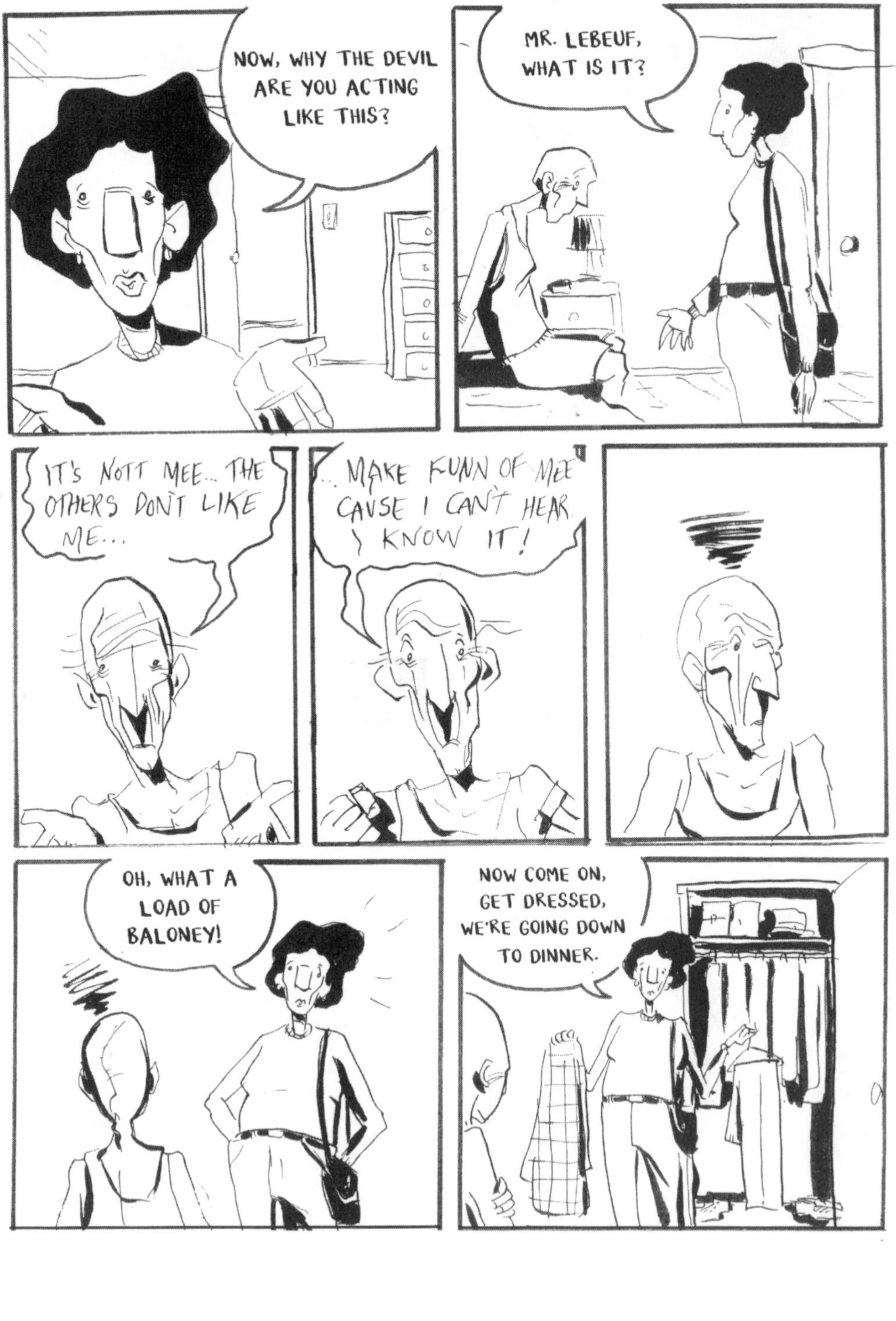
NOW, WHY THE DEVIL ARE YOU ACTING LIKE THIS?
MR. LEBEUF, WHAT IS IT?
IT'S NOTT MEE... THE OTHERS DON'T LIKE ME...
...MAKE FUNN OF MEE CAUSE I CAN'T HEAR. I KNOW IT!
OH, WHAT A LOAD OF BALONEY!
NOW COME ON, GET DRESSED, WE'RE GOING DOWN TO DINNER.

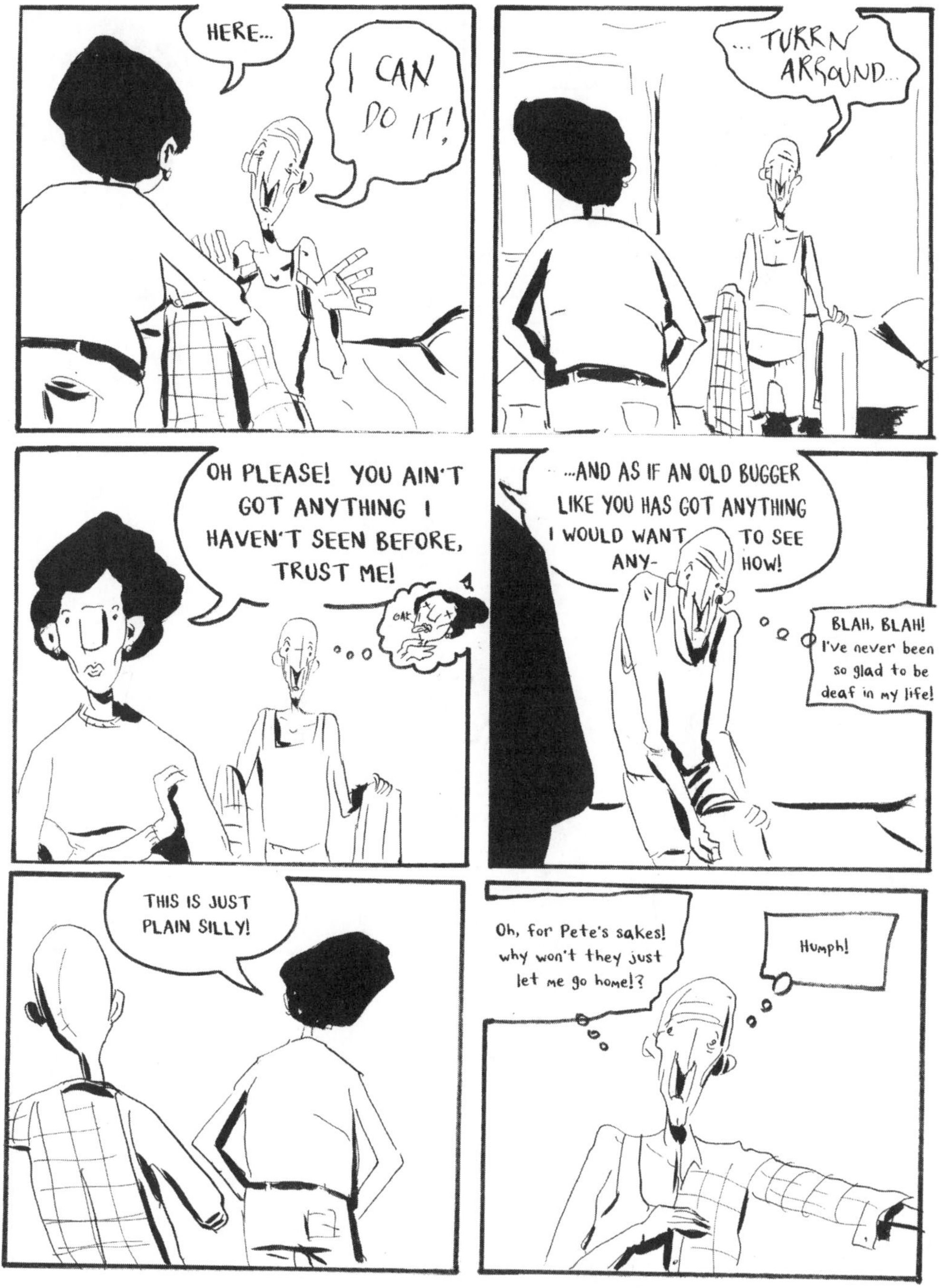
HERE...
I CAN DO IT!
... TURRN ARROUND...
OH PLEASE! YOU AIN'T GOT ANYTHING I HAVEN'T SEEN BEFORE, TRUST ME!
...AND AS IF AN OLD BUGGER LIKE YOU HAS GOT ANYTHING I WOULD WANT TO SEE ANY-HOW!
BLAH, BLAH! I've never been so glad to be deaf in my life!
THIS IS JUST PLAIN SILLY!
Oh, for Pete's sakes! why won't they just let me go home!?
Humph!

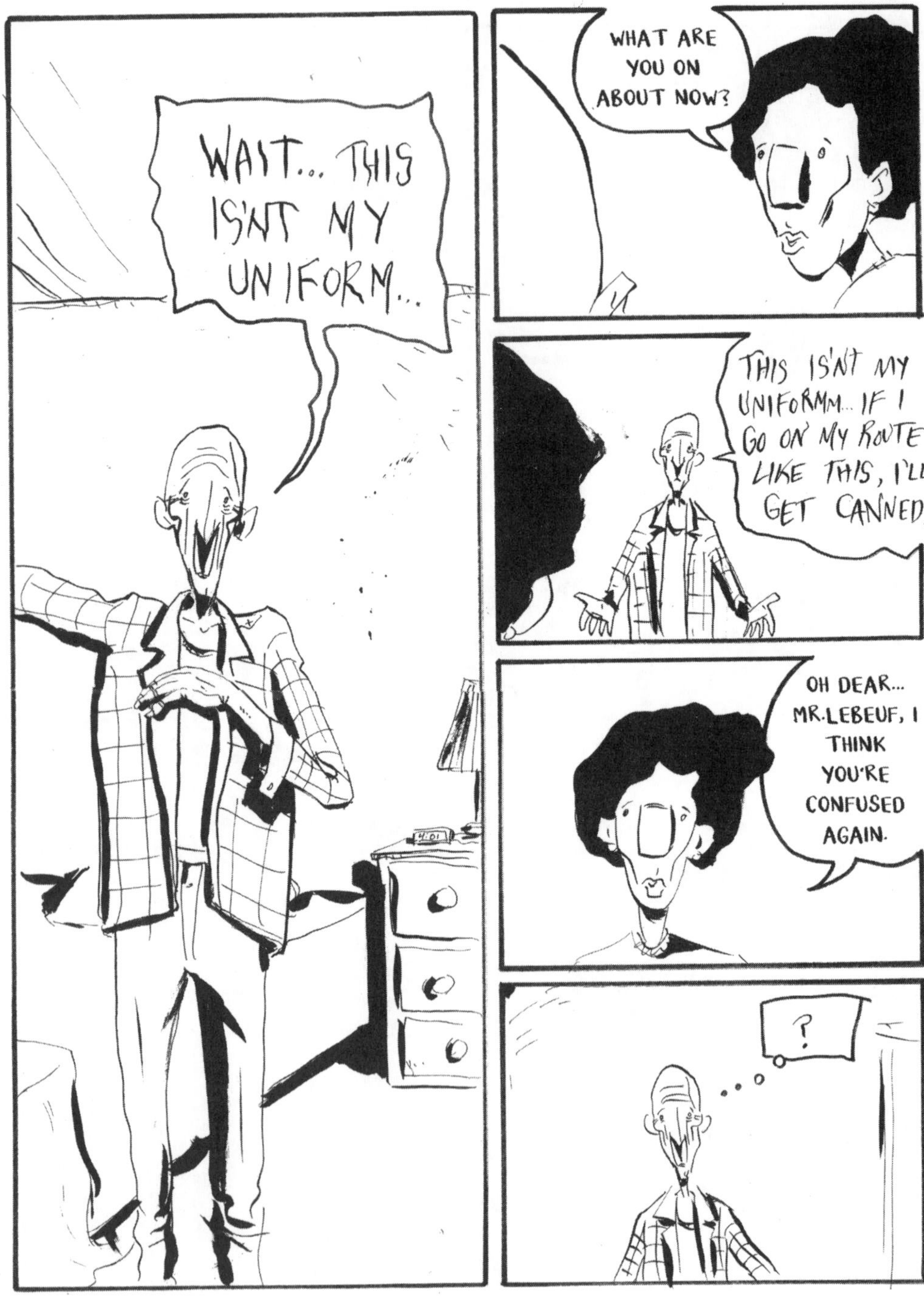
WAIT... THIS IS'NT MY UNIFORM...
WHAT ARE YOU ON ABOUT NOW?
THIS IS'NT MY UNIFORMM... IF I GO ON MY ROUTE LIKE THIS, I'LL GET CANNED!
OH DEAR... MR.LEBEUF, I THINK YOU'RE CONFUSED AGAIN.
?

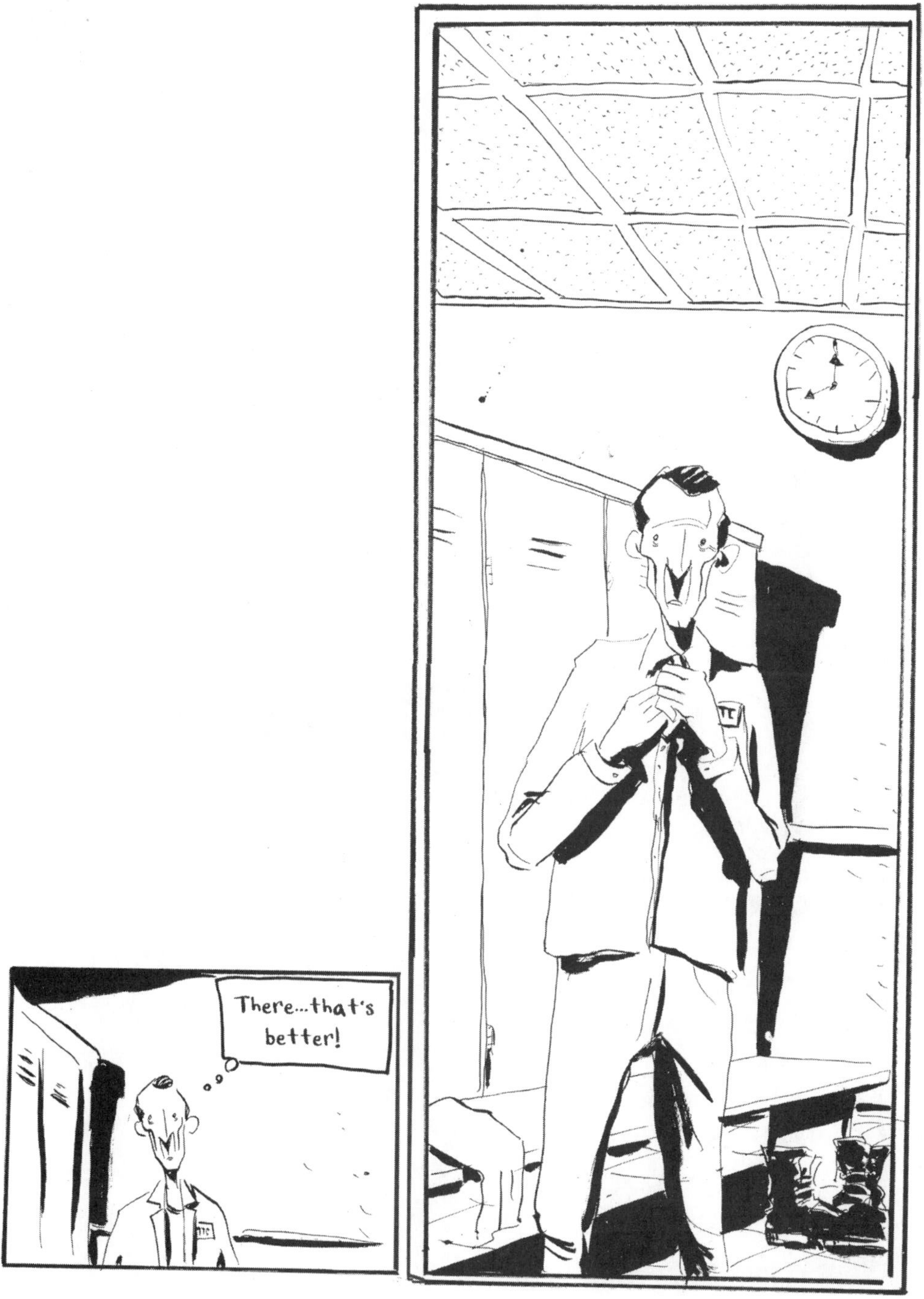
There...that's better!

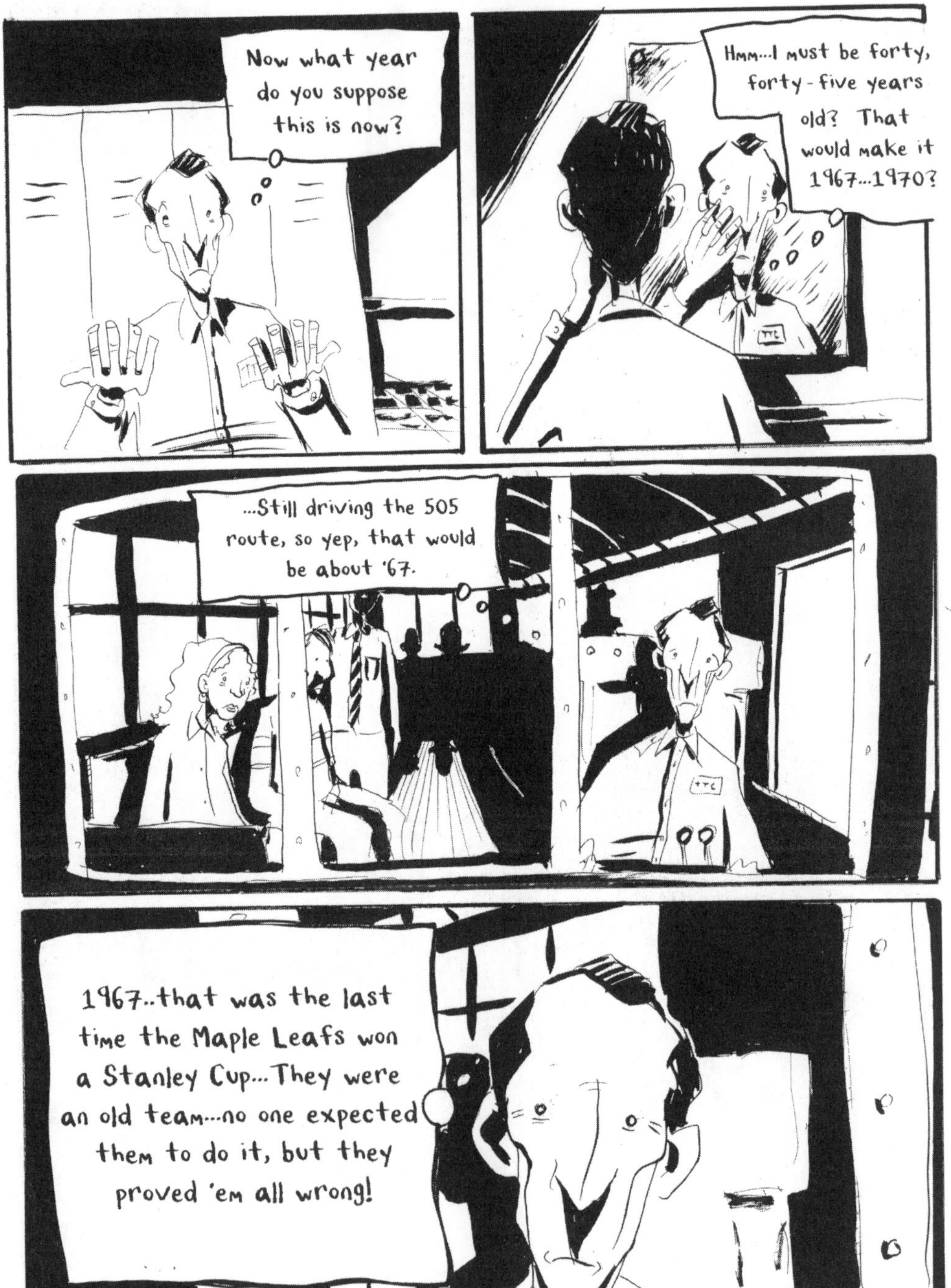
Now what year do you suppose this is now?
Hmm...I must be forty, forty-five years old? That would make it 1967...1970?
TTC
...Still driving the 505 route, so yep, that would be about '67.
TTC
1967..that was the last time the Maple Leafs won a Stanley Cup...They were an old team...no one expected them to do it, but they proved 'em all wrong!

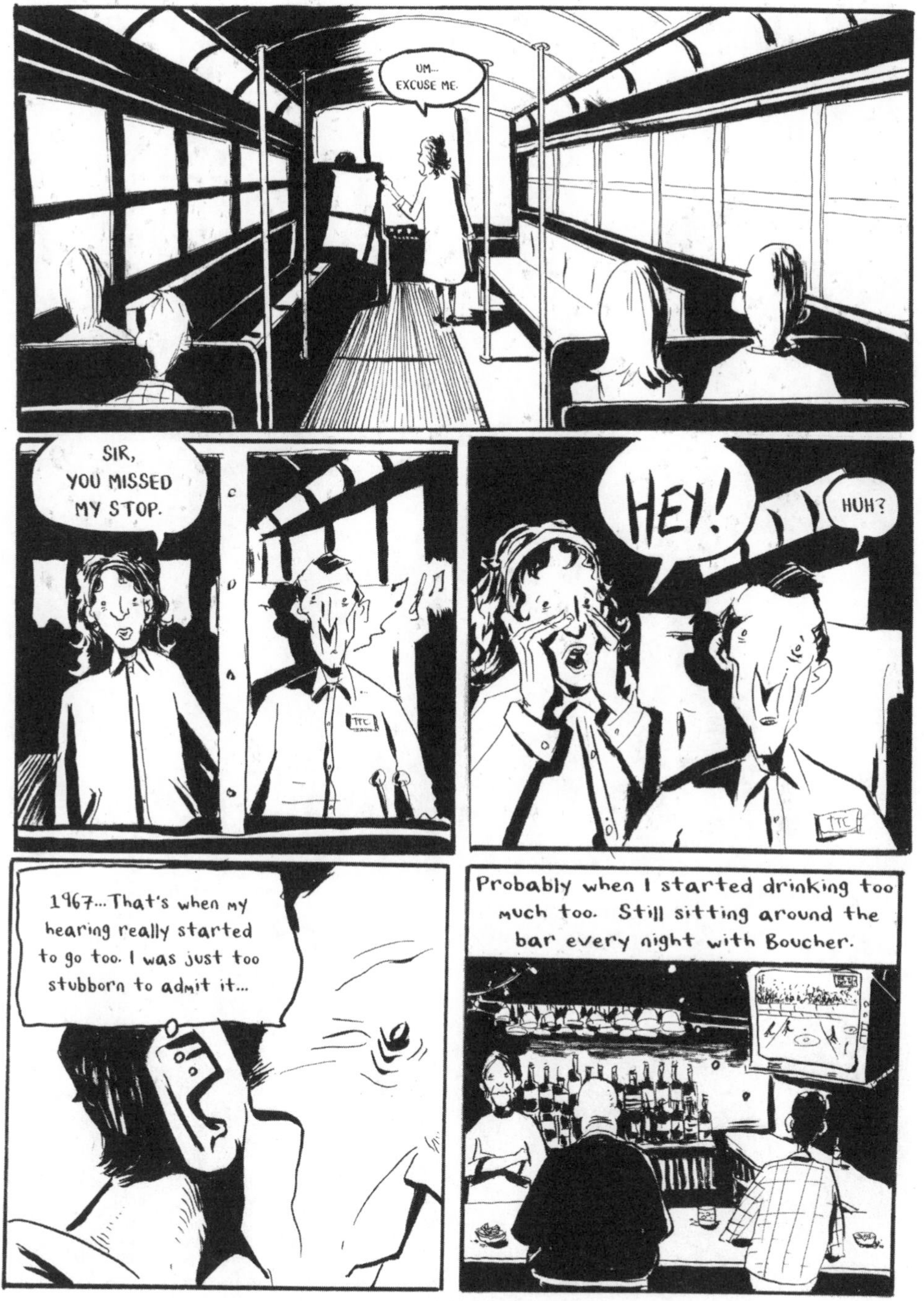
UM... EXCUSE ME.
SIR, YOU MISSED MY STOP.
HEY!
HUH?
1967... That's when my hearing really started to go too. I was just too stubborn to admit it...
Probably when I started drinking too much too. Still sitting around the bar every night with Boucher.

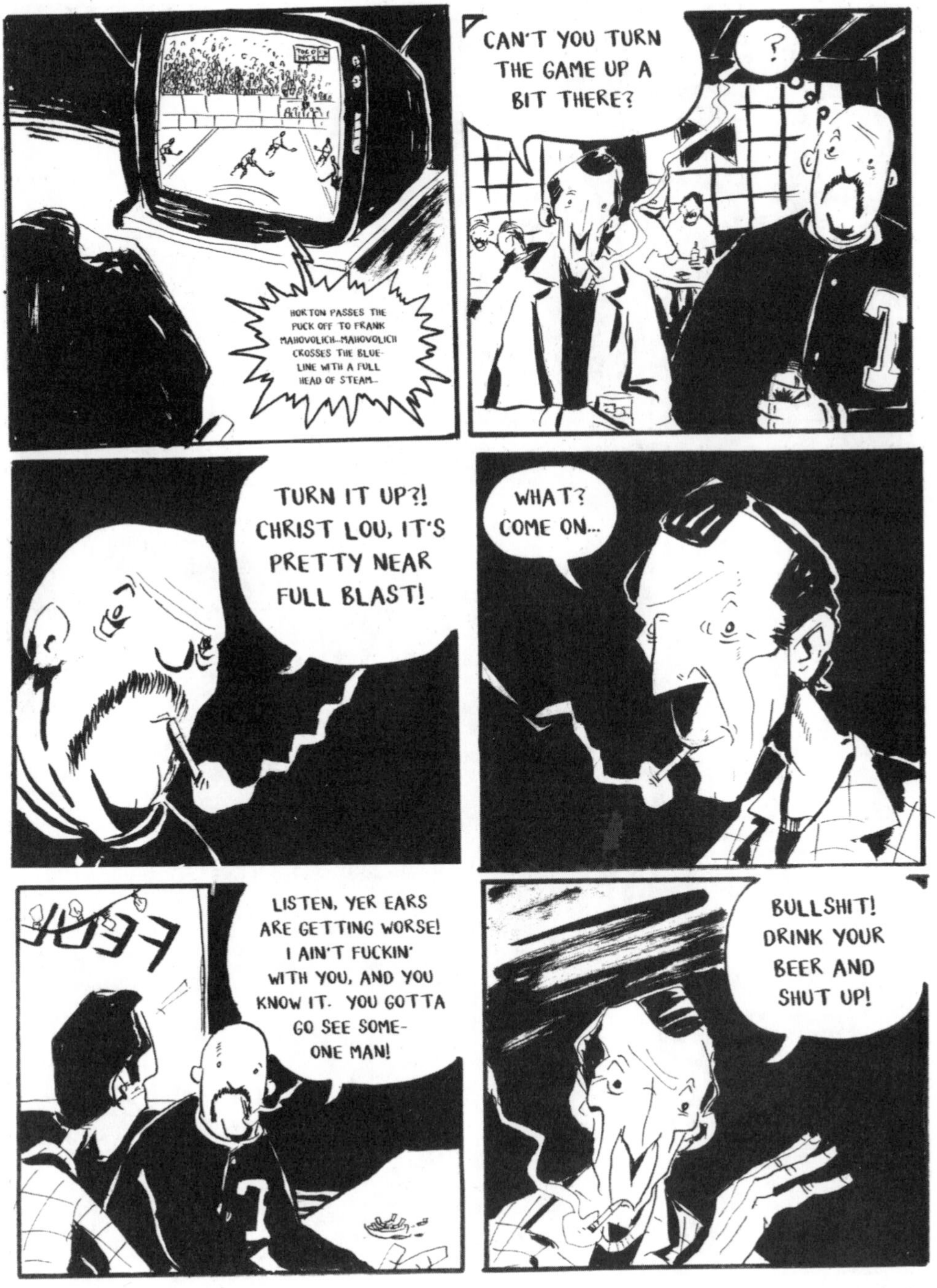
HORTON PASSES THE PUCK OFF TO FRANK MAHOVOLICH...MAHOVOLICH CROSSES THE BLUE-LINE WITH A FULL HEAD OF STEAM...
CAN'T YOU TURN THE GAME UP A BIT THERE?
?
TURN IT UP?! CHRIST LOU, IT'S PRETTY NEAR FULL BLAST!
WHAT? COME ON...
LISTEN, YER EARS ARE GETTING WORSE! I AIN'T FUCKIN' WITH YOU, AND YOU KNOW IT. YOU GOTTA GO SEE SOME-ONE MAN!
BULLSHIT! DRINK YOUR BEER AND SHUT UP!

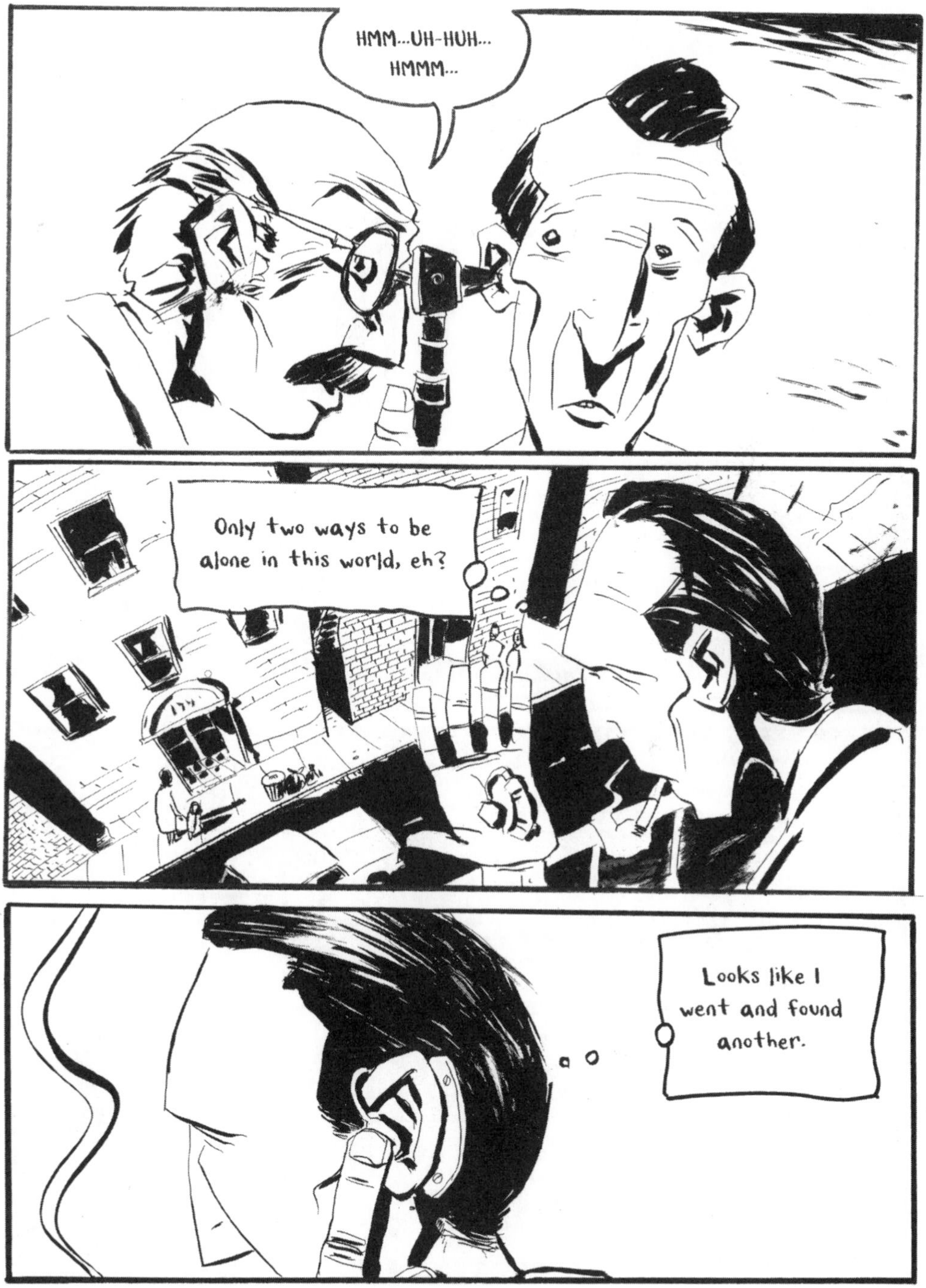
HMM...UH-HUH... HMMM...
Only two ways to be alone in this world, eh?
Looks like I went and found another.

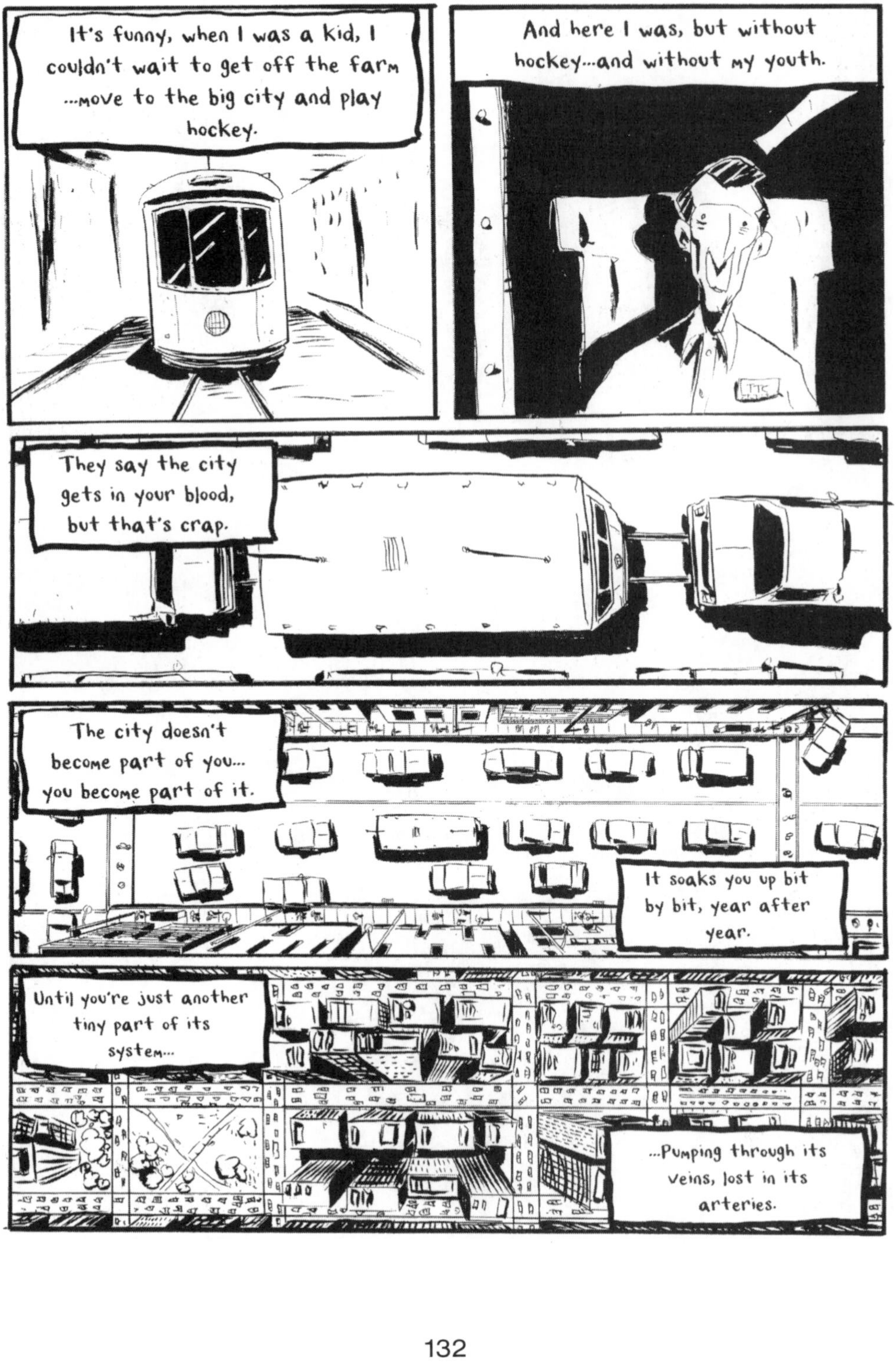
It's funny, when I was a kid, I couldn't wait to get off the farm ...move to the big city and play hockey.
And here I was, but without hockey...and without my youth.
They say the city gets in your blood, but that's crap.
The city doesn't become part of you... you become part of it.
It soaks you up bit by bit, year after year.
Until you're just another tiny part of its system...
...Pumping through its veins, lost in its arteries.

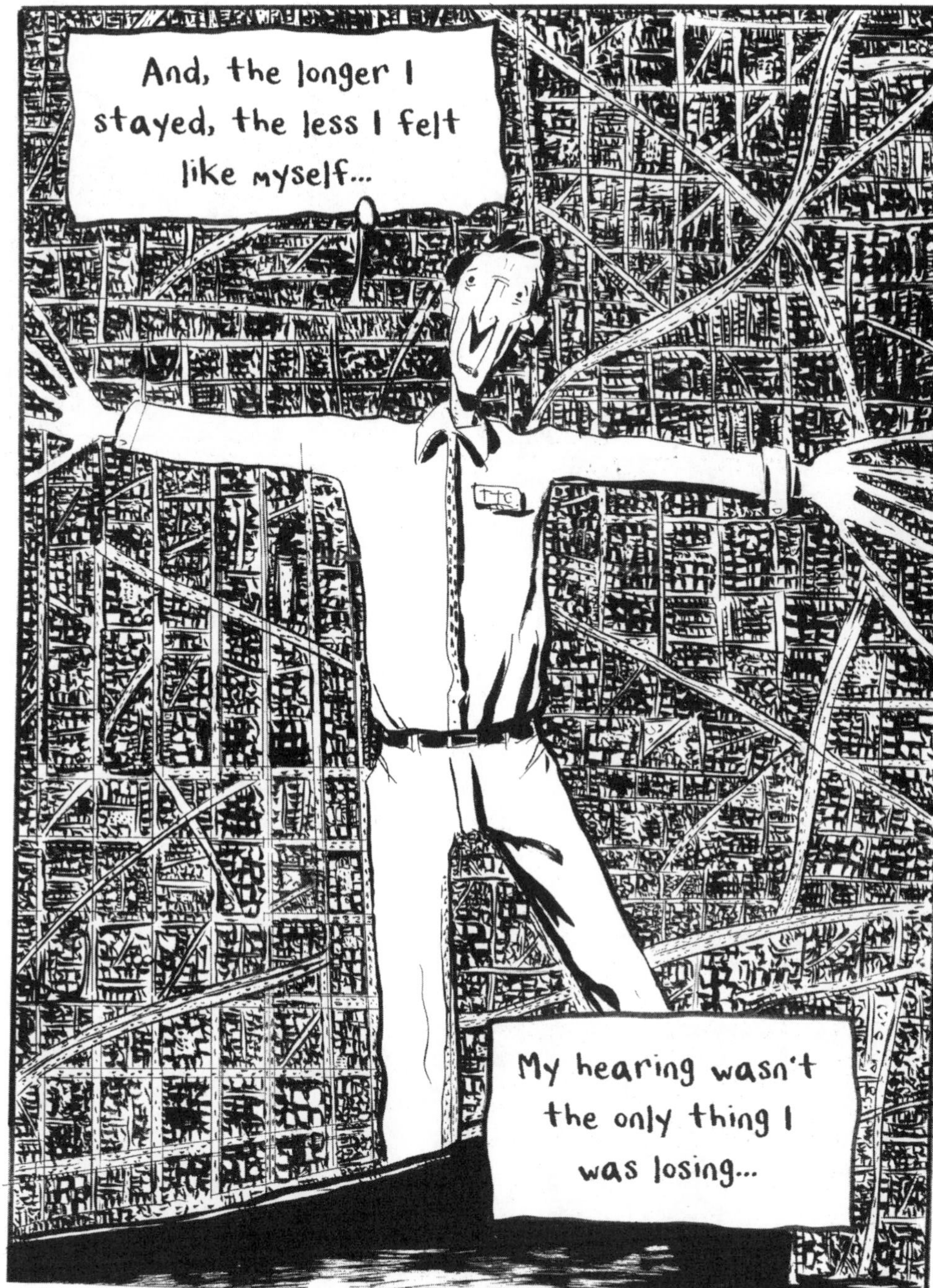
And, the longer I stayed, the less I felt like myself...
My hearing wasn't the only thing I was losing...

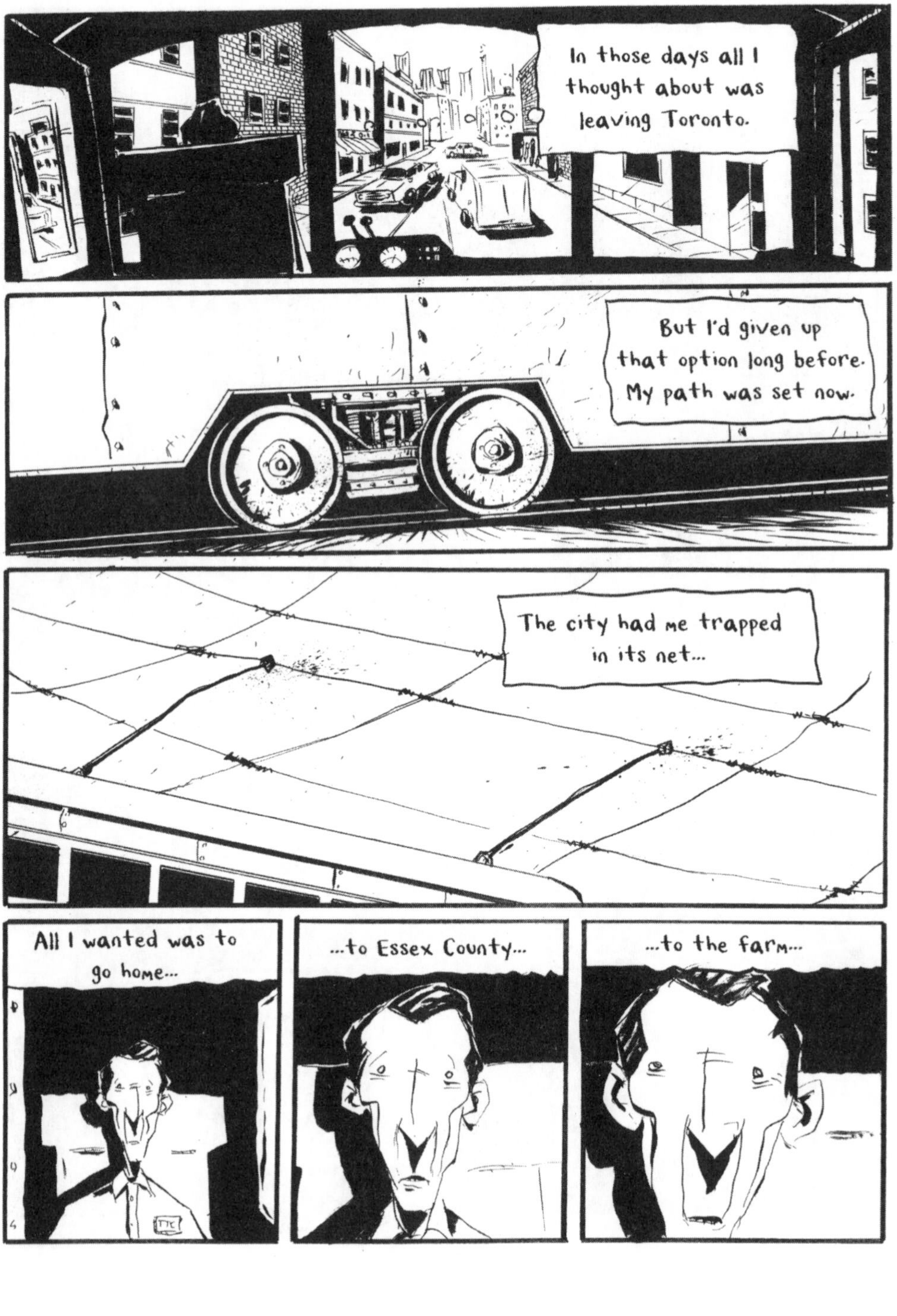
In those days all I thought about was leaving Toronto.
But I'd given up that option long before. My path was set now.
The city had me trapped in its net...
All I wanted was to go home...
TTC
...to Essex County...
...to the farm...

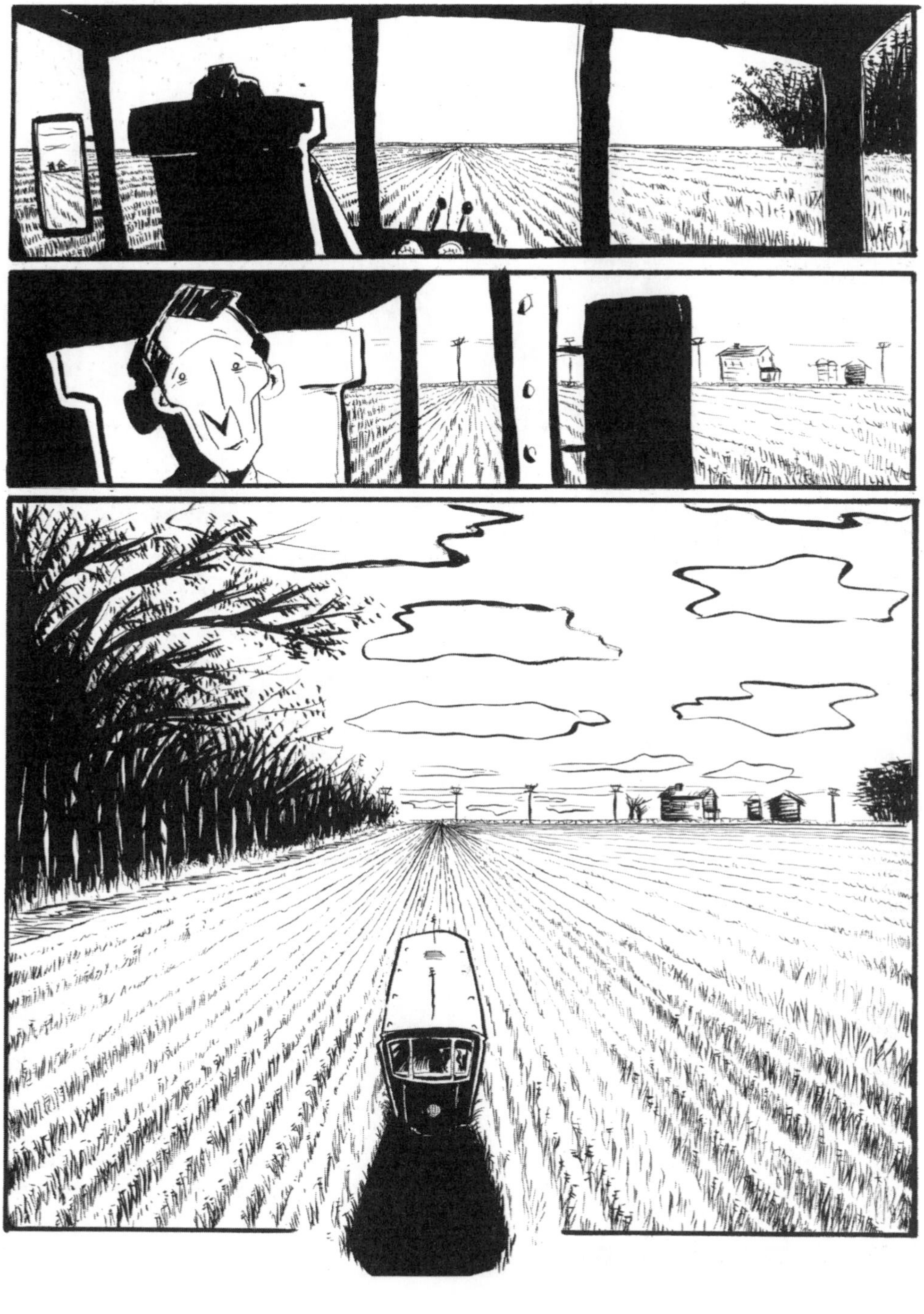

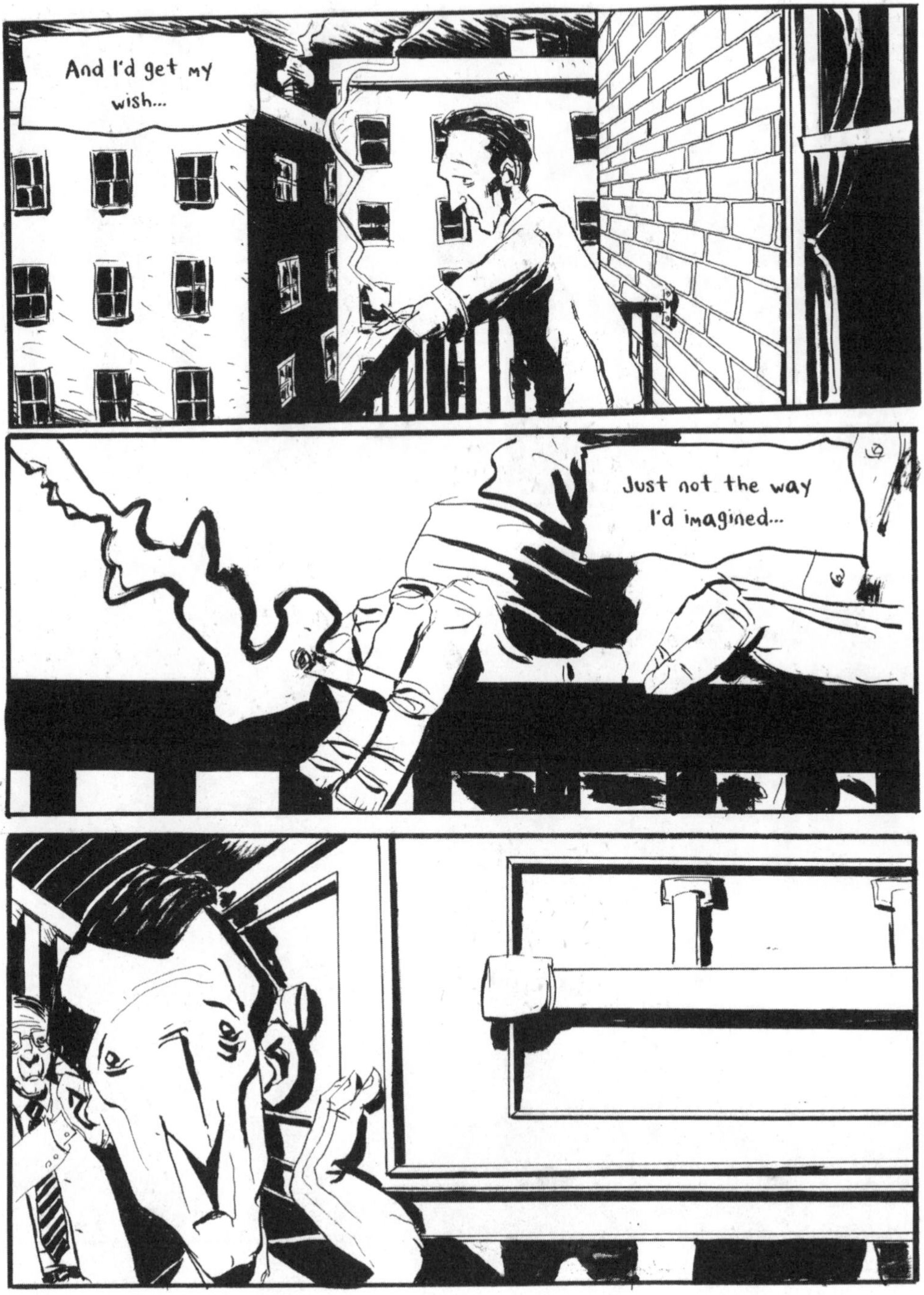
And I'd get my wish...
Just not the way I'd imagined...

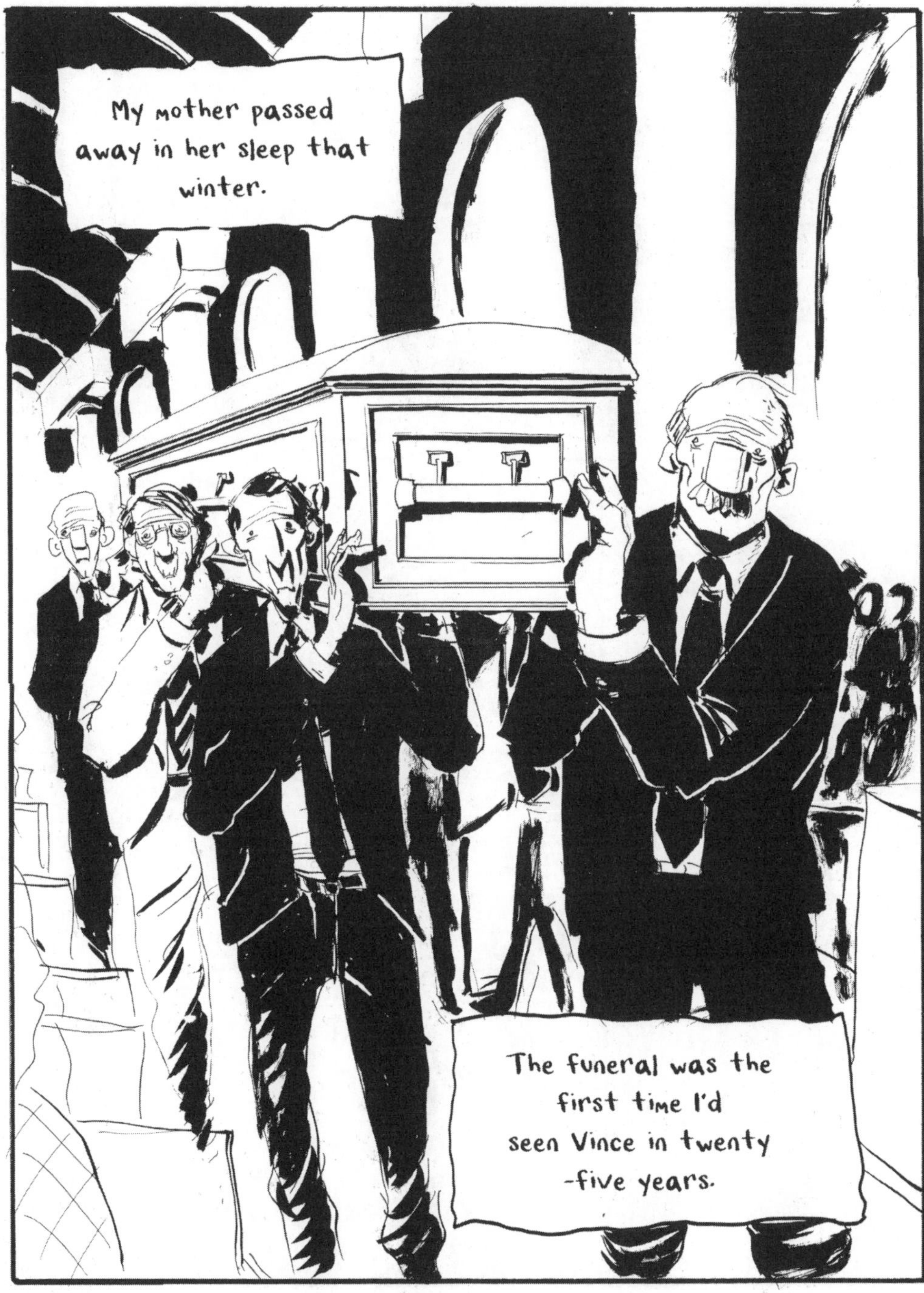
My mother passed away in her sleep that winter.
The funeral was the first time I'd seen Vince in twenty -five years.

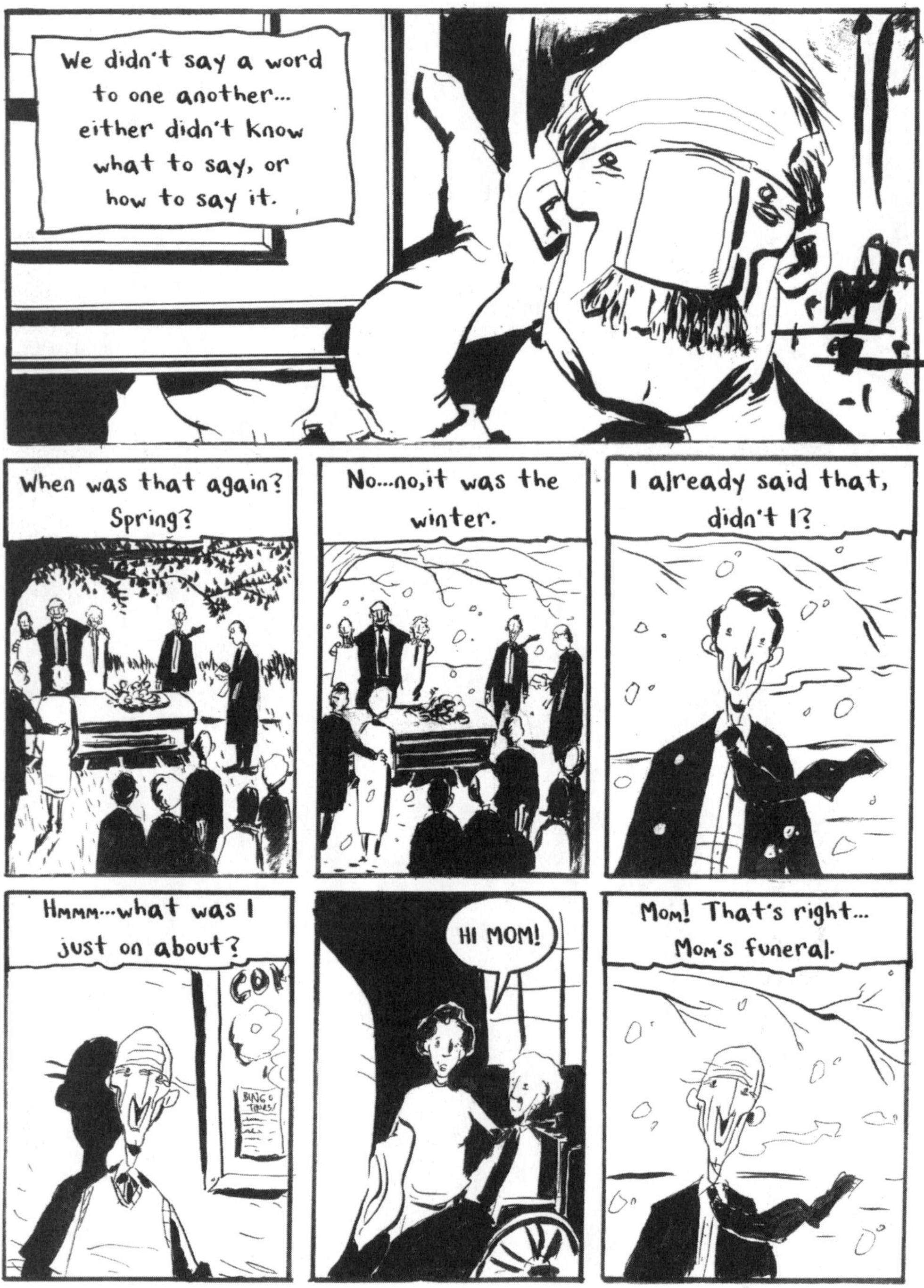
We didn't say a word to one another... either didn't know what to say, or how to say it.
When was that again? Spring?
No...no,it was the winter.
I already said that, didn't I?
Hmmm...what was I just on about?
HI MOM!
Mom! That's right... Mom's funeral.

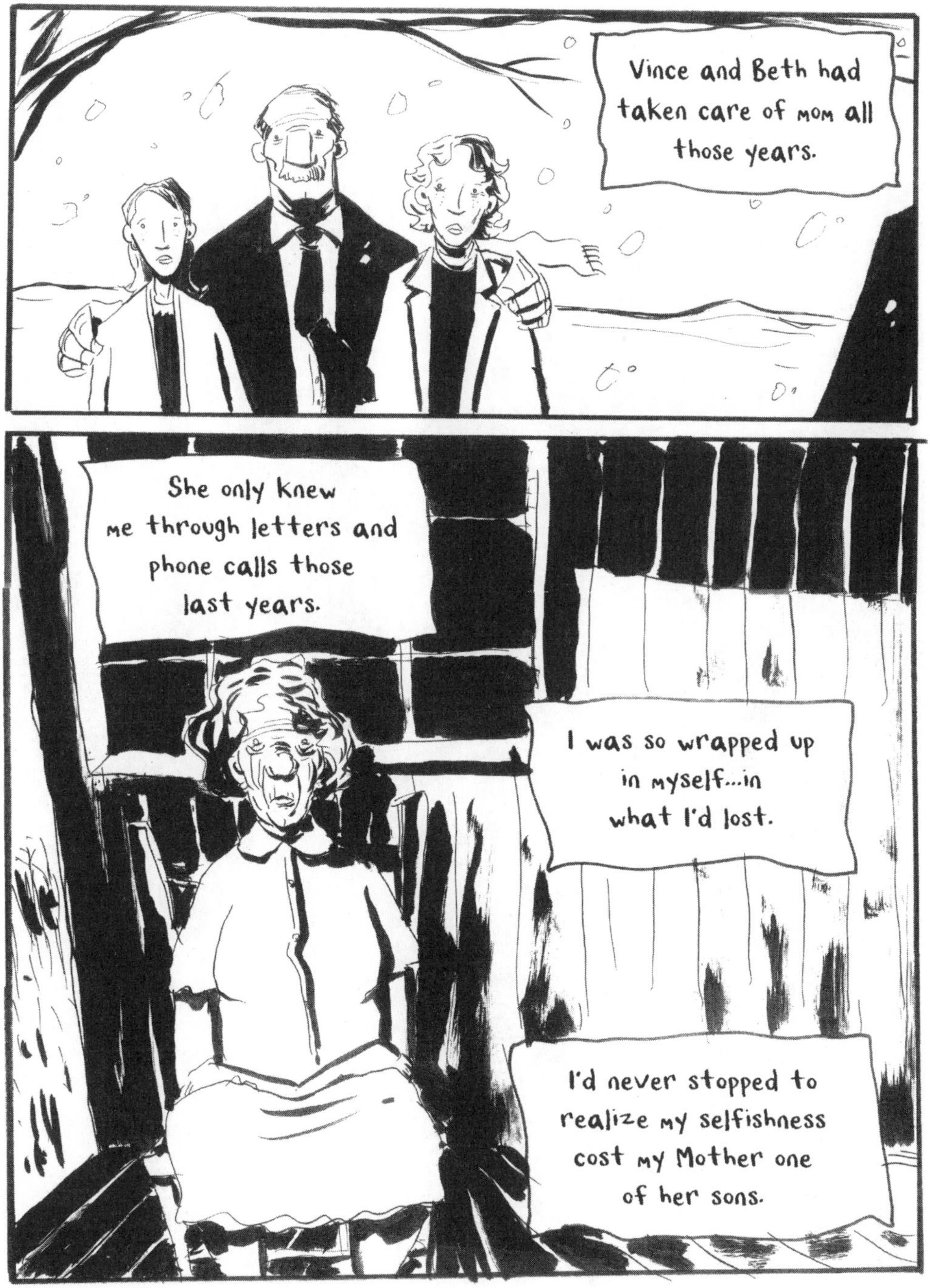
Vince and Beth had taken care of MOM all those years.
She only knew me through letters and phone calls those last years.
I was so wrapped up in myself...in what I'd lost.
I'd never stopped to realize my selfishness cost my Mother one of her sons.

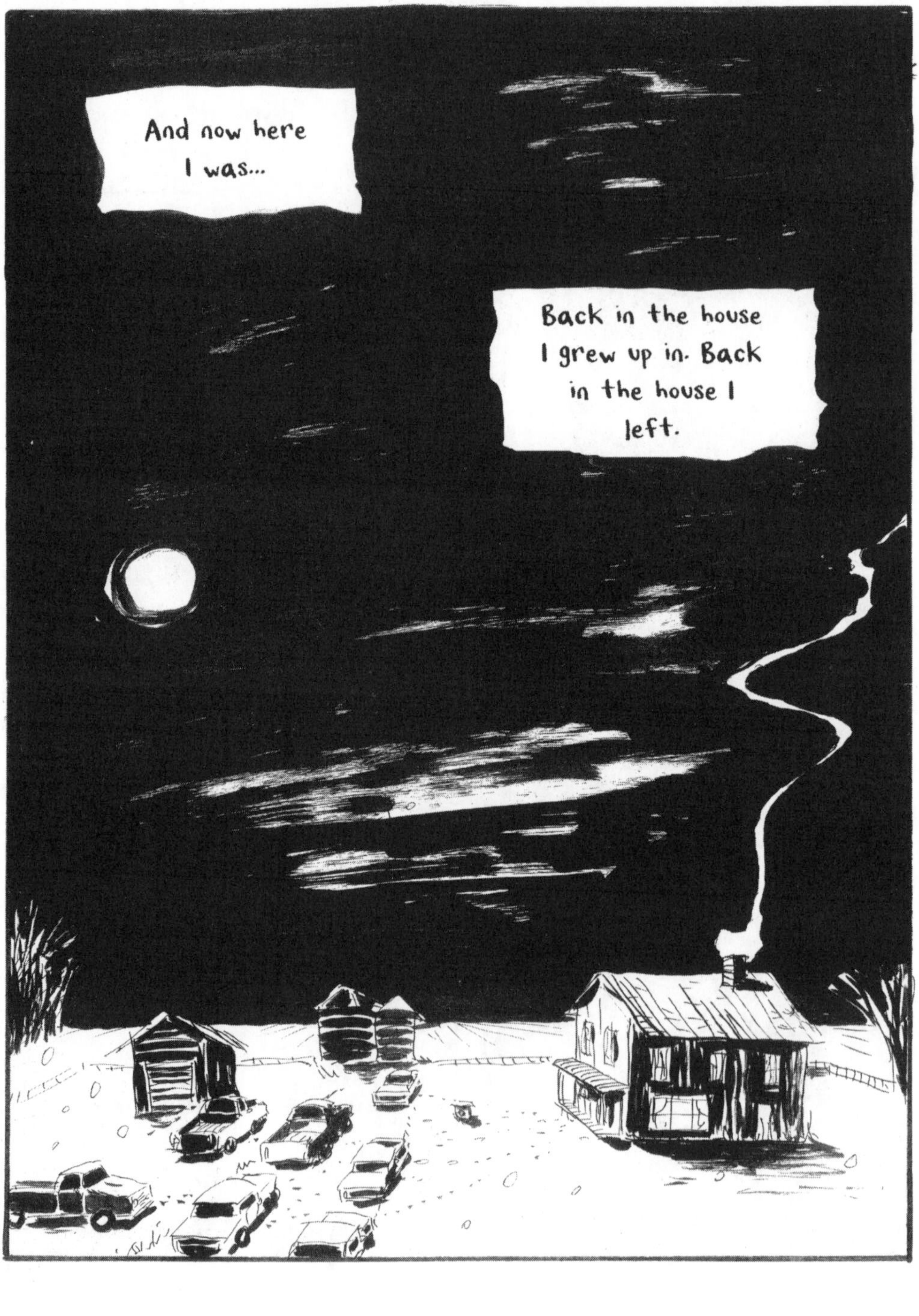
And now here I was...
Back in the house I grew up in. Back in the house I left.

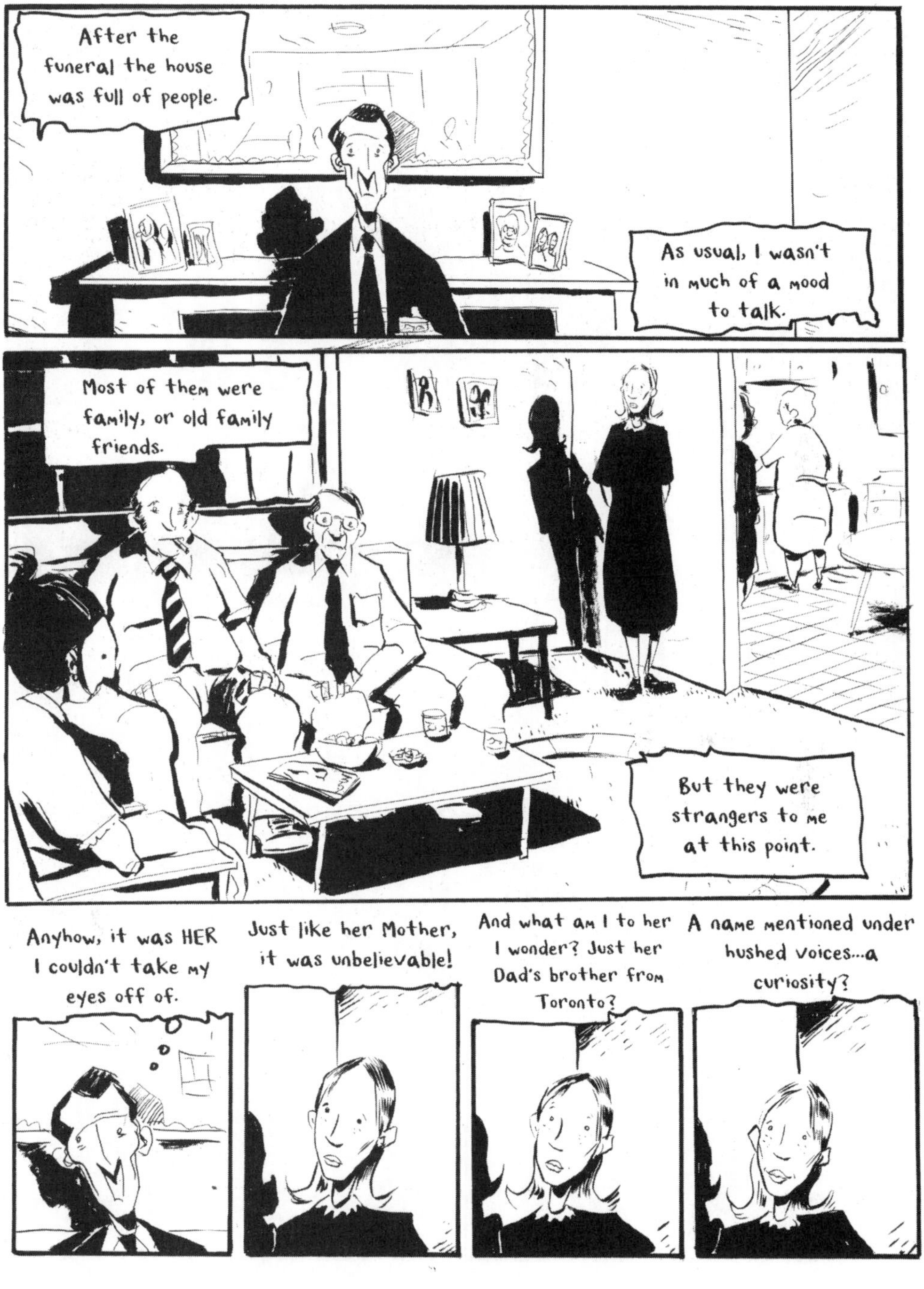
After the funeral the house was full of people.
As usual, I wasn't in much of a mood to talk.
Most of them were family, or old family friends.
But they were strangers to me at this point.
Anyhow, it was HER I couldn't take my eyes off of.
Just like her Mother, it was unbelievable!
And what am I to her I wonder? Just her Dad's brother from Toronto?
A name mentioned under hushed voices...a curiosity?

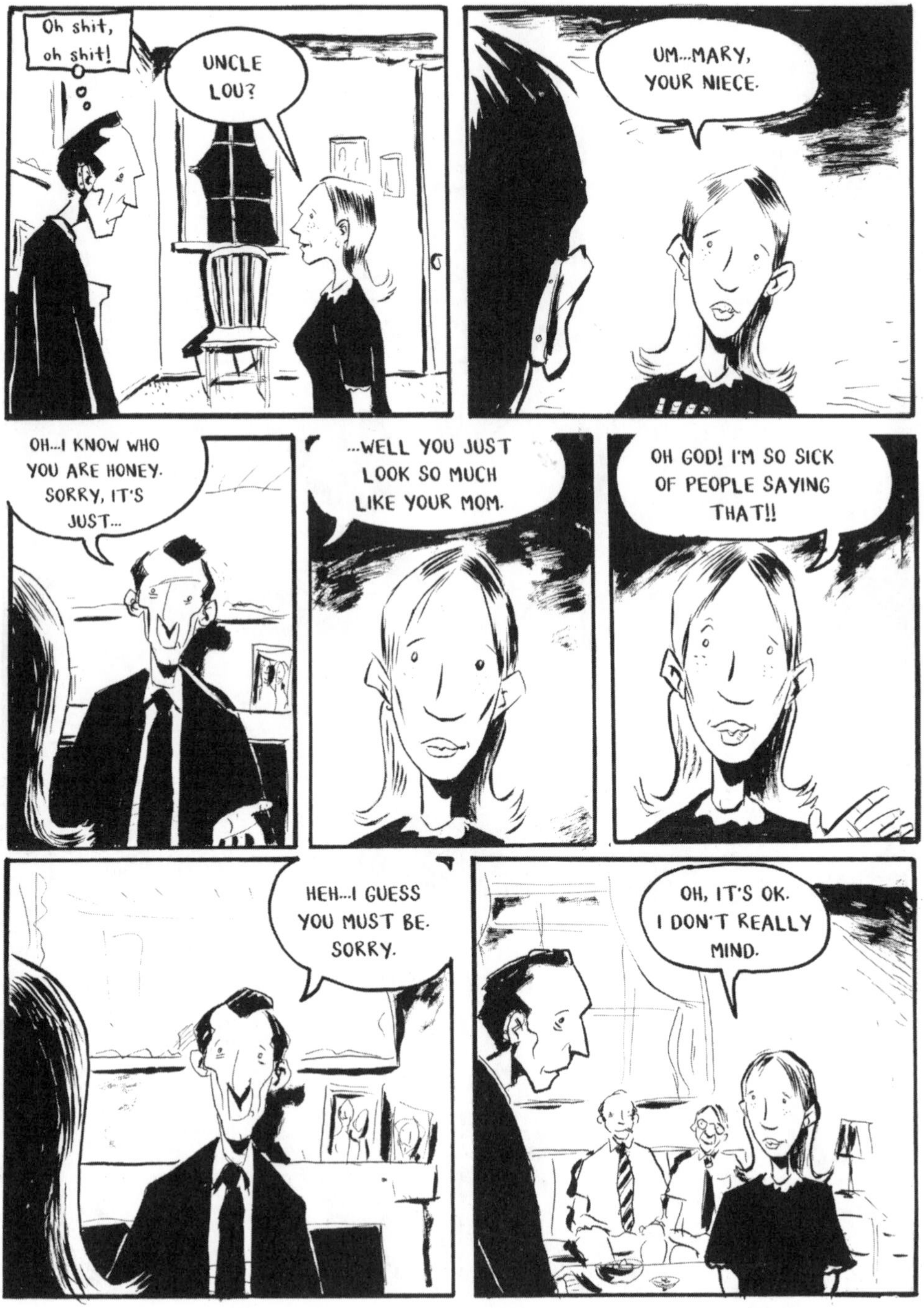
Oh shit,
oh shit!
UNCLE
LOU?
UM...MARY,
YOUR NIECE.
OH...I KNOW WHO
YOU ARE HONEY.
SORRY, IT'S
JUST...
...WELL YOU JUST
LOOK SO MUCH
LIKE YOUR MOM.
OH GOD! I'M SO SICK
OF PEOPLE SAYING
THAT!!
HEH...I GUESS
YOU MUST BE.
SORRY.
OH, IT'S OK.
I DON'T REALLY
MIND.

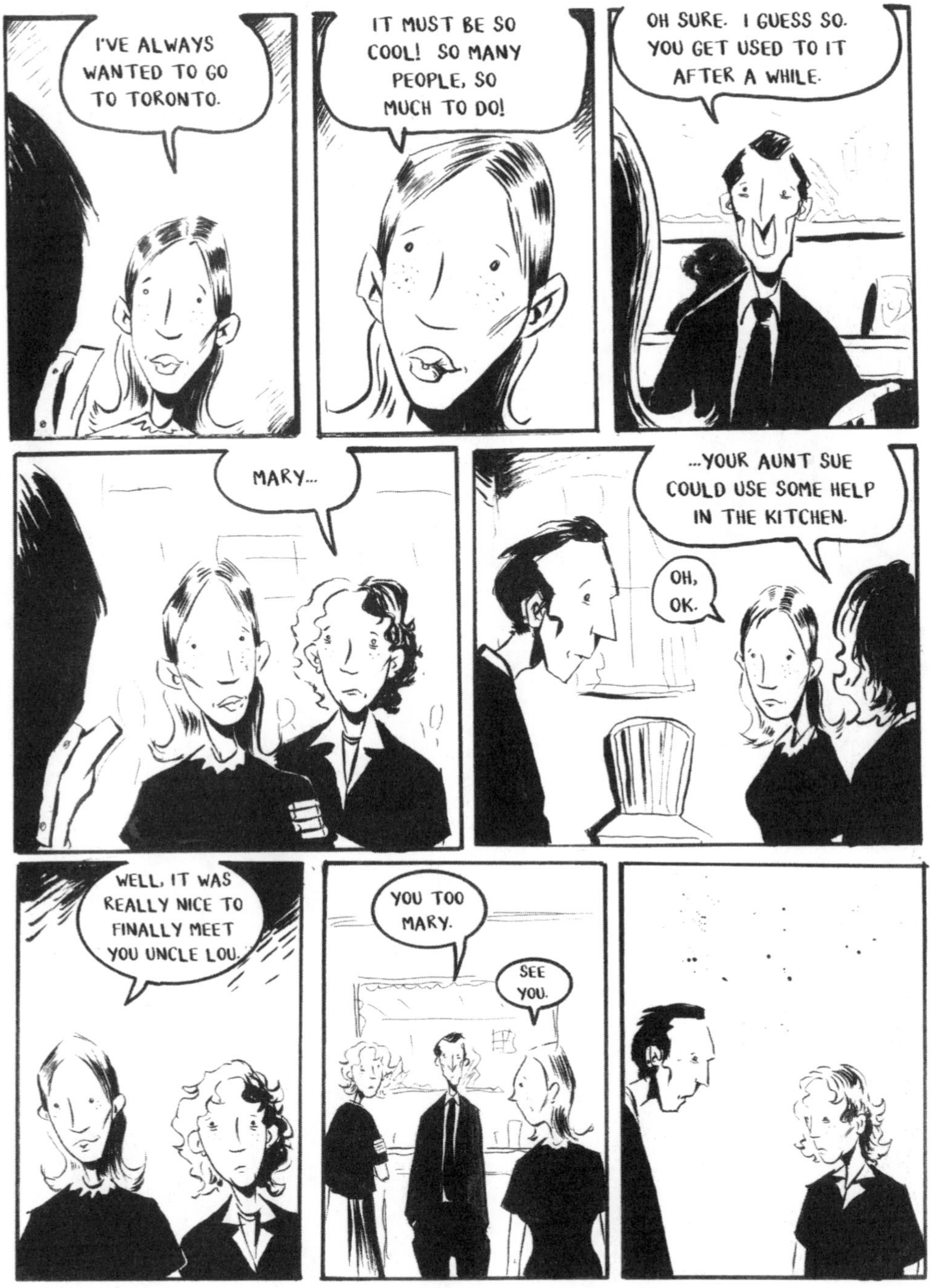
I'VE ALWAYS WANTED TO GO TO TORONTO.
IT MUST BE SO COOL! SO MANY PEOPLE, SO MUCH TO DO!
OH SURE. I GUESS SO. YOU GET USED TO IT AFTER A WHILE.
MARY...
...YOUR AUNT SUE COULD USE SOME HELP IN THE KITCHEN.
OH, OK.
WELL, IT WAS REALLY NICE TO FINALLY MEET YOU UNCLE LOU.
YOU TOO MARY.
SEE YOU.

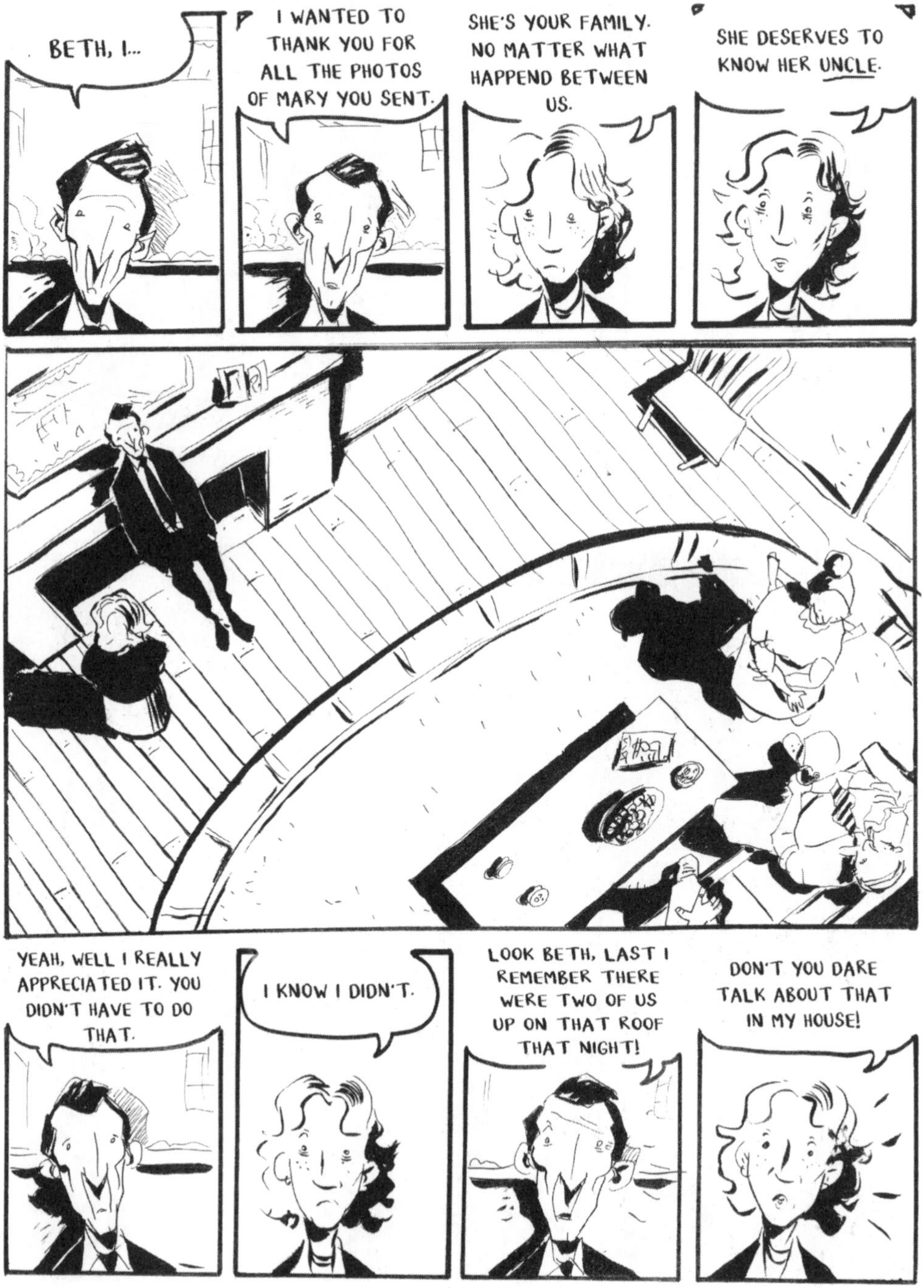
BETH, I...
I WANTED TO THANK YOU FOR ALL THE PHOTOS OF MARY YOU SENT.
SHE'S YOUR FAMILY. NO MATTER WHAT HAPPEND BETWEEN US.
SHE DESERVES TO KNOW HER UNCLE.
YEAH, WELL I REALLY APPRECIATED IT. YOU DIDN'T HAVE TO DO THAT.
I KNOW I DIDN'T.
LOOK BETH, LAST I REMEMBER THERE WERE TWO OF US UP ON THAT ROOF THAT NIGHT!
DON'T YOU DARE TALK ABOUT THAT IN MY HOUSE!

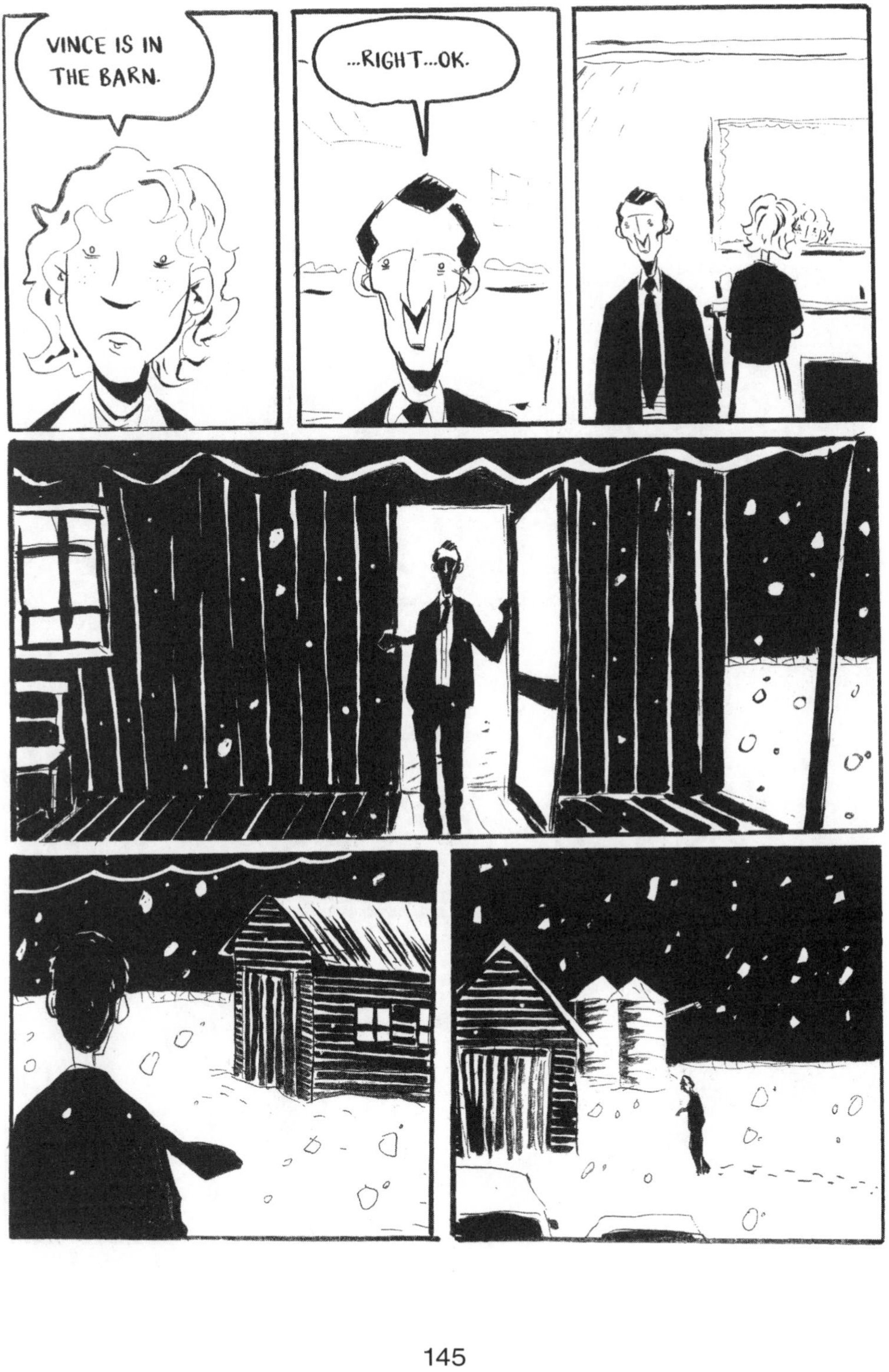
VINCE IS IN THE BARN.
...RIGHT...OK.

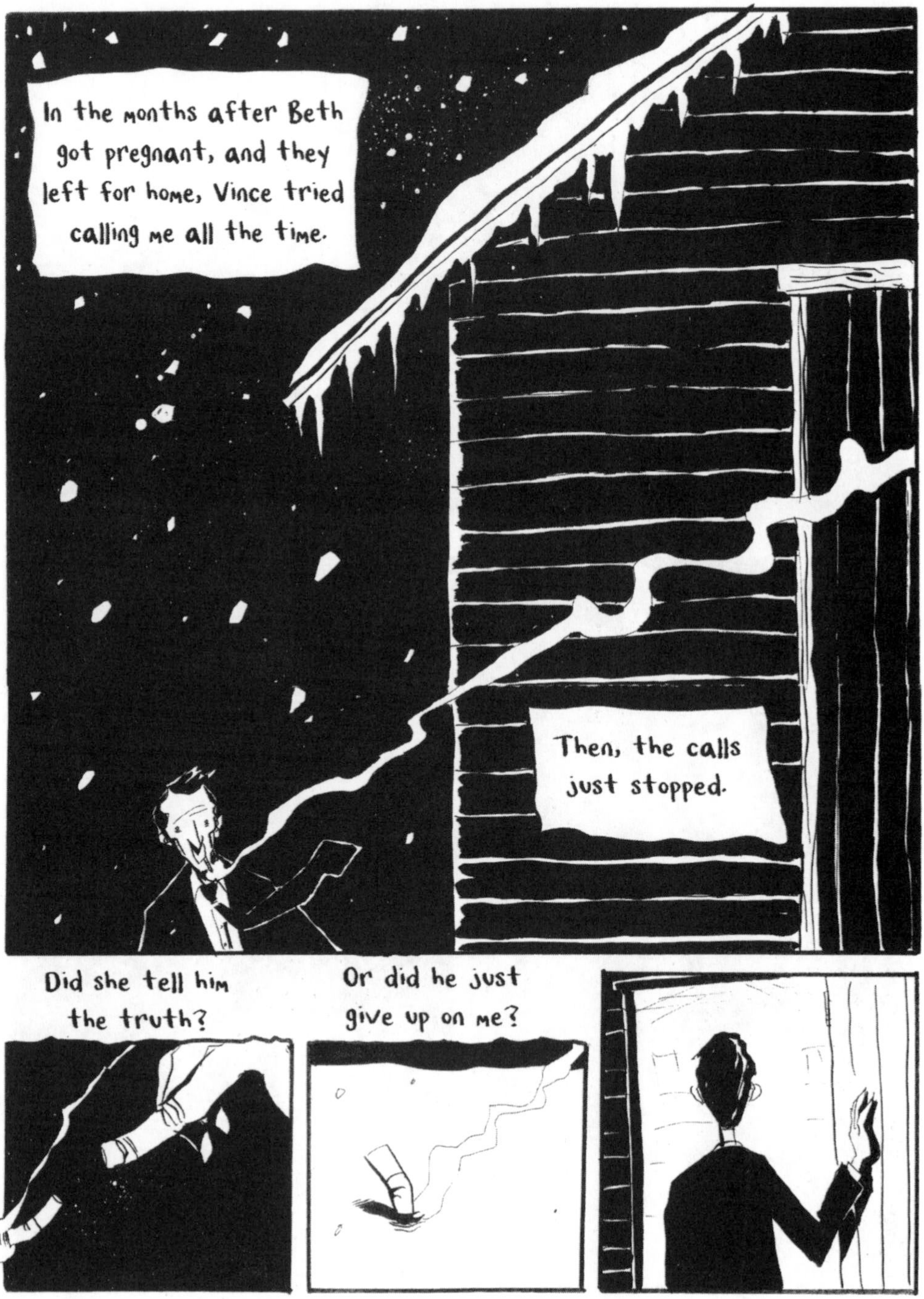
In the months after Beth got pregnant, and they left for home, Vince tried calling me all the time.
Then, the calls just stopped.
Did she tell him the truth?
Or did he just give up on me?

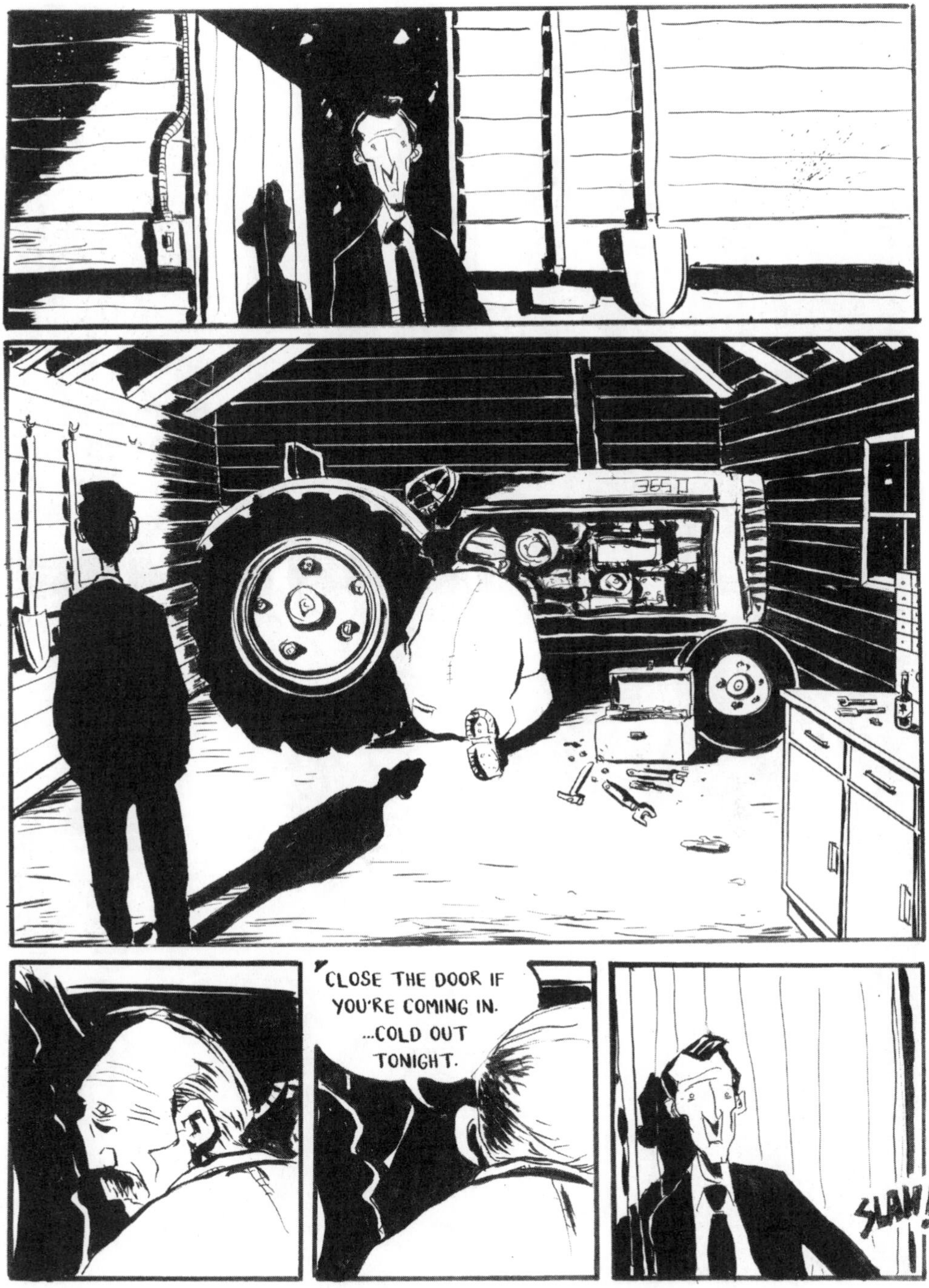
CLOSE THE DOOR IF YOU'RE COMING IN. ...COLD OUT TONIGHT.
SLAM!

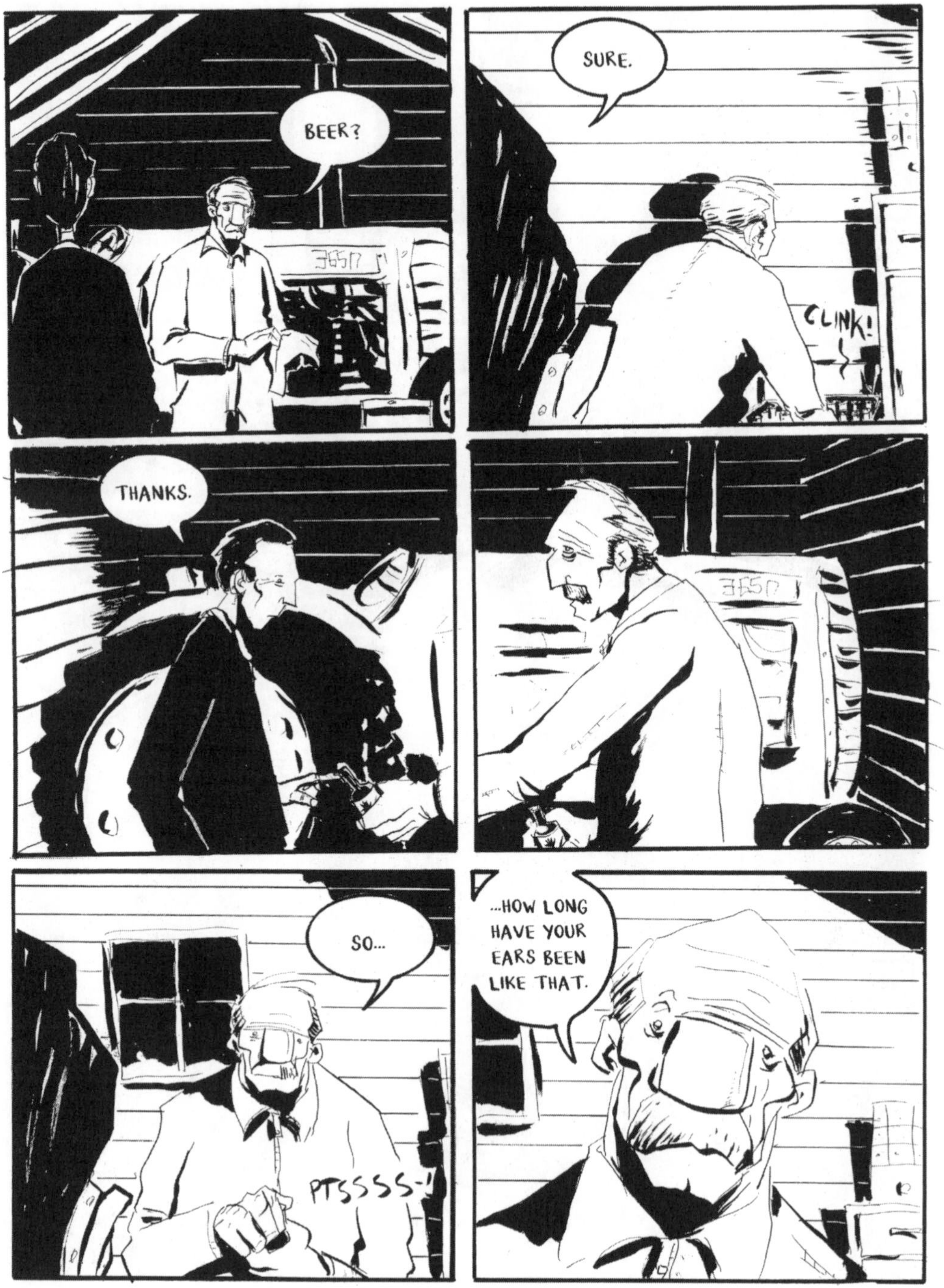
BEER?
SURE.
CLINK!
THANKS.
SO...
PTSSSS-!
...HOW LONG HAVE YOUR EARS BEEN LIKE THAT.

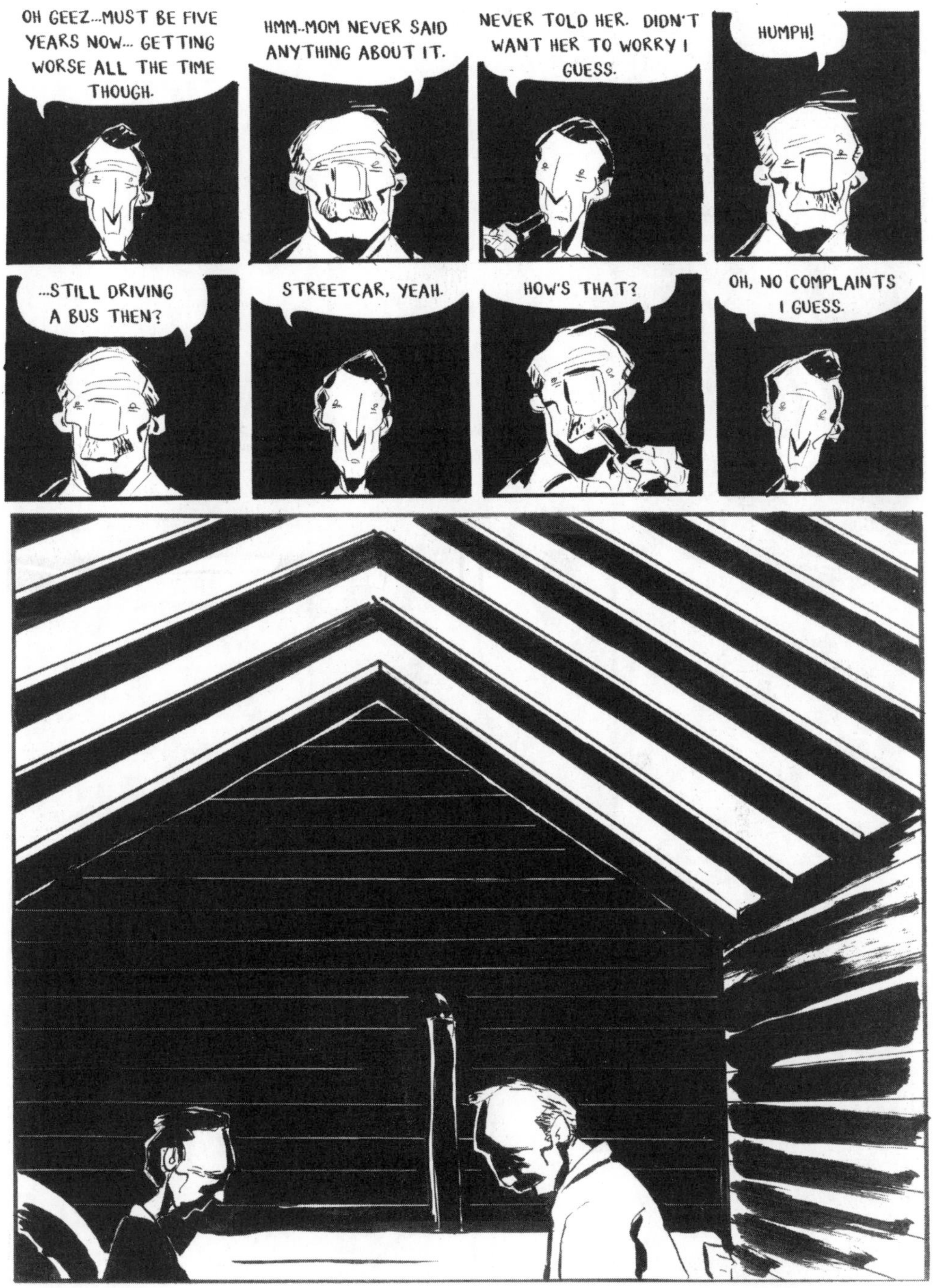
OH GEEZ...MUST BE FIVE YEARS NOW... GETTING WORSE ALL THE TIME THOUGH.
HMM..MOM NEVER SAID ANYTHING ABOUT IT.
NEVER TOLD HER. DIDN'T WANT HER TO WORRY I GUESS.
HUMPH!
...STILL DRIVING A BUS THEN?
STREETCAR, YEAH.
HOW'S THAT?
OH, NO COMPLAINTS I GUESS.

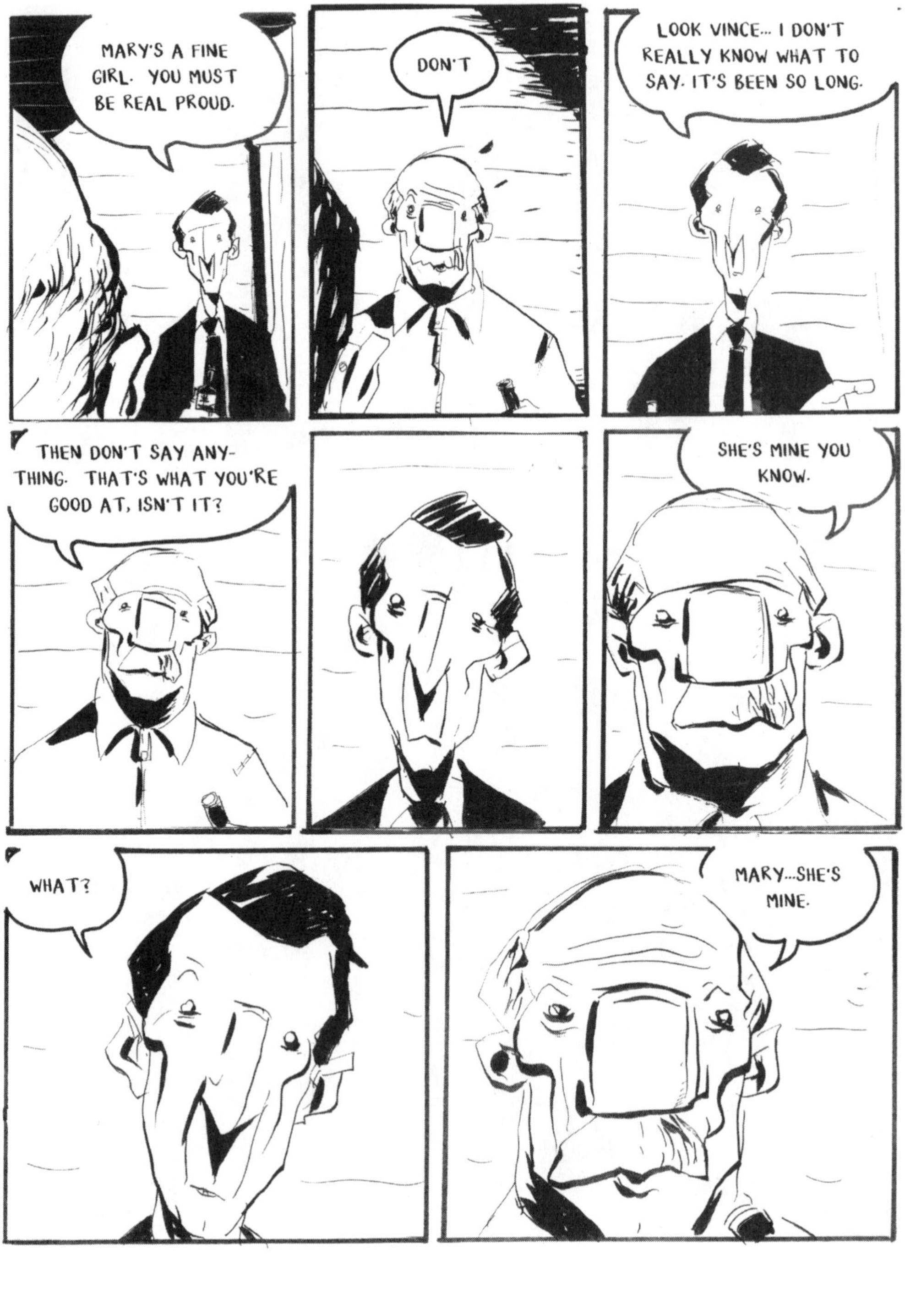

MARY'S A FINE GIRL. YOU MUST BE REAL PROUD.
DON'T
LOOK VINCE... I DON'T REALLY KNOW WHAT TO SAY. IT'S BEEN SO LONG.
THEN DON'T SAY ANYTHING. THAT'S WHAT YOU'RE GOOD AT, ISN'T IT?
SHE'S MINE YOU KNOW.
WHAT?
MARY...SHE'S MINE.

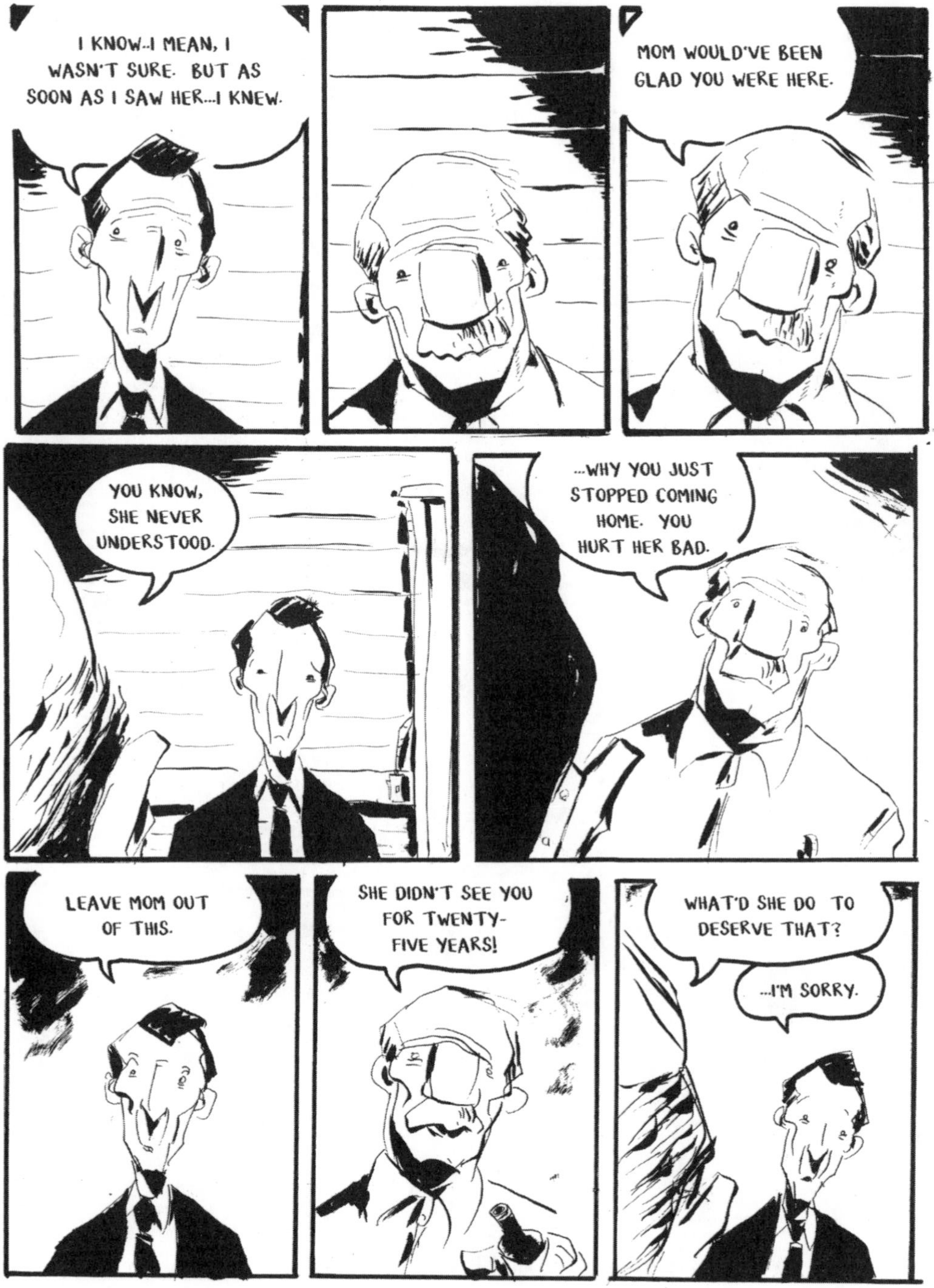
I KNOW..I MEAN, I WASN'T SURE. BUT AS SOON AS I SAW HER...I KNEW.
MOM WOULD'VE BEEN GLAD YOU WERE HERE.
YOU KNOW, SHE NEVER UNDERSTOOD.
...WHY YOU JUST STOPPED COMING HOME. YOU HURT HER BAD.
LEAVE MOM OUT OF THIS.
SHE DIDN'T SEE YOU FOR TWENTY-FIVE YEARS!
WHAT'D SHE DO TO DESERVE THAT?
...I'M SORRY.

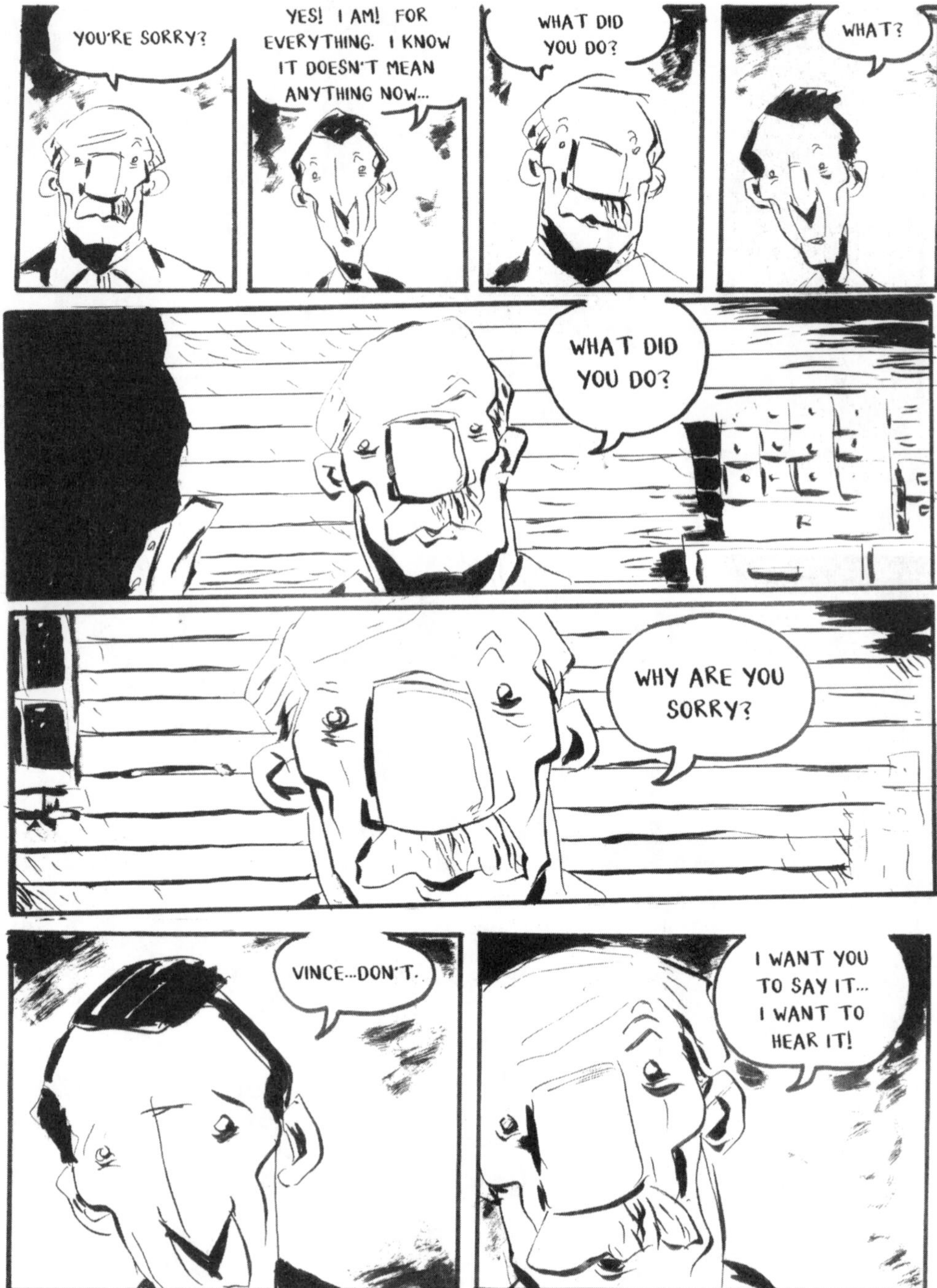
YOU'RE SORRY?
YES! I AM! FOR EVERYTHING. I KNOW IT DOESN'T MEAN ANYTHING NOW...
WHAT DID YOU DO?
WHAT?
WHAT DID YOU DO?
WHY ARE YOU SORRY?
VINCE...DON'T.
I WANT YOU TO SAY IT... I WANT TO HEAR IT!

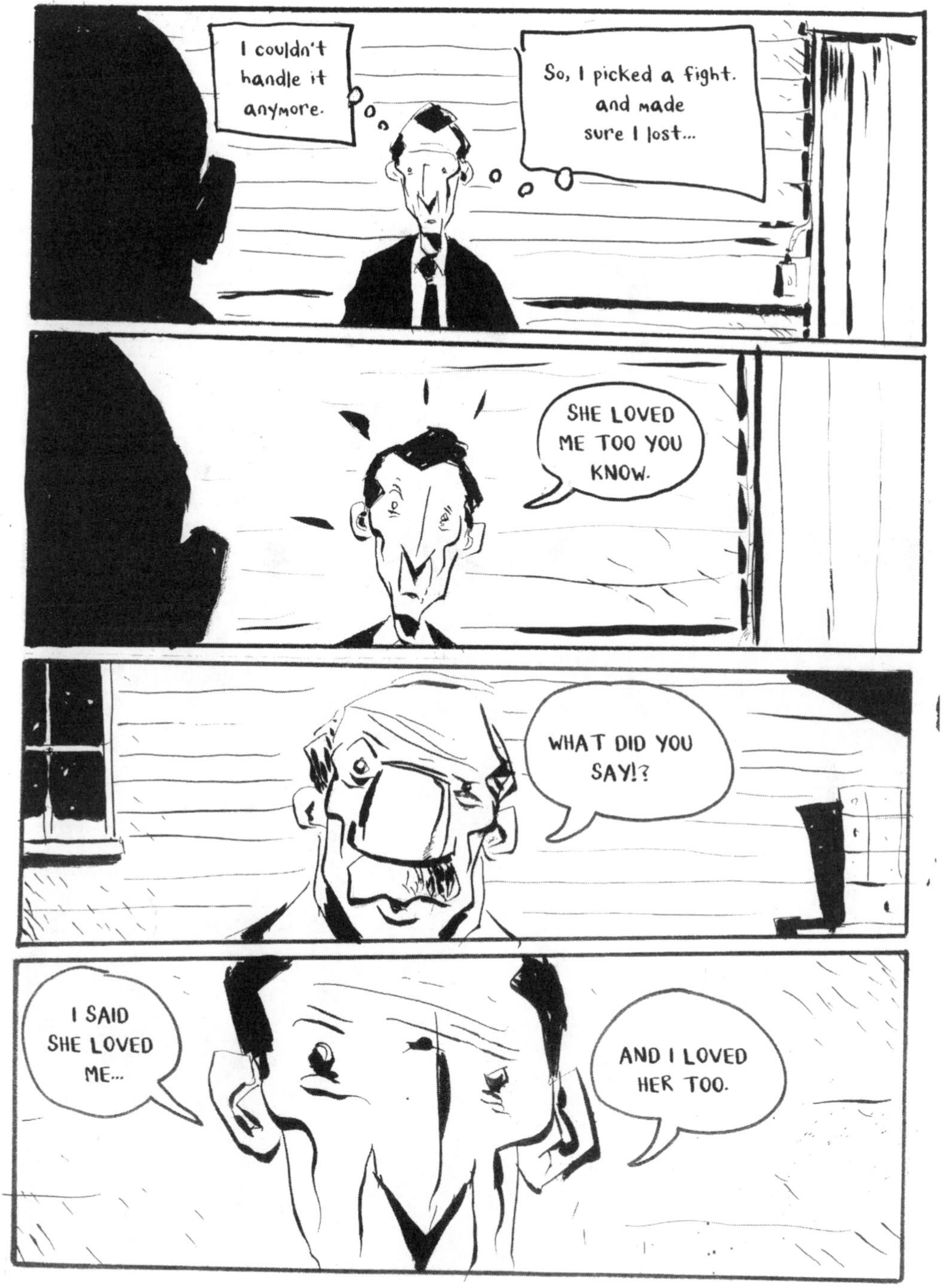
I couldn't handle it anymore.
So, I picked a fight. and made sure I lost...
SHE LOVED ME TOO YOU KNOW.
WHAT DID YOU SAY!?
I SAID SHE LOVED ME...
AND I LOVED HER TOO.

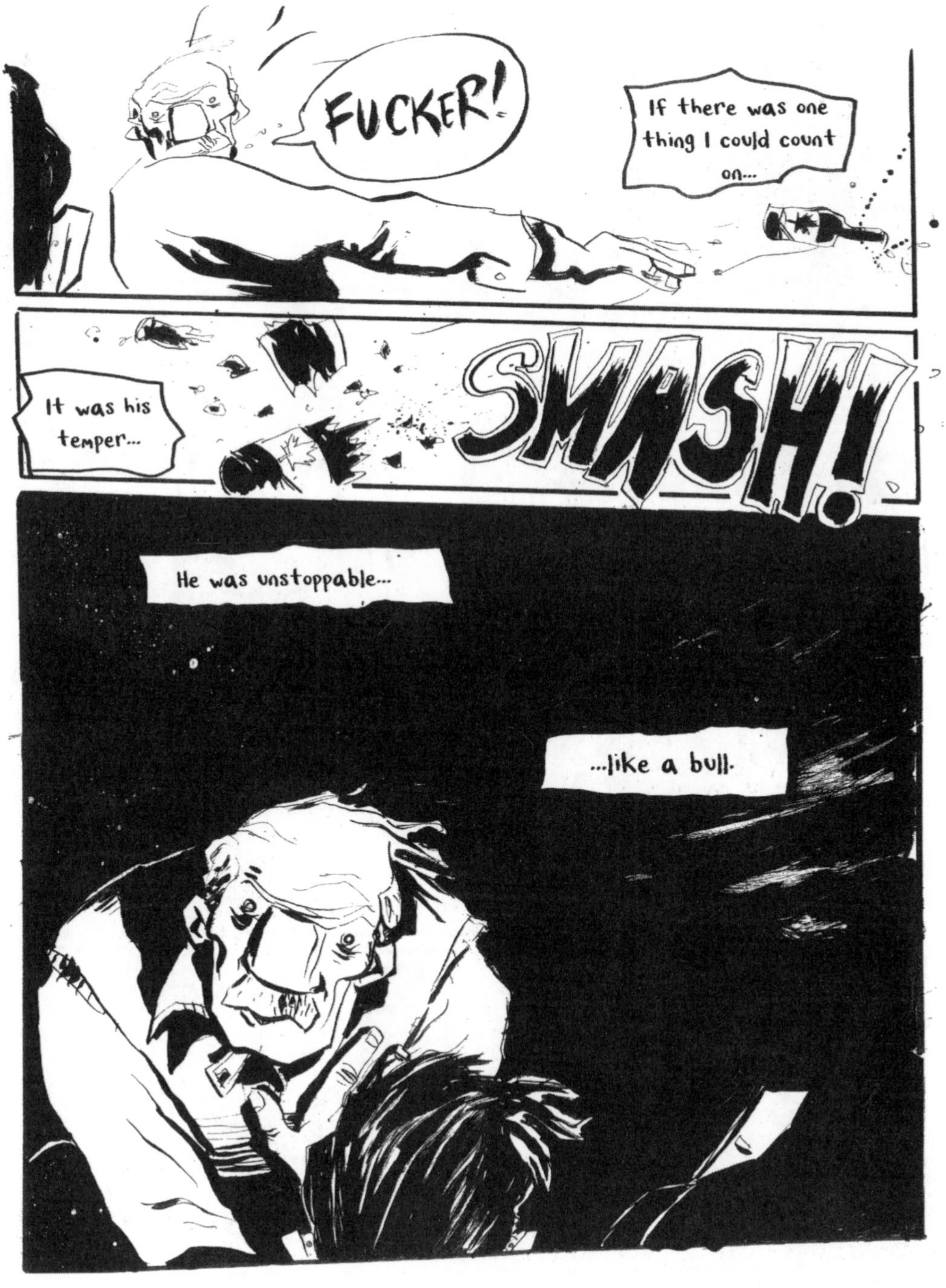
FUCKER!
If there was one thing I could count on...
It was his temper...
SMASH!
He was unstoppable...
...like a bull.

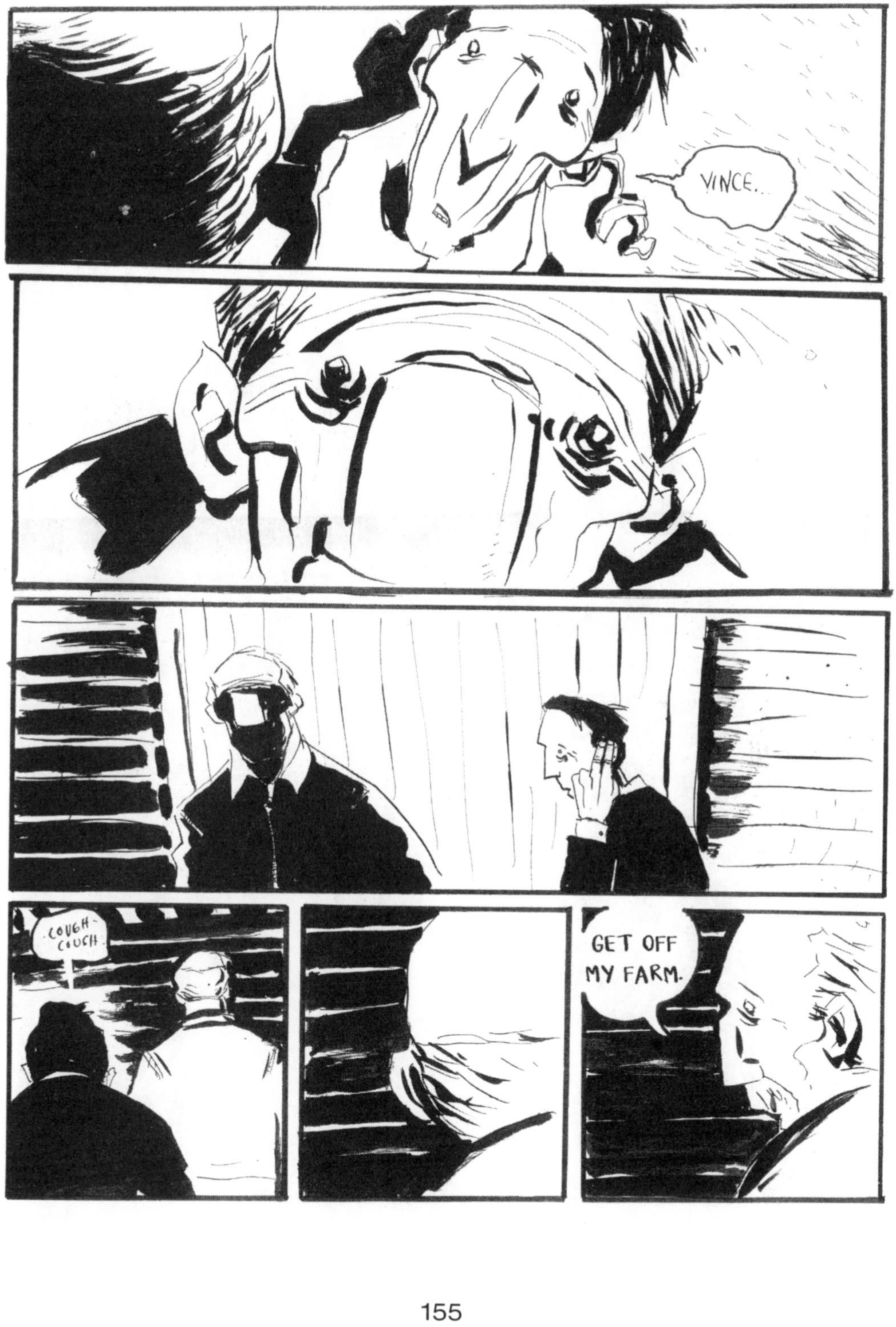
VINCE..
COUGH-
COUGH
GET OFF
MY FARM.

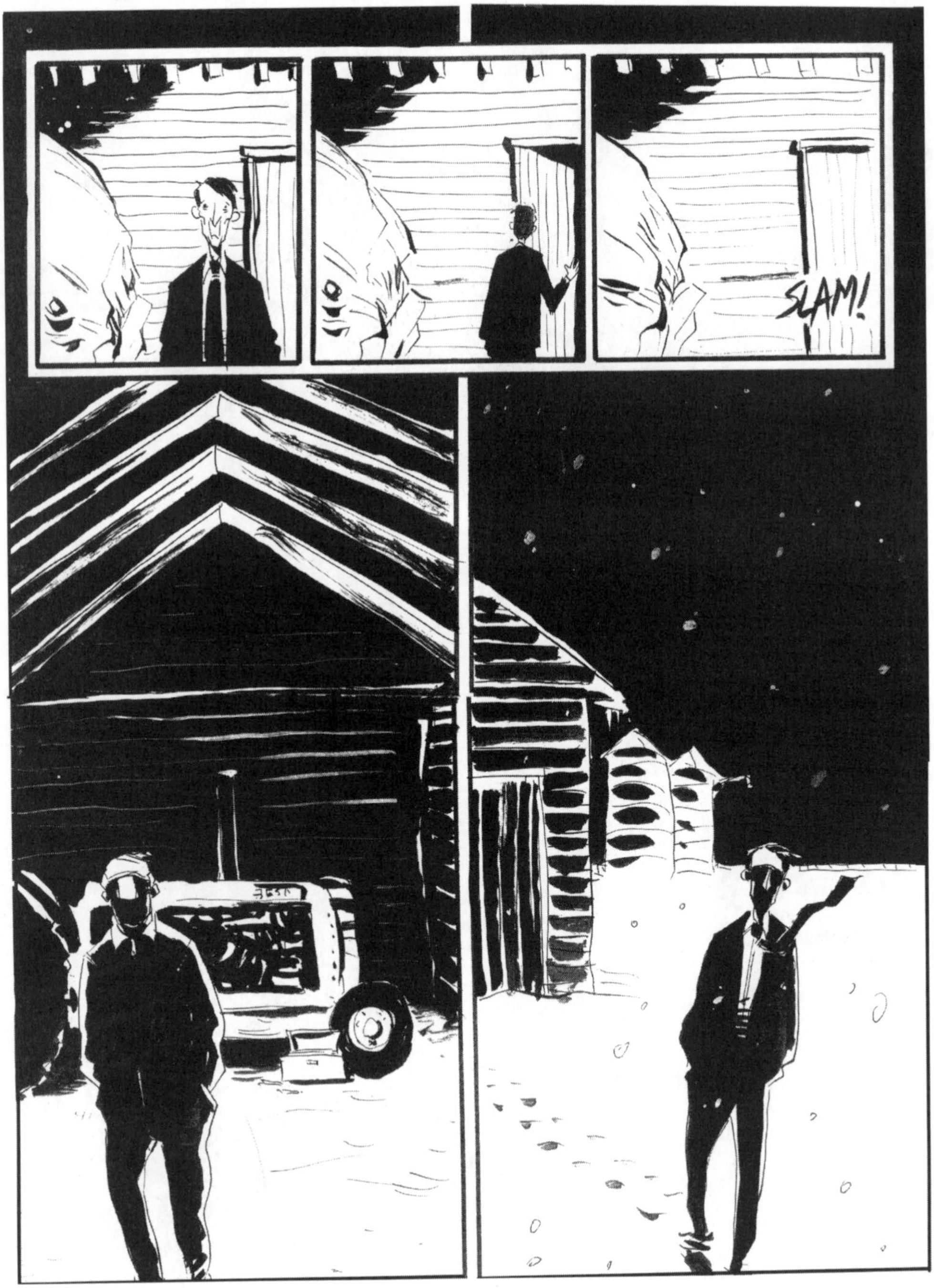
SLAM!

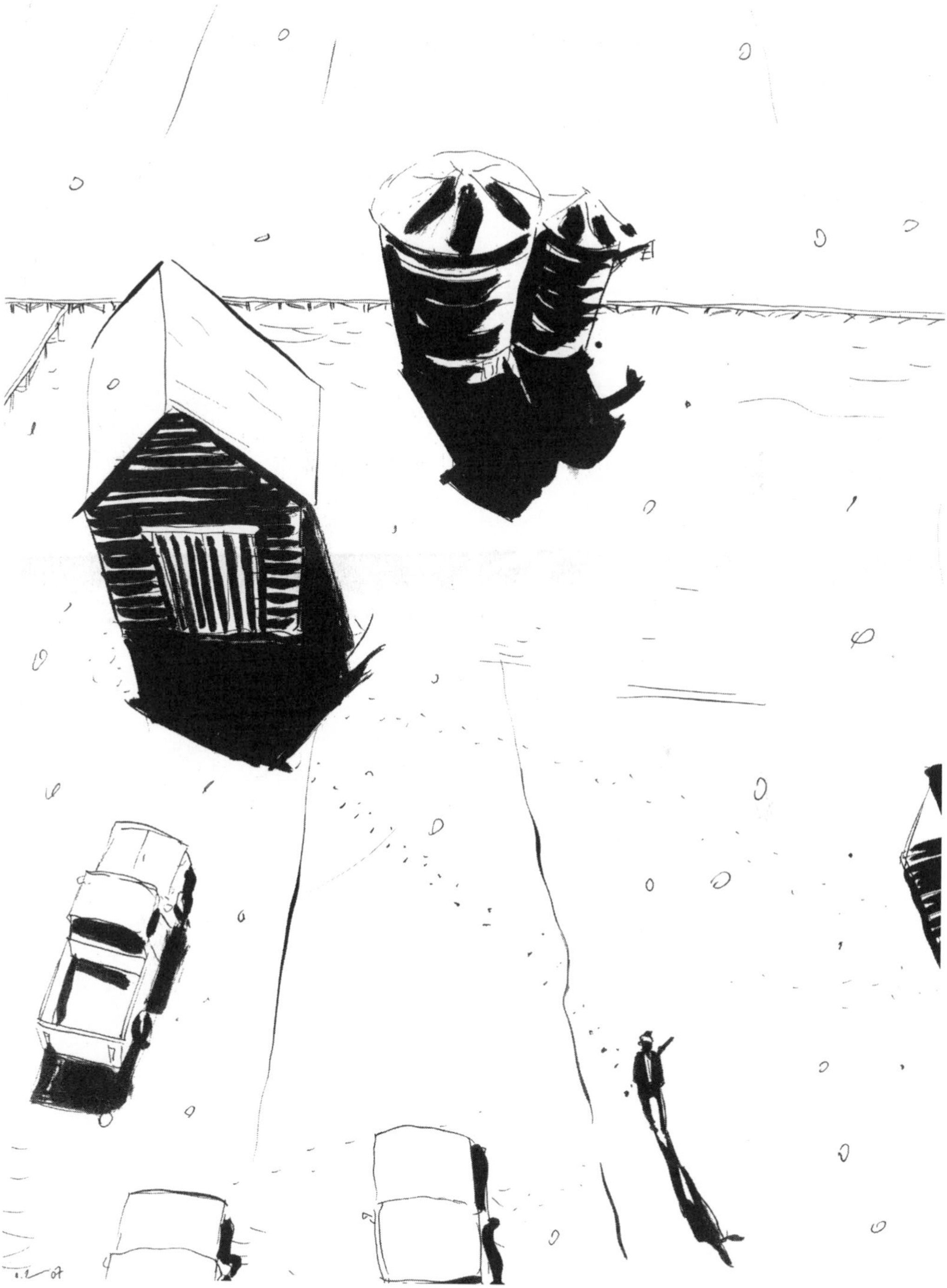

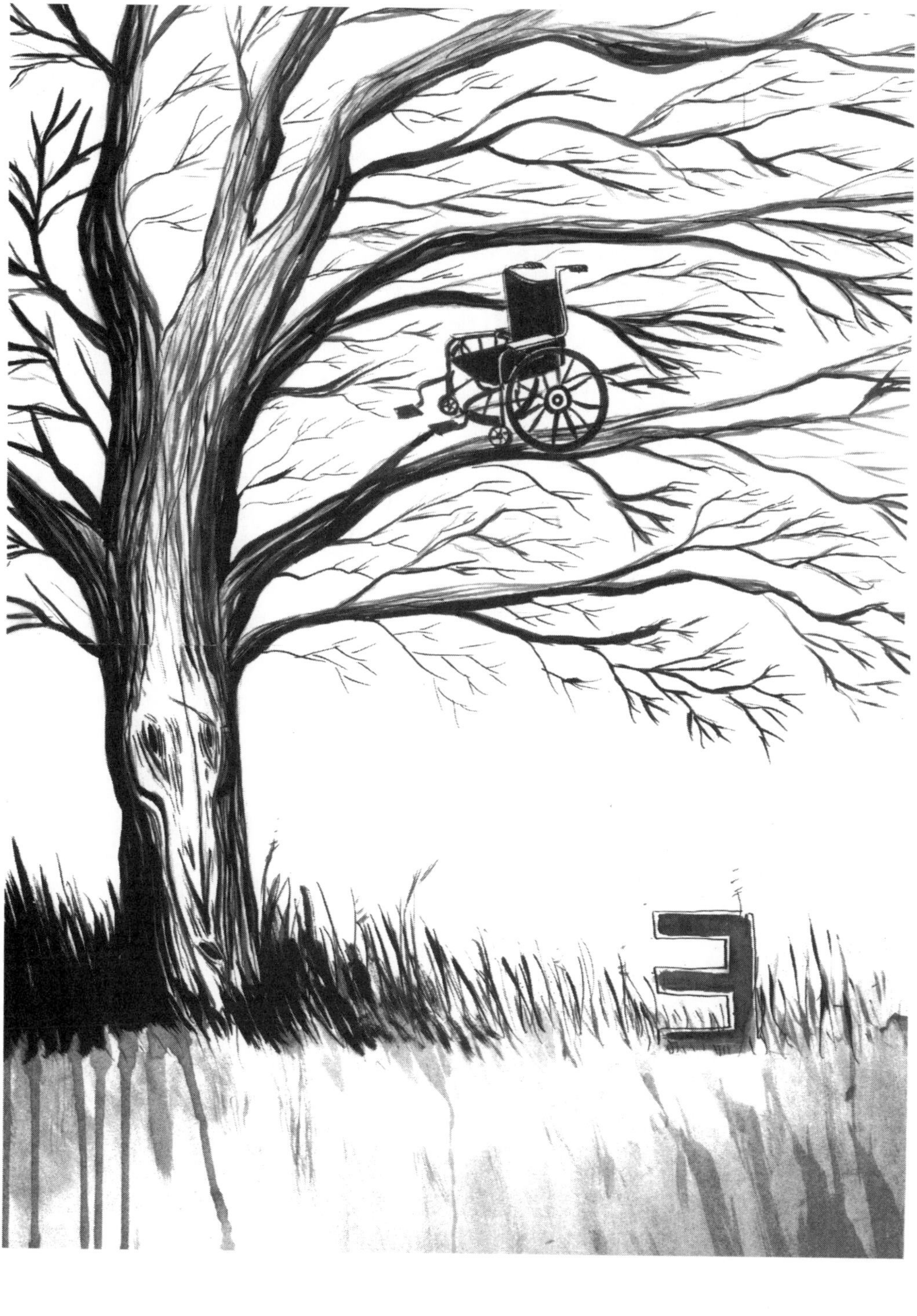

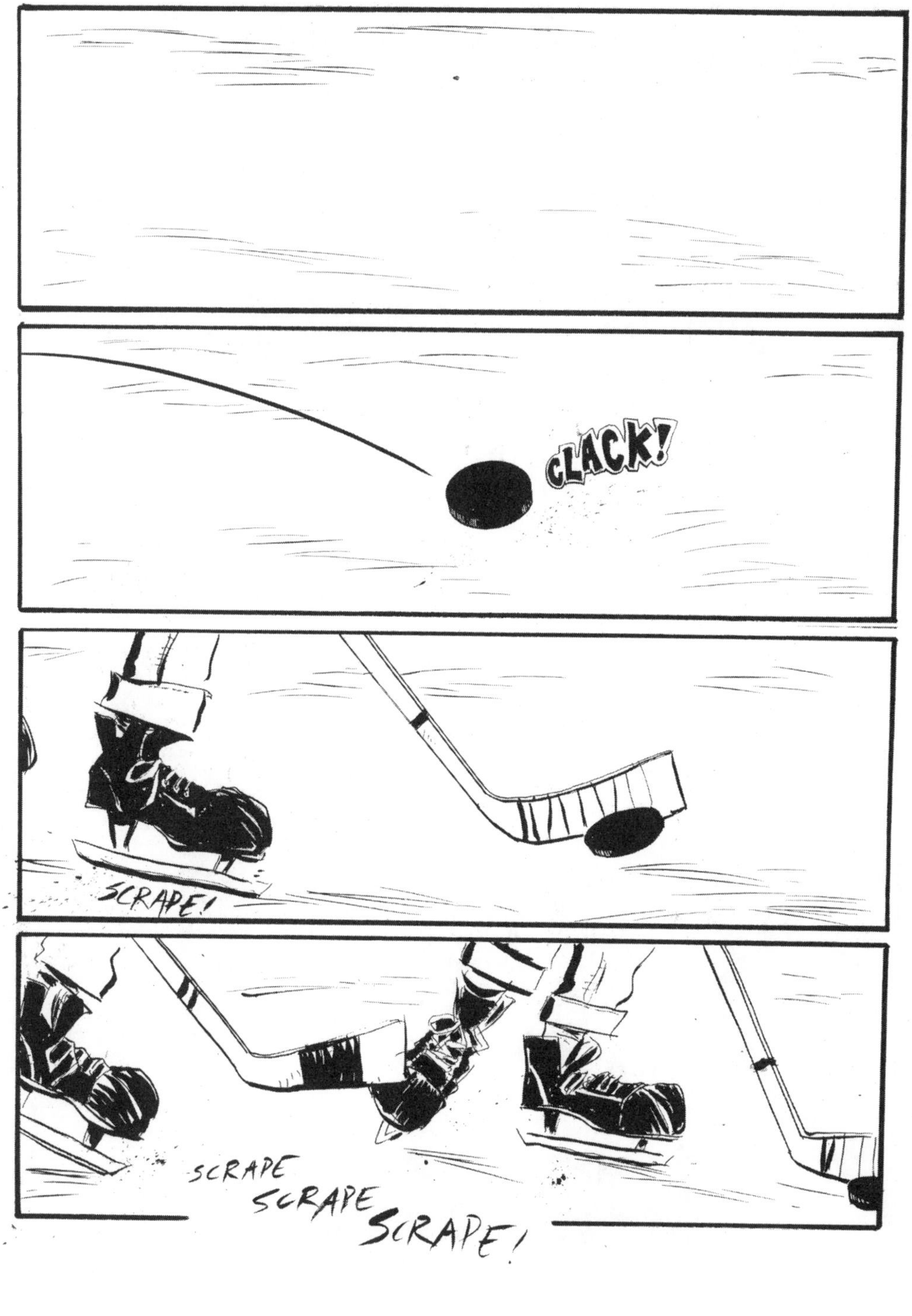
CLACK!
SCRAPE!
SCRAPE
SCRAPE
SCRAPE!

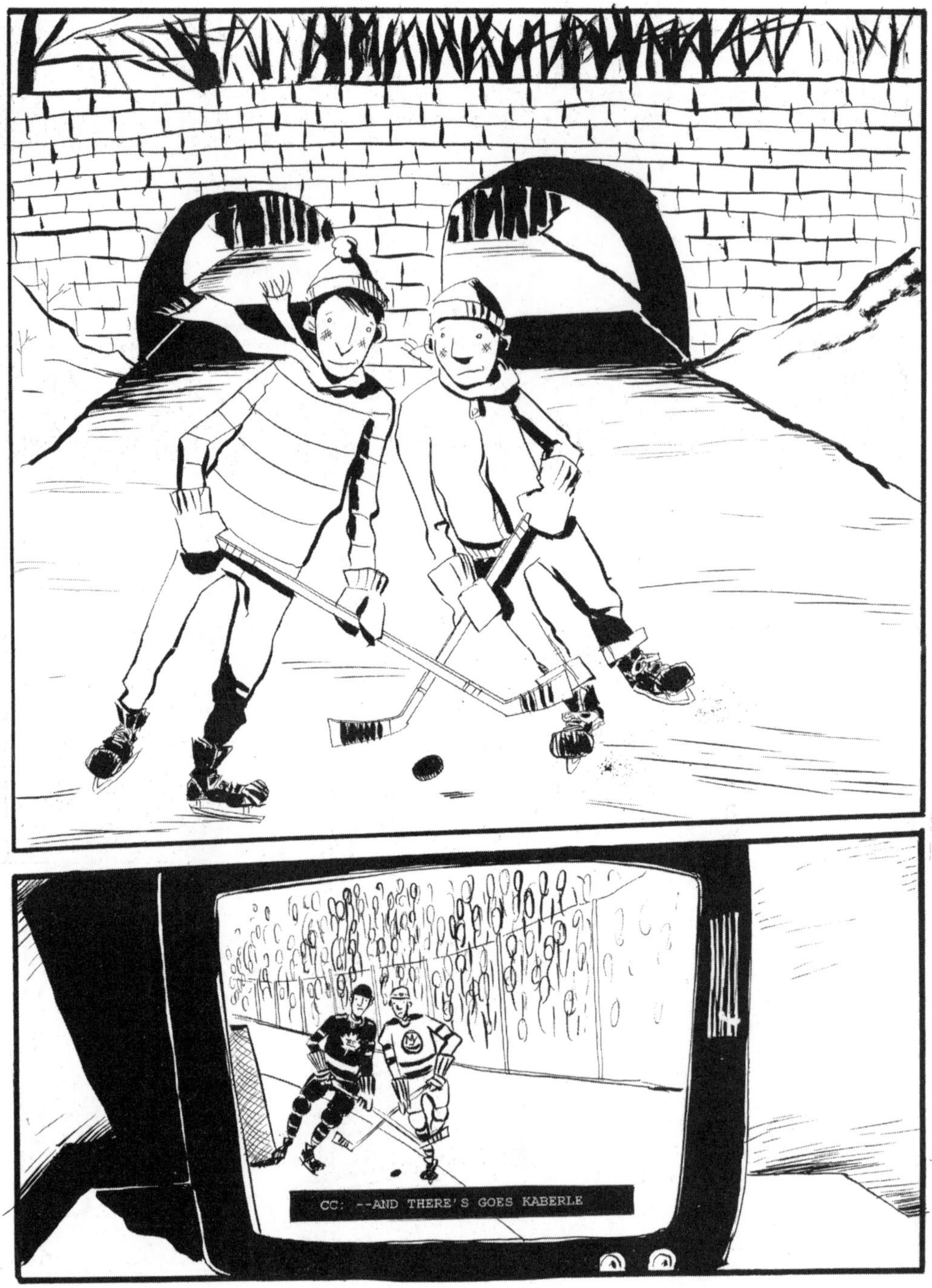
CC: --AND THERE'S GOES KABERLE

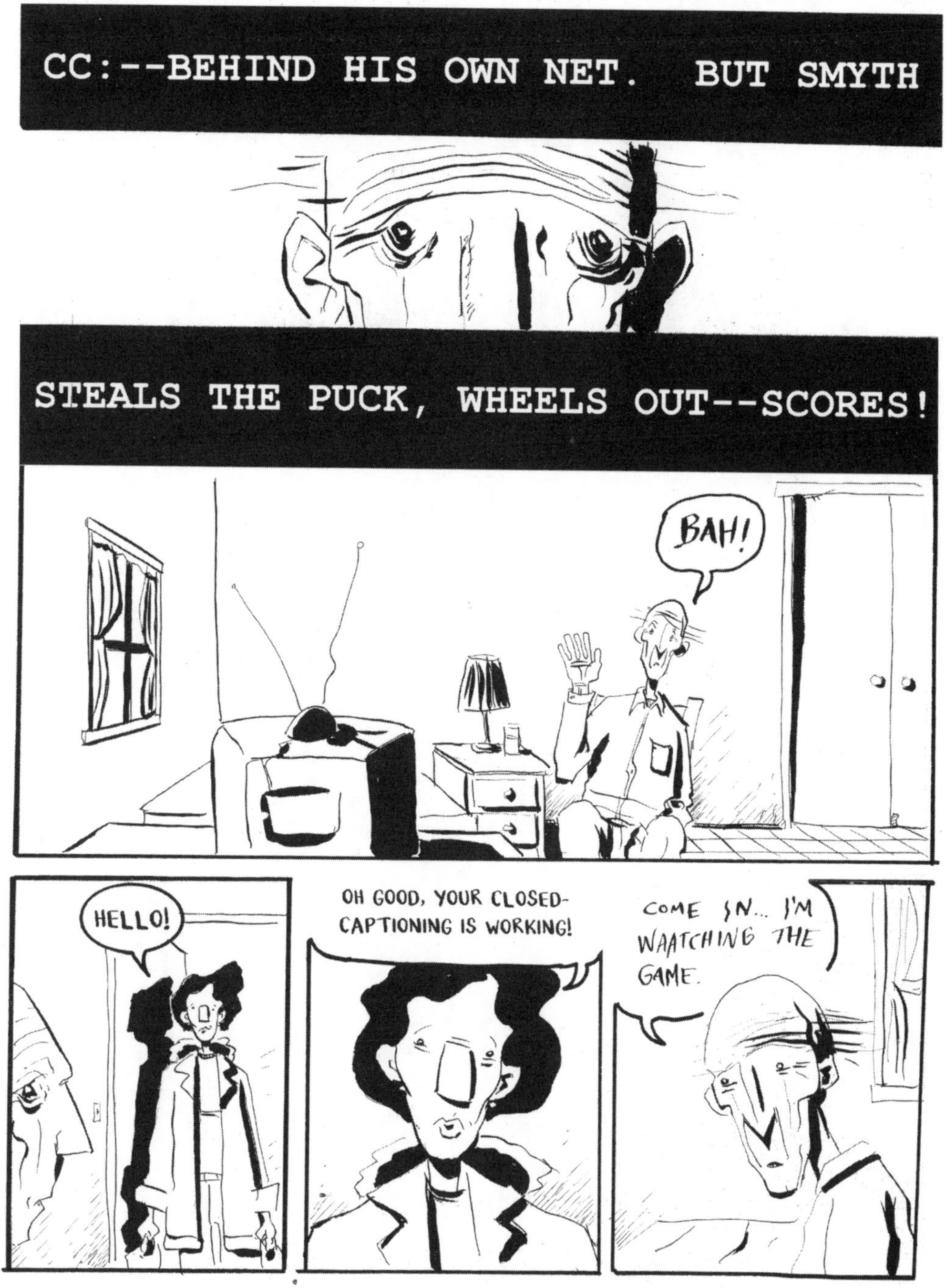
CC:--BEHIND HIS OWN NET. BUT SMYTH
STEALS THE PUCK, WHEELS OUT--SCORES!
BAH!
HELLO!
OH GOOD, YOUR CLOSED-CAPTIONING IS WORKING!
COME IN... I'M WAATCHING THE GAME.

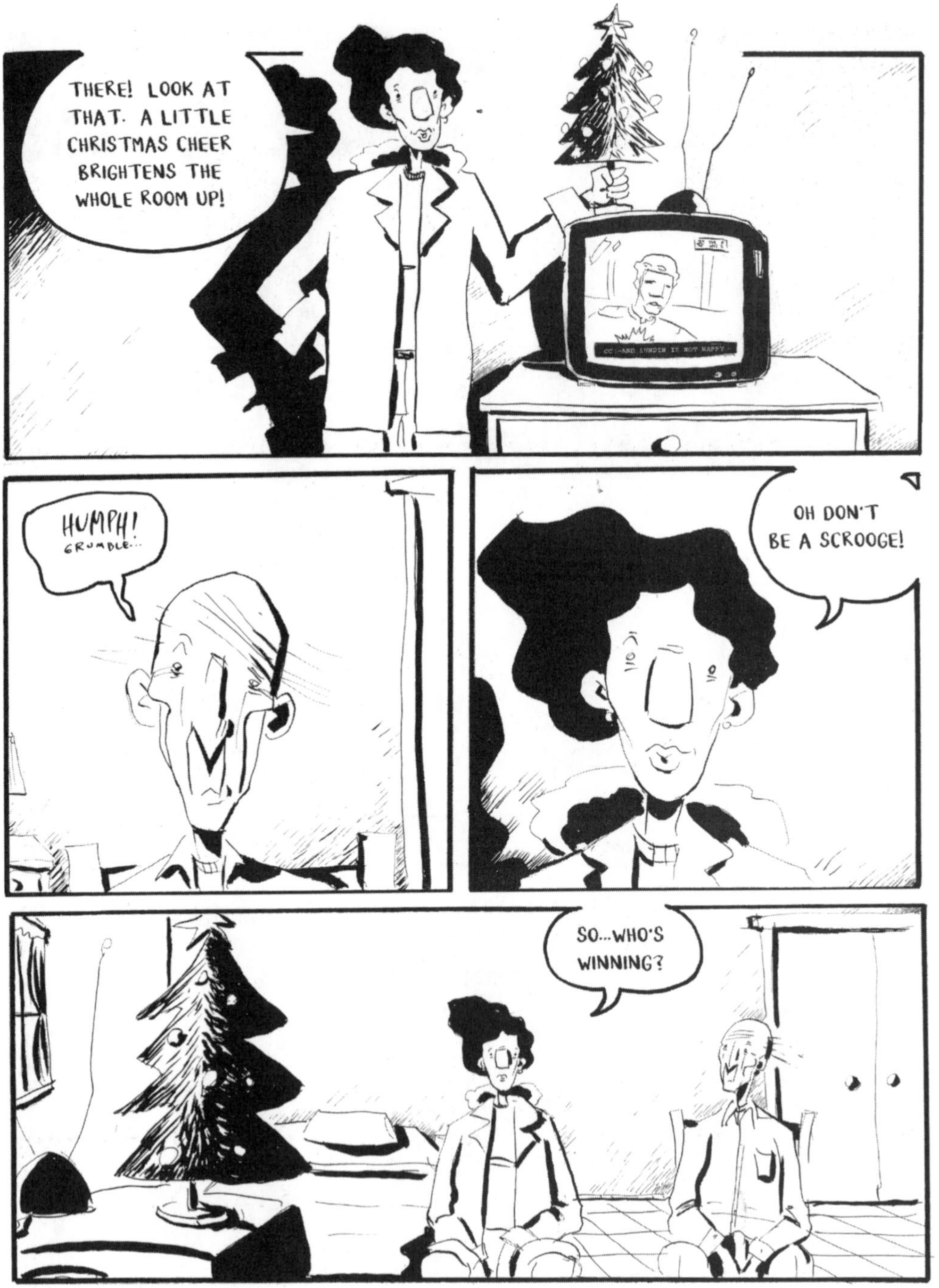
THERE! LOOK AT THAT. A LITTLE CHRISTMAS CHEER BRIGHTENS THE WHOLE ROOM UP!
CC:-AND SUNDIN IS NOT HAPPY
HUMPH!
GRUMBLE...
OH DON'T BE A SCROOGE!
SO...WHO'S WINNING?

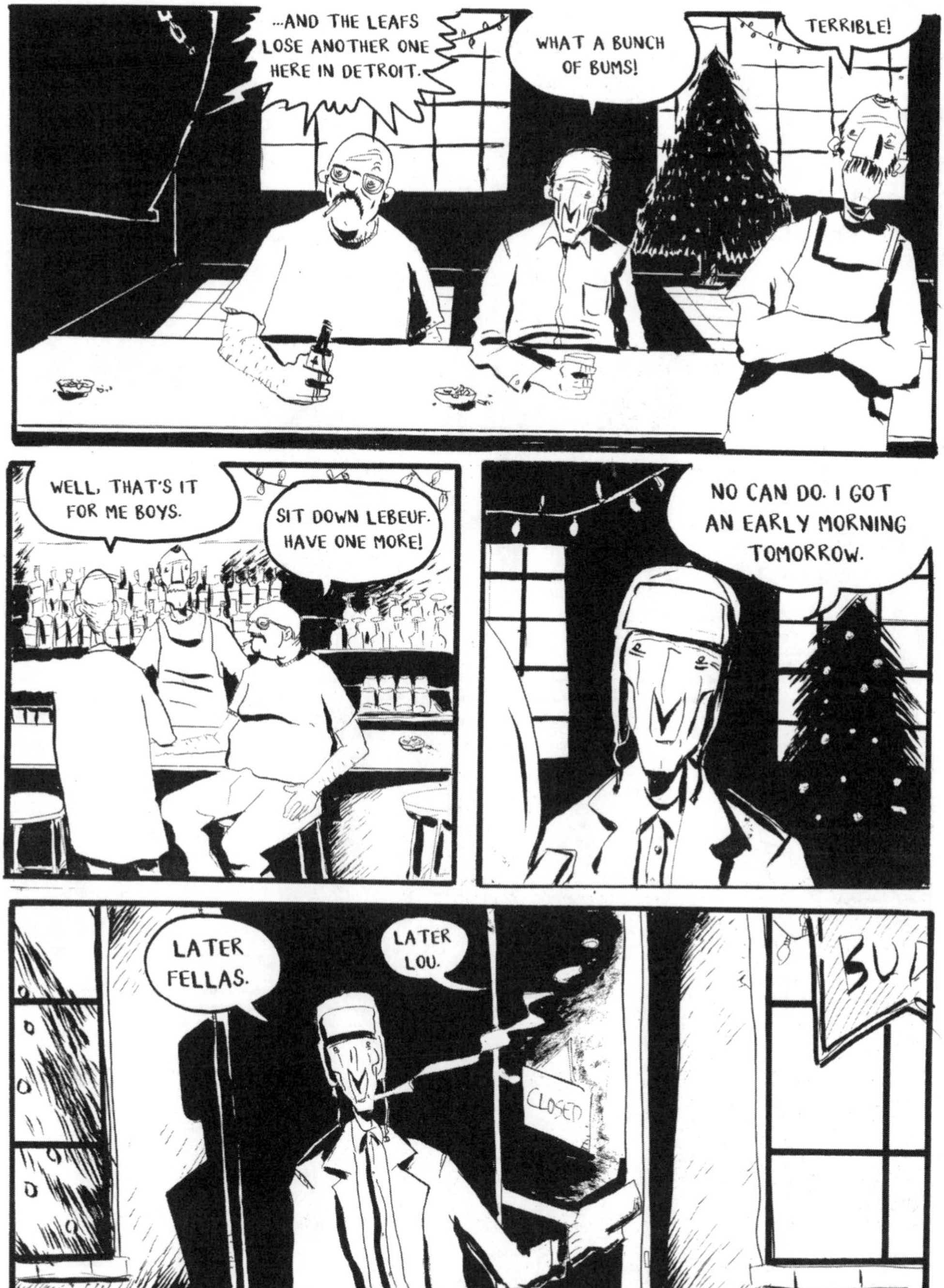
...AND THE LEAFS LOSE ANOTHER ONE HERE IN DETROIT.
WHAT A BUNCH OF BUMS!
TERRIBLE!
WELL, THAT'S IT FOR ME BOYS.
SIT DOWN LEBEUF. HAVE ONE MORE!
NO CAN DO. I GOT AN EARLY MORNING TOMORROW.
LATER FELLAS.
LATER LOU.
CLOSED

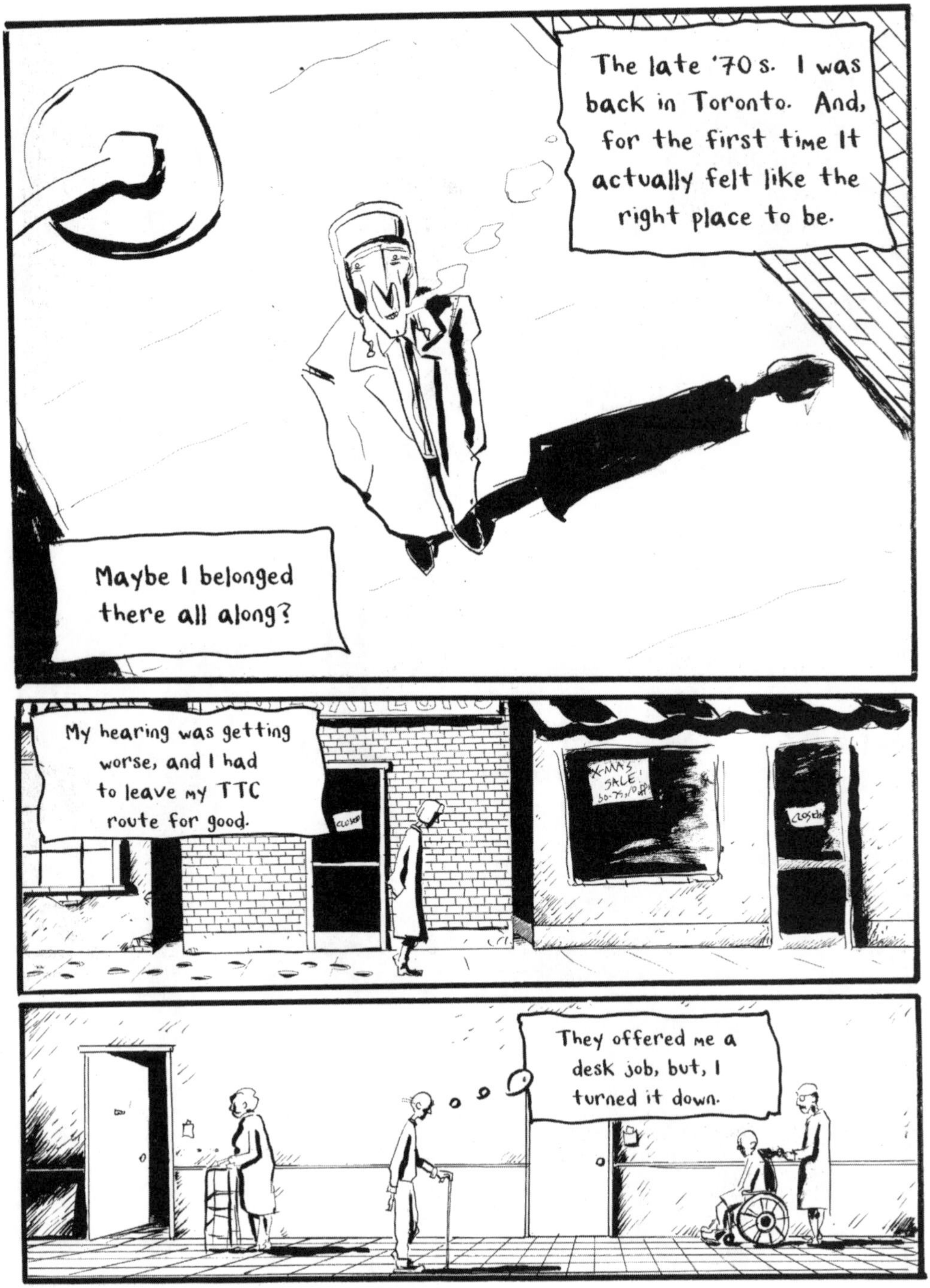
The late '70s. I was back in Toronto. And, for the first time It actually felt like the right place to be.
Maybe I belonged there all along?
My hearing was getting worse, and I had to leave my TTC route for good.
X-MAS SALE!
CLOSED
CLOSED
They offered me a desk job, but, I turned it down.

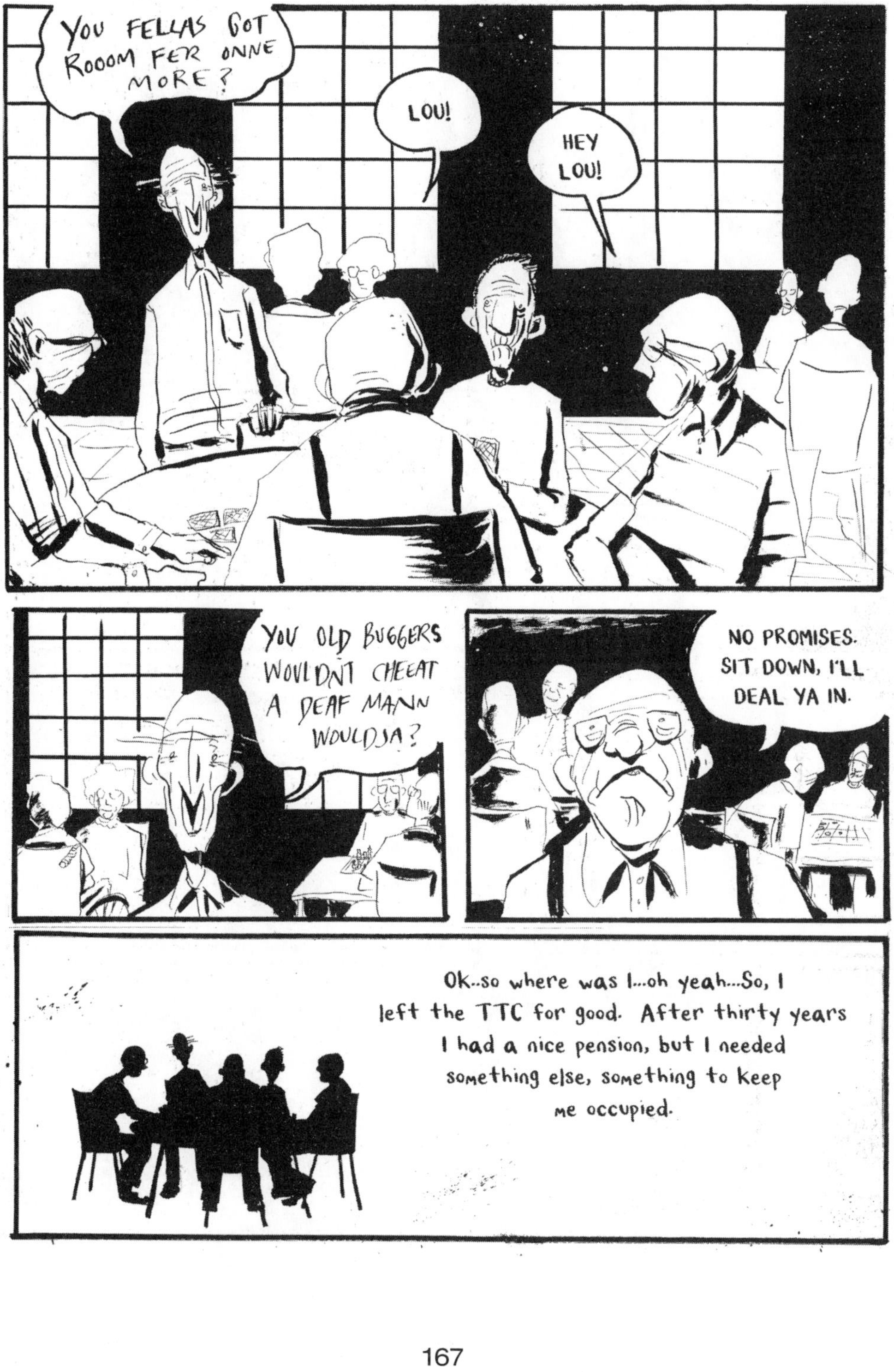
YOU FELLAS GOT ROOOM FER ONNE MORE?
LOU!
HEY LOU!
YOU OLD BUGGERS WOULDN'T CHEEAT A DEAF MANN WOULDJA?
NO PROMISES. SIT DOWN, I'LL DEAL YA IN.
Ok..so where was I...oh yeah...So, I left the TTC for good. After thirty years I had a nice pension, but I needed something else, something to keep me occupied.

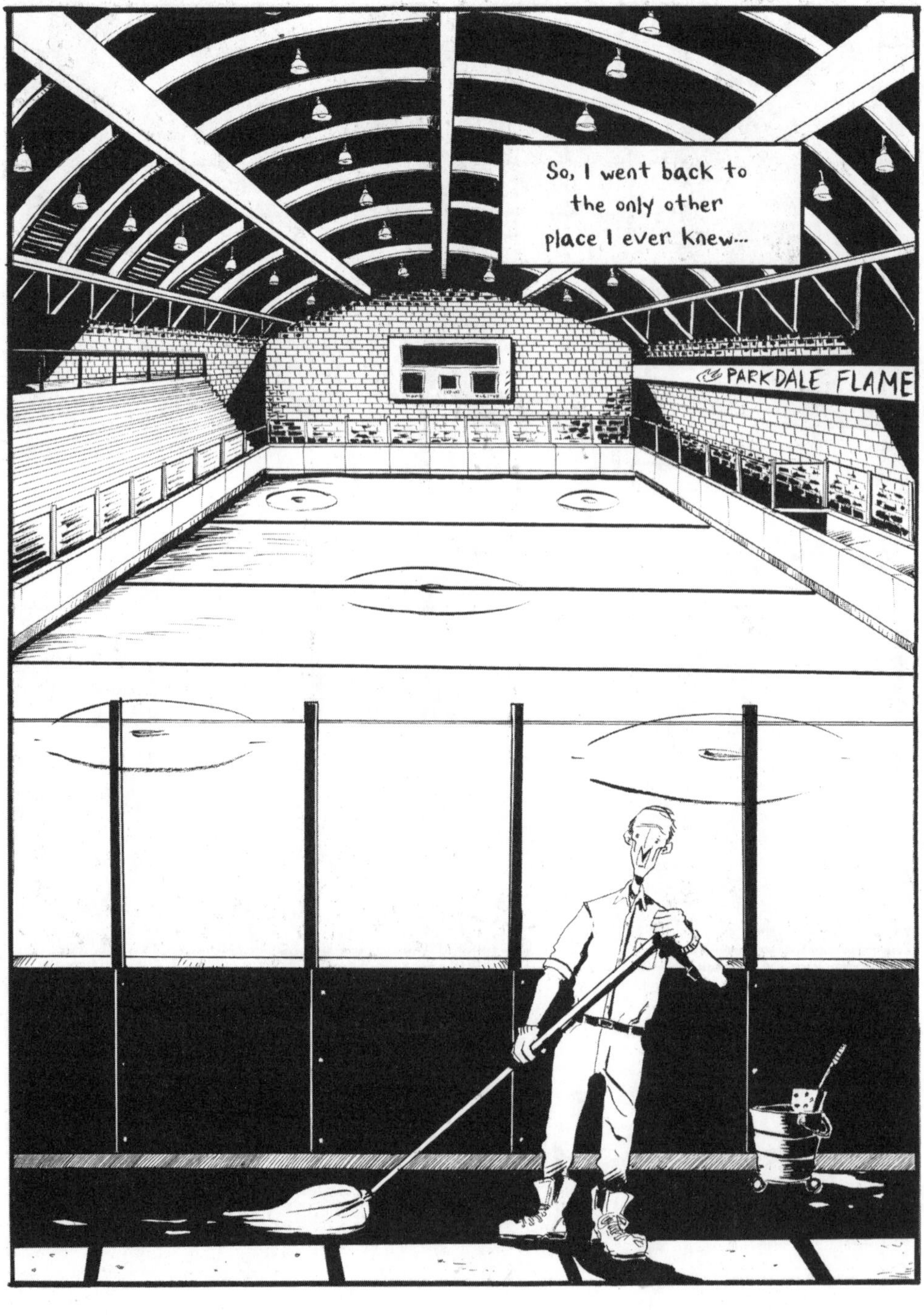
So, I went back to the only other place I ever knew...
PARKDALE FLAME

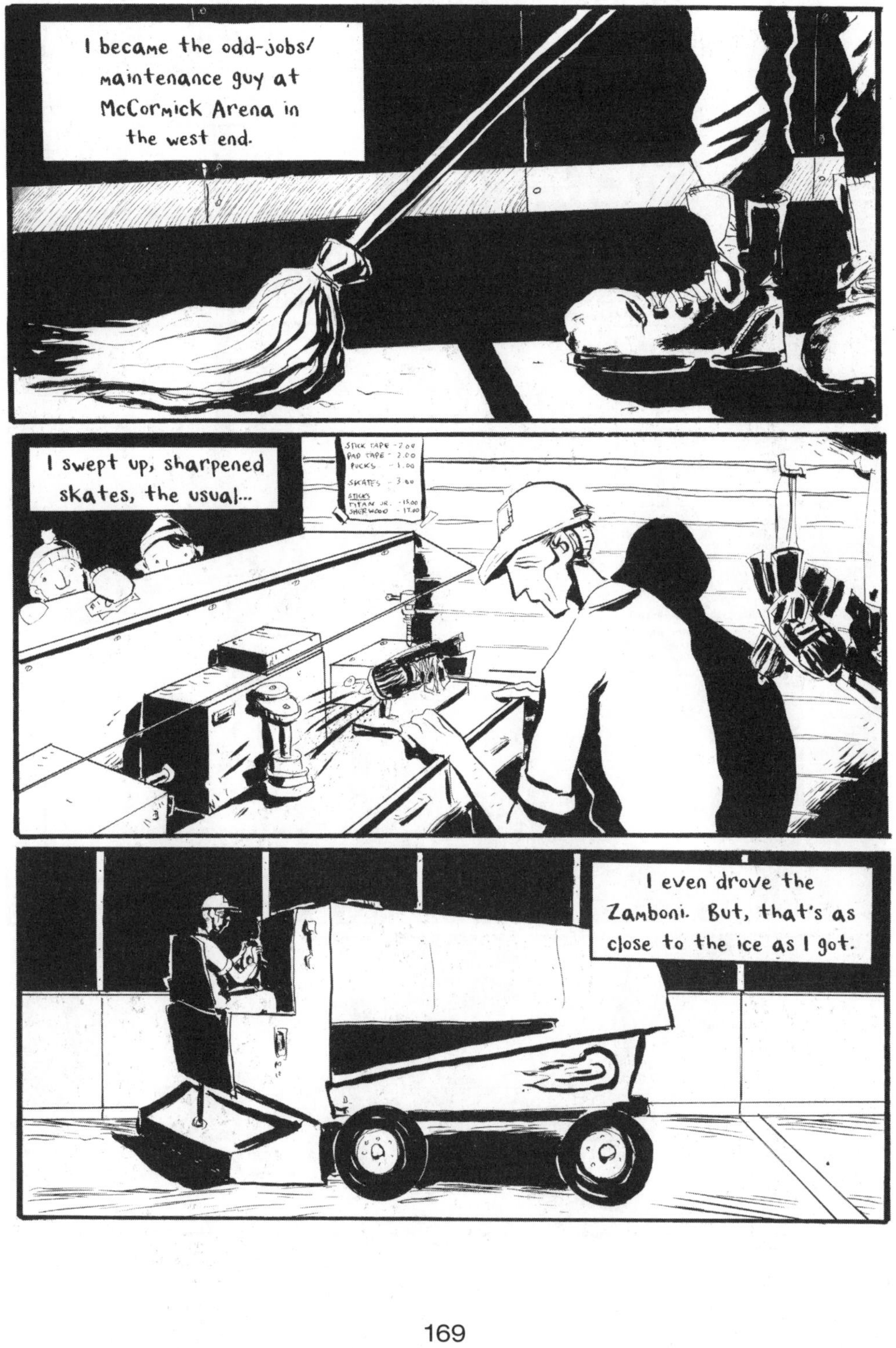
I became the odd-jobs/ maintenance guy at McCormick Arena in the west end.
I swept up, sharpened skates, the usual...
STICK TAPE - 2.00
PAD TAPE - 2.00
PUCKS - 1.00
SKATES - 3.00
STICKS
TITAN JR. - 15.00
SHERWOOD - 17.00
I even drove the Zamboni. But, that's as close to the ice as I got.

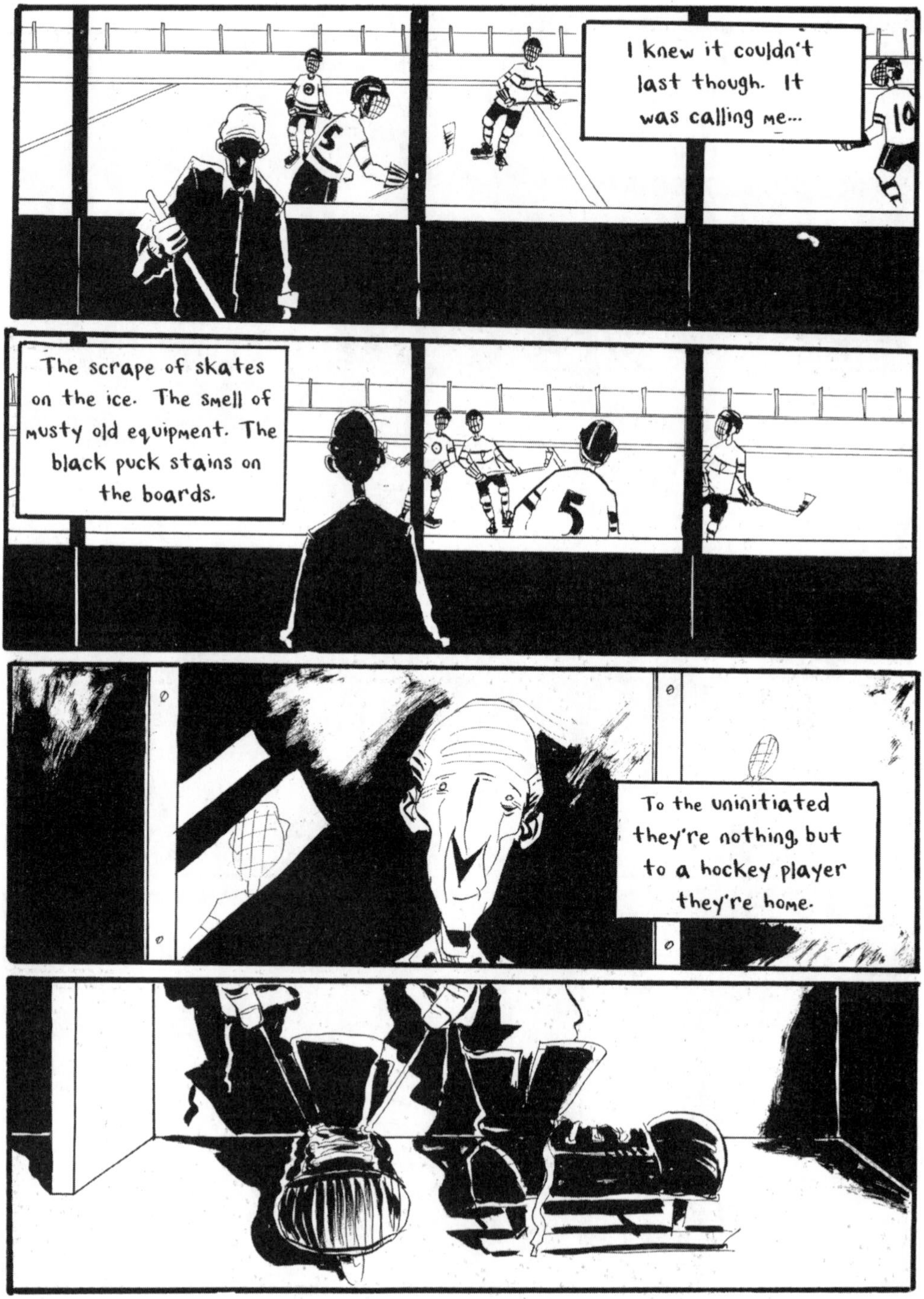
I knew it couldn't last though. It was calling me...
The scrape of skates on the ice. The smell of musty old equipment. The black puck stains on the boards.
To the uninitiated they're nothing, but to a hockey player they're home.

One Sunday morning I snuck out early, before the Peewee game.

I had a ratty old pair of skates, and a new stick I'd bought at Canadian Tire.

SCPAPE!

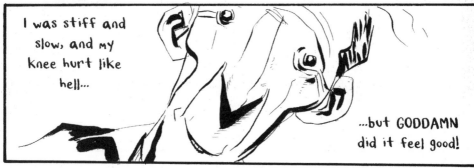

I was stiff and slow, and my knee hurt like hell...

...but GODDAMN did it feel good!

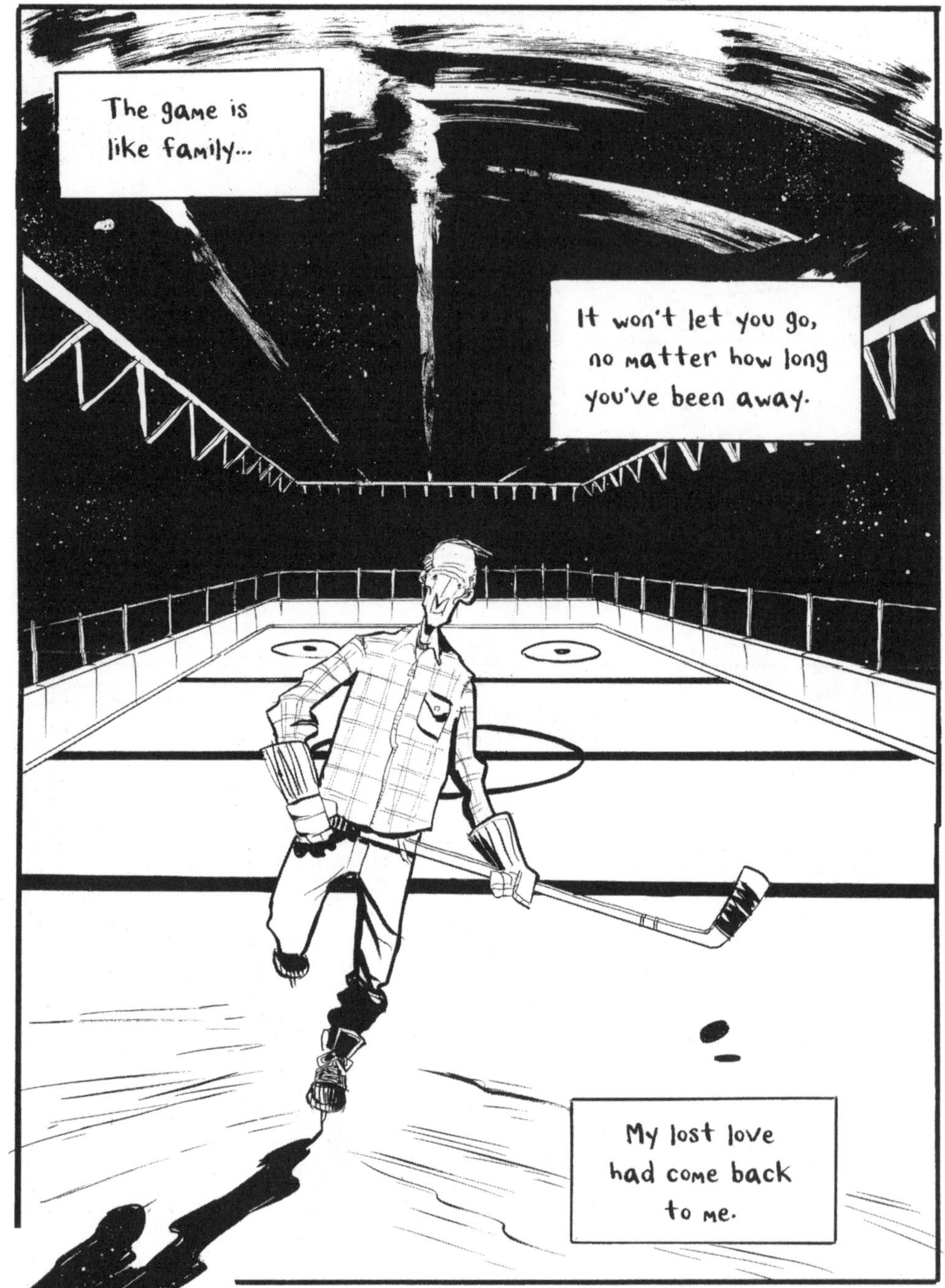
The game is like family...
It won't let you go, no matter how long you've been away.
My lost love had come back to me.

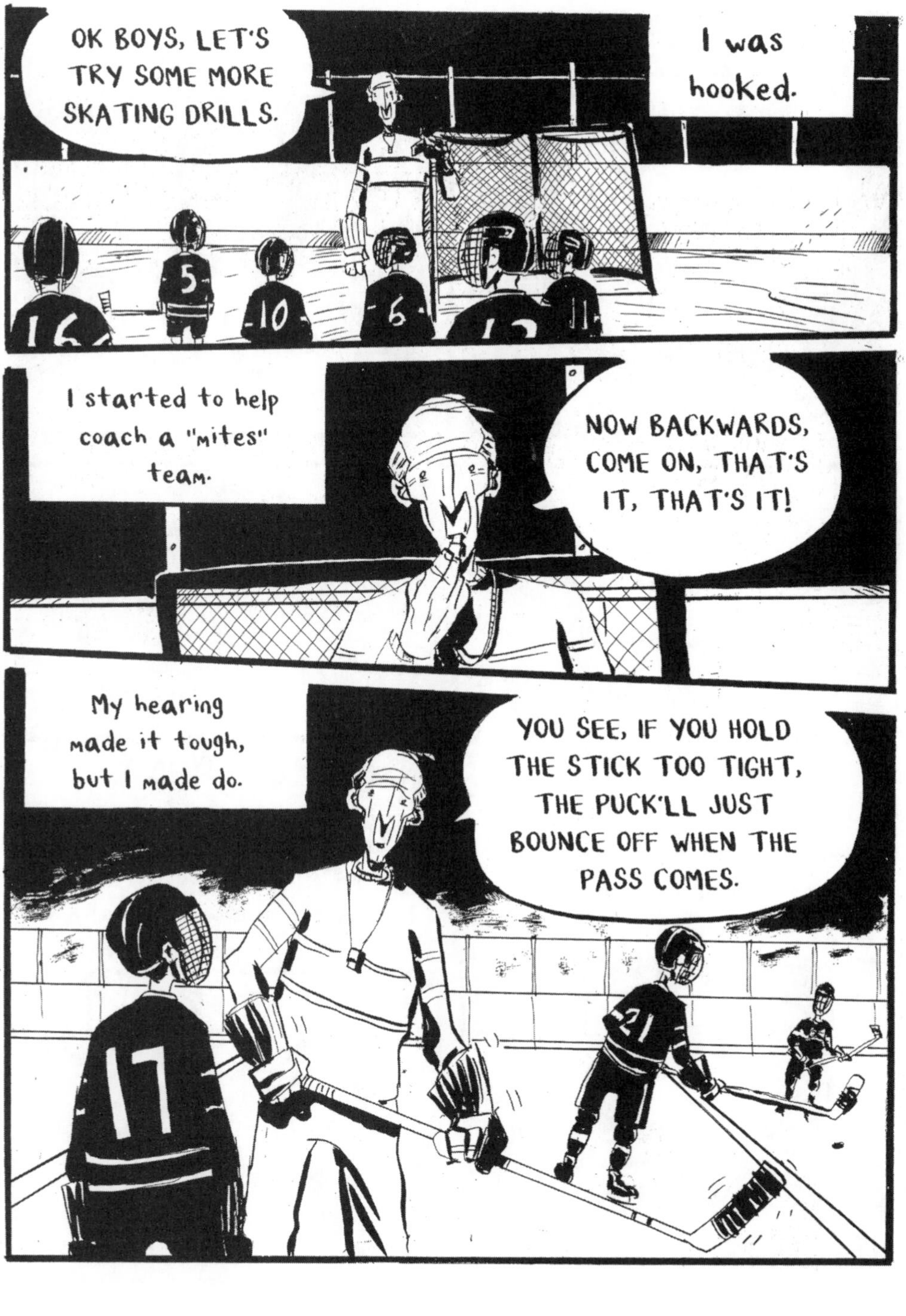
OK BOYS, LET'S TRY SOME MORE SKATING DRILLS.
I was hooked.
I started to help coach a "mites" team.
NOW BACKWARDS, COME ON, THAT'S IT, THAT'S IT!
My hearing made it tough, but I made do.
YOU SEE, IF YOU HOLD THE STICK TOO TIGHT, THE PUCK'LL JUST BOUNCE OFF WHEN THE PASS COMES.

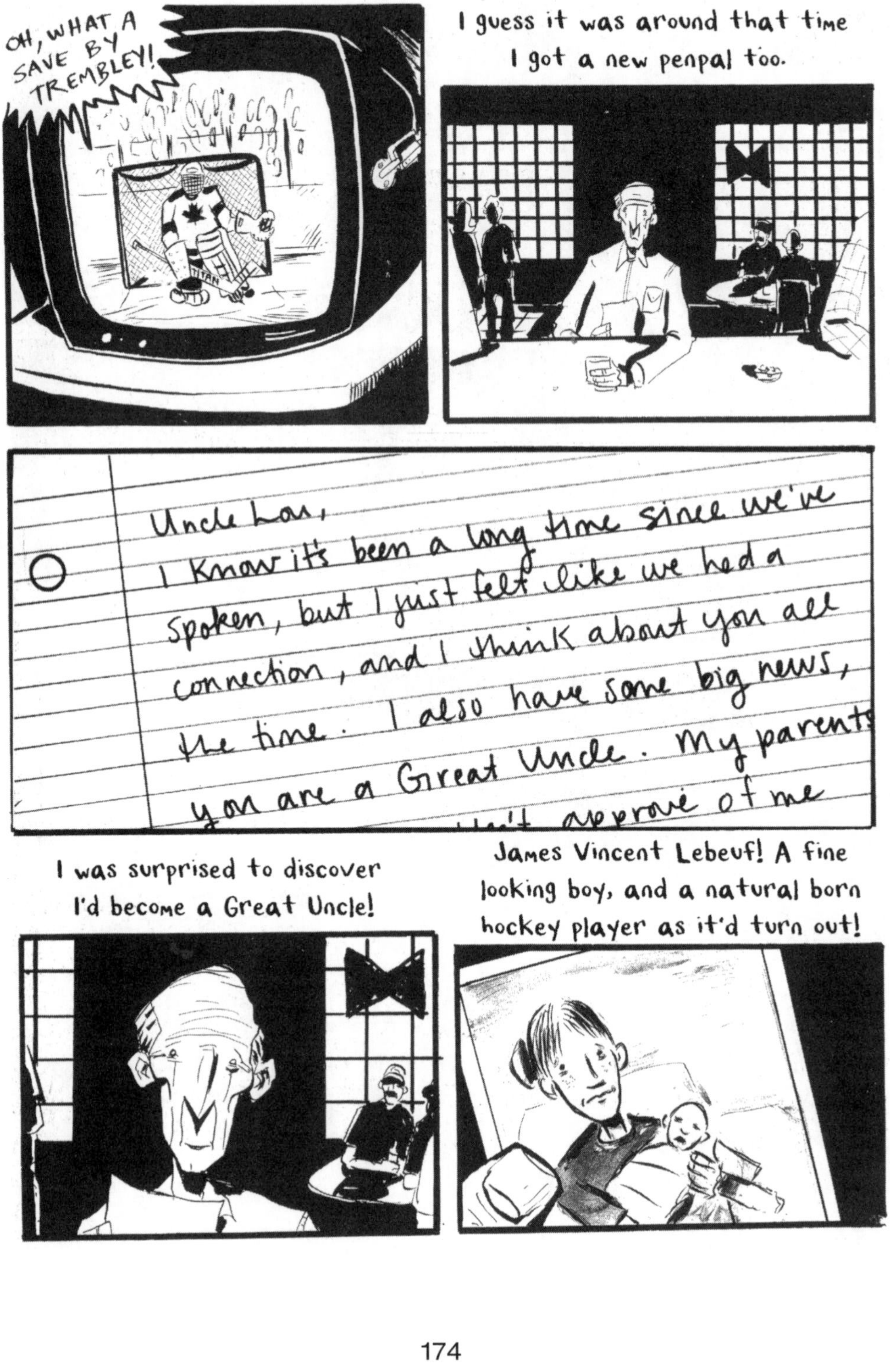
OH, WHAT A SAVE BY TREMBLEY!
TITAN
I guess it was around that time I got a new penpal too.
Uncle Lou,
I know it's been a long time since we've
spoken, but I just felt like we had a
connection, and I think about you all
the time. I also have some big news,
you are a Great Uncle. My parents
approve of me
I was surprised to discover I'd become a Great Uncle!
James Vincent Lebeuf! A fine looking boy, and a natural born hockey player as it'd turn out!

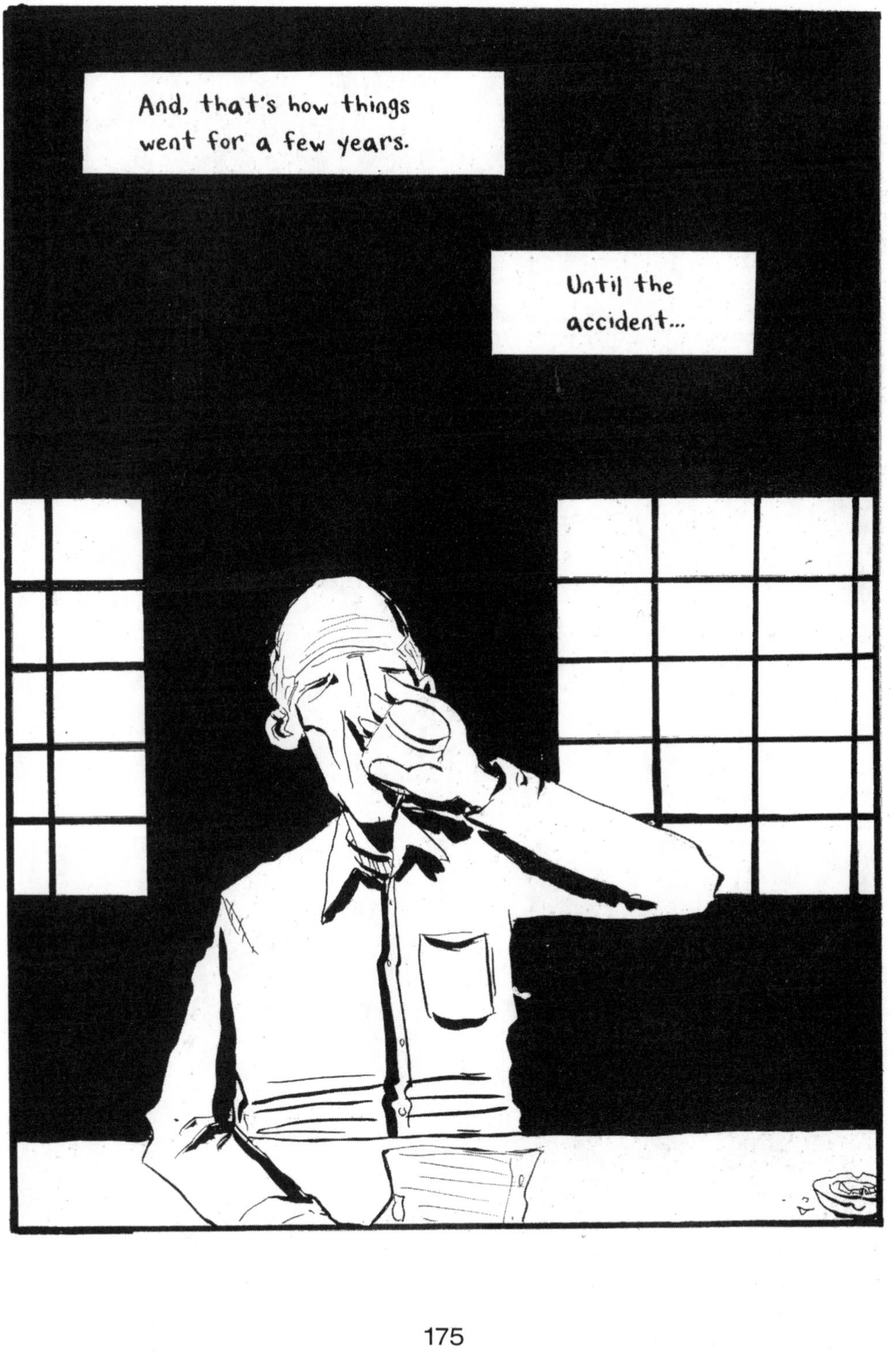
And, that's how things went for a few years.
Until the accident...

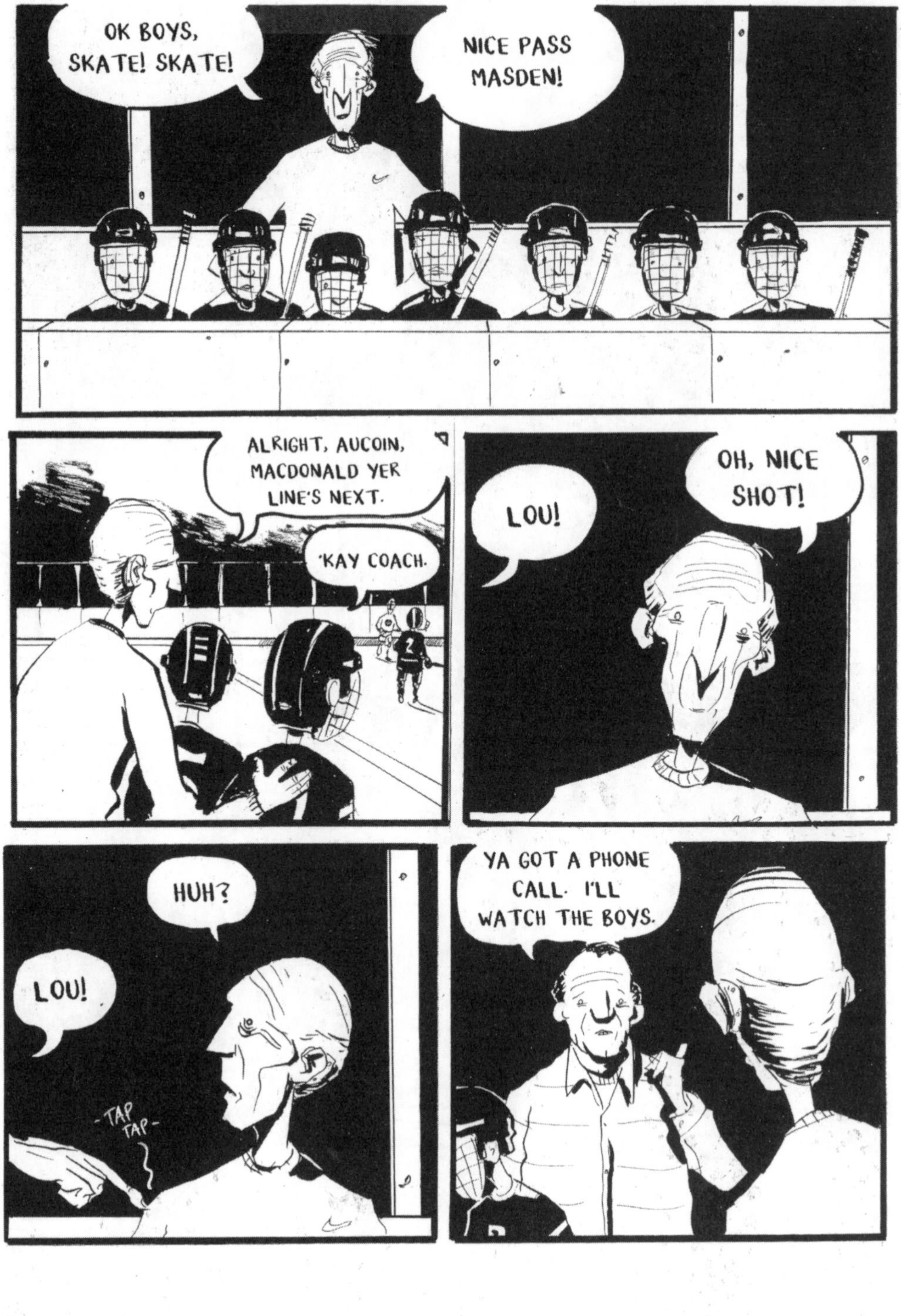
OK BOYS, SKATE! SKATE!
NICE PASS MASDEN!
ALRIGHT, AUCOIN, MACDONALD YER LINE'S NEXT.
'KAY COACH.
LOU!
OH, NICE SHOT!
HUH?
LOU!
-TAP TAP-
YA GOT A PHONE CALL. I'LL WATCH THE BOYS.

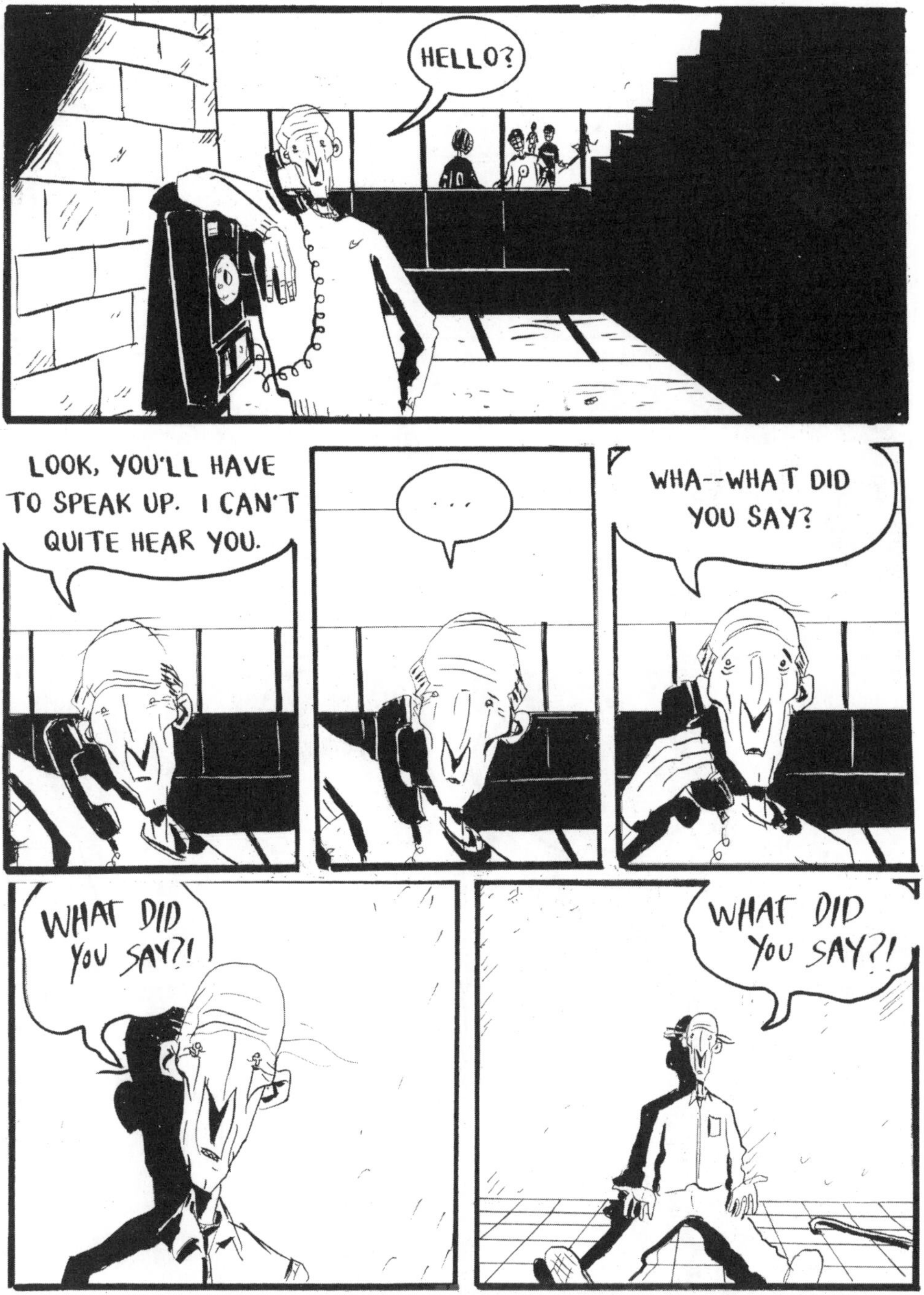
HELLO?
LOOK, YOU'LL HAVE TO SPEAK UP. I CAN'T QUITE HEAR YOU.
. . .
WHA--WHAT DID YOU SAY?
WHAT DID YOU SAY?!
WHAT DID YOU SAY?!

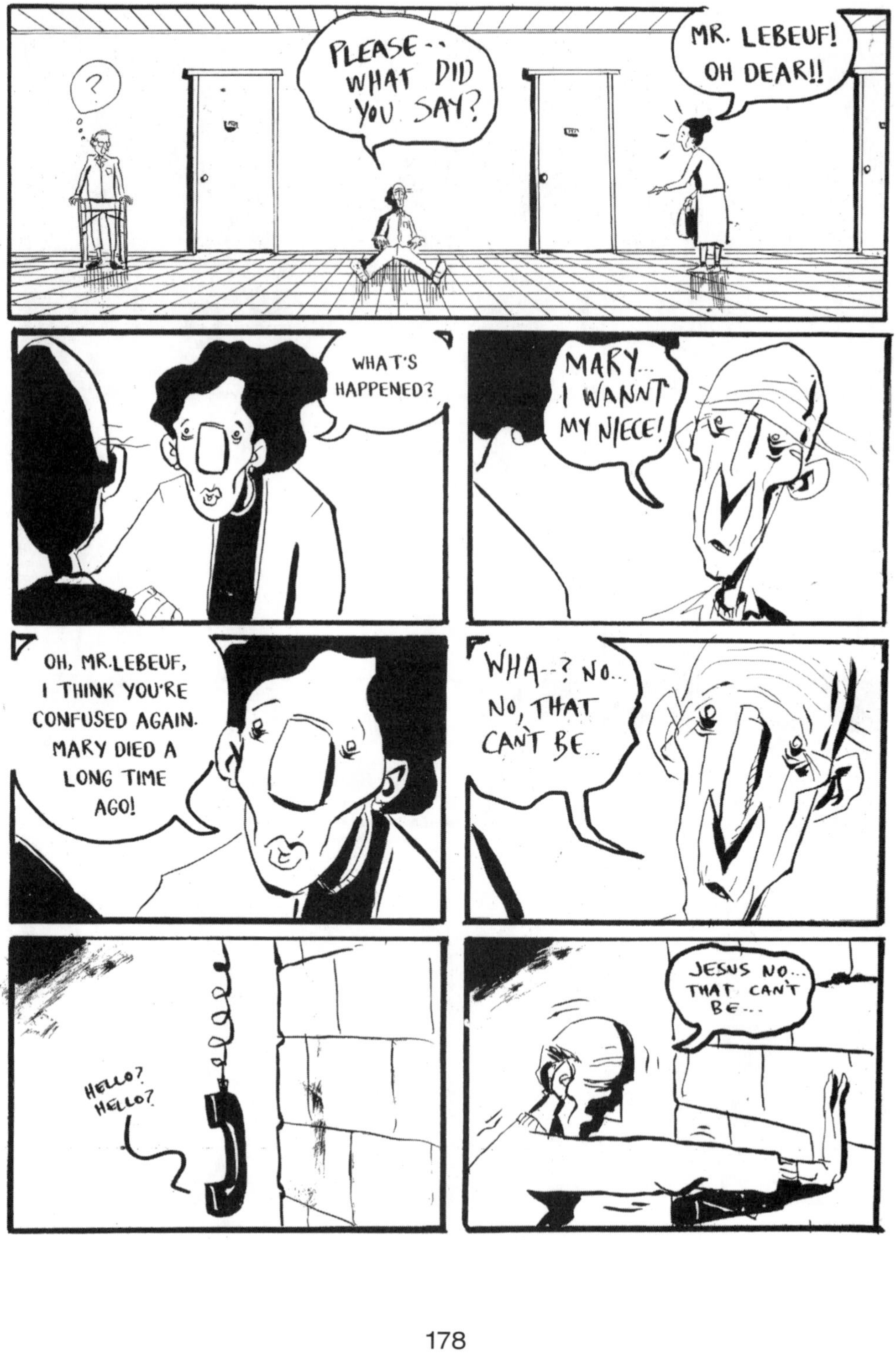
?
PLEASE.. WHAT DID YOU SAY?
MR. LEBEUF! OH DEAR!!
WHAT'S HAPPENED?
MARY... I WANNT MY NIECE!
OH, MR. LEBEUF, I THINK YOU'RE CONFUSED AGAIN. MARY DIED A LONG TIME AGO!
WHA--? NO... NO, THAT CAN'T BE...
HELLO? HELLO?
JESUS NO... THAT CAN'T BE...

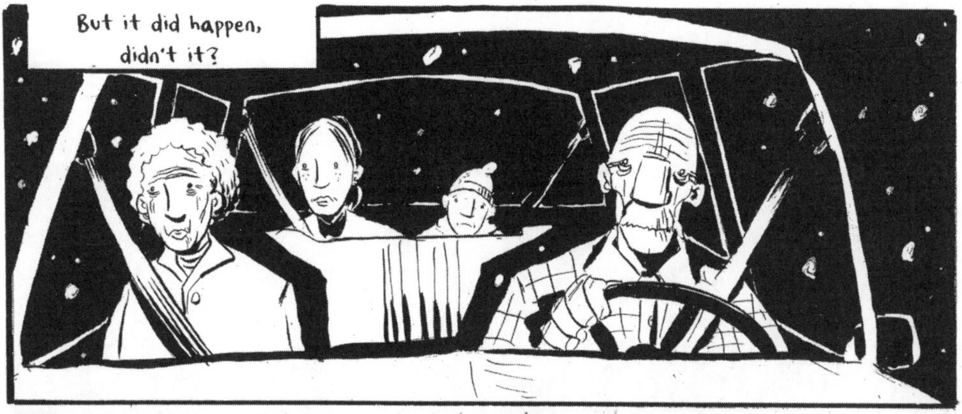
But it did happen, didn't it?

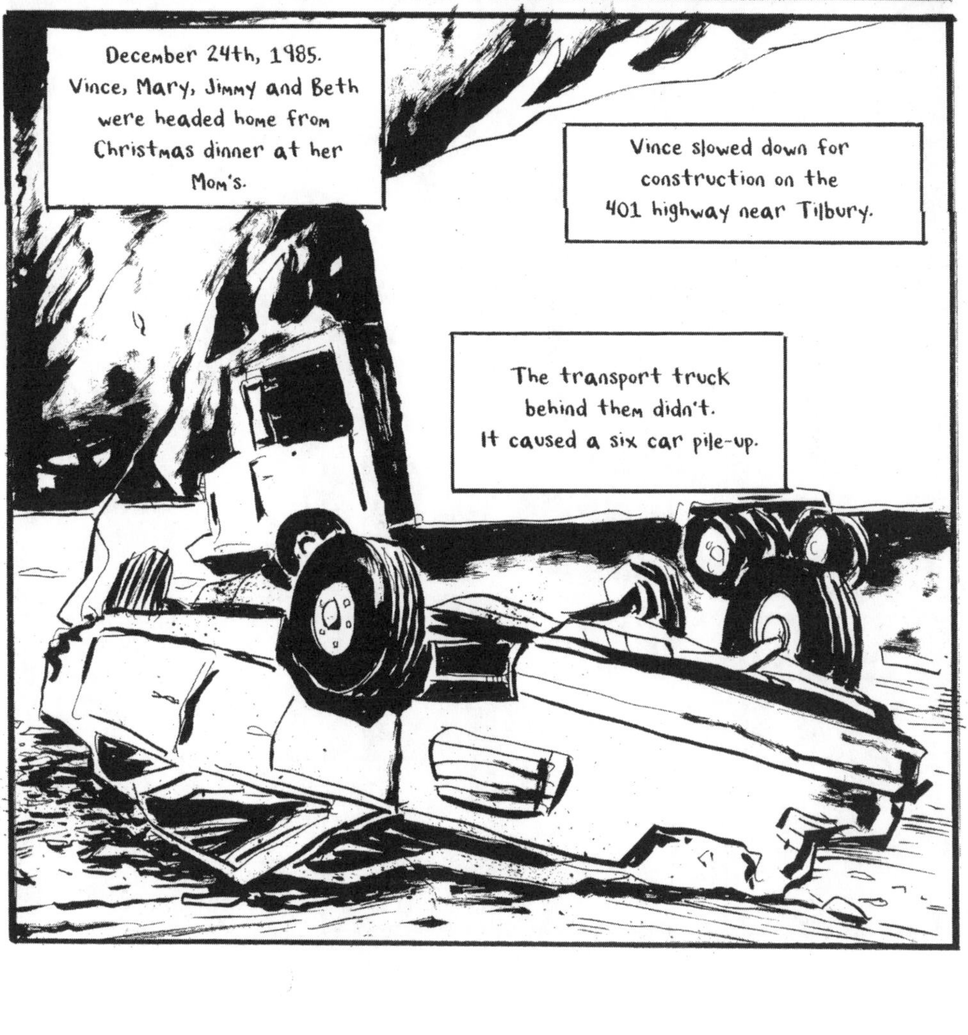
December 24th, 1985. Vince, Mary, Jimmy and Beth were headed home from Christmas dinner at her Mom's.
Vince slowed down for construction on the 401 highway near Tilbury.
The transport truck behind them didn't. It caused a six car pile-up.

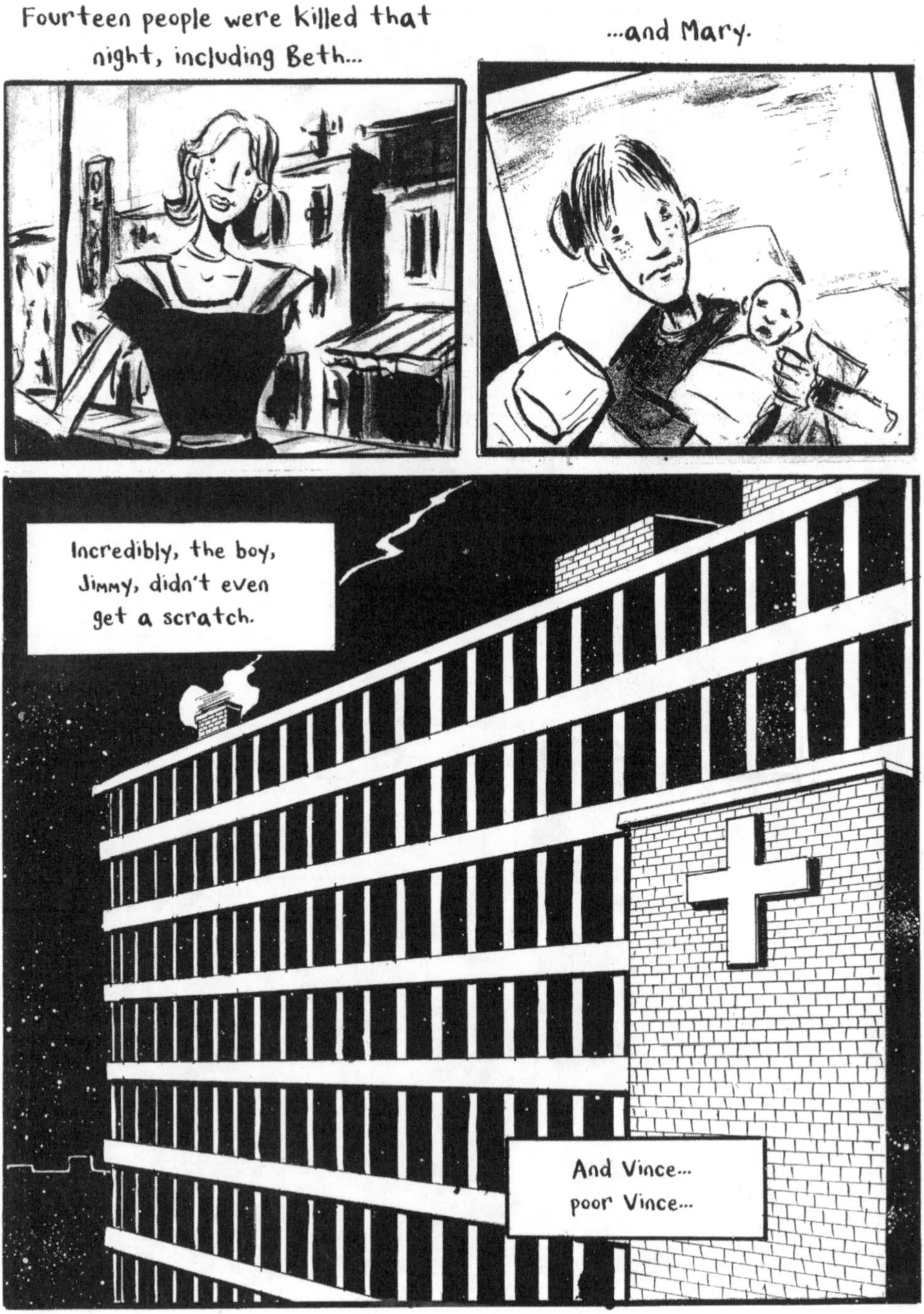
Fourteen people were killed that night, including Beth...
...and Mary.
Incredibly, the boy, Jimmy, didn't even get a scratch.
And Vince... poor Vince...

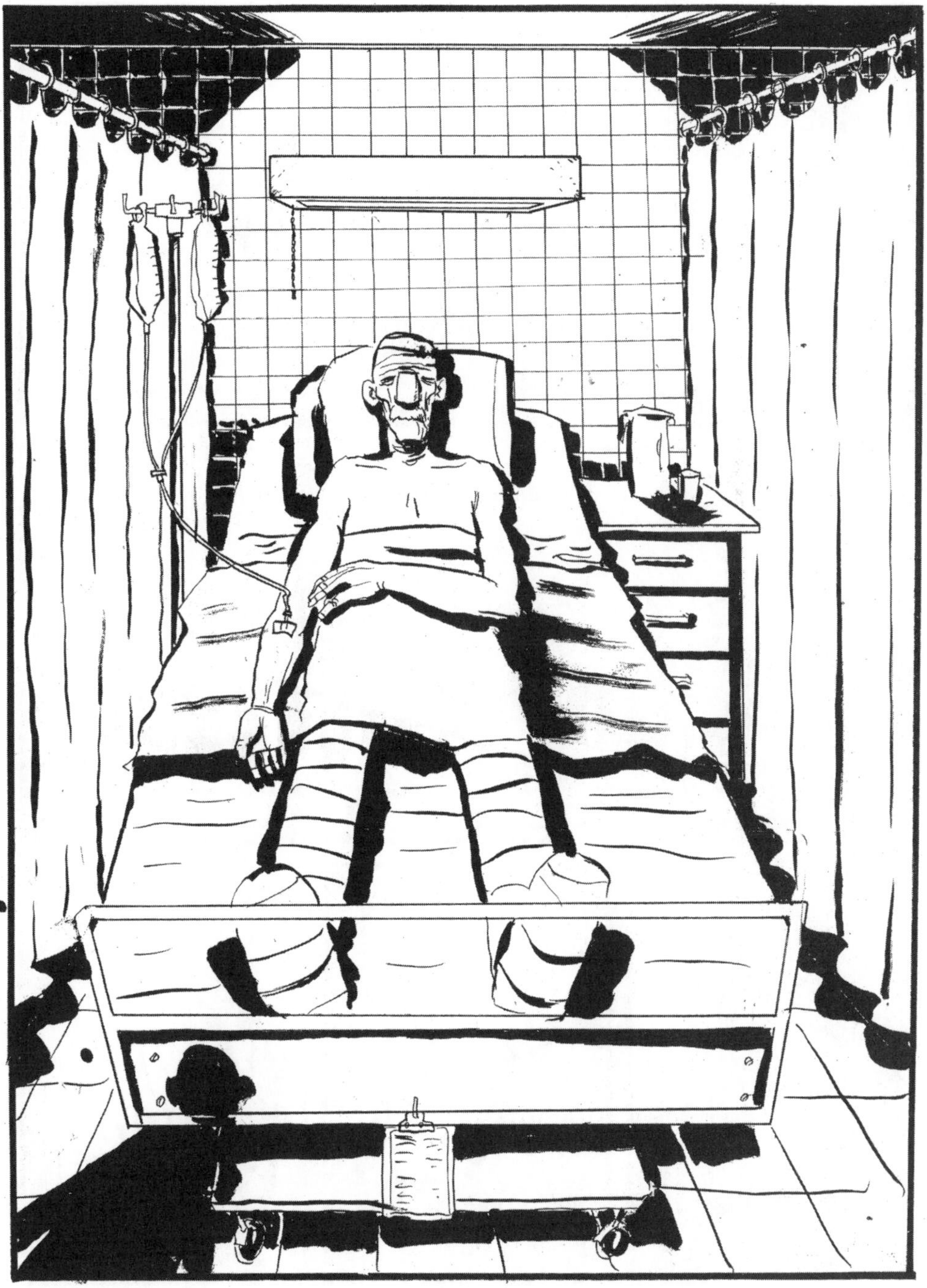

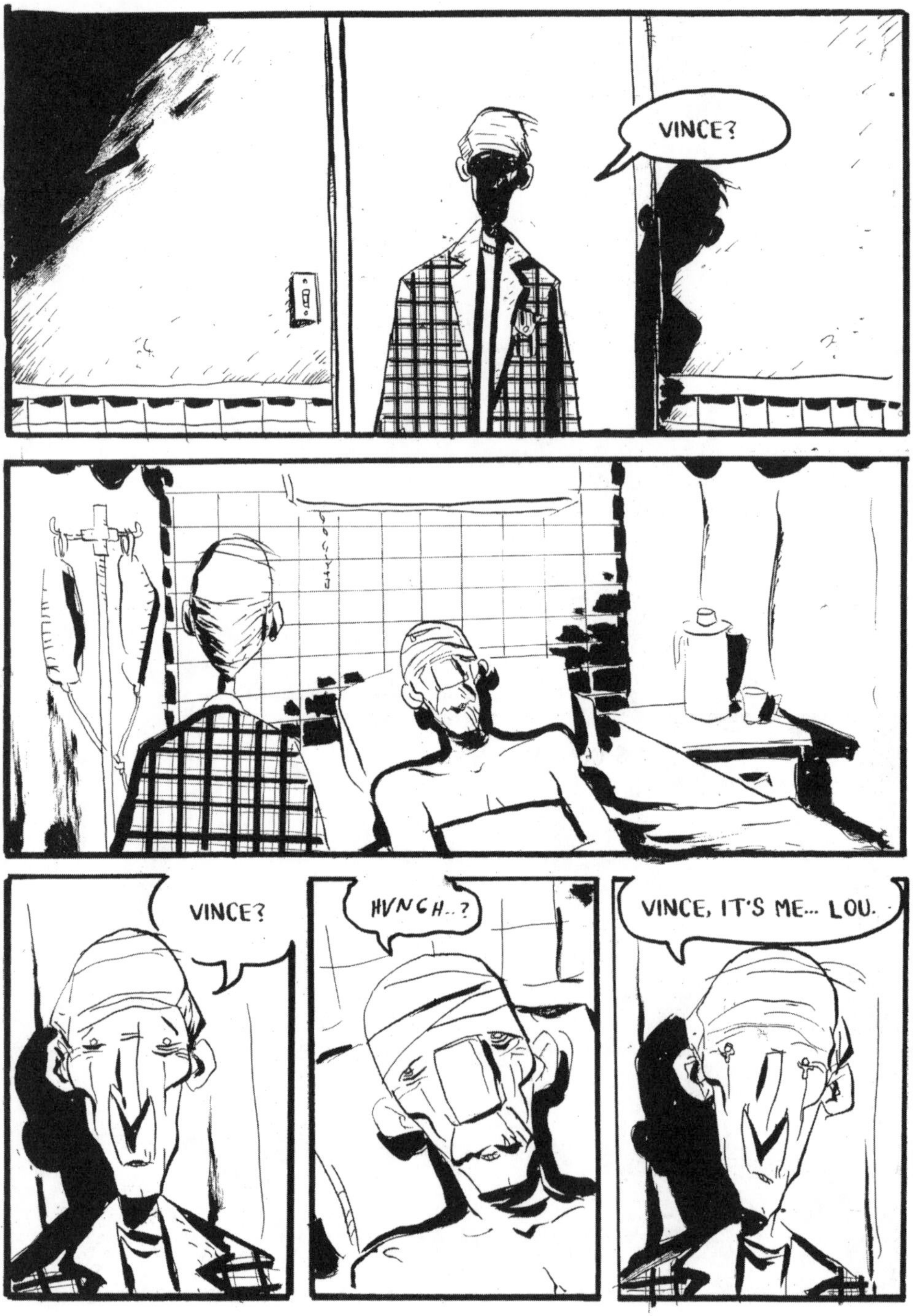
VINCE?
VINCE?
HVNGH..?
VINCE, IT'S ME... LOU.

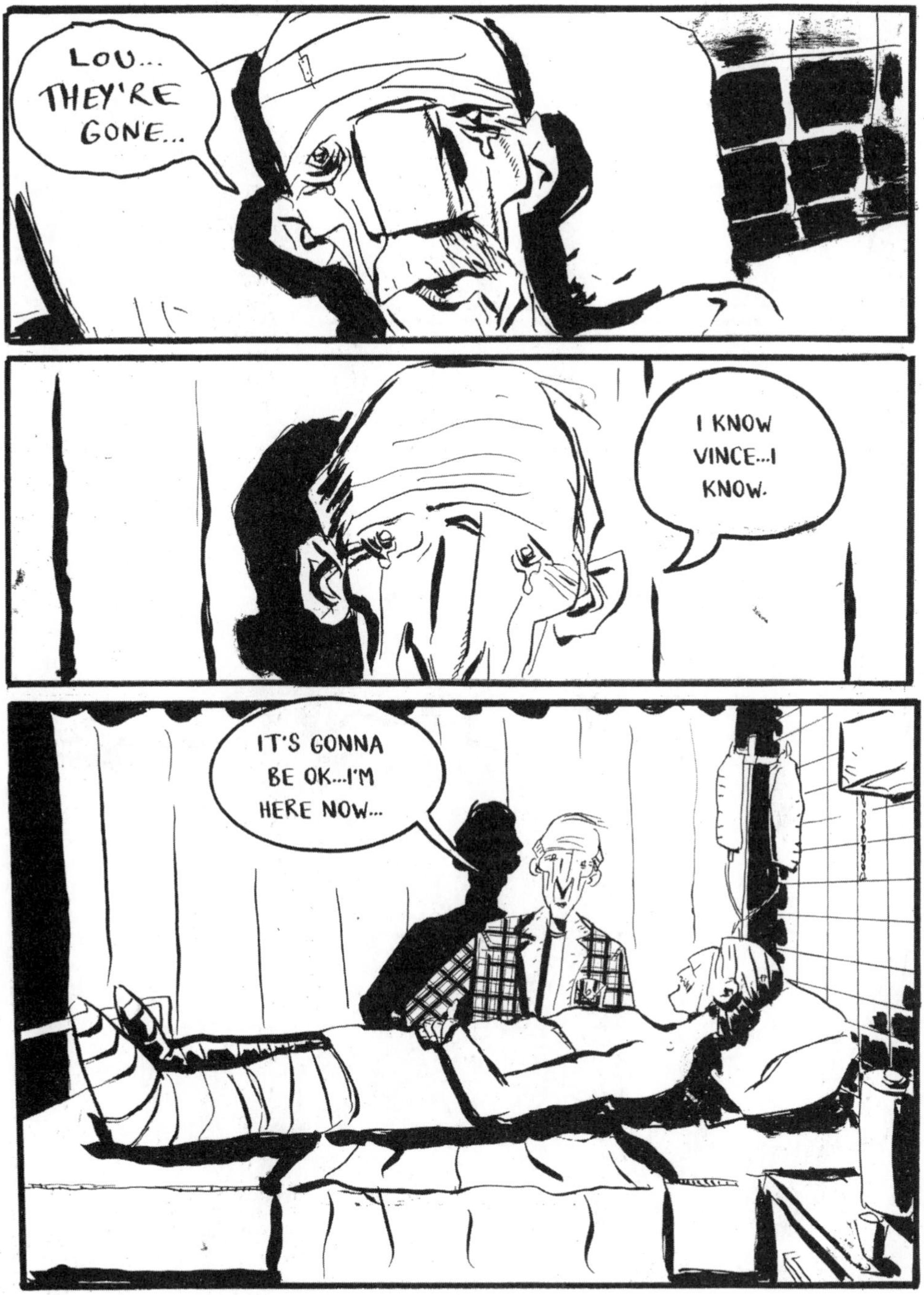
LOU... THEY'RE GONE...
I KNOW VINCE...I KNOW.
IT'S GONNA BE OK...I'M HERE NOW...

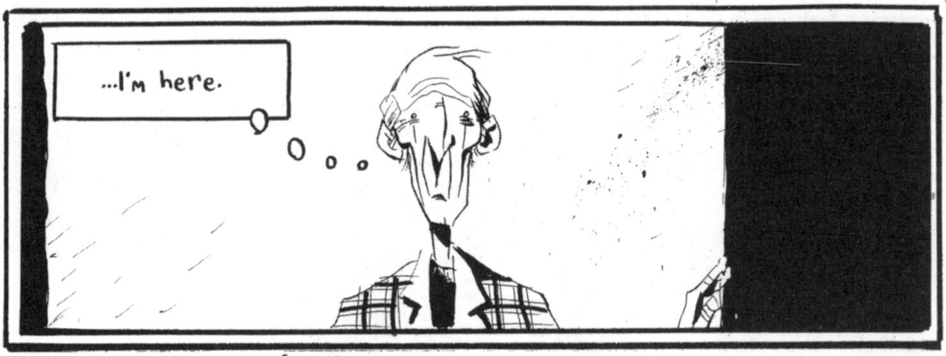
...I'm here.

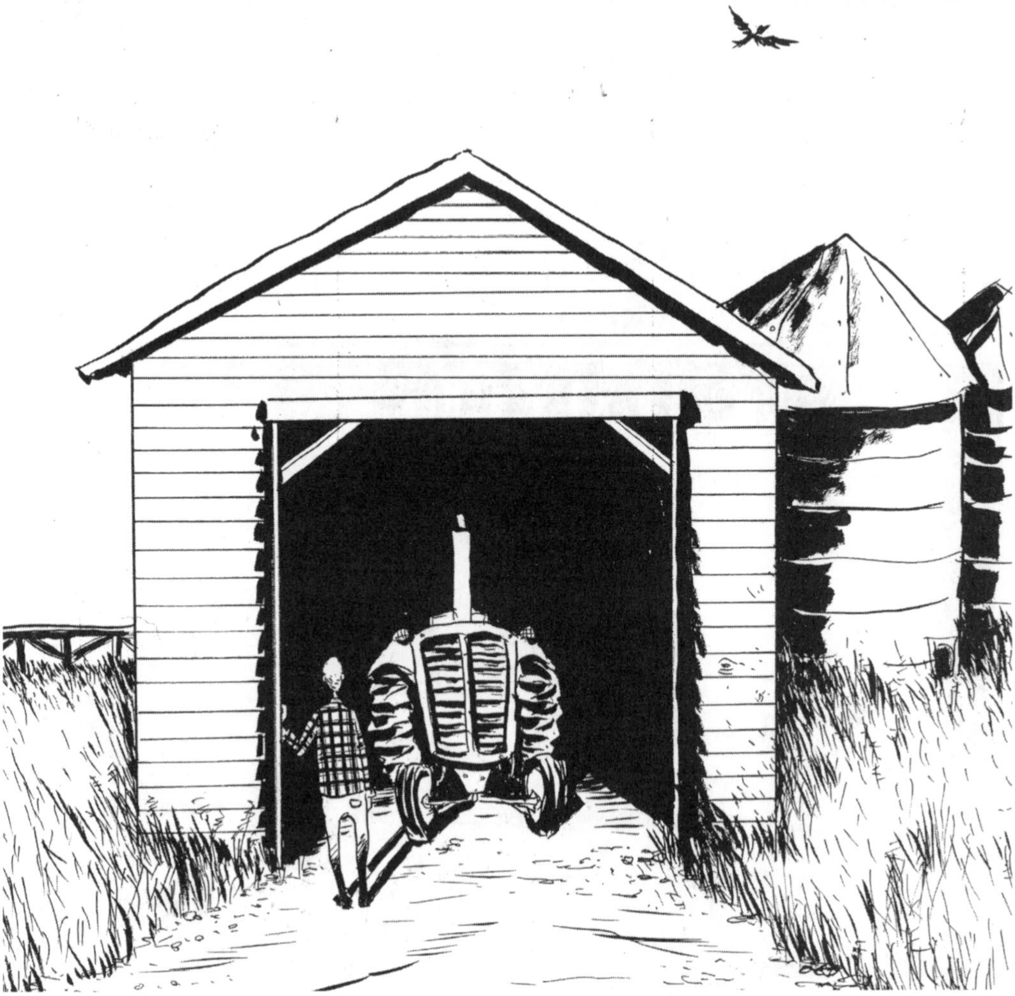

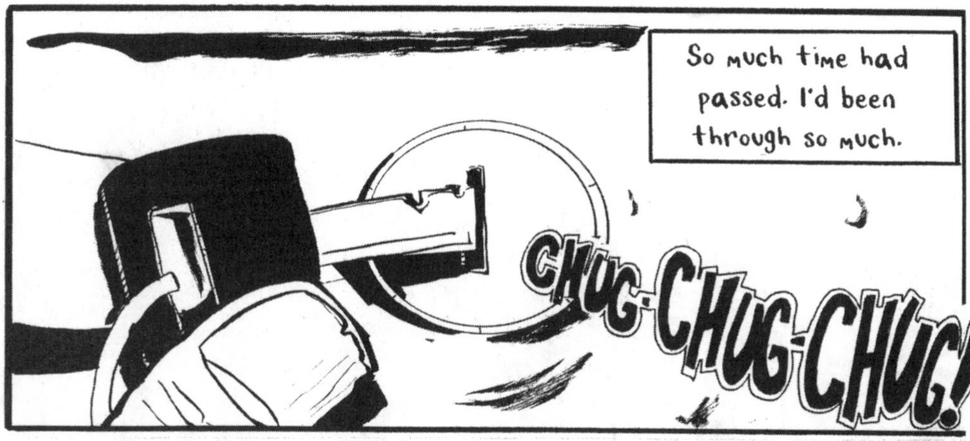
So much time had passed. I'd been through so much.
CHUG-CHUG-CHUG!

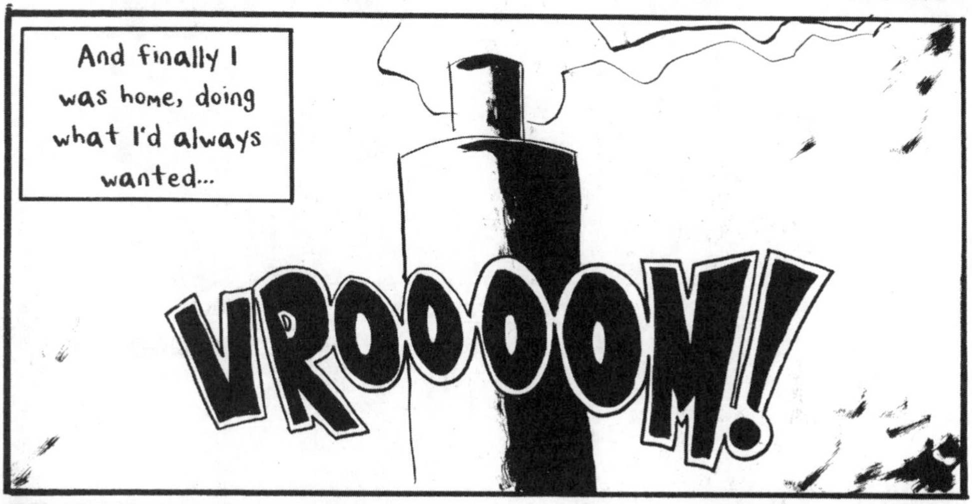
And finally I was home, doing what I'd always wanted...
VROOOOM!

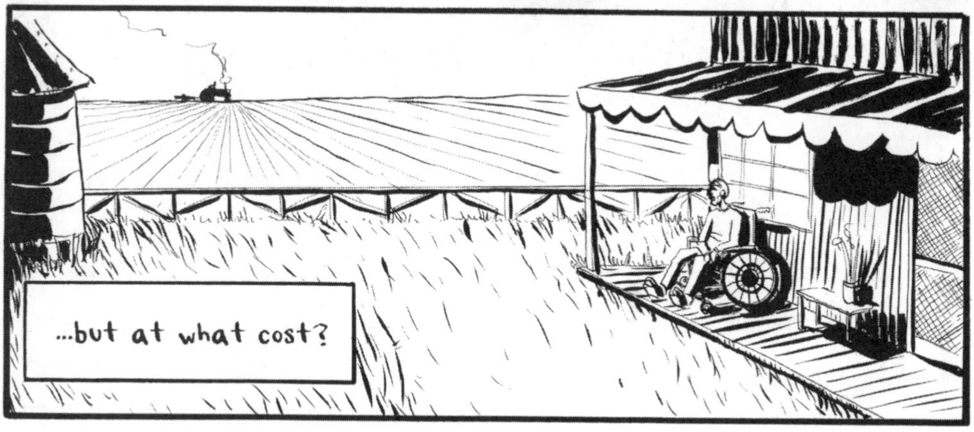
...but at what cost?

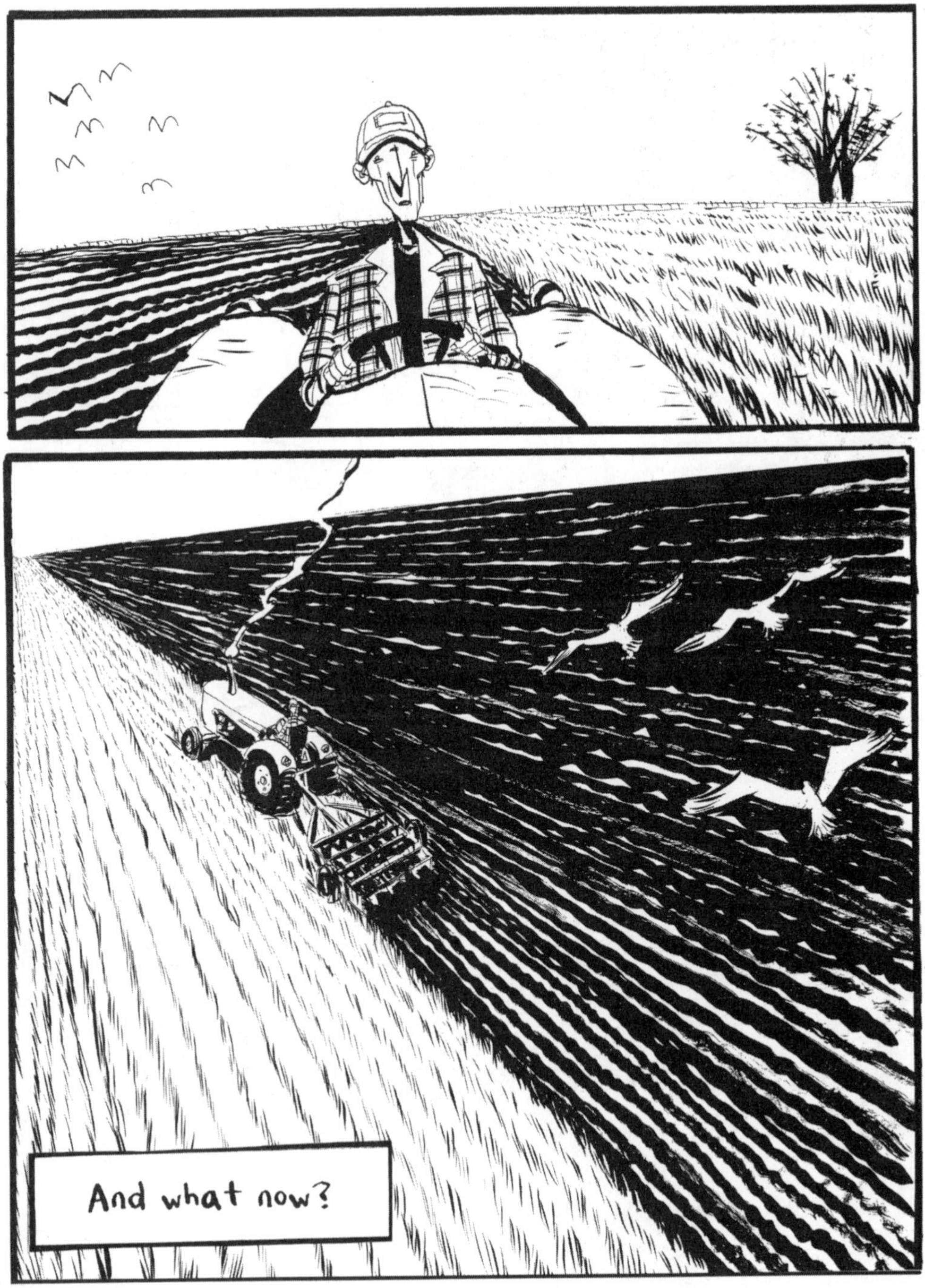
And what now?

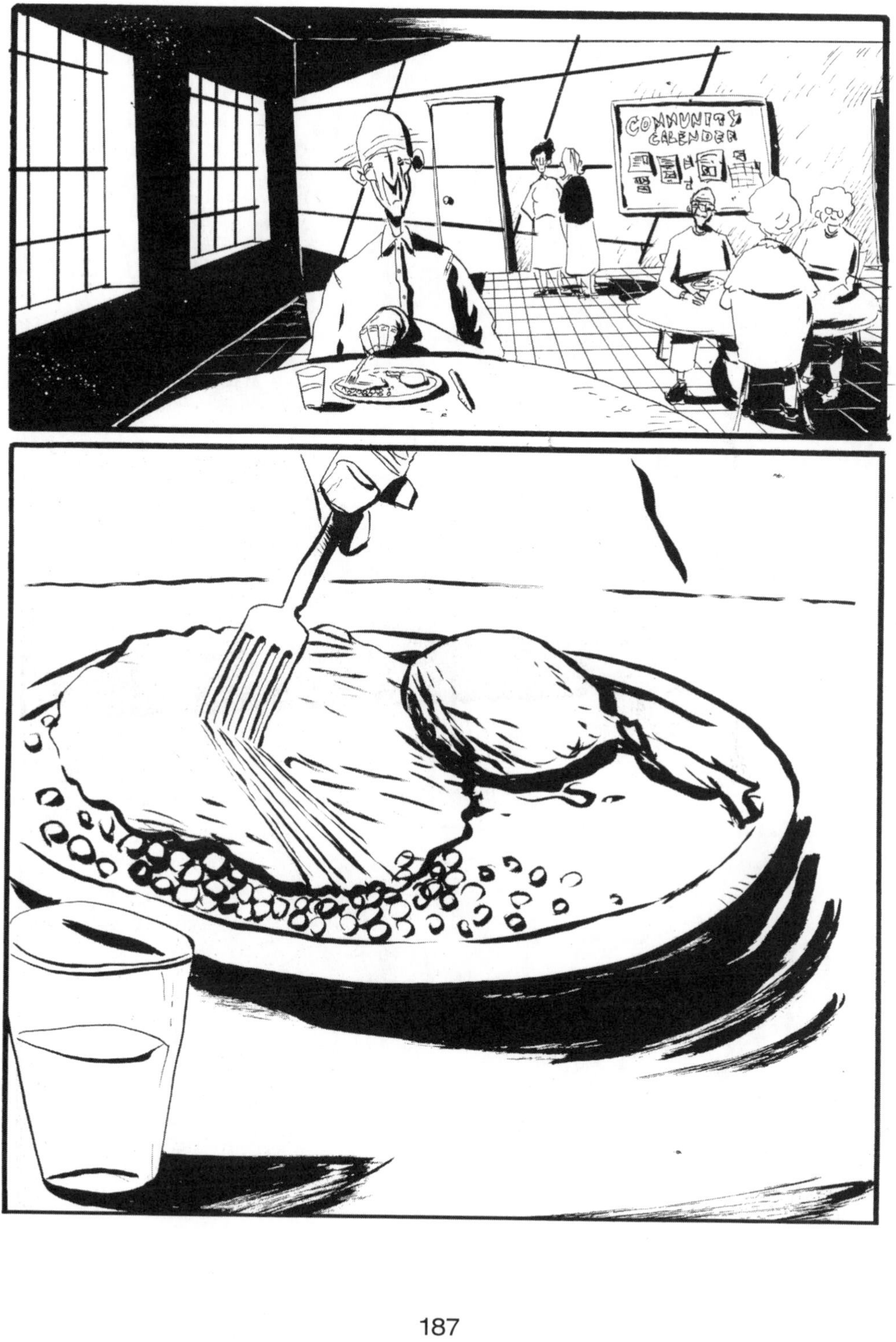
COMMUNITY
CALENDER

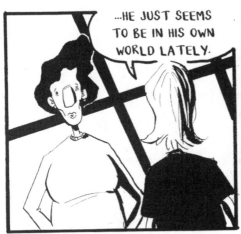

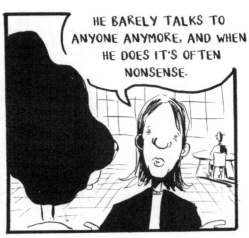

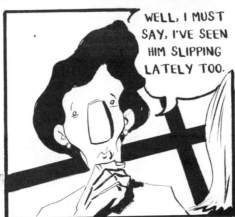

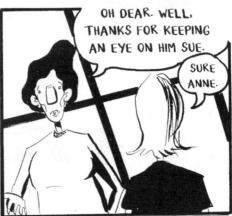

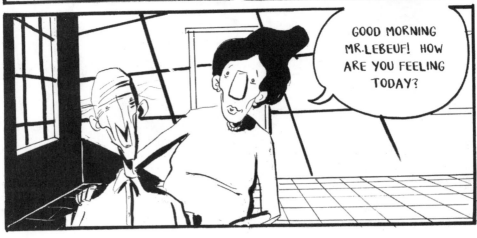

188

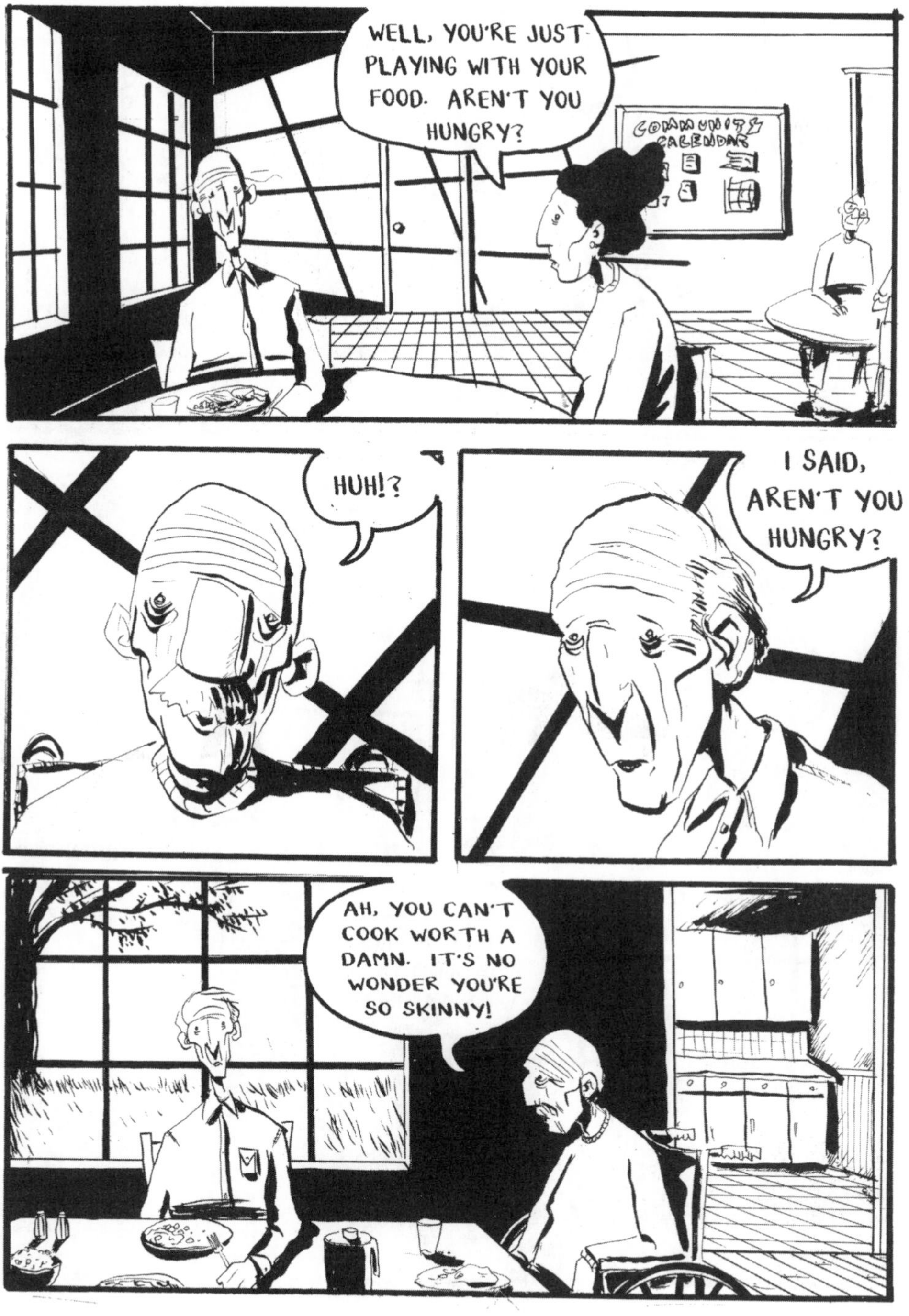
WELL, YOU'RE JUST-PLAYING WITH YOUR FOOD. AREN'T YOU HUNGRY?
HUH!?
I SAID, AREN'T YOU HUNGRY?
AH, YOU CAN'T COOK WORTH A DAMN. IT'S NO WONDER YOU'RE SO SKINNY!

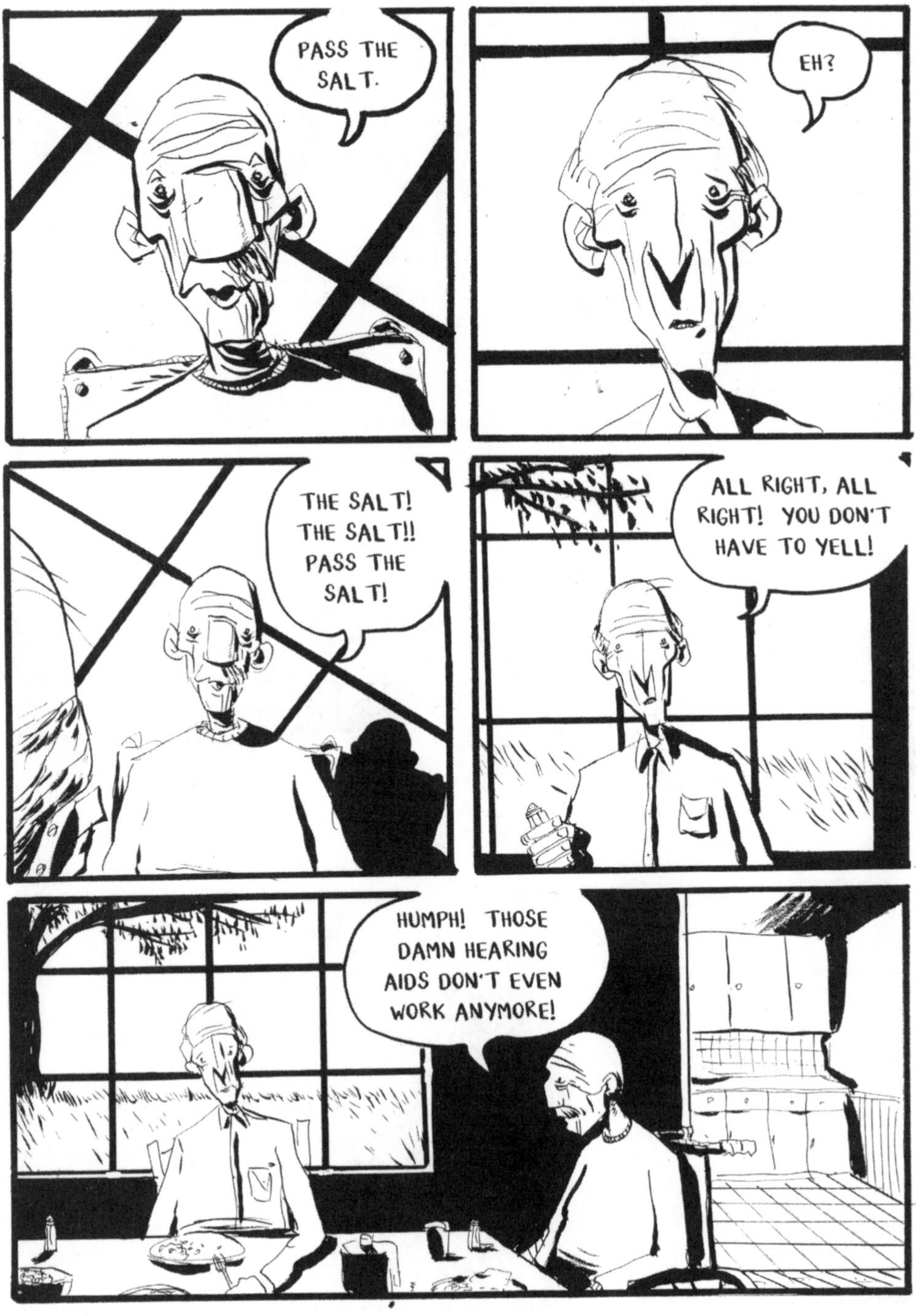
PASS THE SALT.
EH?
THE SALT! THE SALT!! PASS THE SALT!
ALL RIGHT, ALL RIGHT! YOU DON'T HAVE TO YELL!
HUMPH! THOSE DAMN HEARING AIDS DON'T EVEN WORK ANYMORE!

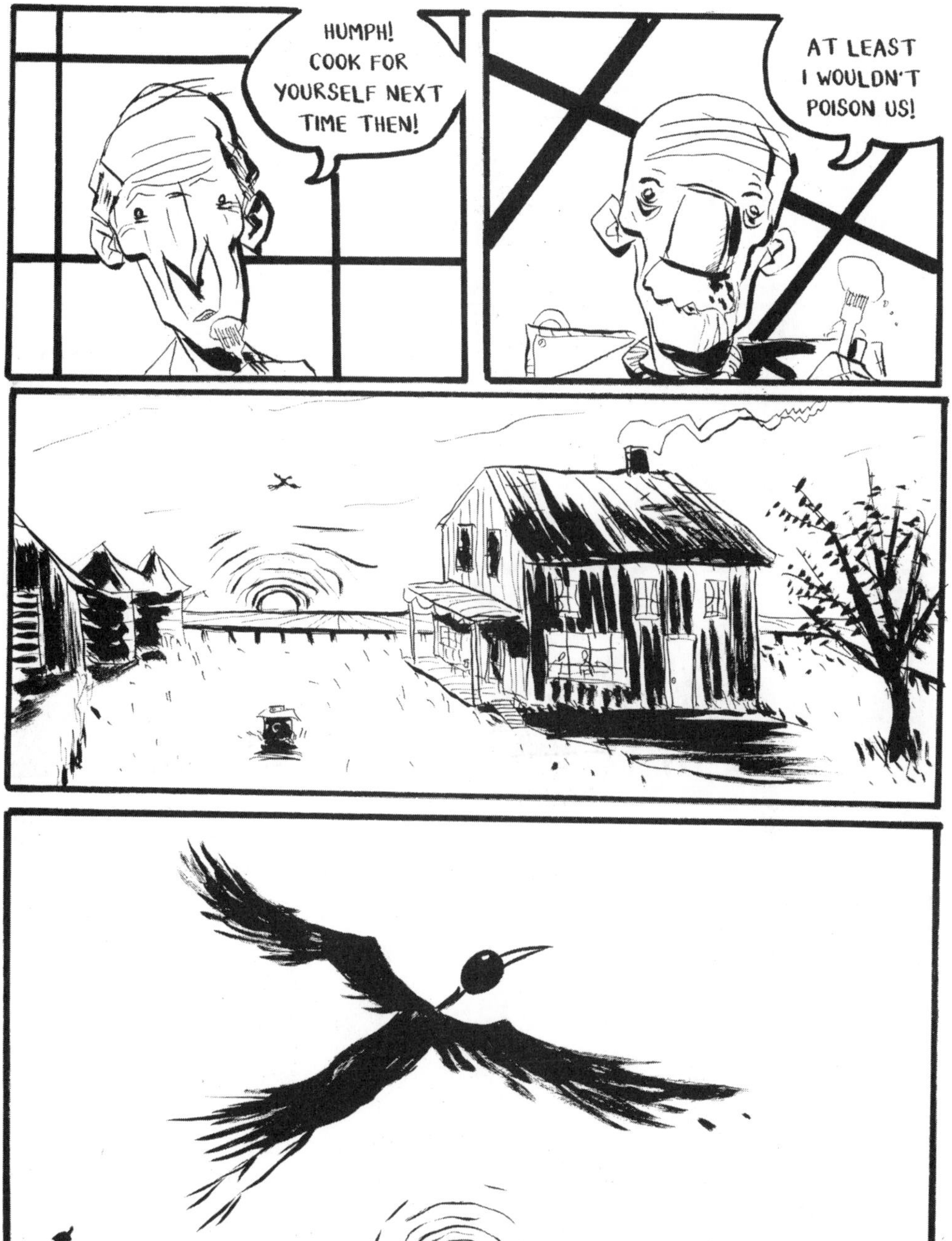
HUMPH! COOK FOR YOURSELF NEXT TIME THEN!
AT LEAST I WOULDN'T POISON US!

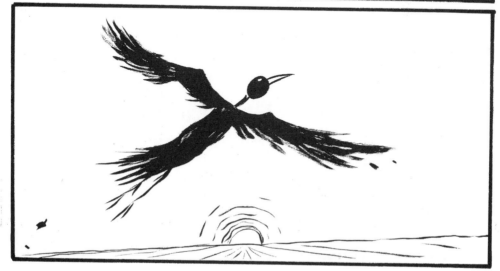

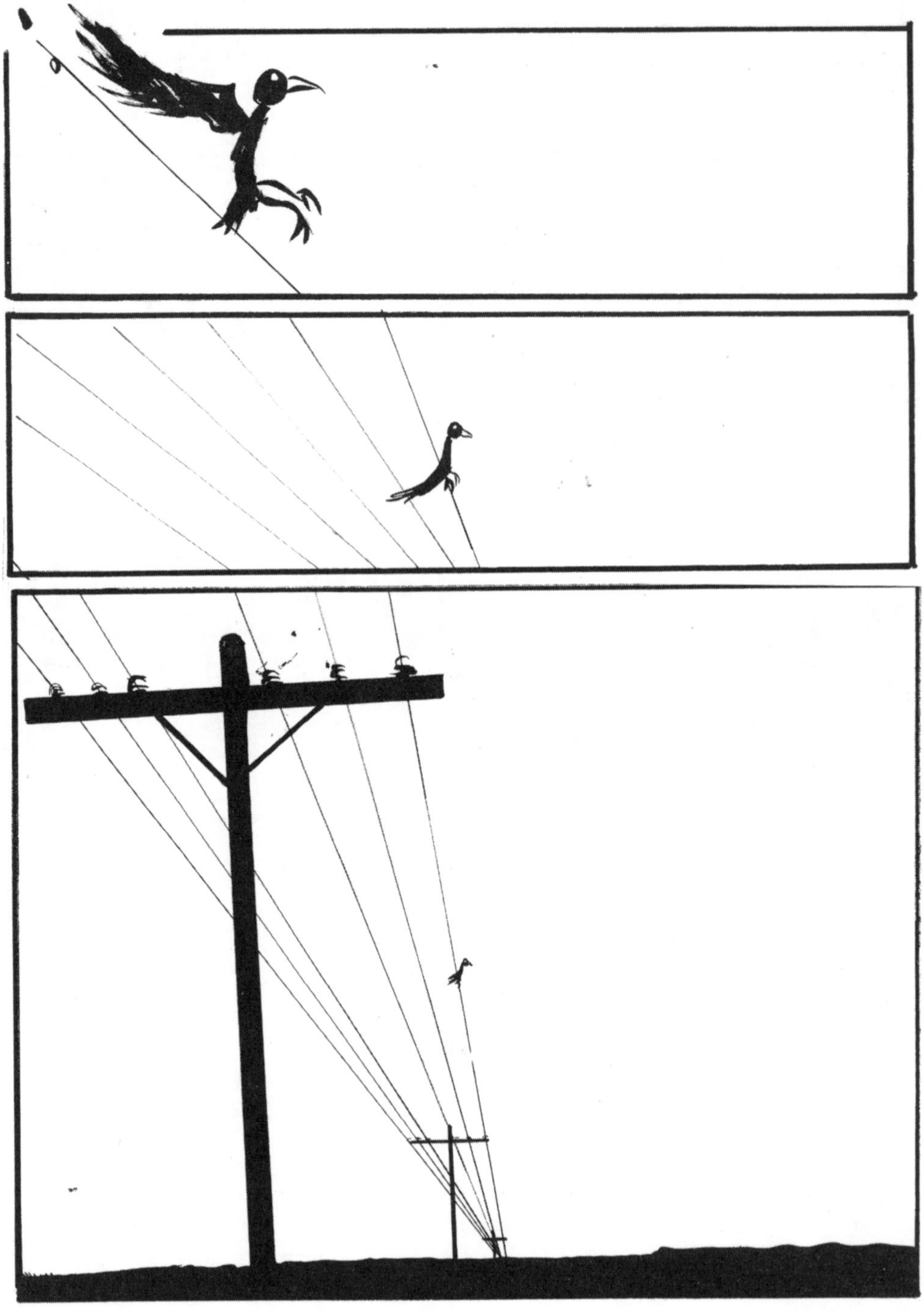

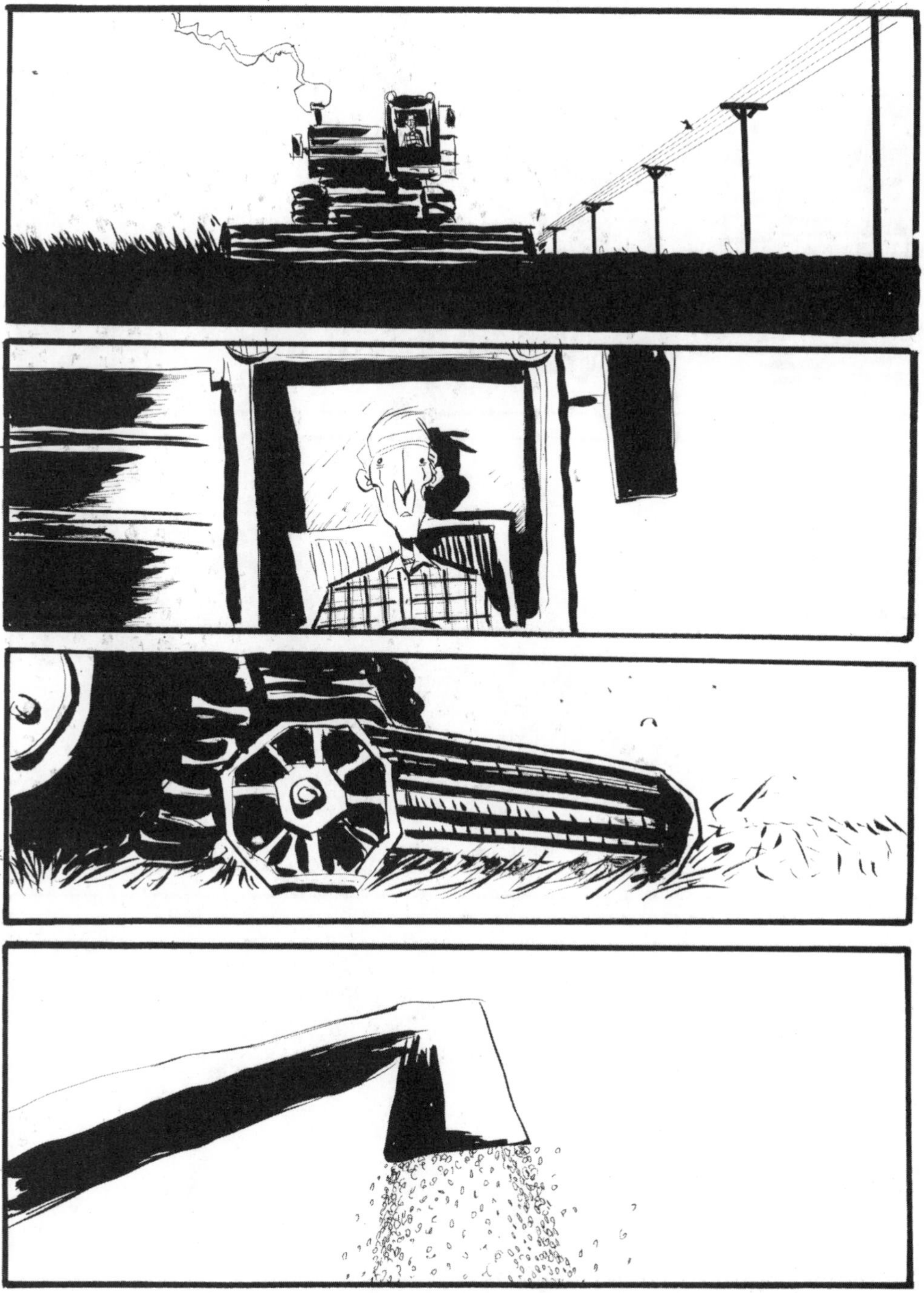

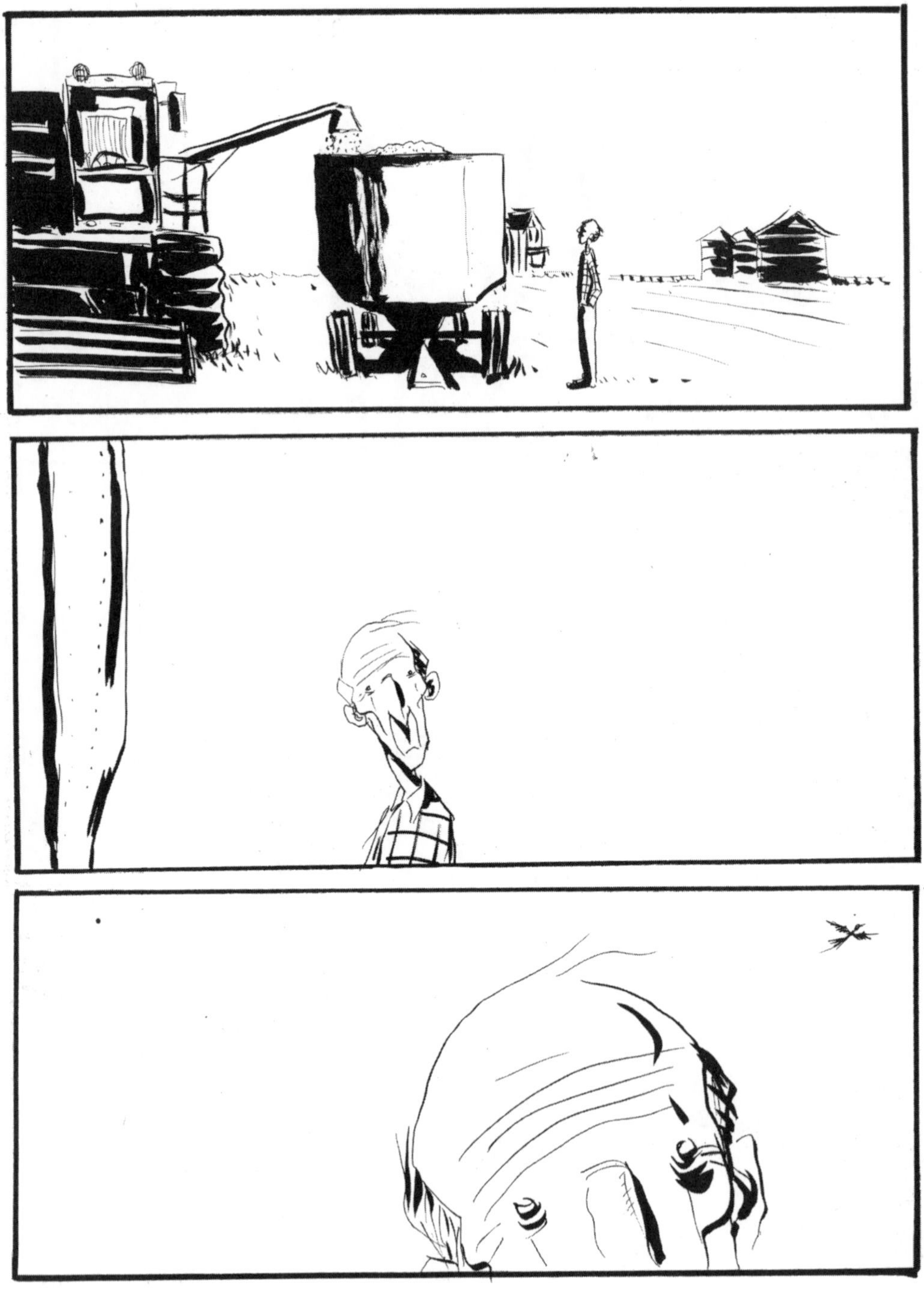

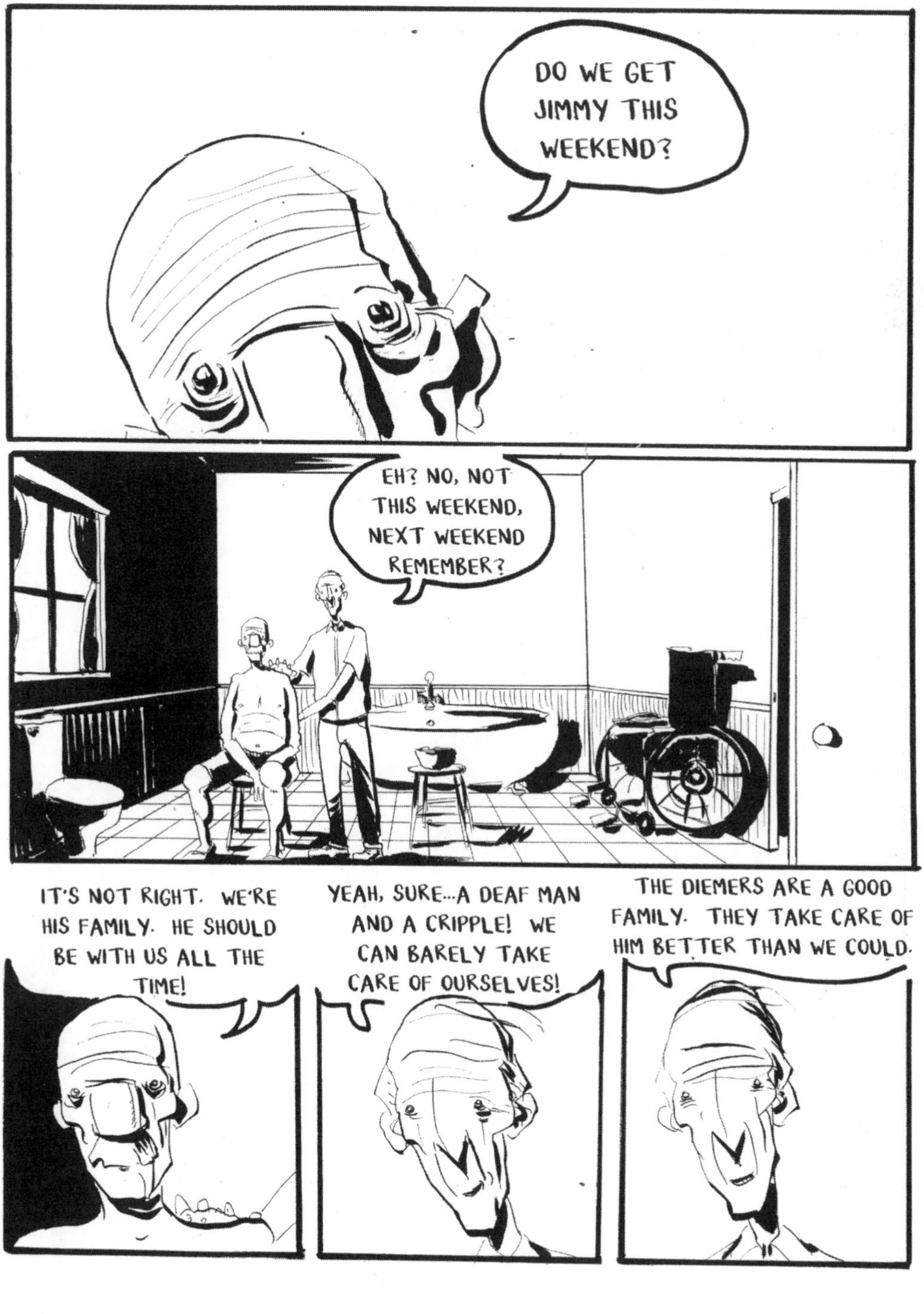
DO WE GET JIMMY THIS WEEKEND?
EH? NO, NOT THIS WEEKEND, NEXT WEEKEND REMEMBER?
IT'S NOT RIGHT. WE'RE HIS FAMILY. HE SHOULD BE WITH US ALL THE TIME!
YEAH, SURE...A DEAF MAN AND A CRIPPLE! WE CAN BARELY TAKE CARE OF OURSELVES!
THE DIEMERS ARE A GOOD FAMILY. THEY TAKE CARE OF HIM BETTER THAN WE COULD.

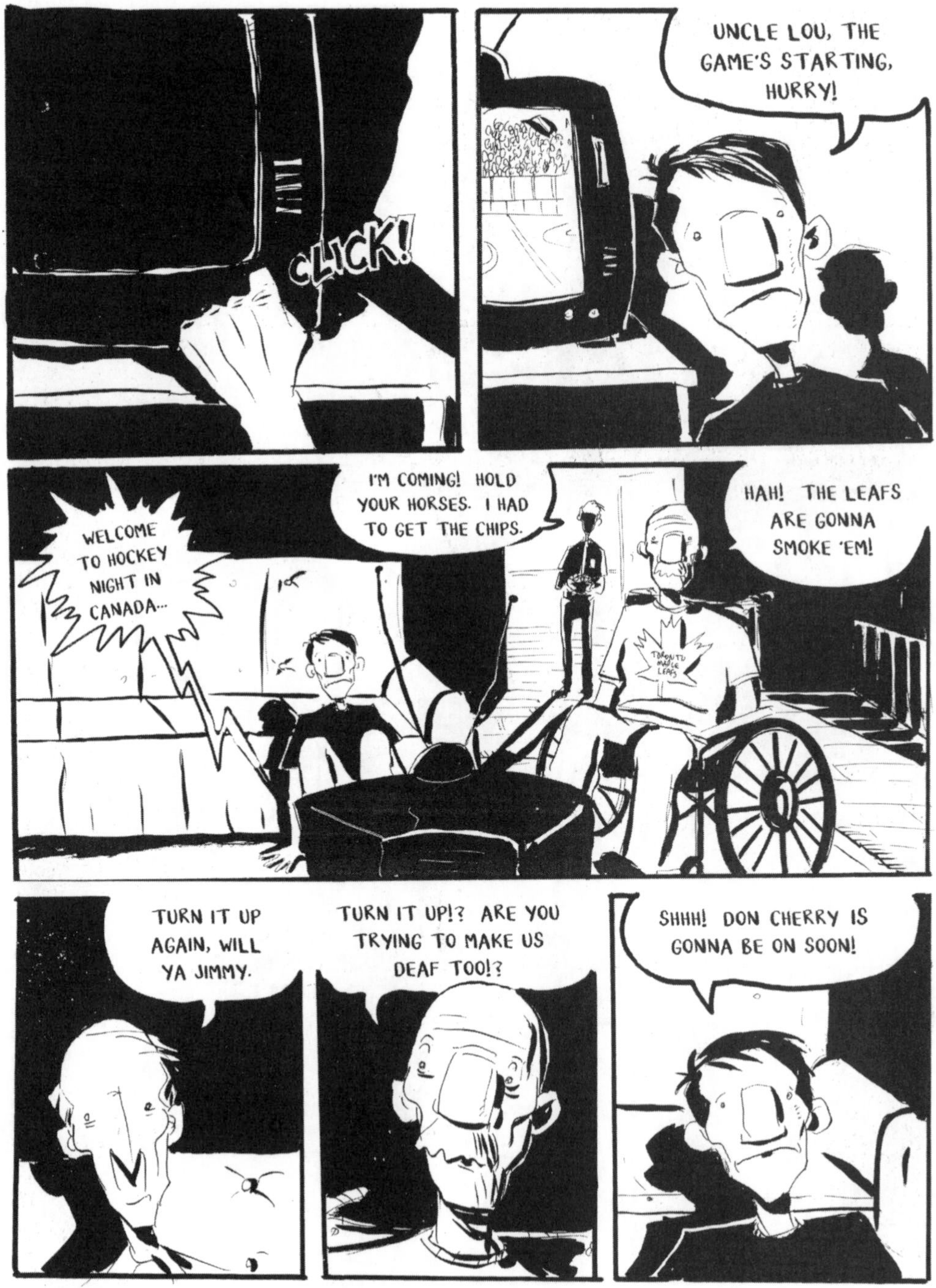
CLICK!
UNCLE LOU, THE GAME'S STARTING, HURRY!
WELCOME TO HOCKEY NIGHT IN CANADA...
I'M COMING! HOLD YOUR HORSES. I HAD TO GET THE CHIPS.
HAH! THE LEAFS ARE GONNA SMOKE 'EM!
TORONTO MAPLE LEAFS
TURN IT UP AGAIN, WILL YA JIMMY.
TURN IT UP!? ARE YOU TRYING TO MAKE US DEAF TOO!?
SHHH! DON CHERRY IS GONNA BE ON SOON!

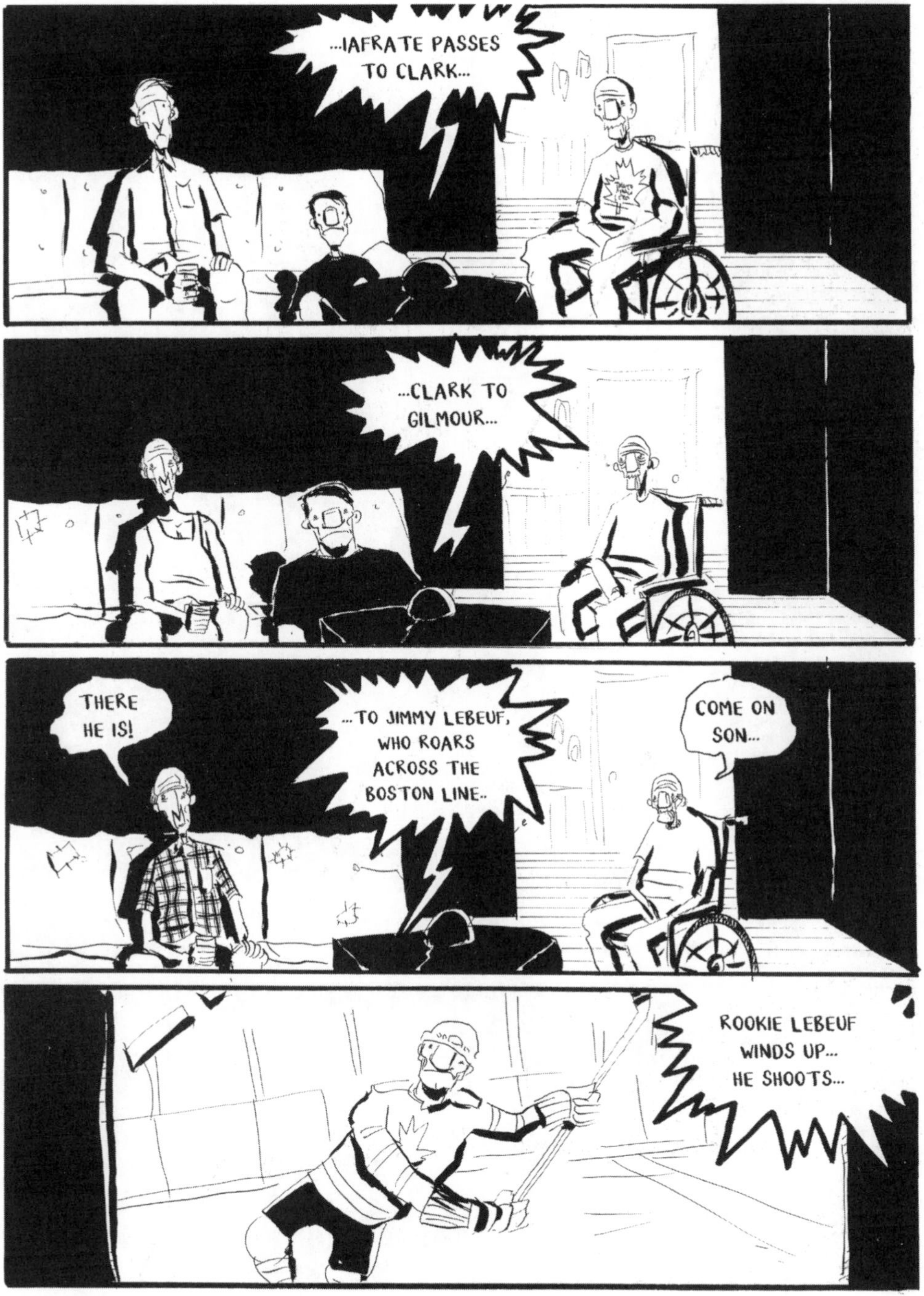

...IAFRATE PASSES TO CLARK...
...CLARK TO GILMOUR...
THERE HE IS!
...TO JIMMY LEBEUF, WHO ROARS ACROSS THE BOSTON LINE..
COME ON SON...
ROOKIE LEBEUF WINDS UP... HE SHOOTS...

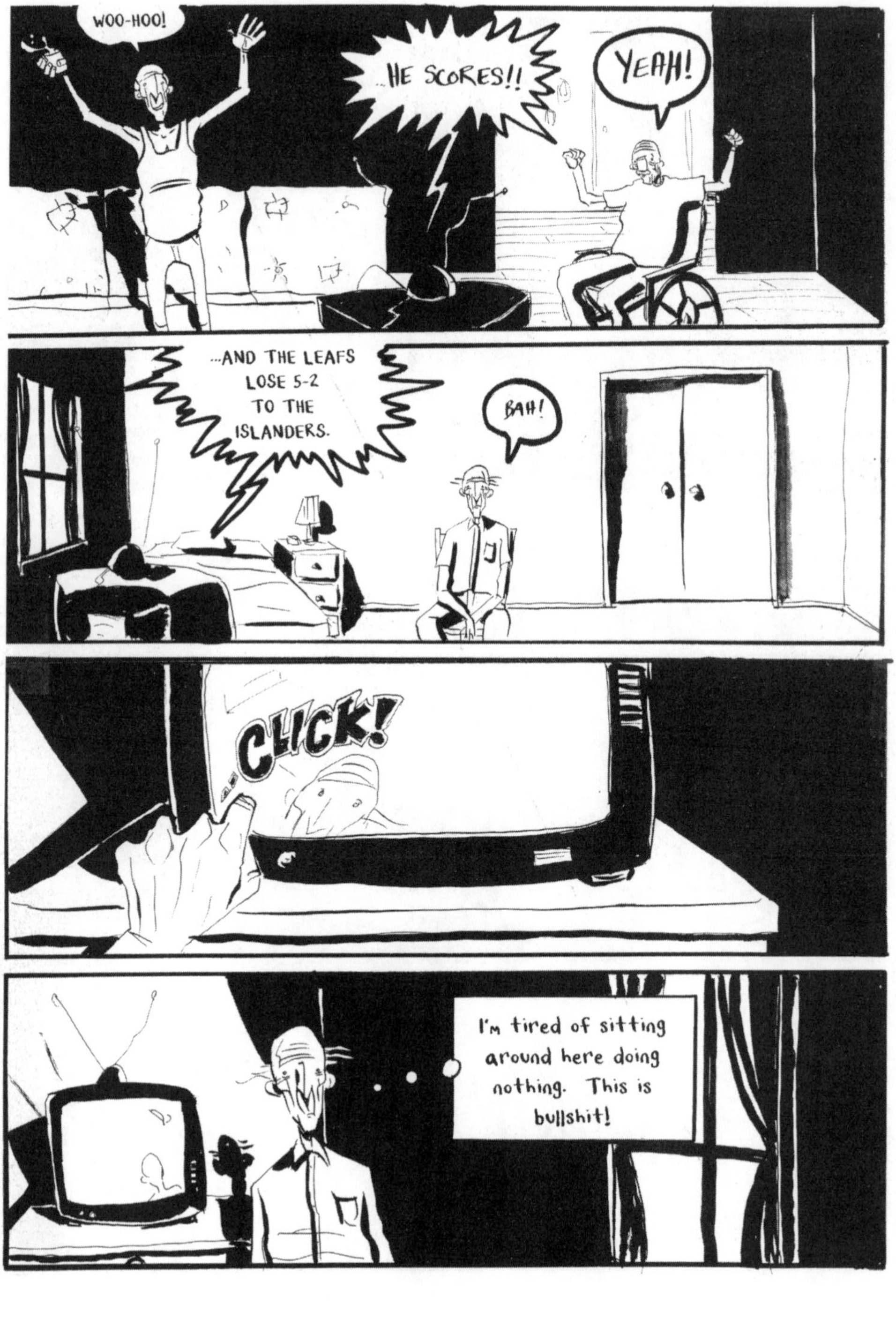
WOO-HOO!
...HE SCORES!!
YEAH!
...AND THE LEAFS LOSE 5-2 TO THE ISLANDERS.
BAH!
CLICK!
I'm tired of sitting around here doing nothing. This is bullshit!

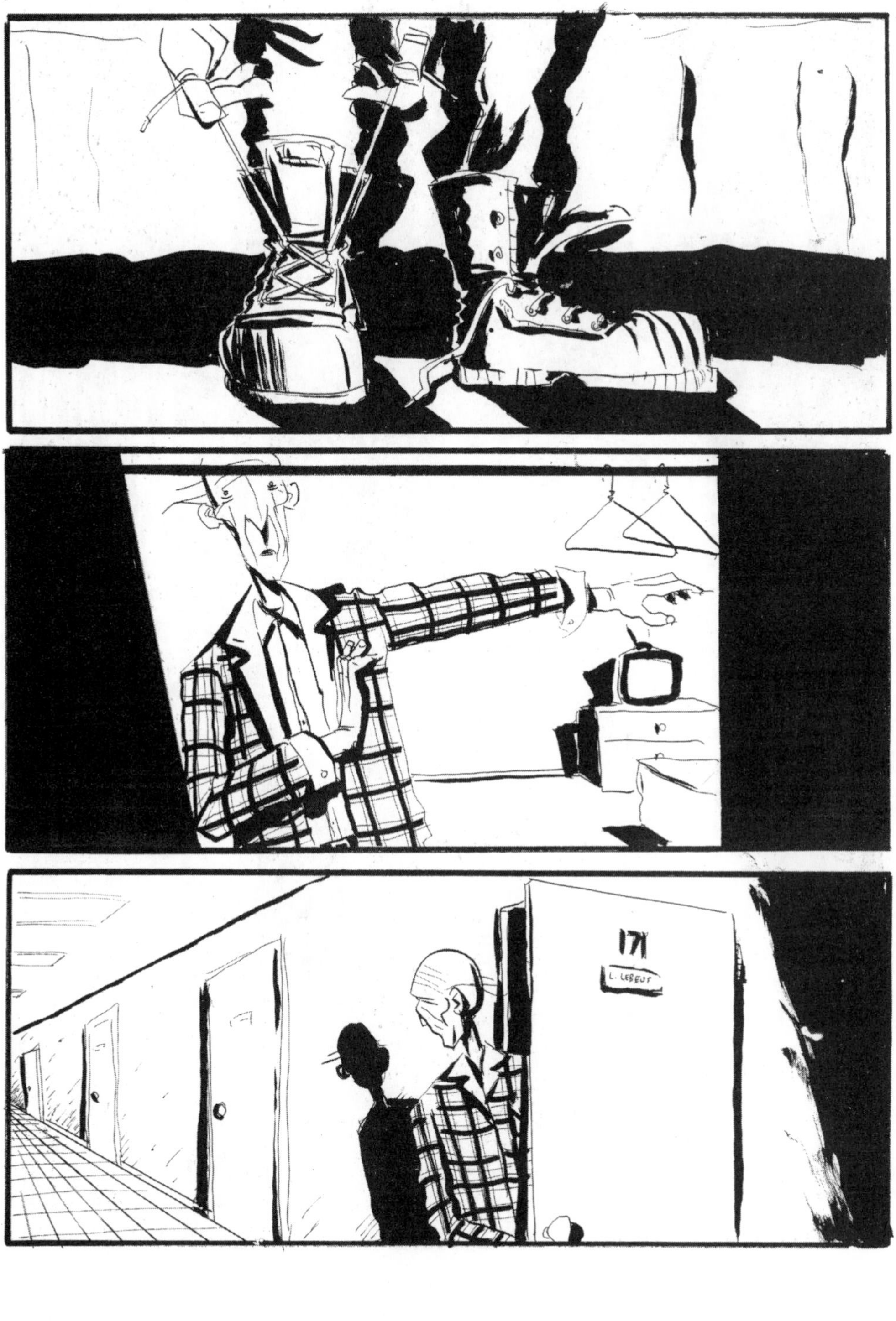
171
L. LEBEUF

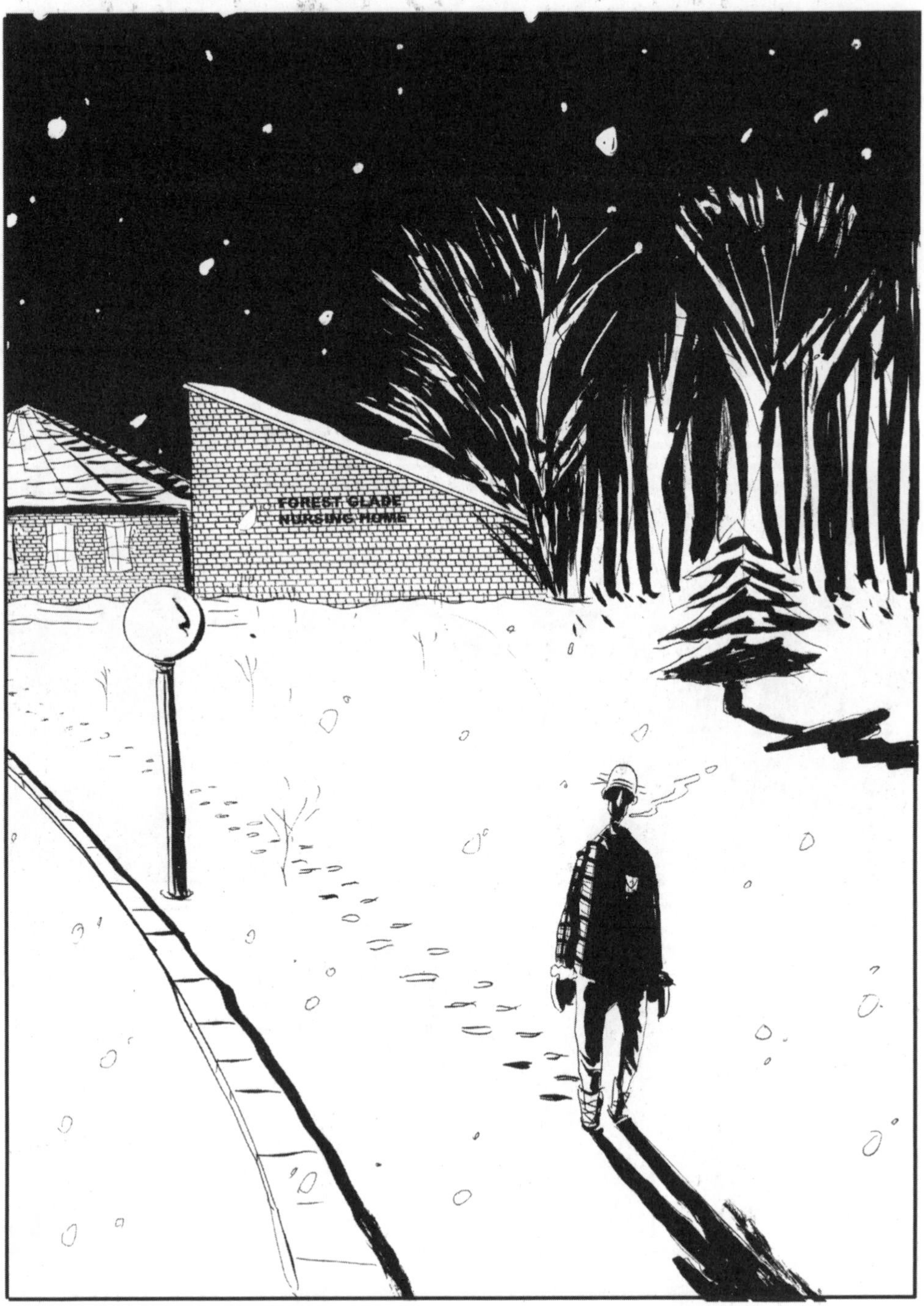
FOREST GLADE
NURSING HOME

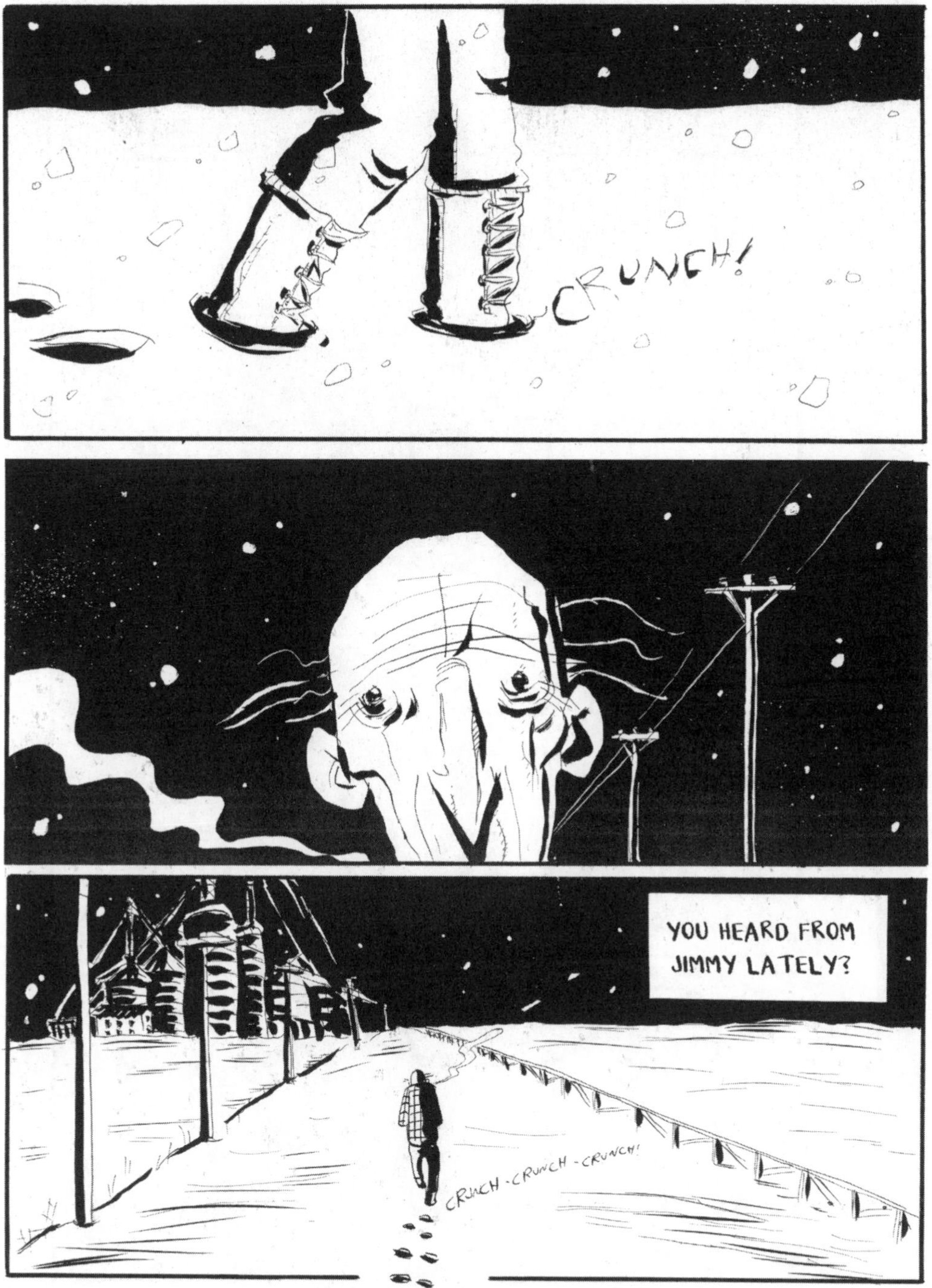
CRUNCH!
YOU HEARD FROM JIMMY LATELY?
CRUNCH-CRUNCH-CRUNCH!

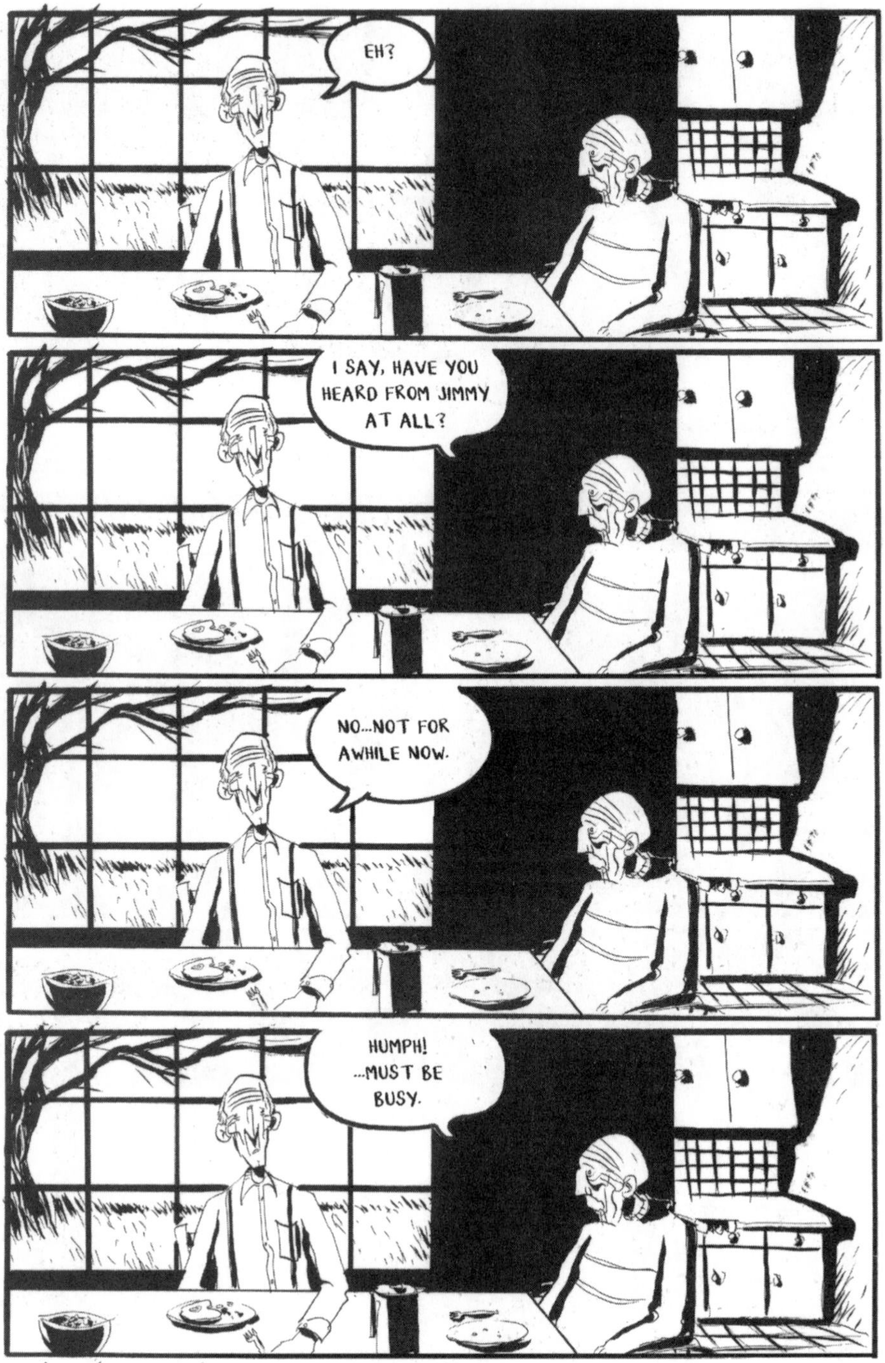
EH?
I SAY, HAVE YOU HEARD FROM JIMMY AT ALL?
NO...NOT FOR AWHILE NOW.
HUMPH! ...MUST BE BUSY.

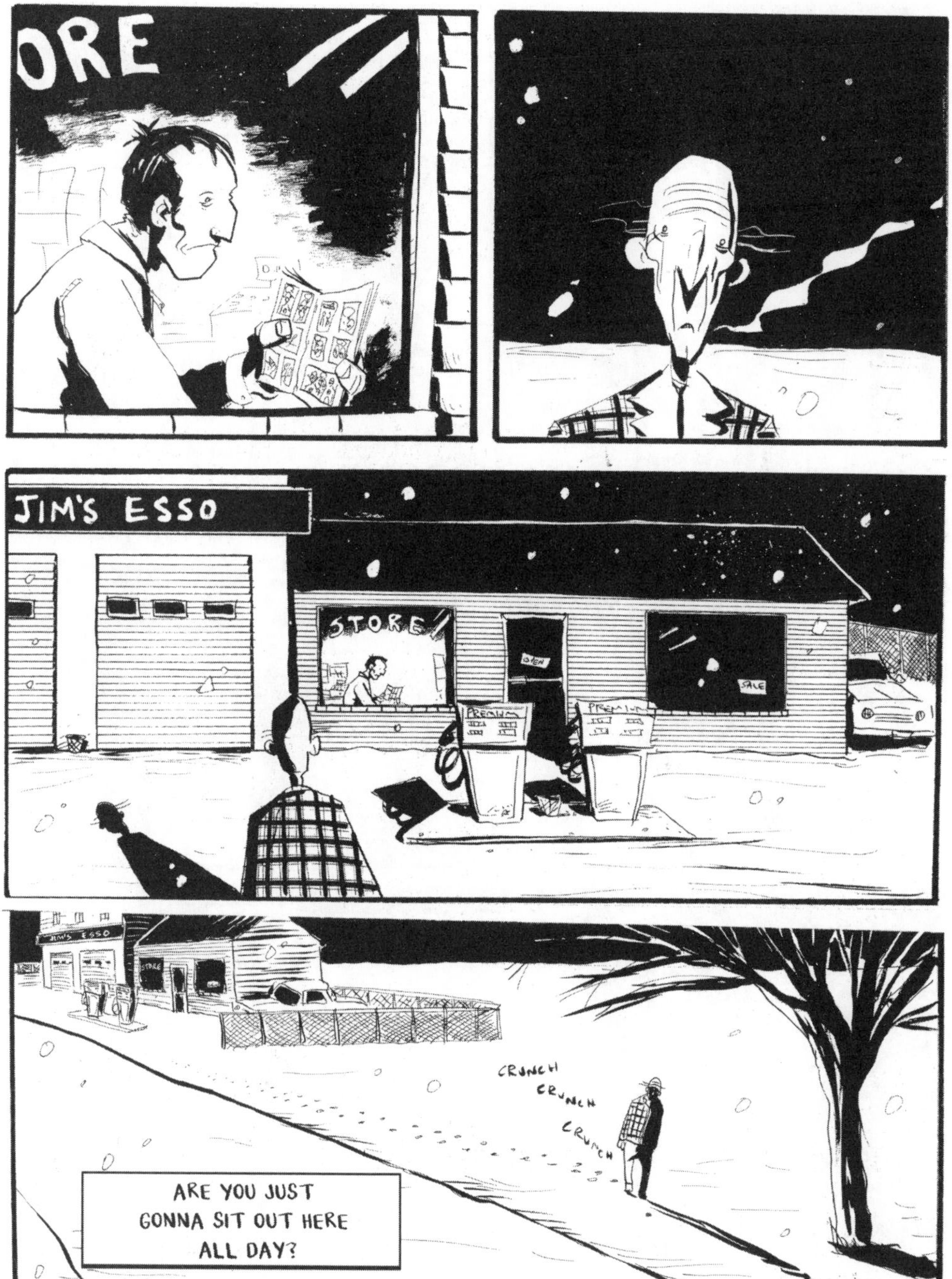
ORE
JIM'S ESSO
STORE
JIM'S ESSO
STORE
CRUNCH
CRUNCH
CRUNCH
ARE YOU JUST GONNA SIT OUT HERE ALL DAY?

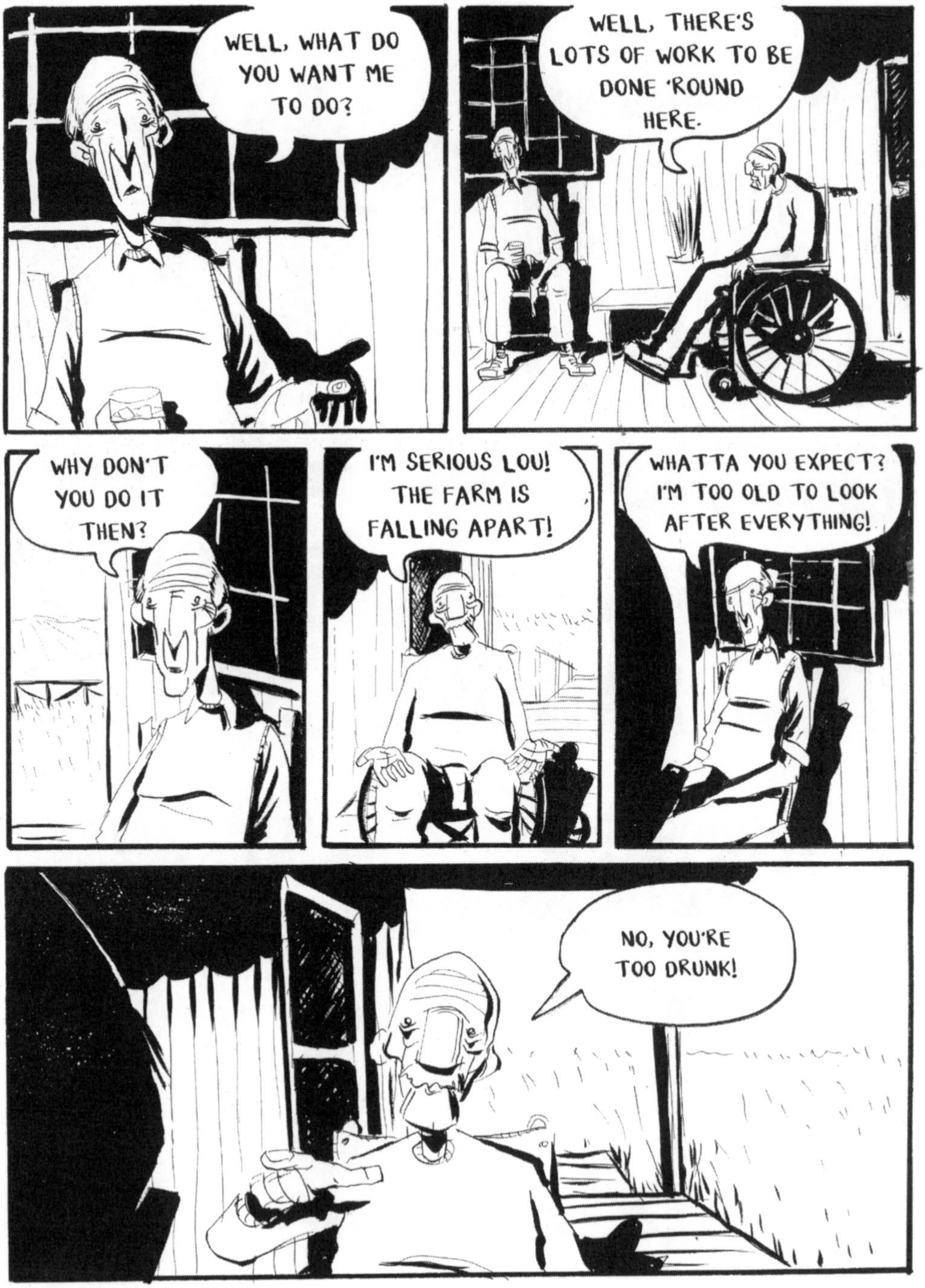
WELL, WHAT DO YOU WANT ME TO DO?
WELL, THERE'S LOTS OF WORK TO BE DONE 'ROUND HERE.
WHY DON'T YOU DO IT THEN?
I'M SERIOUS LOU! THE FARM IS FALLING APART!
WHATTA YOU EXPECT? I'M TOO OLD TO LOOK AFTER EVERYTHING!
NO, YOU'RE TOO DRUNK!

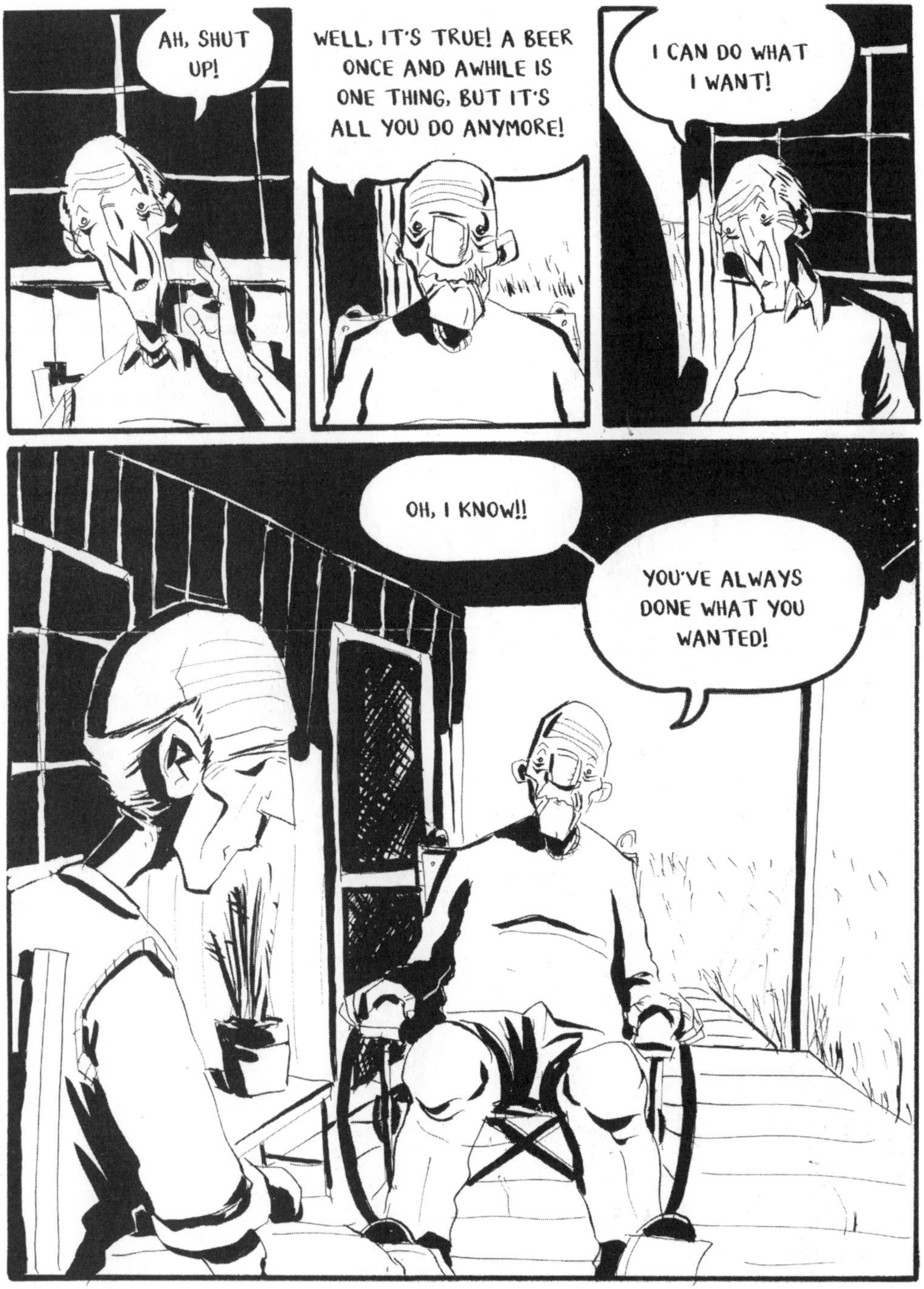
AH, SHUT UP!
WELL, IT'S TRUE! A BEER ONCE AND AWHILE IS ONE THING, BUT IT'S ALL YOU DO ANYMORE!
I CAN DO WHAT I WANT!
OH, I KNOW!!
YOU'VE ALWAYS DONE WHAT YOU WANTED!

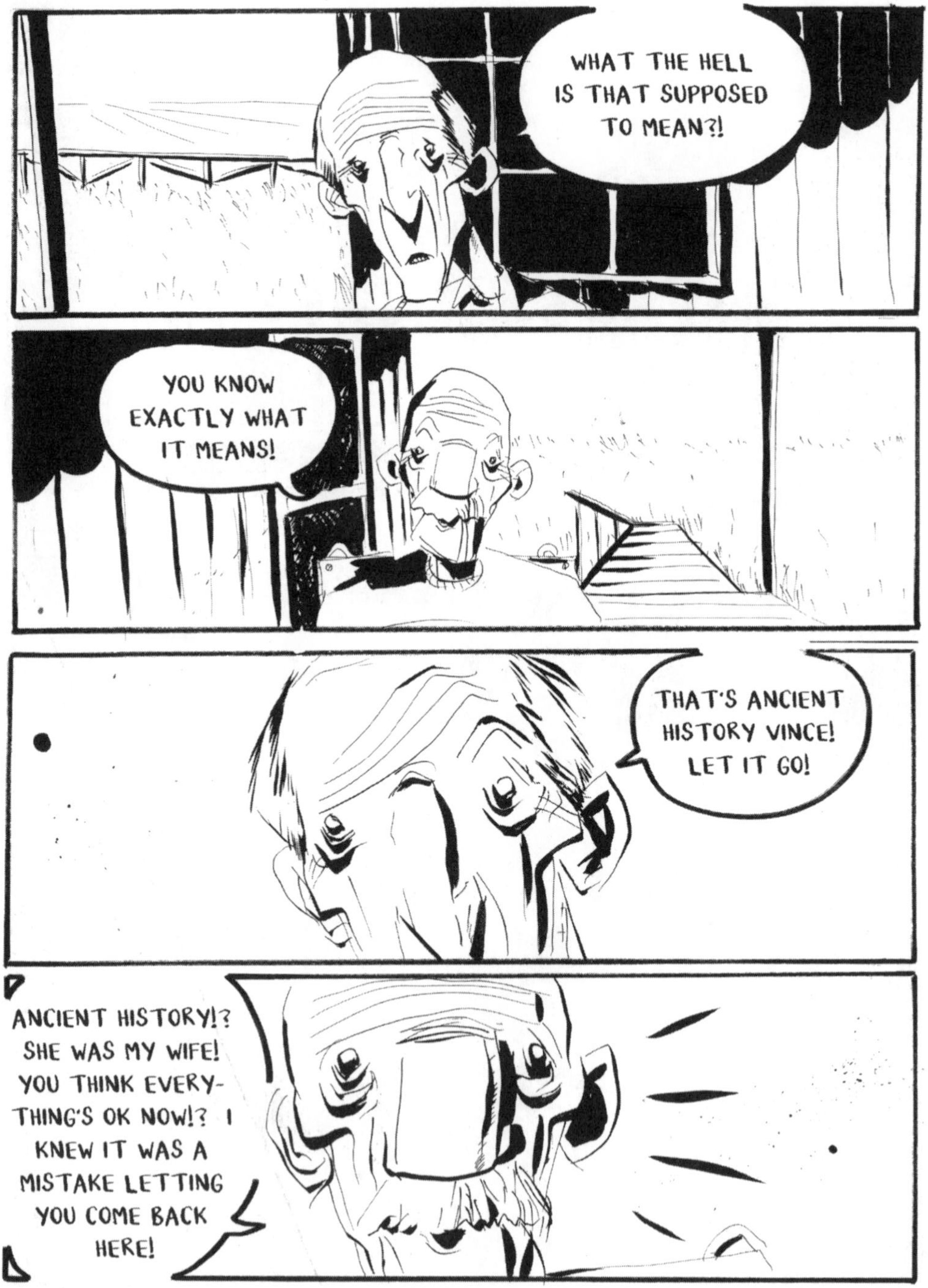
WHAT THE HELL IS THAT SUPPOSED TO MEAN?!
YOU KNOW EXACTLY WHAT IT MEANS!
THAT'S ANCIENT HISTORY VINCE! LET IT GO!
ANCIENT HISTORY!? SHE WAS MY WIFE! YOU THINK EVERY-THING'S OK NOW!? I KNEW IT WAS A MISTAKE LETTING YOU COME BACK HERE!

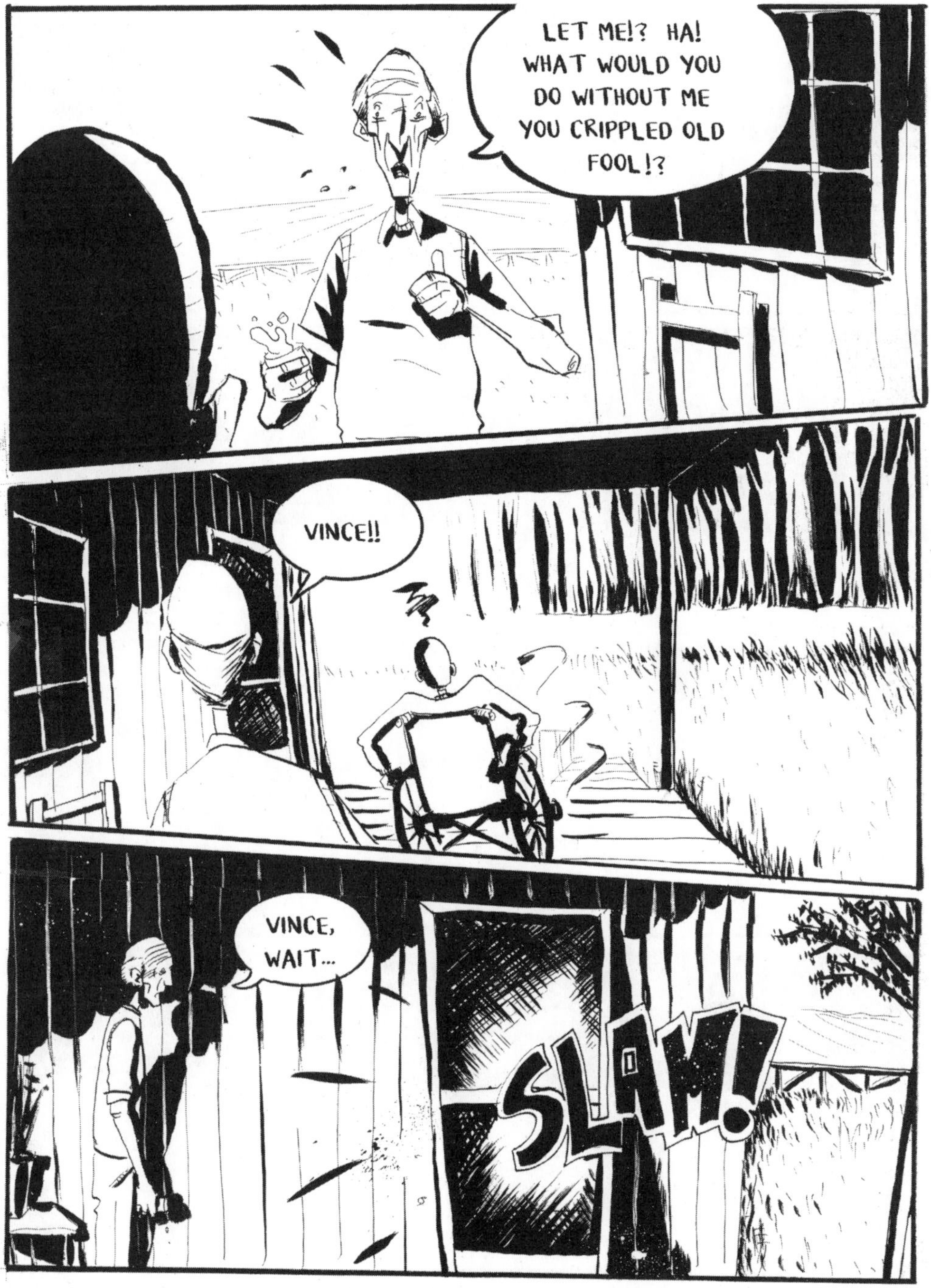
LET ME!? HA! WHAT WOULD YOU DO WITHOUT ME YOU CRIPPLED OLD FOOL!?
VINCE!!
VINCE, WAIT...
SLAM!

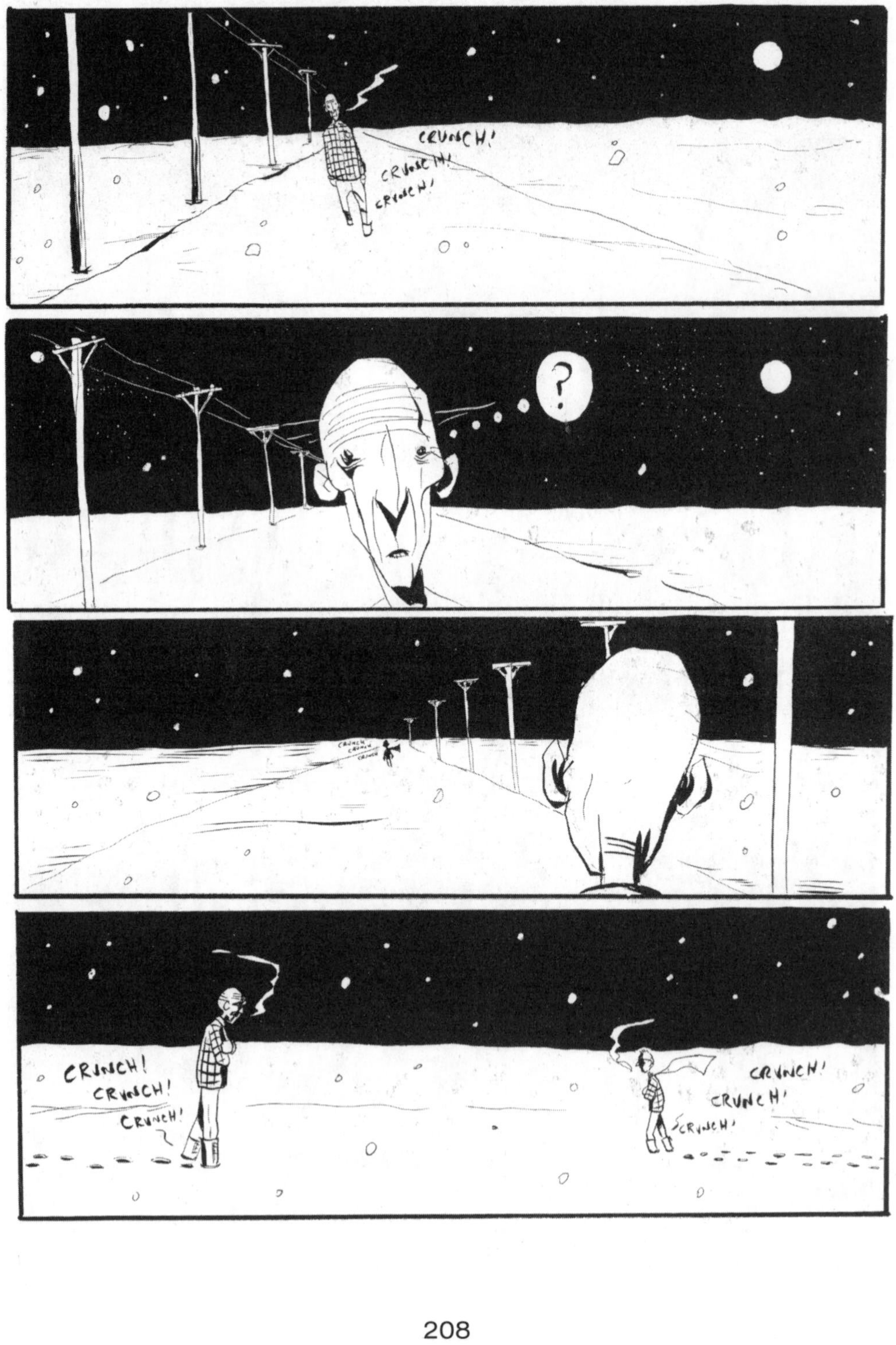
CRUNCH!
CRUNCH!
CRUNCH!
?
CRUNCH!
CRUNCH!
CRUNCH!
CRUNCH!
CRUNCH!
CRUNCH!

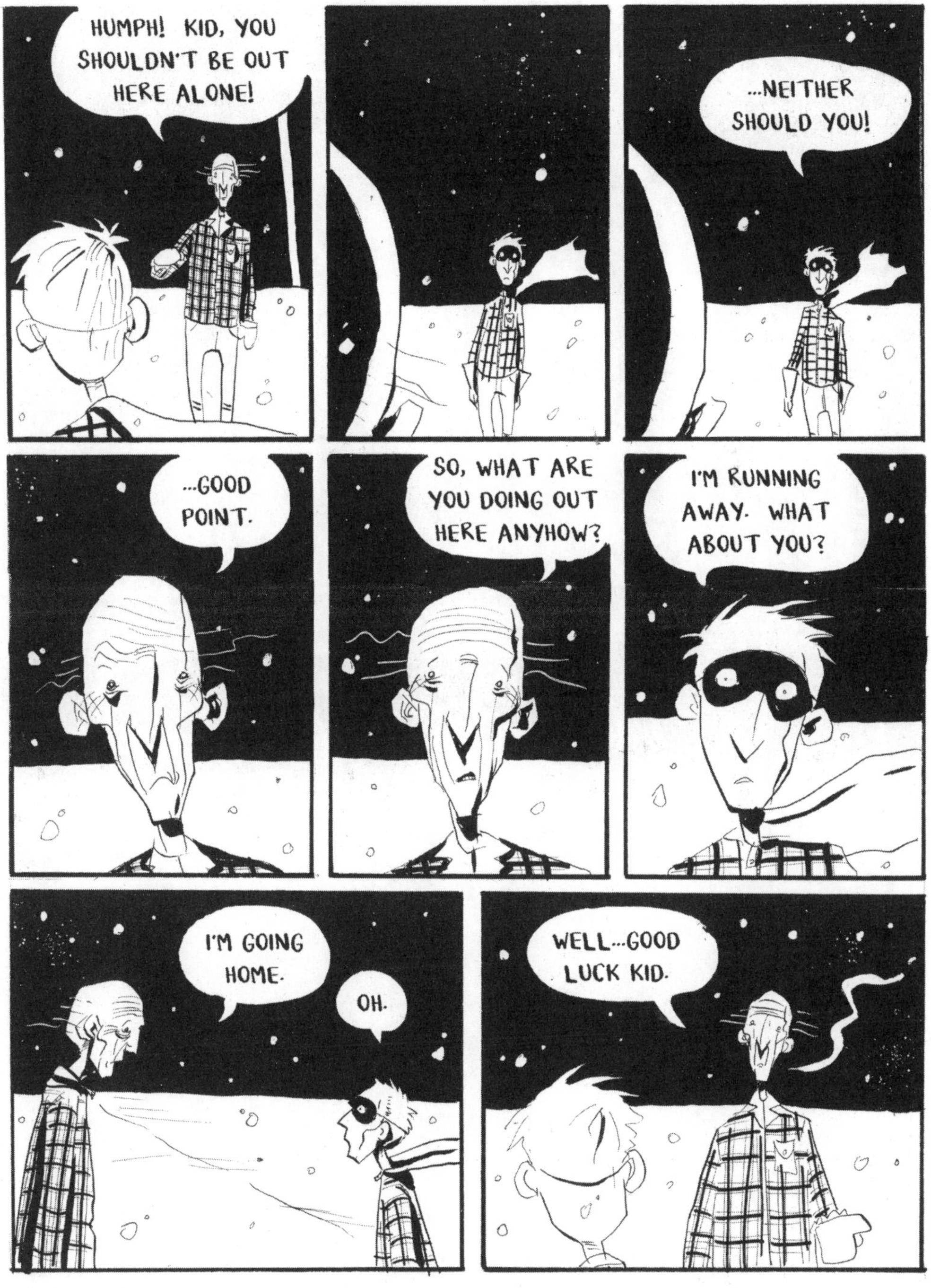
HUMPH! KID, YOU SHOULDN'T BE OUT HERE ALONE!
...NEITHER SHOULD YOU!
...GOOD POINT.
SO, WHAT ARE YOU DOING OUT HERE ANYHOW?
I'M RUNNING AWAY. WHAT ABOUT YOU?
I'M GOING HOME.
OH.
WELL...GOOD LUCK KID.

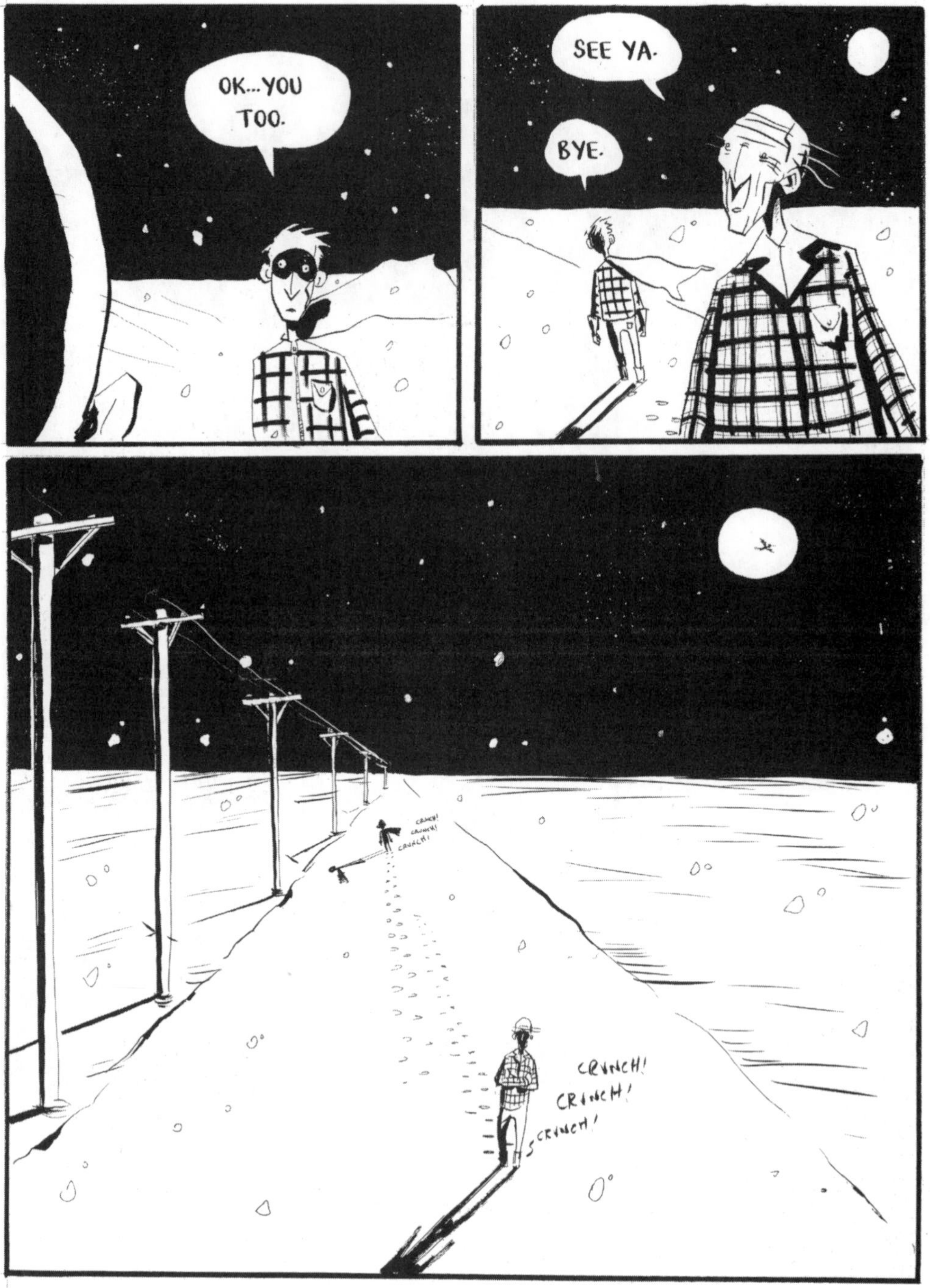
OK...YOU TOO.
SEE YA.
BYE.
CRUNCH!
CRUNCH!
CRUNCH!

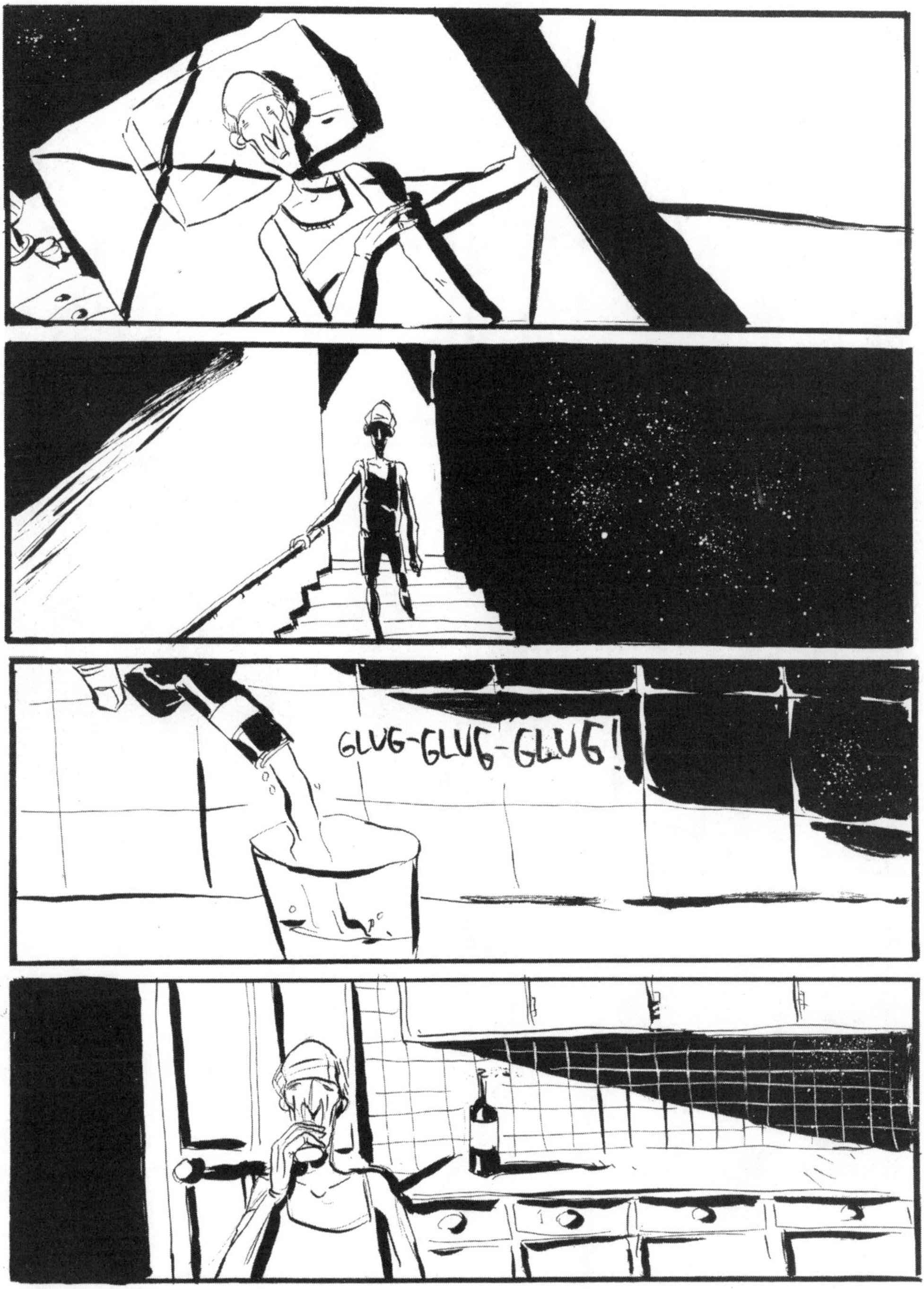
GLUG-GLUG-GLUG!

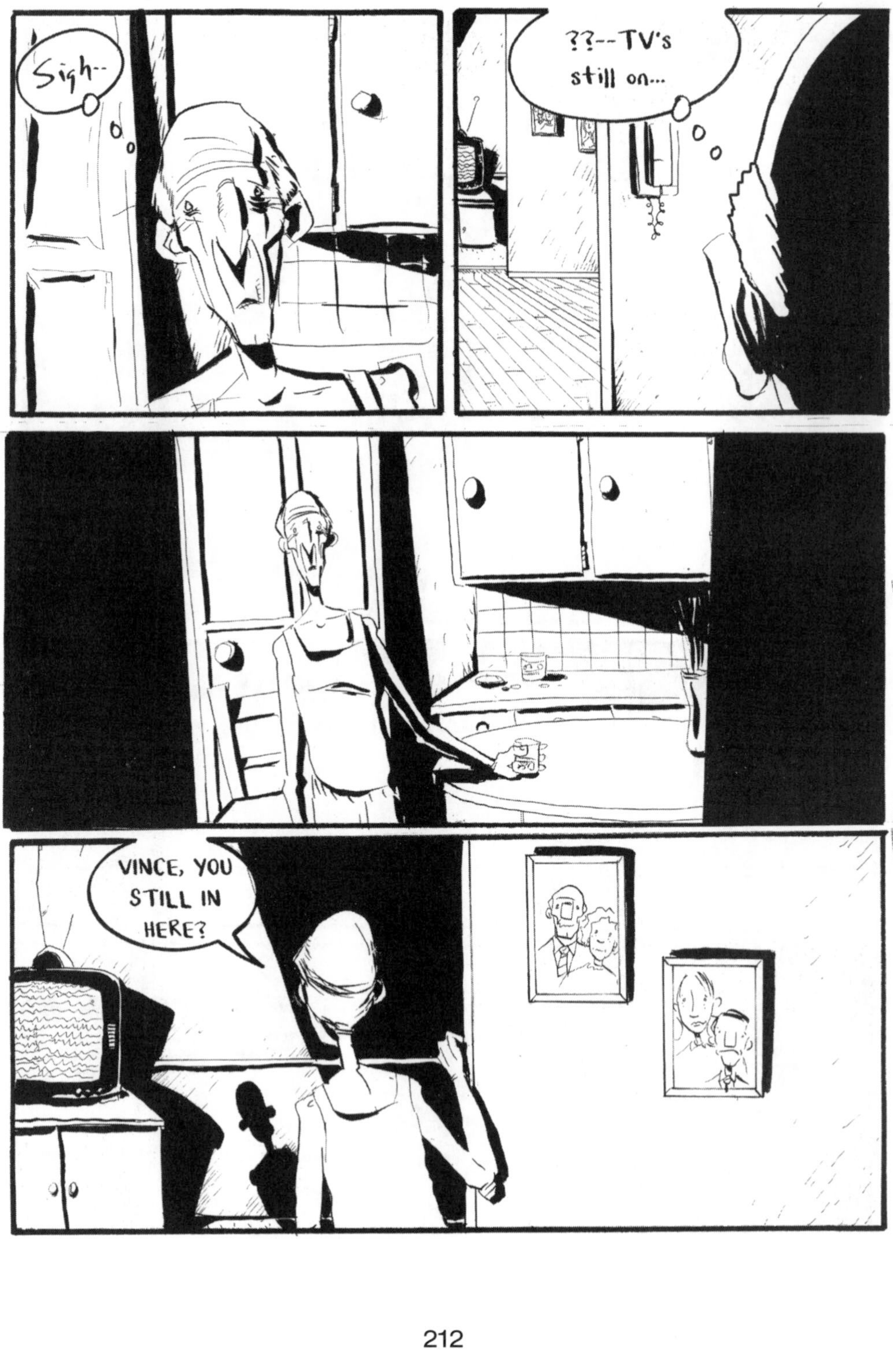
Sigh--
??--TV's still on...
VINCE, YOU STILL IN HERE?

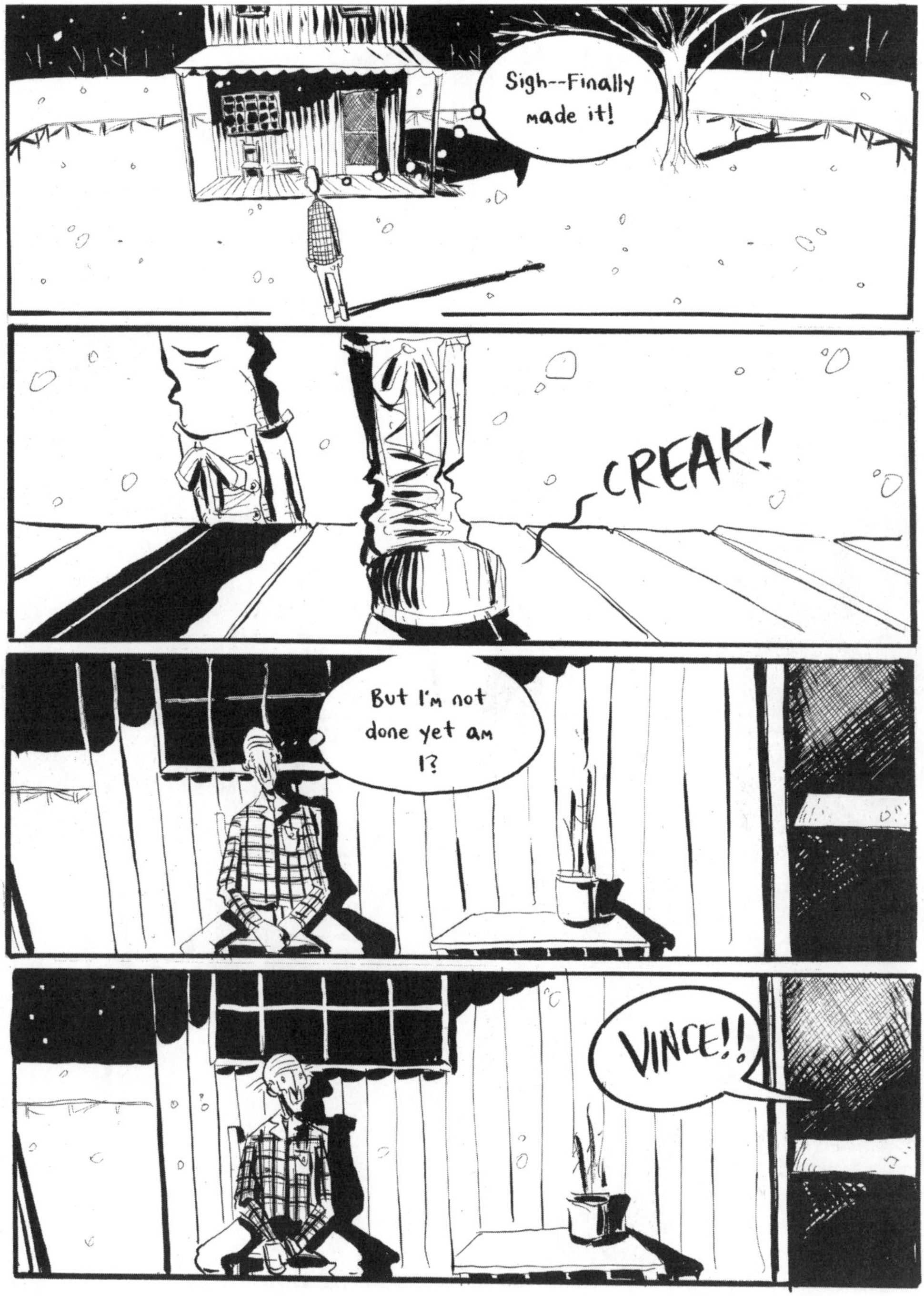
Sigh--Finally made it!
CREAK!
But I'm not done yet am I?
VINCE!!

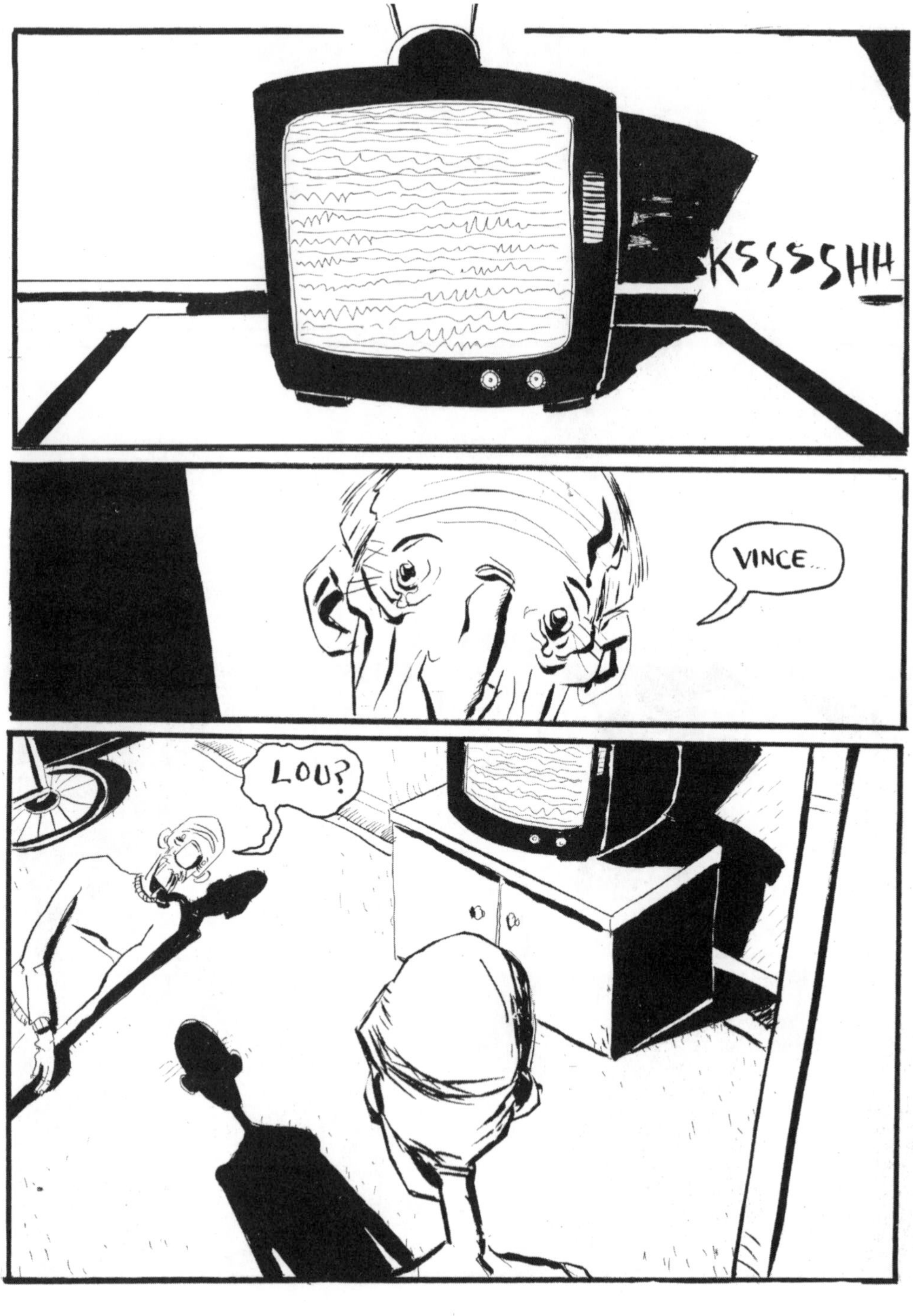
KSSSSHH
VINCE...
LOU?

LOU, WHAT HAPPENED?
IT'S OK... I JUST FELL...
I DON'T KNOW VINCE. YOU DON'T LOOK SO GOOD. I'M GONNA CALL FOR AN AMBULANCE...
NO! NO... DON'T GO LOU... JUST STAY...
OK, OK...I'M HERE.

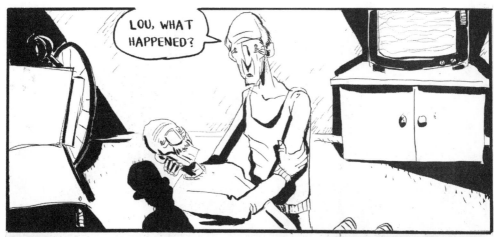

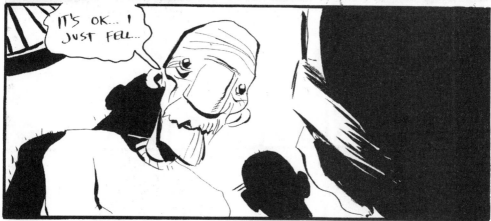

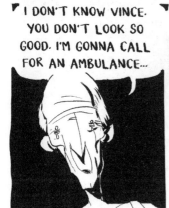

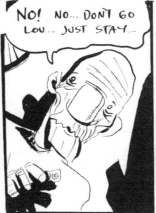

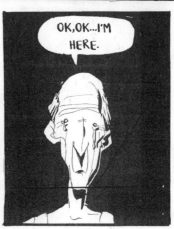

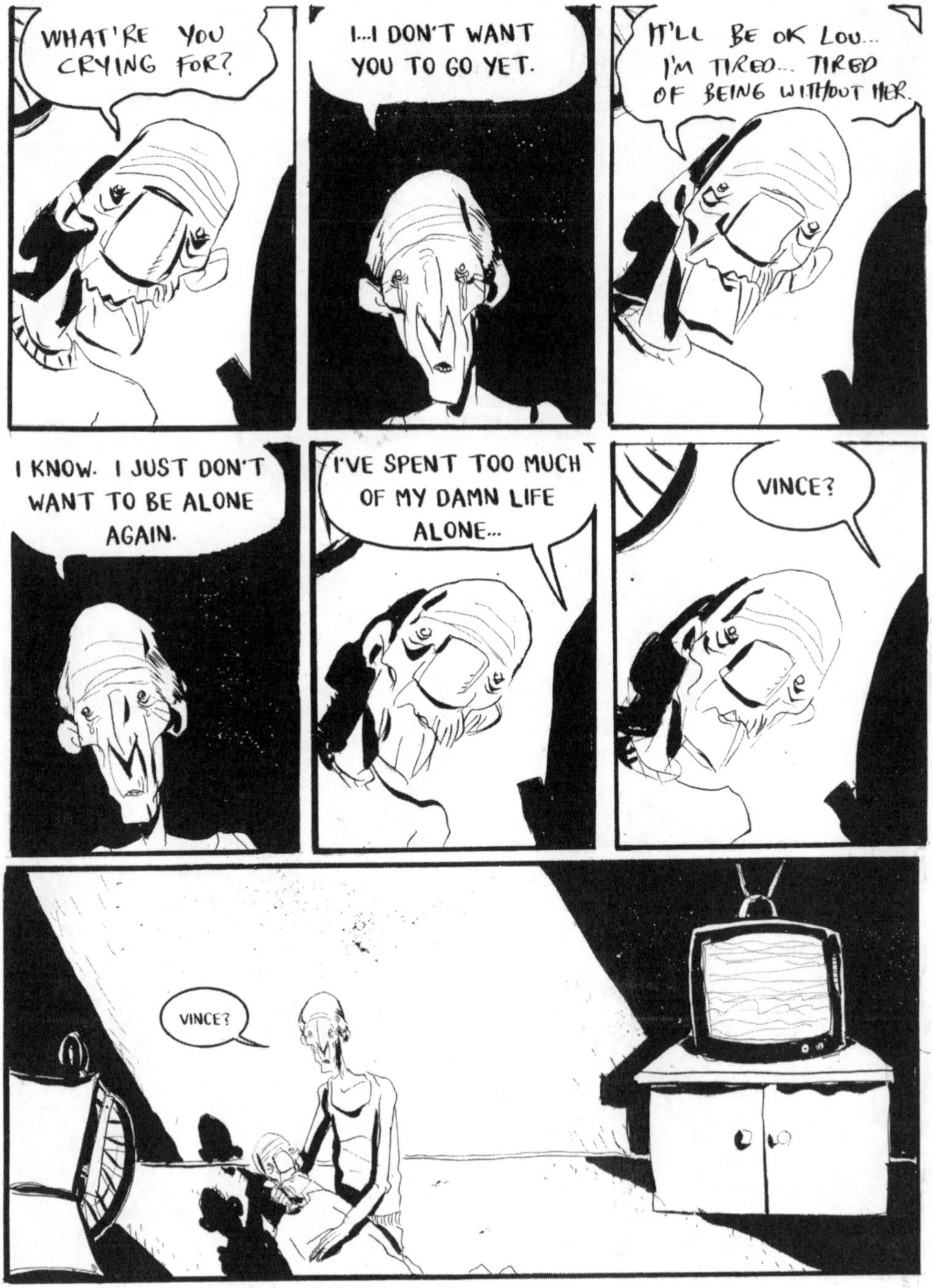
WHAT'RE YOU CRYING FOR?
I...I DON'T WANT YOU TO GO YET.
IT'LL BE OK LOU... I'M TIRED... TIRED OF BEING WITHOUT HER.
I KNOW. I JUST DON'T WANT TO BE ALONE AGAIN.
I'VE SPENT TOO MUCH OF MY DAMN LIFE ALONE...
VINCE?
VINCE?

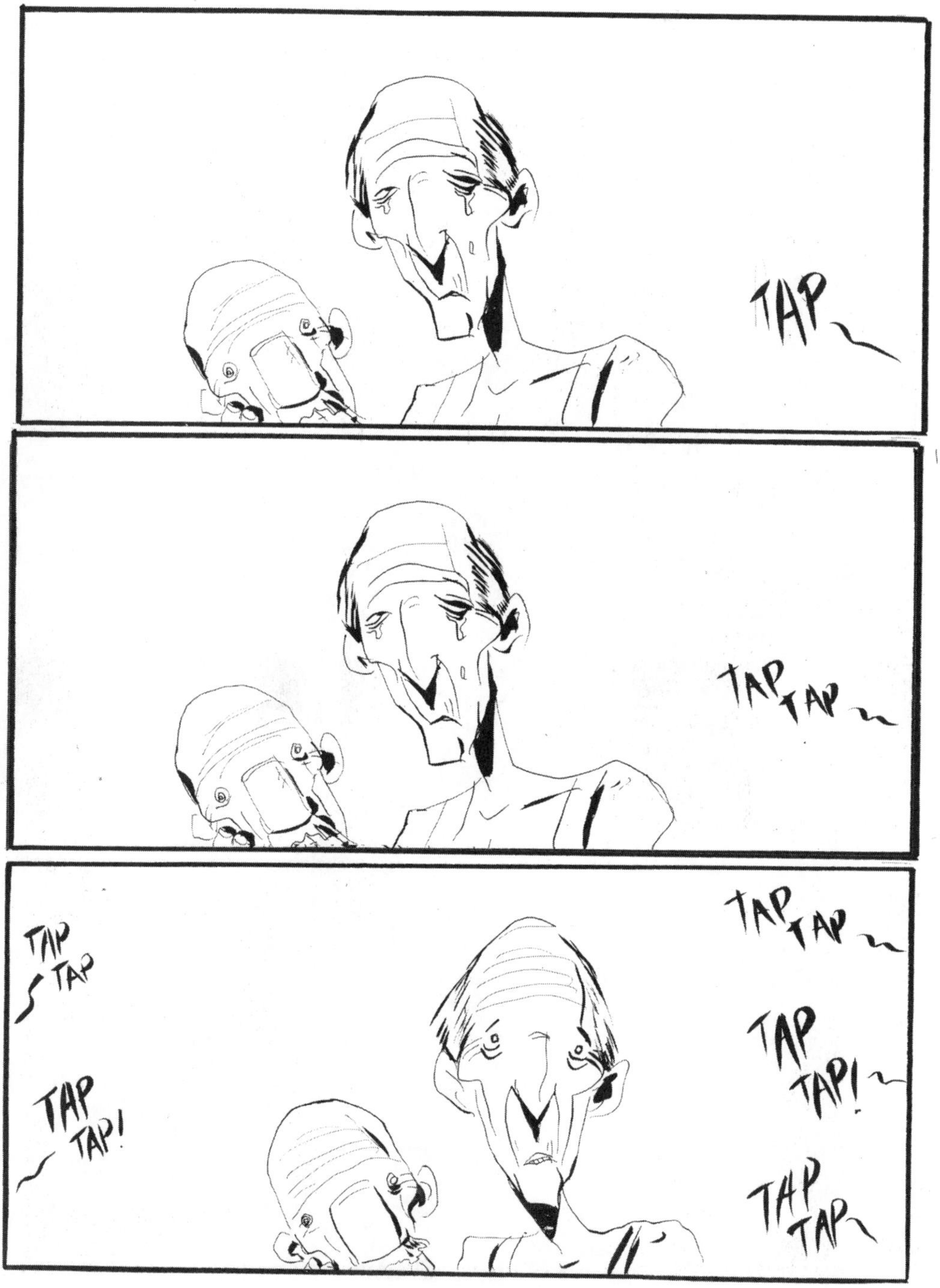
TAP
TAP TAP
TAP TAP
TAP TAP
TAP TAP!
TAP TAP!
TAP TAP

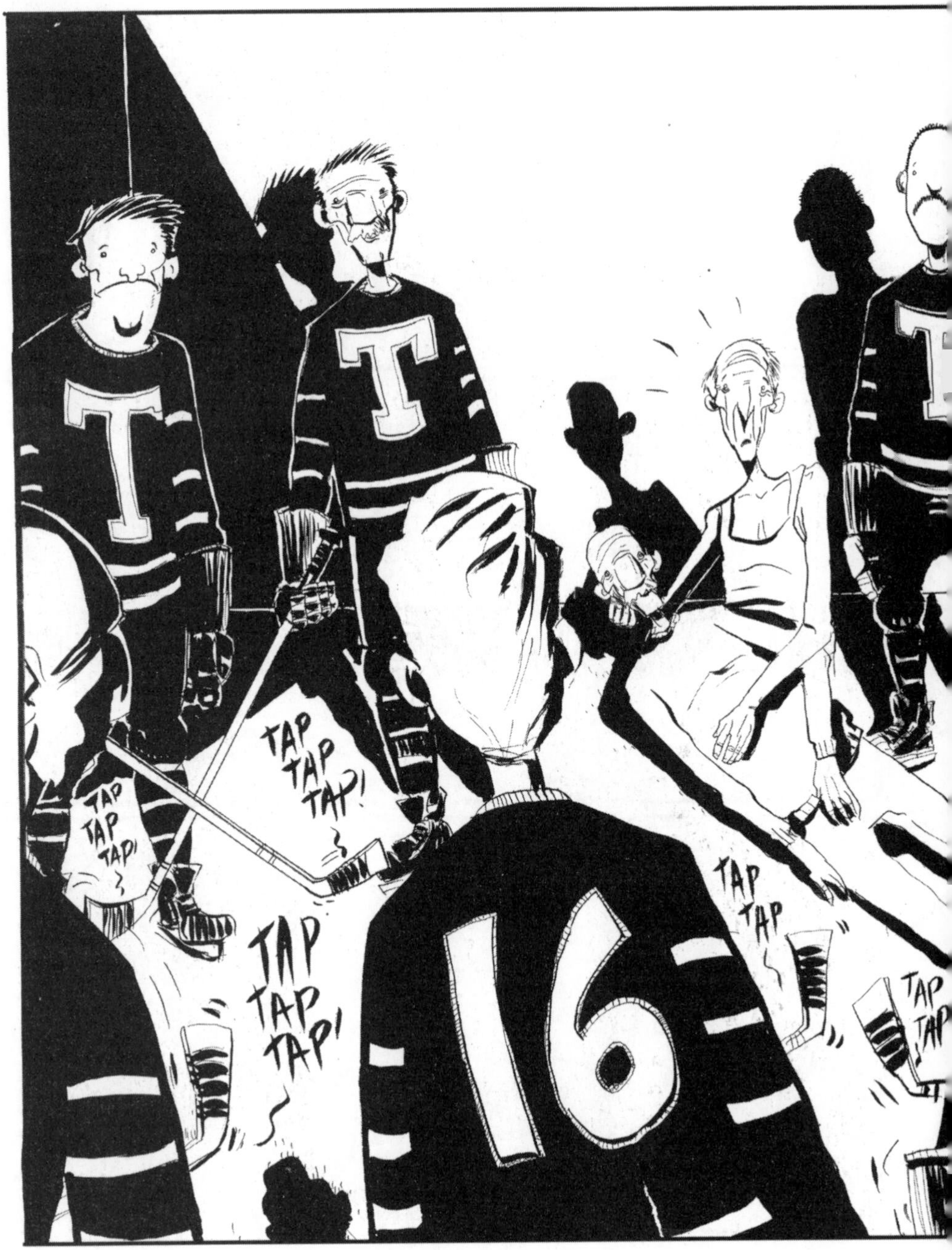
TAP
TAP
TAP!
TAP
TAP
TAP!
TAP
TAP
TAP!
TAP
TAP
16

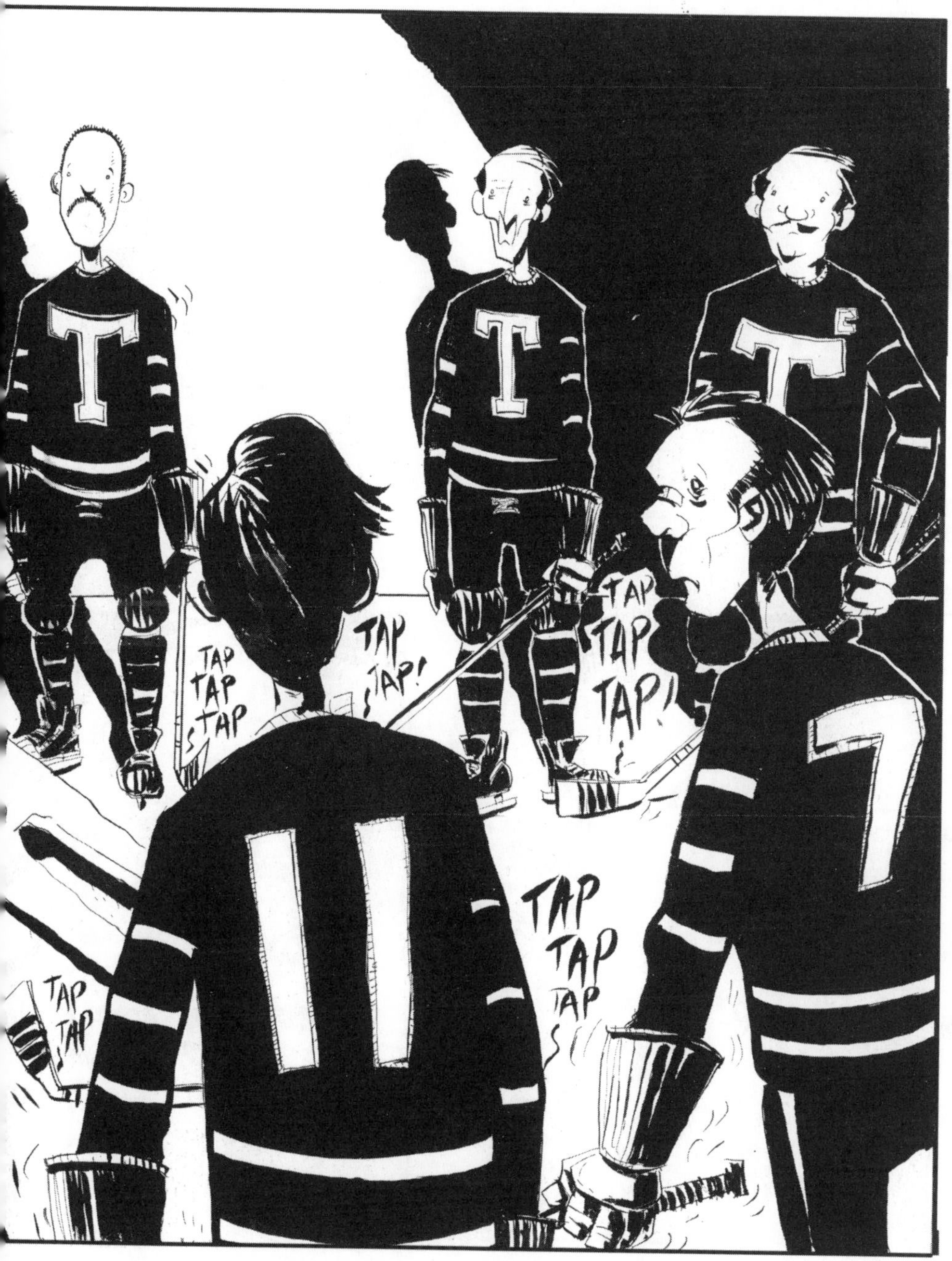
TAP
TAP
TAP
TAP
TAP!
TAP
TAP
TAP!
TAP
TAP
TAP
TAP
TAP

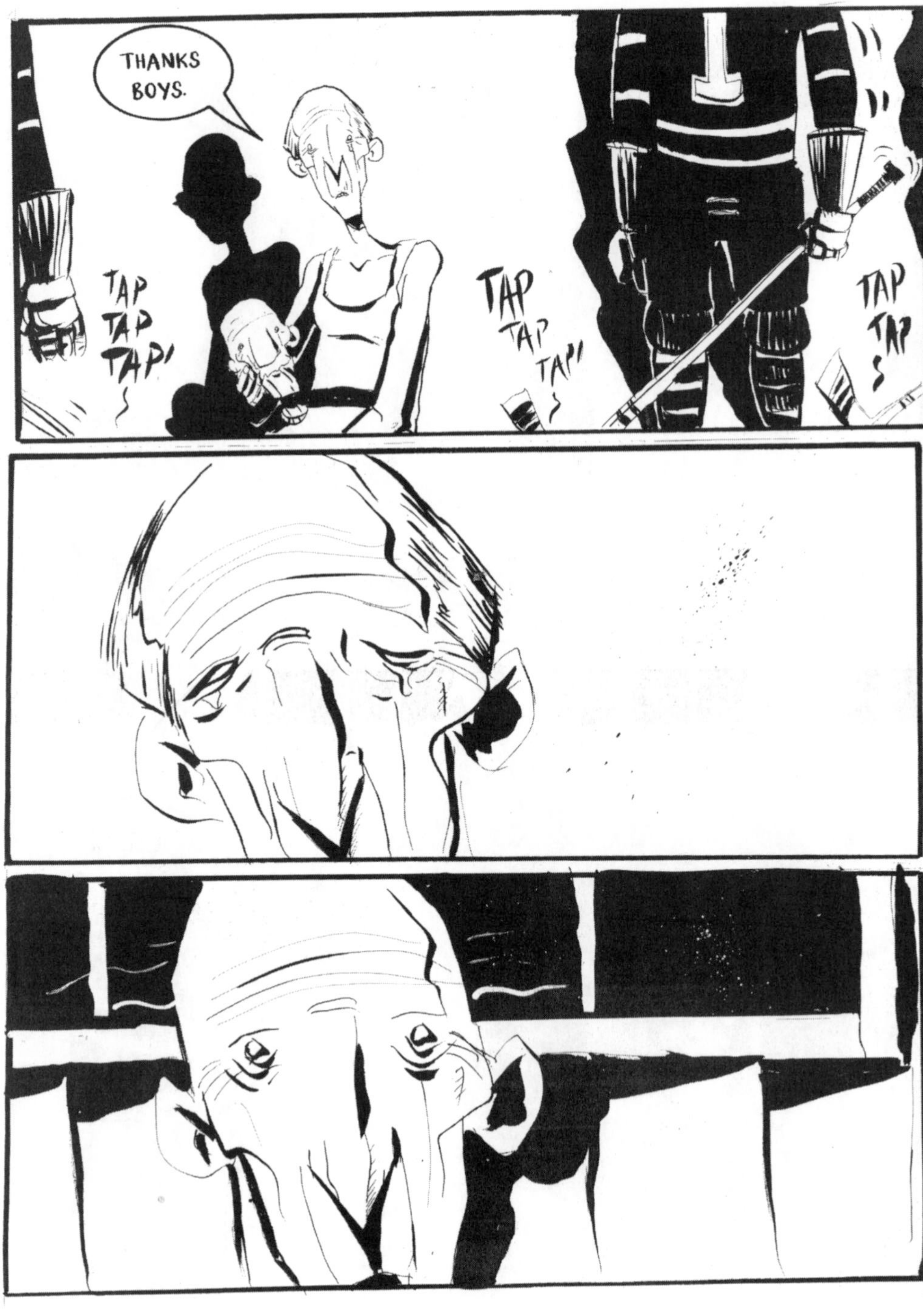
THANKS BOYS.
TAP TAP TAP!
TAP TAP TAP!
TAP TAP

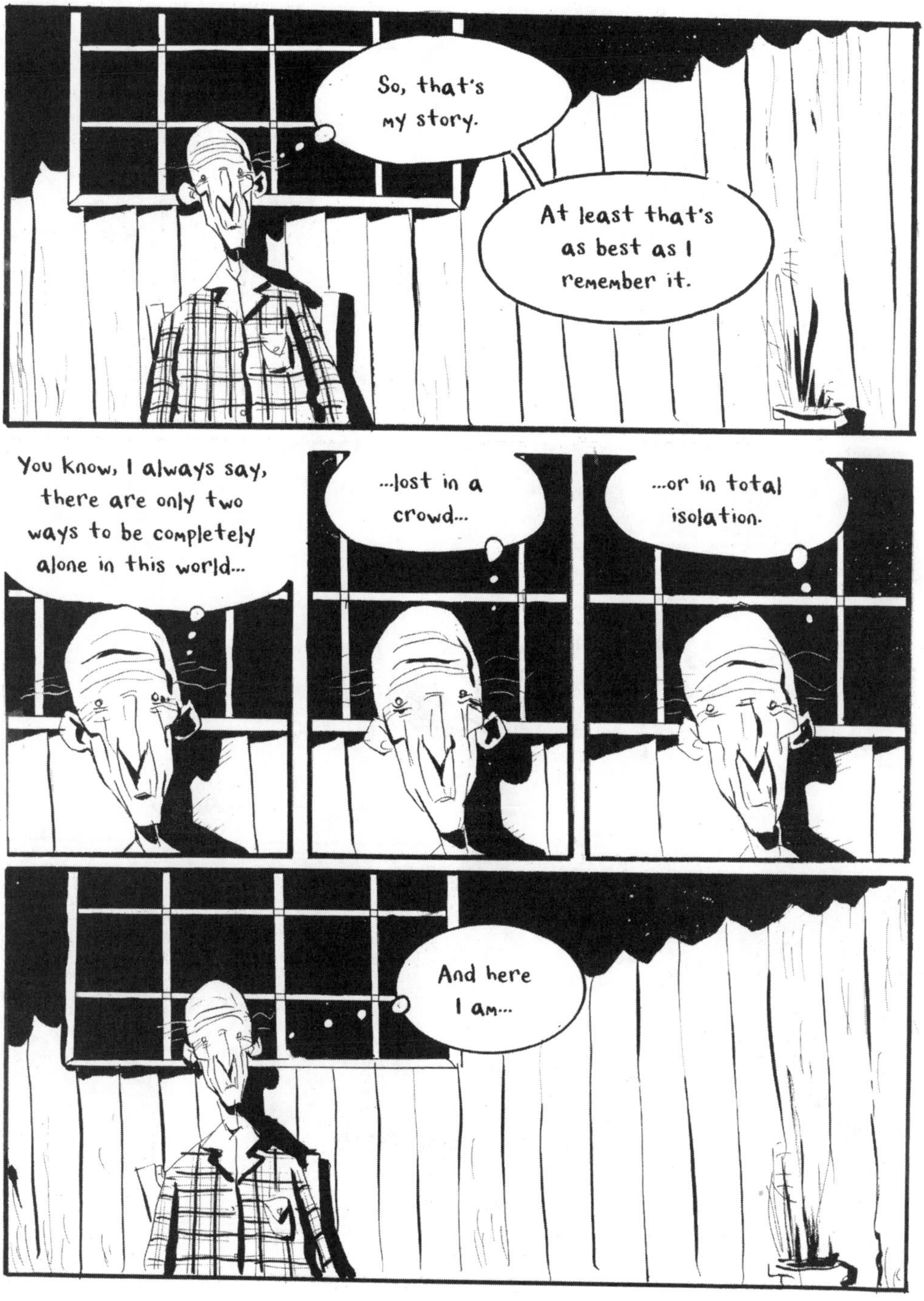
So, that's my story.
At least that's as best as I remember it.
You know, I always say, there are only two ways to be completely alone in this world...
...lost in a crowd...
...or in total isolation.
And here I am...

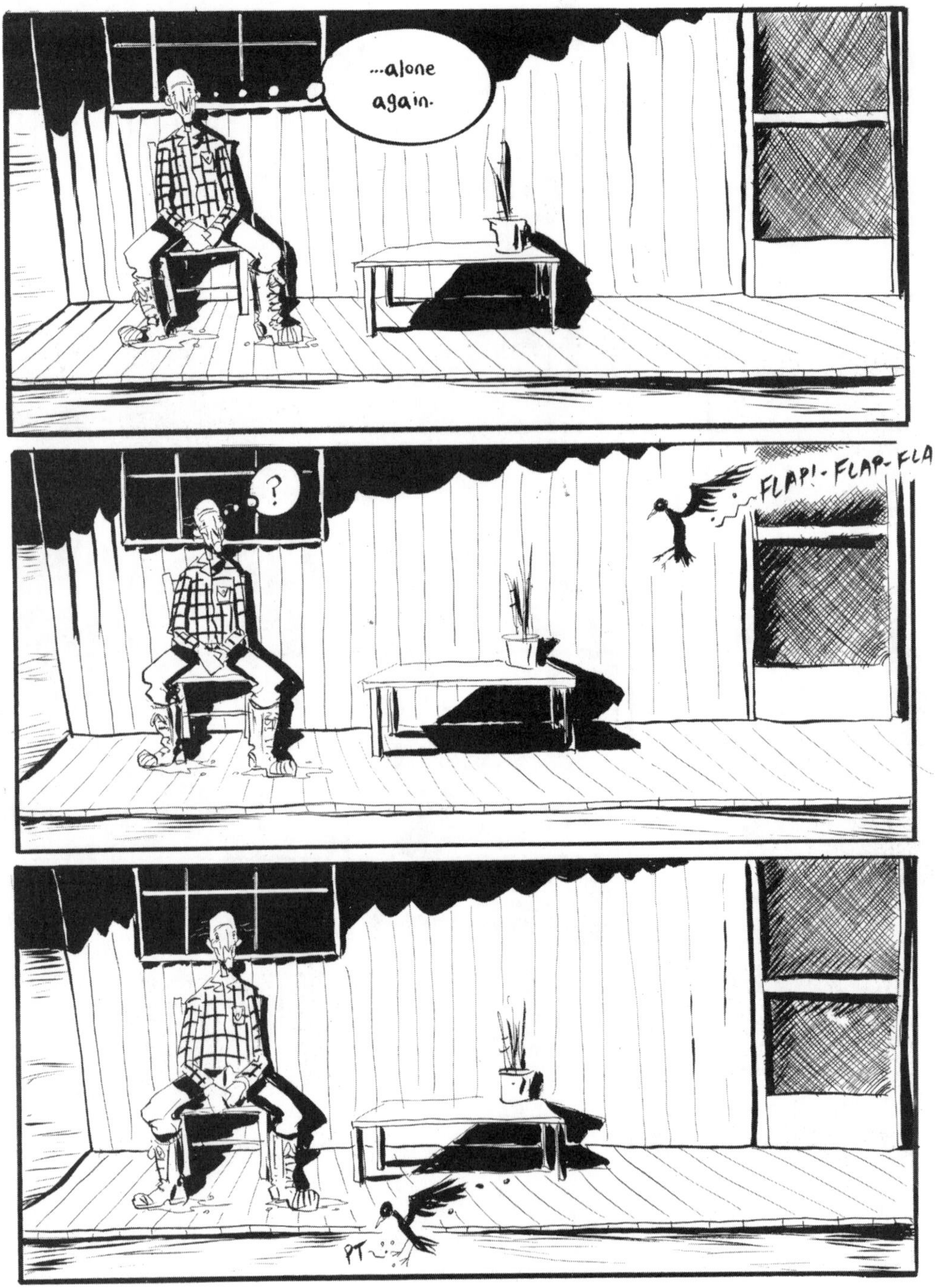
...alone again.
?
FLAP!-FLAP-FLA
PT

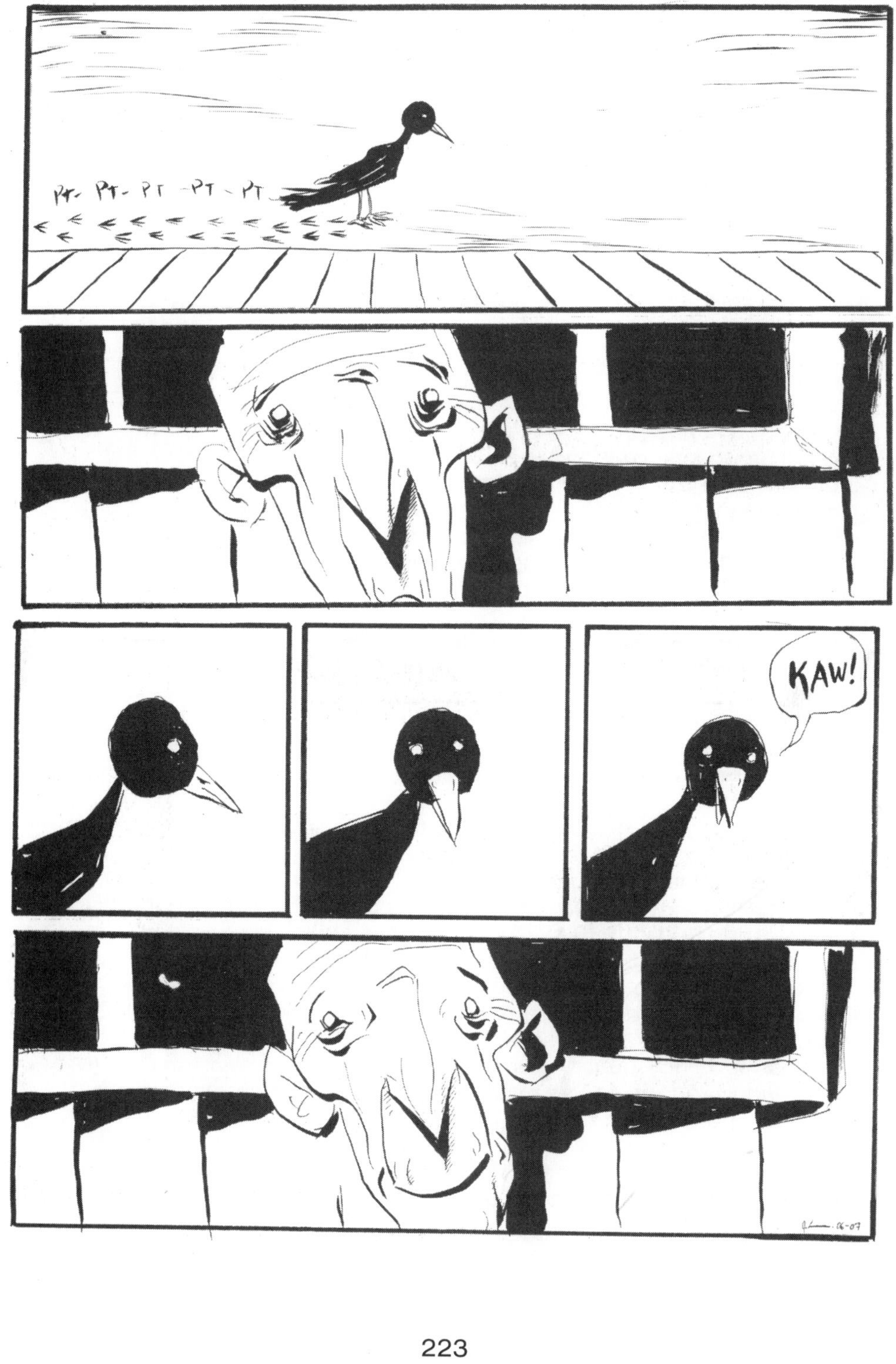
PT- PT- PT -PT - PT
KAW!

I would like to acknowledge the following works for inspiring me to create *Ghost Stories*, and keeping me excited me along the way: *The Game* by Ken Dryden, *The Tropic of Hockey* by Dave Bidini, *The Game of Our Lives* by Peter Gzowski, *Slap Shot* by George Roy Hill, *Searching For Bobby Orr* by Steven Brunt, *The Golem's Mighty Swing* by James Sturm, and *Road To America* by Baru.

Also, a special thank you goes out to Neko Case, whose beautiful song "I WIsh I Was the Moon," from her album *Blacklisted*, provided the initial spark for this story.

The quote that opens this book was by the great Canadian author, educator and humorist Stephen Leacock (1869-1944).

I would like to cite the following books for providing invaluable reference while working on *Ghost Stories*: *Toronto Maple Leafs: Images of Glory* by James Duplacey and Joseph Romain (published in 1990 by McGraw-Hill), and *Hockey: An Illustrated History* by Dan Diamond and Charles Wilkins (published in 1985 by Doubleday Canada).

I used many images as inspiration and reference for the book. One image in particular, however, proved so powerful and iconic that it couldn't be escaped. Therefore, I would like to specifically acknowledge Ray Lussier's photograph of Bobby Orr's Stanley Cup-winning goal (May 1970), widely recognized as one of the single greatest images in the history of sport. It made its way almost directly into *Ghost Stories* on page 79 as the panel of Lou's game-winning goal.

And last, but not least, I would like to give a huge thank you to Chris Staros and Brett Warnock for their support.